No words had yet been exchanged between the two women. It wasn't until after Chloe was sleeping snugly in the guest bedroom, the old gray tom curled up contentedly beside her, that Steffie handed her old friend a glass of wine and said, "Okay, spill."

"I brought in a hooker late last night for solicitation."

"And that would be news because . . . ?"

"She offered to trade some information with me in exchange for not booking her."

"By the look on your face, I'd say she had something big to trade." Steffie tucked her legs under her on the sofa.

"She told me that Anthony Navarro knows that the child I adopted four years ago is his daughter, and he's coming after her." Her friend nodded slowly. "I'd say that was big."

"You think she knows what she's talking about?"

"You think there's any chance she could have made that up and, just coincidentally, got the facts right?"

"Okay, so we pick him up—"

"First, you have to find him. Stef, you've been after him for years, and you haven't come close."

"So we look a little harder while we wait for him to show."

"He won't be coming himself. He won't have to. He's offered twenty-five thousand dollars to the person who brings him his daughter."

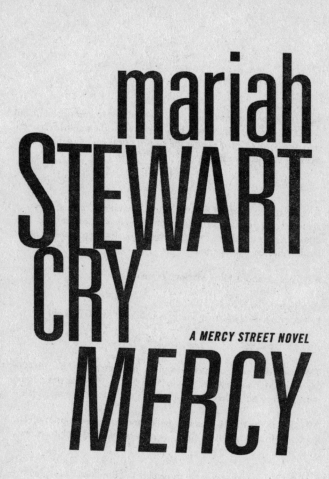

mariah STEWART
CRY MERCY

A MERCY STREET NOVEL

BALLANTINE BOOKS • NEW YORK

Cry Mercy is a work of fiction. Names, characters, places, and incidents are the products of the author's imagination or are used fictitiously. Any resemblance to actual events, locales, or persons, living or dead, is entirely coincidental.

A Ballantine Books Mass Market Original

Copyright © 2009 by Marti Robb
Excerpt from *Acts of Mercy* copyright © 2009 by Marti Robb

This book contains an excerpt from the mass market edition *Acts of Mercy* by Mariah Stewart. This excerpt has been set for this edition only and may not reflect the final content of the forthcoming novel.

Published in the United States by Ballantine Books, an imprint of The Random House Publishing Group, a division of Random House, Inc., New York.

BALLANTINE and colophon are trademarks of Random House, Inc.

ISBN 978-0-345-50613-9

Printed in the United States of America

www.ballantinebooks.com

OPM   9   8   7   6   5   4   3   2   1

To the doggie divas—
JB, Mama Jean, Mary
and South Philly Phil

ACKNOWLEDGMENTS

Thanks as always to the ever-fabulous team at Ballantine Books—Linda Marrow, Kate Collins, Kelli Fillingim, Sarina Evan, Scott Shannon, Libby McGuire, and Kim Hovey (hopefully, I didn't leave anyone out), and to my agent, Lorretta Barrett, and her staff—Nick Mullendore and Jennifer Didik.

Huge appreciation to FBI Special Agent Pam Stratton, and to Special Agent Jack Martinelli, who met with us on the firing range and taught me how to always get my man (and I have the target to prove it!).

The Nora Roberts Foundation received a donation from Debra Newhouse via her purchase of a raffle ticket that turned out to be a winner, and bought her the right to have a character named after her in this book. Thanks to the ladies at ADWOFF—especially Phyllis Lannik—for running this fund-raiser that supports literacy and so many other good causes.

PROLOGUE

August 2008

His chest heaving from exertion, he dumped his burden unceremoniously on the ground, leaned against the nearest tree, and gulped in air, trying to catch his breath. Who would have believed a 110-pound girl could be so unwieldy, so hard to control? Well, if he was ever going to do something like this again—and he knew he would—he was going to have to get in shape. No question about it—first thing Monday morning, he was going to join a gym.

He looked at the heap that lay at his feet. Damn, but she'd been a pretty thing. He knelt down and touched her hair, running his fingers through the long brown strands and holding them up in the sunlight where shades of red and gold glinted and gleamed in his hand. Beautiful, really.

He sat next to her and studied her face. Her eyes had been warm and brown and her smile eager when they'd first met. They'd talked and laughed, compared notes, noticed how much they had in common. The brown eyes, the love of sushi, the ocean. They'd both collected shells as children, both had played tennis, and neither ever missed an episode of *South Park*. Uncanny, she'd declared, that we're so much alike.

He'd offered to meet her at the train station and she accepted without a second thought. They'd chatted and gone to lunch and she got into his car without hesitation. When he stopped along the lonely back road and told her he wanted to show her something, she never questioned his motives. Even when he struck her that first time, she seemed not to comprehend what was happening. It wasn't until he had her on the ground, and the beast had taken over, that he'd seen the terror in her eyes. The beast had been like a living thing, and for a moment, it was him against it. The beast, of course, won.

Her fear had bled from every pore in her body and the smell of it had ignited him like nothing he'd ever experienced. She cried and pleaded and begged. No words had ever sounded sweeter to his ears.

God, he'd had no idea that it would be like this.

He'd never imagined that anything could feel so good. That sex could be so exhilarating, that such power could flow through his hands to ignite his entire body.

He'd never known how completely he could connect with another human being.

Before lifting her and continuing on his way, he gently smoothed her hair from her face. There was still a long way to go. He wanted to find the perfect place for her. She deserved a special place to rest in the peace she now enjoyed, the peace he'd brought to her. She should have sunlight and wildflowers in return for the wonders he'd discovered through her. After all, she had been his first.

He smiled, remembering every delicious moment, and reveled in the knowledge that she would not be his last.

ONE

Robert Magellan stood on the front steps of his Tudor-style mansion and looked over the crowd gathered on the paved circular drive that was wide enough to accommodate three vehicles.

"I want to be able to park three cars across," he'd told the contractor, and that's exactly what he got.

Today there were people, not cars, lining the driveway.

"Are you sure this is a good idea?" Robert's personal assistant and right hand, Susanna Jones, asked from just inside the front door.

"It's a great idea," he assured her.

"You've always avoided the press," she reminded him.

"Yes, but this time I have something important to say."

"There were those who thought you might have had something important to say when you sold your stock in Magellan Express a few years back," she said dryly.

"My ex-partner talked enough for both of us," he recalled. "There wasn't much for me to add."

And of course, he'd had little enough to say to the media when his wife and son went missing more than two years earlier. At the request of the police, he'd made the televised pleas for anyone with any knowledge of their whereabouts to call the numbers that flashed on the screen, but beyond that, he'd been silent. His reluctance to speak on camera about his family had led some to speculate that perhaps he'd had a hand in their disappearance, but no one who knew him took *that* seriously. Robert had always worn his heart on his sleeve, and even now, speaking publicly about Beth and Ian was acutely painful, something he'd rather not do.

"Mr. Magellan, if you're ready . . ." The young assistant to the head of the public relations firm Robert had hired to organize his press conference placed the microphone on the podium that had been brought in that morning.

"Let's do it." Robert smiled and stepped up to the mike.

"Ladies and gentlemen, thanks for coming today on such short notice."

As if anyone from the local newspapers or television stations would have missed the first press conference Robert Magellan had ever called. His gated property had hummed with a buzzing undercurrent for the past hour.

"What do you suppose he's up to? Think he's going to announce that he's starting up another business?" The whispers floated on a light late spring breeze.

"What do you think it is this time? Energy? Or do you think he's sticking with technology?"

"Whatever it is, I'm calling my broker and telling him to buy me some of whatever it is he's selling. Everything he's ever touched turned to gold."

"Well, except for that business with his wife and kid . . ."

"Yeah, that was tough. Still haven't found either of them."

"You think maybe that's what he's—"

"Shhhh. I want to hear what he's saying."

"Recently, my cousin, Father Kevin Burch of Our Lady of Angels parish here in Conroy, reminded me of an oath we made to each other when we were kids." Robert made eye contact with Trula Comfort, who, as his late grandmother's best friend, had been invited to come along for the ride when he made his fortune. Trula winked, knowing, he suspected, how he planned to introduce his latest venture.

" 'When I grow up, I'm going to make a lot of money,' we promised ourselves and each other, 'and I'm going to use it to help people who can't help themselves.' Well, I grew up and did, in fact, make a lot of money, and Kevin has devoted his life to helping others. But until now, I haven't done a whole lot of good for too many people outside of my immediate circle."

Robert paused momentarily. "Father Kevin recently reminded me of that, too."

When the light laughter died down, Robert said, "As I'm sure you all know, more than two years ago, my wife, Beth, and our son, Ian, disappeared without a trace. Because I have unlimited resources, I was able to hire private investigators to search for them when the police came up dry. The fact that our local, state, and federal law enforcement agencies were unsuccessful doesn't negate the diligence of their work, but the reality is that, eventually, as every lead turned into a dead end, they had to turn their attention to other cases.

"Not too long ago, Father Kevin enlisted my assistance in finding two Conroy teenagers who'd also gone missing. I know that some of you covered the story of the successful return of these kids to their families. And once again, Father Kevin took the opportunity to remind me of that oath we'd made long ago."

Robert cleared his throat before continuing. "There are countless people whose loved ones have disappeared. There are thousands of parents who go to bed each night wondering where their missing children are, whether they're dead or alive. Over time, their cases go cold, the police are pulled in other directions, and the investigations often cease, leaving the families praying for a miracle. Well, I'm here today to announce the formation of what I like to think of as a catalyst for miracles, the Mercy Street Foundation. Funded by me, the foundation will employ the best talent available from all avenues of law enforcement, and put them to work to try to solve those unsolvable cases. Missing persons and homicides will be our focus."

A reporter in the back row raised his hand, and without waiting for acknowledgment from Robert asked, "Are you talking about a private police force?"

"More like a private investigative firm," Robert told him.

"When you say this is funded by you, what exactly does that mean?"

"It means that I will be paying the investigators, whatever staff I have to hire, whatever expenses we incur to get the job done."

"How is this going to work?" someone asked.

"Suppose you have a sister who's been missing for a couple of months—maybe even a couple of years—and the police are no longer actively looking for her. The trail is cold. You'd go to our website and you'd fill out a form. We've streamlined the process as much as possible. Answer all the questions about the case, tell us why we should choose your case to work on. You'd apply pretty much the way you would for a scholarship. You fill out the paperwork, then you wait for a response," Robert said. "To start, we'll choose one case each month to work on. It'll be up to the applicant to convince us to choose his or her request. Each one will be evaluated. The one we feel we're most able to help is the one we'll choose that month."

"Who's 'we'?" someone asked.

"Right now, the evaluation committee consists of my assistant, Susanna Jones; Mallory Russo, a former Conroy detective who was the first person I hired; and myself." He nodded in the direction of an attractive blond woman who stood close to the podium. "Mallory will be pretty much calling the shots on how the investigations will proceed, and since she has nine years of experience in law enforcement, her opinion will carry the most weight. She'll also be the bottom line on new hires. That's our committee."

"A-hem." Someone coughed nearby.

"Oh. Right. And Father Kevin Burch," Robert grinned. "He doesn't have any law enforcement experience, but he'll be trying to channel some divine guidance."

On the sidelines, Kevin laughed.

"You're saying you'll work on one case each month. Is that how long you're giving yourselves to solve a case? One month?" one of the local TV anchors asked.

"We will work each case until it's solved or until we or the applicant feels the investigation has run its course and is no longer productive." Robert stacked the index cards containing his few notes on the podium. "Look, I of all people know that there are some cases that will never be solved. Some missing persons will never be found, some killers will never be brought to justice. But we'll do our best on every case. For some victims, there will be justice. For some families, there will be closure."

"How much staff do you anticipate?"

"We'll grow as we need to. Right now, we have only one investigator, but she's going to have her hands full evaluating the submissions. We're going to have to hire at least one more immediately just to take on the first case." He looked directly into the camera and added, "We're looking for law enforcement personnel with experience in all avenues. Crime-scene investigators, crime-scene analysts and reconstruction experts, criminologists, profilers—we'll need them all, sooner or later. I'm also hoping to set up our own lab within the next year so that we can analyze evidence on our own without being a burden to the state and county labs. So if you're tops in your field and you're looking for a real challenge, go to our website and fill out an application."

"That's pretty ambitious," someone in the crowd noted.

"Yes." Robert smiled. "We know."

"When will you start hiring?"

"We'll begin the interview process with our first strong applicant. We intend to be well on our way to being fully staffed within six to nine months."

The conference lasted another half hour, with Robert fielding questions and repeating the website address several times for prospective applicants for the foundation's services as well as for potential employees. The young man from the PR firm passed out copies of the press release, and when the last question had been asked and answered, Robert waved to the crowd from the front porch before retreating into his house with his small inner circle.

"How soon do you think before we'll start hearing from people?" Mallory asked as she closed the door behind them.

"Before Trula gets the coffee made," Robert replied. "You're going to be a very busy woman over the next few weeks."

"Good." She smiled and followed the others into the large kitchen at the back of the house. "I like busy. I *need* busy. I can hardly wait."

"You won't have to," Trula said. "I just heard a

'ping' on the computer over there on the desk. That's one of the computers Robert had set up to receive email only through the website."

She pulled out a chair and gestured for Mallory to take a seat. "Make yourself comfortable, honey. I think you're going to be working late tonight. . . ."

.

In Southern California, a woman leaned closer to her television and listened with great interest to the mid-day press conference she'd found by accident while channel surfing, wasting time until she had to pick up her daughter at preschool. Intrigued, she went to the Mercy Street Foundation website and read about Robert Magellan's latest brainstorm. Using Magellan Express, the Internet search engine he'd developed and later sold for a king's ransom, she typed in *Conroy, PA*, and found it to be a small, working-class city surrounded by farms and gently rolling hills. She studied the photographs and liked what she saw. Returning to the website for the foundation, she filled out the online application for employment, but hesitated when it came to submitting it.

A conversation she'd had in the wee hours of that morning came back to her in full force, a conversation that had set her on edge and had made the prospect of a change—one involving a quick relocation—more appealing than it might otherwise have been.

Fifteen minutes later, she was still deliberating whether to submit the application, when the sound of a slamming car door drew her attention to the street outside. In this mostly blue-collar neighborhood, there was little traffic during the afternoon hours. She rose and peered through the front window, and her blood froze in her veins. A late model car was parked directly across the street, and two men were standing next to it on the sidewalk, their gaze fixed on her house.

She knew what they were there for, even if she did not know their names. It had been less than eight hours since she'd been warned, and once warned, she'd been a fool to think there'd be time.

Turning back to the laptop, she made one quick change on the application before hitting send.

Almost without thinking, she ran up the steps. Practically diving into her closet, she dragged out the large duffel bag she'd kept packed for just such a day. She ran across the hall into her daughter's room where she grabbed a few things she knew they could not leave behind—Chucky the dog and Buggy the glowworm—then slipped back downstairs. The men were still there, debating, perhaps, the likelihood of finding her home in the middle of the day. She picked up her laptop from the sofa and hurried into the kitchen. Grabbing her handbag from the counter, she shoved in her Glock and grabbed a plastic bag from the pantry. She stuffed in her daughter's things then quietly passed through the back door into the yard.

Her heart pounding, she ran the length of the backyard to the alley behind her house where she'd parked her car. Driving carefully to make certain she was not being followed, she took a roundabout way to her daughter's preschool. She parked on a side street, out of view of the front of the building, took a deep calming breath, and entered through a side door, just in case.

Once inside, she waved to the head teacher, indicating that she'd arrived to pick up her daughter.

"Hey, you're early today," the teacher said.

"Just a little." She searched the group for her child.

"Chloe Nolan, your mommy's here," the teacher called into the next room.

A tiny girl with dark curls and darker skin, yellow paint on her clothes and her cheek, skipped through the doorway.

"Can I go home with Natalie today?" The little girl flung herself onto her mother's legs and held on. "Please?"

"Not today, sweetie," her mother replied softly. "Go get your things and tell Natalie maybe another day."

"Tomorrow?"

"We'll see."

"*We'll see* means no." Chloe pouted.

"It means, we'll see what tomorrow brings. And we will. So go get your things now and—"

"I have my things. There, by the door." The girl pointed to the pile of backpacks.

"Say good-bye to your teacher, then, and let's go."

"Bye, Miss Maria. Bye, Natalie. Bye, Kelly." The little girl's voice trailed off as she picked up her belongings. Reaching up to hold her mother's hand, she babbled brightly all the way to the car.

"Are we going home?" Chloe asked as she strapped herself into her seat.

"We're going to Aunt Steffie's for a while."

"Are we eating dinner there?"

"We might even stay all night."

"Yay! I get to play with Mr. Mustache." Chloe's small feet kicked the seat gleefully. "He's my favorite cat in the whole entire world."

"He's a pretty special cat, all right," her mother agreed.

"Mommy, are you having a bad day?"

"Why? Do I look like I'm having a bad day?"

"You're not smiling."

She forced the biggest smile she could muster.

"Better?" she asked.

"Uh-huh," Chloe agreed.

She took the long way to her friend Stephanie's house, and parked two blocks away. She gathered up the things she'd brought with her, and locked the door. She'd have to remember to ask Steffie to have the car towed to the police impound lot for safekeeping.

"Why do we have to walk so far?" Chloe grumbled as she trudged along, lugging her backpack.

"Because it's a good day for a walk, and we want to see what we can see."

"It's cold," Chloe complained.

"Then we'll cross and walk on the sunny side of the street." She remembered there used to be a song about that, but she couldn't remember the words. Someone used to sing it to her, long ago, but she didn't remember who. "But we're almost there already. See? Just three more houses and we're there."

They crossed the street and walked up the driveway to the backyard.

"Her car's not here. She isn't home." Chloe looked as if she were about to cry.

"She'll be here soon."

"What if she isn't? We'll have to walk all the way back to the car. . . ." Chloe's eyes widened dramatically at the thought.

"She said she'd be home by . . . oh, there she is, see? I told you."

The blue and white Crown Victoria pulled slowly into the driveway and parked. A tall woman in her early forties got out. If she was surprised to see she had visitors, Chief Stephanie Jenkins of the Silver Hills, California, police department didn't show it.

"Hey, cuteness," she called to Chloe. "What's happening?"

"I'm happening," Chloe grinned.

"You bet your buttons you are." She kissed the top of the child's head. "Come on inside. Let's see what old Mr. Mustache is up to. I'll bet he's sleeping like a big old slug."

"Mommy said we might eat dinner here and maybe sleep here, too." Chloe dropped her backpack inside the door and took off in search of the cat.

"*Mi casa es su casa,*" Steffie told her.

"What?" Chloe turned to ask.

"It means, my house is your house. That means you are welcome to stay as long as you like."

"Yay." Chloe grinned happily. "Does that mean that your cat is my cat, too?"

"Sure enough, sugar."

No words had yet been exchanged between the two women. It wasn't until after Chloe was sleeping snugly in the guest bedroom, the old gray tom curled up contentedly beside her, that Steffie handed her old friend a glass of wine and said, "Okay, spill."

"I brought in a hooker late last night for solicitation."

"And that would be news because . . . ?"

"She offered to trade some information with me in exchange for not booking her."

"By the look on your face, I'd say she had something big to trade." Steffie tucked her legs under her on the sofa.

"She told me that Anthony Navarro knows that the child I adopted four years ago is his daughter, and he's coming after her." Her friend nodded slowly. "I'd say that was big."

"You think she knows what she's talking about?"

"You think there's any chance she could have made that up and, just coincidentally, got the facts right?"

"Okay, so we pick him up—"

"First, you have to find him. Stef, you've been after him for years, and you haven't come close."

"So we look a little harder while we wait for him to show."

"He won't be coming himself. He won't have to. He's offered twenty-five thousand dollars to the person who brings him his daughter."

Steffie whistled. "Jesus. He's serious."

"As a heart attack."

"So we pick up whoever he sends—"

"They'll just keep on coming, Steffie. He wants his daughter."

"Why?"

"The word on the street is, eight months ago, he had measles. It left him sterile. No more baby Navarros."

"So he wants the one he had with . . . wait a minute, how did he find out who adopted her? Tameka died while she was in prison. The court terminated his rights because he never showed up at any of the hearings. How all of a sudden does he know who has his kid?"

"He bribed someone at children's services. This hooker this morning, she knew the whole story, Stef. She even knew the name of Chloe's birth mother."

"Well, shit." Steffie stood and began to pace. After a moment, she said, "Okay, we do this. We stake out your house—"

"You'll have to get in line. It's already being staked out."

"You know this for certain?"

"I saw them. Two of them, parked right across the street from my house."

"When was this?"

"They were there when I left to pick up Chloe from school. Which is why I left when I did, and why I came here instead of going home."

"You think Navarro sent them?"

"I'd bet my life on it. I won't bet Chloe's."

Steffie reached for the radio she had strapped onto her waistband, but her friend stopped her.

"Uh-uh. It won't do any good, Stef. It won't stop until he gets her. He'll get her at her school or he'll have someone come into the house in the middle of the night, but he will get her." She shook her head, her face white with fear. "As long as we're here, and he knows we're here, it won't stop. There aren't enough police in this part of the state to take on his whole family, and he won't care how many of us or how many of them die."

"So we call in the FBI."

"Steffie, the FBI has been after him for longer than you have."

"So what are you going to do?"

"Let me tell you what I saw on TV this afternoon. . . ." She related what she'd heard and what she'd learned from the Mercy Street Foundation website.

"You're thinking about applying?"

"I already did, online."

"You're just going to pack up and move East?"

"No time to pack." She shook her head. "I don't dare go back to the house, Stef. I have to protect my daughter. No way can I let that animal or any of his relatives get within a country mile of her. I've always had a bag packed with clothes and cash and some things I couldn't leave behind. Chloe's baby pictures . . . some of her baby things."

"What made you think you'd need to do that?"

"I spent my entire childhood on the move. I've never felt that anyplace, anything in my life was permanent. Which is why I rented, instead of buying that house."

"Give me a few days to see what we can do."

"There's nothing you can do. No one's gotten close to him, ever. No one knows where he is. He has a huge network, his brothers, his sisters, his cousins, his uncles. We're talking about one of the biggest drug families operating between Mexico and Southern California."

"Sooner or later—"

"Later will be too late for my daughter. I can't give her up to the kind of life she'd have, growing up as the daughter of a major drug dealer."

"So you move across the country, you think he won't be able to find you?"

"He won't be looking for Emme Caldwell."

"You'd change your name?"

"My *name*?" she snorted. "What is my name, Stef? I don't even know what my real name is."

Steffie held her head in her hands. "You know that Emme Caldwell died five months ago."

"Robert Magellan won't know that."

"He will when he checks her references."

"That would be you."

Steffie fell silent.

"I know it's a lot to ask. If you're not comfortable with it, God knows, I'll understand. I can reapply, with a different name."

"You already applied as Emme?"

"Yes."

"Well, that pretty much seals the deal."

"Oh, God. I should have thought this through a little more. Stef, I am so sorry. It's just that, after hearing all this from that hooker this morning, then going off my shift and seeing this press conference on TV, then those two goons were outside my house . . ." She blew out a long stream of air. "It just seemed like a sign, like someone was telling me something. But I was wrong to put you in a position where you'd have to lie. It'll be okay. I'll come up with something else."

"It's not okay," Steffie told her. "You're the best friend I ever had. You saved my life twice in the past five years. I can save yours this once. Besides, if anything happened to you or to that precious girl . . ."

Steffie visibly shivered. They'd both seen firsthand what happened to those who crossed the Navarro family in the past.

"Just tell me what you want me to do. . . ."

TWO

"Mommy, do I go to school tomorrow?" Chloe looked up from the picture book she'd been quietly looking at for the last eighteen miles.

"Not tomorrow, pumpkin." The newly self-christened Emme Caldwell met her daughter's eyes in the rearview mirror. She'd been trying to think of herself as Emme and banish all thoughts, all reminders of her old name. *Emme Caldwell,* she'd repeated to herself over and over. *My name is Emme Caldwell.*

Even her newly purchased ID reminded her that she was, indeed, Emme Caldwell. It had gone against everything she'd believed in to pay money for falsified documents, but in the end, survival trumped everything else.

"When?" Chloe banged the heels of her sneakers on the car seat to emphasize her displeasure. "I haven't gone to school in *days*! When can I go to school again?"

"Pretty soon," her mother told her.

"But not my school," Chloe said softly.

"You'll go to a new school," she said brightly as

she tried to picture introducing herself to Chloe's new teacher. *Hi. I'm Emme Caldwell. . . .*

"I liked my old school." Chloe's feet banged with increased vigor.

"I'll bet you'll like your new school, too."

"Natalie won't be there." Chloe's eyes filled with tears. "I won't know anyone. I won't have anyone to play with."

"You didn't know anyone at Miss Maria's either, until you went the first day, remember?"

"Why can't I go to my old school anymore?" It was more a demand than a question.

"Do you remember what I told you?"

"That you're going to have a new job and it would be too far away to go to the old school." Chloe's face held the promise of a major whine on the way. "Why couldn't you keep your old job?"

"Sometimes change is good, Chloe, sometimes—"

"I could stay with Aunt Steffie."

"Aunt Steffie works a lot, much more than I do."

"I could have a babysitter, like when you have to work and I don't have to go to school." She brightened. "I could stay with Mr. Mustache."

"It isn't that simple, baby."

"I'm not a baby." To prove her point, Chloe wiped away the tears that had begun to spill over with the back of her hand.

"I know, sweetie. And I'm sorry that this move is upsetting you. But it's what we have to do."

"I don't like it," Chloe grumbled from the backseat.

They'd had the same conversation no fewer than three times each day since they left California.

Outside of Denver, Emme pulled off Route 70 and followed the signs for Highway 36, which had appeared on the map to be the quickest way east. It was closing in on 6 P.M., and she suspected that part of Chloe's problem was hunger and fatigue. Even though the child had slept for a short time earlier in the afternoon, being confined in the car seat all day was taking its toll.

"We're going to have some dinner and find a nice place to stay tonight," Emme told her. "So you're going to have to help me find a restaurant."

Chloe sat up straight in her seat and peered out the window.

"I see golden arches," she said excitedly.

"Let's look for someplace with a better selection of dinners."

Several minutes later, the sign for a hotel with a decent-looking restaurant came into view, and Emme turned in to the parking lot.

"Look, Chloe," she said as she turned off the engine. "We can have dinner, swim in the pool, and sleep in a nice bed. What do you say?"

"Do they have spaghetti?"

"We can go in and ask." Emme got out and opened the rear door. "What if they don't have spaghetti? What else would you like?"

"Macaroni and cheese. The orange kind Aunt Steffie makes. It comes in a box." Chloe undid her seat belt and with her mother's help, hopped down to the ground. She continued to rattle off dinner possibilities all the way to the reception desk and all the way to the room they'd share that night.

There'd been spaghetti on the menu and a heated

indoor pool for a swim before bedtime, so Chloe was not only a happy girl, but a very tired one by the time they turned in for the night. She fell asleep almost immediately after getting into her pajamas. Her mother was more than ready for a good night's sleep herself, but took the time to chart the next day's route before turning off the light. She was hoping to get to somewhere between St. Joseph, Kansas, and Springfield, Illinois, by the following night. She fell asleep trying to calculate how many more days they'd be on the road before they finally arrived in Conroy, Pennsylvania. Home of the Mercy Street Foundation. And with any true luck, future home to Emme and Chloe Caldwell.

"Just a heads-up," Stephanie said when she called Emme's disposable cell phone the next morning. "I did get a call from a Mallory Russo from the Mercy place wanting to know about Emme Caldwell."

"What did you tell her?"

"I told her that she'd have to submit her request in writing, along with the release of information you agreed to when you filled out your application online, but that I could tell her that you were one of the best officers I ever worked with and that I was much saddened by your resignation."

"Thank you, Stef."

"It's true."

"I appreciate it. More than I can say. I know you're going out on a limb for me." Emme paused. "Did she send in the release?"

"She faxed it over. She'll have my recommendation by this time tomorrow." Steffie added, "Maybe sooner, if no one gets shot between now and six o'clock today."

"I hope my chance for future employment doesn't really hang on that little detail."

"Don't worry. I'll take care of it. But she did seem really curious about the fact that you'd already resigned."

"What did you tell her?"

"That she'd have to speak directly with you because there were some personal issues involved. I didn't know what else to say."

"That's fine. I'm sure she'll ask me. I'll have something prepared."

"By the way, how's my baby girl doing?"

"She isn't a very happy girl right now," Emme admitted. "She misses school and her friends."

"She'll be okay. She'll adjust as soon as you get settled and she has a new school. She'll make new friends."

"We can only hope."

"She will. Think positively."

"I'm trying to."

"So what's your plan from here?" Stephanie asked.

"I'm hoping to get as far as Missouri today. Tomorrow, hopefully, Indiana. I'd like to be in Pennsylvania by Monday."

"You should be able to make that."

"The drive has been pretty hard on Chloe. She gets pretty fussy. I have to look for places to stop for lunch where there's a playground or a park nearby so she can run some of it off. Then at night, we look for places that have indoor pools. It slows us down but we both need some exercise after sitting in the car for the entire day."

"Flying would have been faster."

"I hate to fly. Besides, I'll need the car once we get out there." She walked to the window and peered out through the drapes. Even though she knew positively that they had not been followed, she suspected that she might never stop looking over her shoulder. "Thanks, Stef, for everything. The reference, the credit card . . ."

"We couldn't have you leaving a paper trail from one state to the next. We don't know what connections he has, or who he's bribed. Using your own cards would have been the equivalent of dropping crumbs behind you as you trekked across the country."

"No one's ever had a better friend than you, Stef."

"I could say the same to you. Emme." Stephanie laughed. "God, that sounds so strange."

"Imagine how I feel. I have to remind myself to think of myself as Emme. But it isn't the first time I had to get used to a new name, so I'm okay with it. It's just a word, when you get right down to it."

"What are you going to tell Chloe?"

"I haven't decided yet. I'm thinking maybe that we'll make a game of it, a secret game between us. Not great, I know, but that's all I've been able to come up with. The thing is, once she's Chloe Caldwell, she has to remember that she's Chloe Caldwell."

"Chloe is a smart girl. She loves to play pretend. She'll remember." Stephanie paused, then asked, "Do you have enough cash?"

"I do, thanks. I've been saving for a rainy day for a

long time. Somehow, I always knew that something like this would happen." She added, "I'm not saying I foresaw this, just that I felt there was a good possibility I'd be pulling up stakes quickly at some point. Like I said before, as a kid I always needed to be able to leave at the drop of a hat. I've kept cash in the house for when I'd have to leave again, and I've been adding to the stash for years. So we're good. We'll be good for a while."

"Do you think you should call this Mallory Russo before you get to Conroy? I don't know if just popping up and saying 'Hi, just thought I'd drop in' is the best way to deal with this. Russo sounded like she was all business on the phone."

"I'm thinking if I'm already there, she's more likely to give me an interview."

"What are you going to do if you get there and she tells you that she's already filled the job?"

"It's hard to believe anyone could have acted faster than I have. And they did say they wanted to be fully staffed in less than a year, so they have to be looking for more than one investigator. If worse comes to worse, I'll see if the local police have an opening. The one thing I won't be doing is heading back to California. But we should be in Conroy by Monday night, so I'll give her a call on Tuesday morning and see if she can fit me in."

"Look, if she says no, we'll think of something else. Over the past few years, I've met a lot of law enforcement people, other police chiefs, at conferences. I can make some calls, see who needs a good cop." Steffie paused before adding, "A great cop."

"Thanks, Stef. If this falls through, we'll do that.

But I have a good feeling about this. Like it's meant to be." She walked to the window and looked out, ignoring the lump in her throat. Steffie had been kinder to her than anyone in her life ever had. Would she ever see her again? "We'll be okay. But thank you. You'll never know how much I appreciate everything you've done for me."

The lump was still in her throat after she quietly snapped shut her cell phone. She lifted one edge of the curtain and stared out on the busy highway where cars buzzed by and the lights from a dozen fast-food places and gas stations obscured the stars. She thought of all the nights she and Chloe had taken a blanket to the backyard and lay back, looking up, watching for shooting stars.

Maybe in our new town, we'll be able to see the stars, she told herself as she dropped the curtain and put the phone down on the bedside table.

She tried to remember everything she'd read online about Conroy. Beyond the town proper, it had looked to be somewhat rural, so chances were good that they'd have a backyard again, and stars overhead at night.

She finished in the bathroom and plugged in the little nightlight she'd brought with them so that Chloe wouldn't be in total darkness if she woke up in the middle of the night. She carefully crawled into the bed next to her sleeping child and tucked the blanket around her before resting her head on her own pillow. She stared at the ceiling and tried to calm the doubts that plagued her when she was alone with her thoughts. She drew on that well of strength she'd drawn from since she was a child in foster care and moved from home to home. As an adult looking back on those days, she'd not been able to remember the number of times she'd been moved.

And always, she'd been the girl without a name.

Well, now she had a name, she reminded herself. Not one that had been chosen for her, but one she'd chosen for herself. Emme Caldwell.

From this day forward, she *would* be Emme Caldwell.

THREE

So what's eating you this morning?" Trula bustled into Mallory's office with a mug of coffee in one hand and a napkin wrapped around a freshly baked muffin in the other. With a slight hint of accusation, she added, "You didn't come for a second cup of coffee with Susanna and you didn't follow your nose to the kitchen for a muffin."

Mallory forced a smile and reached out for the napkin and the mug. "You didn't have to do this, but I thank you." She sniffed the muffin. "Ummm. You put pecans in these, didn't you?"

She turned the mug around to see which of Trula's pithy sayings she'd gotten that morning. *The truth is rarely pure and never simple.*

Amen to that.

"I did." Trula took a seat without waiting to be offered one. "So . . . I'm waiting."

"For? . . ." Mallory took a bite of muffin and smiled. "Delicious. You could package these and sell them and make big bucks, Trula."

"Don't change the subject. You know what for."

"You don't take no for an answer very often, do you." It wasn't a question.

"Not if I can help it."

Mallory sighed, resigned.

"I got a call this morning from one of the applicants for the investigator job."

"So? That's what you wanted. That's why we went through that whole press conference thing and did the website. What's the problem? Is the applicant unqualified?"

"No. She appears to be as qualified as most, I guess. Some may be better, some may be not as. Her qualifications aren't the problem."

"So?"

"So she's in Conroy and she wants an interview."

"Again," Trula sighed, "I say, so?"

"So she was a cop in California. She applied online the day the application was posted, quit her job, packed it all up, drove east, and is counting on us hiring her."

"Do I have to repeat myself a fourth time?"

"So who does that?" Mallory frowned. "Who quits their job and drives across the country, demands an interview for a job she may not get?"

"Asked or demanded?"

"Asked. But I had the feeling if I'd said no, she'd have begged until I said I'd see her."

"When is she coming in?"

"This afternoon. I told her I could see her around two."

"Doesn't give you much time to check her references."

"I already did that. Actually, I do a preliminary

check of the ones who look qualified as soon as I get the app. If I know up front that someone isn't going to be a contender, that's one less interview I have to arrange."

"Did she check out?"

Robert wandered in and took the chair next to Trula's.

"Did who check out?" he asked.

Mallory filled him in on the conversation thus far.

"So did she?" Trula repeated.

"She did. Actually, her former boss gave her a glowing reference." Mallory took a sip of coffee. "It was as if she couldn't say enough about her. I can't explain why, but it just sounded . . . I don't know, too pat or something."

"Why's that?" asked Susanna, who'd been listening at the doorway.

"You're chief of police in a town not far from the Mexican border. One of your best officers quits the force with no notice—I mean, how much notice could she have given? The application just went online two weeks ago, and this woman is already here after having driven from California. And yet you still give her the highest possible recommendation? You never mention the fact that she left you high and dry and a man short?" Mallory shook her head. "Something about that just isn't sitting right with me."

"So maybe after you talk to her, you'll have an idea why." Robert stood and stretched. "I trust your instincts, Mal. It's up to you whether or not to hire her."

"Well, I'd sure like to have an opportunity to interview some of the competition."

"There isn't going to be a whole lot of time to deliberate. If it looks like she can't cut it, cross her off the list and go on to the next one. We're going to need staff pronto."

"We're going to need the *right* staff," Mallory reminded him. "You want the best person for the job, not just *any* investigator."

"True enough. But you can't tell me that in that entire bunch of applicants you can't find someone who fits the bill who can start really soon. We set the first of the month as our deadline to kick off that first case, and the first is closing in on us very quickly," he pointed out. "Kevin will be here late this afternoon and we'll be deciding which case gets the privilege of being number one."

"I have it down to three," Mallory told him. "The write-ups are on your desk." She turned to Susanna. "Yours, too."

"I already read through them. Interesting. A little something there for everyone," Susanna remarked.

"How many submissions did we get?" Robert asked.

"Six hundred and twelve," Mallory told him.

"How did you cut them down to three?"

"Wasn't easy."

"I should go take a look." Robert stood. "Did Kevin get copies, Mal?"

"I faxed them to the church office this morning."

"Well, then, I'll leave this other thing—the possibly overzealous applicant—in your hands," Robert said as he left the room.

Mallory turned to Susanna, who shrugged and said, "Like Robert said, it's up to you. But we will need to hire someone soon. Over six hundred submissions in two weeks? Craziness." She followed Robert out the door.

Mallory turned to Trula.

"Don't look at me. I'm just the cook."

"My ass."

Smiling, Trula stood and picked up the crumpled napkin and the empty mug.

"Lunch is in thirty minutes."

Emme stopped in front of the ornate iron gates that shut off Robert Magellan's estate from the rest of the world. She put the car in park and stared at the guard who was walking toward her.

"Can I help you, miss?" he asked.

"Is this Robert Magellan's? . . ."

He nodded.

"I have an appointment with Mallory Russo."

"Ms. Caldwell?"

It took a split second for her to realize he was addressing *her*. "Yes."

"You're expected." He smiled and returned to the small booth he'd been sitting in. "Go on through and follow the drive to the circle on the right. You can leave your car there. Someone will meet you at the door."

"Thanks."

More curious than ever, she drove through the opening gates.

"Mommy, is this a castle?" Chloe asked from the backseat. "Are we going to see a prince?"

"Sort of," Emme mumbled and followed the guard's instructions to the front door.

"Who lives here, Mommy?"

"A very wealthy man who puts his money to good use to help people who have problems."

"I have problems," Chloe told her. "I don't have a school."

"Not that kind of problem, sweetie."

"What kind?"

"He helps to find people who are lost."

"Do you think he could help me find Bobo?" One of Chloe's favorite stuffed animals had been inadvertently left behind when her mother had grabbed a few cherished items from Chloe's room.

"I think he only looks for people."

"Bobo was people," she heard Chloe whisper.

When they reached the circle, Emme parked and got out, and couldn't help but stare at the Tudor mansion that seemed to go on forever.

"I bet a princess lives here too." Chloe unbuckled her seat belt and eagerly jumped from the car without waiting for assistance. "Will I get to see her?"

"There's no princess, sweetie," her mother said as she took her hand. Together they started toward the front door.

It opened almost immediately. A woman of indeterminable age stood at the threshold. She was dressed in a denim skirt that had faded from too many washings, a blue chambray shirt with the sleeves rolled to her elbows, and a bright red apron dotted with spots of flour here and there. White tennis sneakers worn without socks were on her feet, her white hair was wrapped into a bun at the nape of her neck, and her glasses sat upon the very end of her nose.

"Come in, Emme Caldwell." She gestured with one

hand. Seeing Chloe, her eyebrows raised almost to her hairline. "And who might this be?"

"This is Chloe, my daughter." Emme's words began to pour out in a rush. "I'm sorry, I know it's highly unusual to bring a child to an interview like this but we just arrived in town last night and I couldn't leave her in the hotel. I probably should have mentioned it when I spoke with Ms. Russo. I promise she won't be a bother to anyone. She's very well behaved. She has a coloring book and her crayons and she can sit on the floor outside the office while I meet with Ms. Russo."

"Nonsense." The woman shut the door behind them. "Chloe can give me a hand in the kitchen. Do you like to bake, Chloe?"

"I baked cookies one time for Mr. Pendergast. He lived next door to us and he had his . . ." Chloe frowned and tugged on her mother's hand. "What did the doctor take out of his stomach?"

"His appendix." Emme stood in the vast entry and fought the urge to gape at the paintings that lined the walls. They all looked authentic.

"That." Chloe stared up at the woman in the apron. "What's your name?"

"Trula."

"Like truly, only not?"

"Exactly." The woman smiled at Emme. "Mallory knows you're here. Her office is the third door down this hall on the left. Chloe and I will be in the kitchen when you're finished. Don't feel the need to rush. Cookies take time."

Emme prayed that Chloe would remember the conversation they'd had several nights ago—and every night since—about their new last name. Convincing Chloe that her name was now Caldwell, not Nolan, and that her mother's first name was now Emme, not Ann, had not been as much as a trial as she'd feared.

"Why, Mommy? Did my name change because I moved?" she'd asked the night before.

"No. It's because . . ." Emme had tried to come up with something plausible. "It's sort of like a game, sweetie."

Even to Emme, that sounded beyond lame.

"That's a silly game."

"I know." Emme sighed, trying to come up with something better. How to explain to a child that it was a matter of life and death?

"Do you like the way it sounds better?" Chloe had asked, saving her.

"I do."

"I do, too." Chloe had begun to sing, ad nauseam, "Chloe Caldwell, Chloe Caldwell, Chloe Caldwell . . ."

Nice of her to have bailed her mother out on that one. Emme still didn't know what reason she'd have ended up giving for the change, but was grateful not to have had to go that route.

She cleared her throat and smoothed the lapels of the white shirt she'd ironed in the hotel room just an hour ago. With some trepidation she watched Chloe disappear into the kitchen with the older woman— the cook? the housekeeper?—and wondered at the wisdom of permitting Chloe to go off into this huge house with a total stranger, however benign and grandmotherly she might have appeared. *Surely it would be okay,* she told herself. Would Robert Magellan have someone of questionable character working in his home?

The kitchen door closed with a whoosh that was audible even at this distance. She was half-tempted to follow, just to make sure, when a tall, good-looking man with dark hair stepped into the hall from a door at the very end.

"Oh." He seemed surprised to see her. He glanced at his watch. "Two o'clock. You're here for Mallory."

He took several steps forward and rapped on a closed door before pushing it open.

"Mal, your appointment is here."

"Thank you." Emme had expected to be nervous—she generally wasn't nervous by nature—but suddenly the import of where she was and what she was doing hit her. She started down the hall in his direction. "You're Mr. Magellan, aren't you?"

"Robert." He nodded, then as an afterthought, extended his hand. "It's Robert. You must be . . . ah . . ."

"Emme Caldwell."

"Yes. Right." He gestured in the direction of the office. "Mallory?"

"Yes. I'm here." A pretty blond woman appeared in the doorway. "Come in, Emme."

The woman stood aside for Emme to enter, then turned to Robert and asked, "Did you want to sit in?"

"No, no." He appeared horrified at the thought. "Your job. Your decision. It's in your hands."

"Right. I'll see you later then." Mallory closed the door behind her. "I am Mallory Russo, by the way. We spoke on the phone."

"Yes. I should apologize for the short notice."

Mallory pointed to a chair and Emme sat.

"I have to admit I was surprised to hear you were in Conroy," Mallory said as she seated herself behind her desk. "I haven't had time to finish reviewing all of the applicants and as you can imagine, we need to vet—"

"I do understand," Emme told her. "I've been thinking about moving east for some time now, but when I saw your press conference and then went to your website, I thought the foundation was worth looking into. You said you were looking for good investigators, I was looking to make a move in this direction and I was going to need a job. I figured, why wait?"

Emme smiled as if there was no need to state the obvious.

"We're looking for the best in the business."

"I believe I qualify. If you check with my former chief of police—"

"I already did that," Mallory cut her off. "She gave you the highest recommendation. But you understand, we have hundreds of applicants for this position."

"I was under the impression that there were a number of positions open. Mr. Magellan's press conference seemed to imply that he was looking for more than one investigator." Was Mallory always this cool, this businesslike to everyone, or has she simply taken an immediate dislike to me? Emme wondered. "And that he was very eager to take on that first case."

"That he is," Mallory conceded. "But Robert has never worked in law enforcement, and he might not be the best person to judge an applicant's qualifications."

"Then by all means, let's talk about mine." Emme settled back, her elbows resting casually on the arms of the chair, and put on her most confident air.

For the next hour, they discussed Emme's training, number of years with the Silver Hills force—seven— and her previous work experience. Mallory appeared to be impressed that Emme had started with the police department as a records clerk right out of high school while taking courses at the local community college. From there, she'd gone on to the police academy, and last year had been sent for special training at the FBI Academy. They talked about the number of cases she'd taken lead on, percentage of cases solved, the number and type of professional courses she'd taken since graduating from the police academy.

"How many homicides have you worked on?" Mallory asked.

"I'd have to go year to year to count them up. I'd say we had roughly a dozen of what I'd consider routine homicides over the past twelve months. That includes domestics, killings that occurred while committing other crimes, hit and runs, and so forth. And then we have the situation where, Silver Hills being very close to the Mexican border, we have significant drug traffic, with the accompanying thugs sliding back and forth between the two countries. It's not unusual to find bodies in the desert or in the mountains right outside of town. The state does pitch in on those, however."

"How many of those 'routine' homicides have you taken lead on?"

Emme paused, debating. It was bad enough she was lying about who she was. She knew Steffie would back anything she said, but if she got the job, she wanted it to be on the merits of her own performance.

"I haven't been lead, per se, on any of them," she answered truthfully. "The detectives take lead on homicides in our department."

"How close do you think you were to making detective, Ms. Caldwell?" Mallory glanced down at her notes.

"I guess you'd have to ask Chief Jenkins that."

"Actually, I did. She said you'd have been given strong consideration for the first available opening . . ."

Thank you, Steffie.

". . . but that she didn't anticipate having any openings for at least another five, possibly ten years." Mallory leaned her forearms on her desk. "She added that you possessed exceptional investigative skills and if she had any reason to think there'd be one sooner, she'd have done whatever she could to have talked you out of this move."

"That was very kind of her." Emme smiled.

"She spoke very highly of you." Mallory put down the paper she'd been scanning and looked Emme directly in the eye. "*Very* highly."

"I appreciate that. What else can I tell you about myself to convince you to hire me?"

"You can tell me why you pulled up stakes to move from California to Pennsylvania just like that." Mallory snapped her fingers.

"I told you on the phone, I saw the press conference. I'd been looking for months to make a move; it just seemed like the right thing to do." Emme fought to keep her nerves from making her voice sound shaky. Was it her imagination, or was Mallory suspicious of her motives? *Better make it good,* she cautioned herself, sensing that her future employment—or lack thereof— could depend on what she said at this moment.

"I mentioned there was a lot of drug trafficking in Silver Hills. Over the past year, there have been several shootings in town involving rival gangs. I have a daughter who is four, Ms. Russo. Her father was Mexican, her mother African American. She is just starting to become aware of the animosity, the name-calling between the two factions. I'd like her to grow up in a different atmosphere, to learn to respect her heritage on both sides."

"I see." Mallory nodded slowly. "She's adopted?"

"Was it the red hair, the green eyes, the pale skin, or the 'map of Ireland' on my face that gave it away?" Her hair wasn't so much red anymore as auburn and she couldn't be certain of an Irish heritage, but everyone seemed to comment on it, so she supposed there might be something to it.

"We can go with all of the above." Mallory smiled with some warmth for the first time since she'd sat down. "I can understand wanting to raise your daughter in a different environment. But why Conroy?"

"Truthfully, when I looked it up on the computer, using Magellan Express, of course"—Mallory laughed—"I saw a town that looked like a place I wish I'd grown up in. I couldn't fill the application out fast enough. And once I did, once I'd hit send, I just felt as if . . . I don't know, I don't want to sound silly, but I just felt as if this was where we were meant to be."

"I see." Mallory played with her pen. "Since you watched the press conference and you went to the website, I'm assuming you read more than the application?"

Emme nodded.

"Then you know that we're going to be taking on some pretty complicated cases, cases that have grown cold because the investigating departments weren't able to solve them. So we're talking about the tough cases, the ones where we will be looking for information that others have overlooked. We'll need instincts that are spot on—not every time, maybe, no one's right one hundred percent of the time, but you're going to have to have a strong track record. We'll need the best skills, the ability to think outside the box. For much of the time, you'll be working alone, because until we get up to snuff with hiring—and that isn't going to happen overnight—there won't be anyone to partner with you."

"I don't mind working alone."

Mallory patted a stack of fat files that towered on one side of her desk.

"These are the submissions we've received in the past week, requests for help from over six hundred people. I expect that will increase as time goes on." She picked up one folder and opened it in front of her. "Here's a case where a woman has been missing for nine years."

Mallory held up a second folder. "This next one, a young boy who went missing when he was seven."

Another. "This one? A father of five who left home

one morning for work and was never seen or heard from again."

Mallory met Emme's eyes across the desk. "These are the kinds of cases you'd be dealing with."

She slid a stack of files across the desk to Emme.

"Pick one at random," Mallory told her, "and tell me how you'd handle it."

Ninety minutes later, they were still discussing the case, Mallory making notes without comment. They were both so engrossed that neither looked up when the door opened and Susanna walked in.

"Mal, I—Oh. Sorry." Susanna paused in midstride. "I didn't realize you were still—"

"It's okay, Suse, come in and meet Emme Caldwell." Mallory looked up from her notes. "We're just doing some hypothetical case analysis."

Emme turned as the tall dark-haired woman came toward her.

"Good to meet you," Susanna said as Emme took her outstretched hand. "If I'm not mistaken, you're our first interviewee."

"She is." Mallory nodded.

"I apologize for interrupting, but there is the most incredible aroma wafting from the kitchen, and I had to follow my nose to see what Trula was up to," Susanna explained. "I was thinking it might be a good time to take a break but I see you're still busy . . ."

"Actually, I think we're done here." Mallory pushed her chair back and rose. "Not because Trula is baking, mind you," she made a point of telling Emme, "but because I think I have enough information for the time being."

"Are there any other questions about my experience I might answer?" Emme asked, concerned by Mallory's sudden dismissal.

"No, I think I have what I need. I have the entire personnel file from Silver Hill, and that has your transcripts and your performance reviews. Thanks for coming in. It was a pleasure to have met you." Mallory walked around the desk to shake Emme's hand.

"So, what happens next?" Emme tried not to appear less than self-confident.

"You'll hear from me once a decision has been made."

"I see." Emme leaned down to pick up her bag, which she'd dropped on the floor when she first took her seat. "Let me give you the number at the hotel and our room number."

"Don't you have a cell phone?" Mallory asked.

"I did. I lost it somewhere between Indiana and Pennsylvania." On purpose, because cell phones can be traced. She'd pick up another throwaway as soon as possible. She'd used most of her prepaid minutes talking to Steffie and the rest of them when she called Mallory. "You don't realize how much you depend on those things until you don't have one. I'll be getting a replacement."

"Well, if we bring you on, we'll give you one. Of course, you might want to have your own before then."

"Yes. Well, then. I suppose we're finished. Thank you so much for seeing me on short notice. I hope it wasn't an imposition, Ms. Russo."

"Not at all. I'm glad you came in." Mallory walked to the door and stood there like a sentinel.

"How would I find Trula?" Emme asked.

"You've already met Trula?"

"She met us at the door when I arrived, and took Chloe—my daughter—to the kitchen." Emme felt a bit of color tinge her cheeks. "I'm sorry, I didn't have anyone to watch her and I couldn't leave her alone in the hotel. I thought I'd leave her in the hall with some of her things to amuse her." Emme held up the bag. "Crayons, coloring book. But Trula met us at the door and sort of swooped up Chloe . . ."

"No need to apologize," Mallory told her. "Trula's swooped up all of us at one time or another. I'm sure she was delighted to have Chloe's company."

"Ahhh, then we have you to thank for what I'm sure must be a wonderful afternoon snack." Susanna grinned. "Well, come along with me, Ms. Caldwell, and we'll track down that child of yours and see just what she and Trula managed to cook up in the time you've been here."

Susanna ushered Emme into the hall, then looked over her shoulder. "Coming, Mallory?"

"I'll be down in a while. Save me some of whatever it is."

"No promises," Susanna called back over her shoulder. To Emme, she said, "I suppose you think we're all very loose around here."

Before Emme could reply, Susanna went on. "Well, I guess we are, in a way. I think that's what happens when your offices are in someone's home."

"Is Trula the cook?"

"The cook, the housekeeper, and all around slave driver. Trula was a very dear friend of Robert's grandmother. She's sort of a family legacy. She'd lived with old Mrs. Magellan, and came to live with Robert when his gran died." Susanna lowered her voice conspiratorially. "She runs the house, watches over Robert and Kevin like a hawk. Kevin is Father Burch, Robert's cousin. Trula loves them both as she'd love her own, if she had her own. Which she doesn't. Actually, she doesn't have any family at all, except for the two of them."

"It's nice of Mr. Magellan to let her stay here," Emme said.

"Ha!" Susanna snorted. "As if he had a choice. He went to close up his grandmother's house after she died and came back with Trula."

"Still, it's nice of him."

"I'm kidding. Of course it's nice of him, but he adores her. They squabble and pick at each other, but they love each other fiercely." Susanna held up a hand to push open the kitchen door. "All of which is probably too much information for someone who has just had her first interview.

"So let's see what we've got going on in the kitchen." Susanna gave the door a shove and called, "Trula, what deliciousness are you cooking up in here?"

FOUR

So Mal, what did you think?" Susanna squeezed in next to Mallory on the banquette in the blue and yellow kitchen.

The Magellan home may have been a mansion, but where Trula ruled, warmth was in abundance. She'd had the large, L-shaped benches built and deep cushions made to match the curtains. The cozy corner had quickly become the favored spot in the house for meetings.

"What did I think about what?" Mallory replied absently.

"The price of gas." Susanna rolled her eyes. "Emme Caldwell. What did you think of her?"

"I think she very well may be as good as her former boss says she is," Mallory told her.

"So do we have a hire?" Robert sat across the large square table from them.

"I don't know."

"Is there a problem with her?" Robert asked.

"I don't know. I just feel that something is off somewhere. She's almost too good to be true."

"Something about her you didn't like?" Robert pressed her.

"I liked her well enough," Mallory conceded.

"I liked her, too." Trula placed a square plate of cookies in the middle of the table. "Not that anyone cares what I think."

"Not true," Mallory protested. "Of course we all care what you think." She picked up one of the cookies and licked the pink frosting. "Are you going to tell us what you liked about her?"

"I liked the way she was with that girl of hers. Came in here to get her, didn't rush the child as if what she was doing wasn't important, the way some folks do to their kids. Listened to what the girl had to say, spoke thoughtfully to her. You can tell a lot about a person by the way they speak to their kids. I like adults who treat children with respect." Trula added a stack of napkins to the table. "And I liked that when she speaks to you, she looks you dead in the eye. 'Course I know that doesn't mean she's a good investigator, but we're talking about liking her." Trula smiled at Mallory. "I liked her."

"You're not fooling anyone. You just liked having a little girl in the kitchen with you," Mallory teased.

"That goes without saying." Still smiling, Trula began to pass around mugs for coffee. She'd been collecting for years and had just received several new ones she'd ordered online. While they each had their favorites, no one ever knew which one they'd end up with if Trula was passing them out.

"Hey, how come I got the one that says *He who dies with the most stuff is still dead*?" Mallory held up her mug.

"Don't complain. She gave me *Sleeps with Dogs*," Susanna said, twirling hers around her index finger. "What's yours say, Robert?"

He picked up the mug, held it up for her to see. "*I am the Gatekeeper.*"

"Oooh, *Ghostbusters*." Mallory's eyes lit up. "Want to trade?"

"Oh, for crying out loud." Trula set the coffeepot on the table and looked from one to the other. "Who cares what your mug says?"

"You obviously do, Trula, because you keep buying them," Susanna pointed out.

Kevin came in through the back door. "Did I miss anything?"

"You missed the children fighting over who got what mug," Trula said dryly.

"Which one did you get?" the priest asked his cousin.

"Don't start it up again," Trula warned. "Just sit down and get on with business."

She poured coffee all around while Kevin hung up his jacket. When he came to the table, she handed him a mug. He raised it to read the saying on it, smiled smugly, and sat next to his cousin.

"Okay, what's it say?" Robert asked.

Kevin held up the mug. *I see dumb people.*

"Trula always did like you best," Robert grumbled.

"Doesn't everyone?" Kevin grinned. "So, where were we before I interrupted?"

"We were discussing the candidate Mallory interviewed today." Susanna filled him in while he helped himself to a cookie.

"Good, bad, indifferent?" Kevin added sugar to his mug.

"She's good," Mallory replied thoughtfully. "Better than good."

"Availability?" Kevin tasted the coffee before adding cream.

"Immediate," Mal told him.

"Don't we need someone immediately?"

Mallory nodded. "If not sooner."

"So what's the problem?"

Mallory ticked off each of Emme's moves on her fingers.

"She saw the press conference on TV, went directly to the website, filled out the application, went in to work the next day—she was a cop in California—quit her job, packed her car, and drove east." She added with emphasis, "With her four-year-old daughter."

"She's enthusiastic about the foundation—that's good, right?"

"Kev, Mal thinks it means something is not right," Susanna said. "That she just up and quit her job and drove out here, expecting to be hired."

"I'm sure you asked her why. What reason did she give?" Kevin asked.

"She said there was a lot of tension between the Mexican and the African-American communities, and since her daughter was half each—she's adopted—Emme thought it would be better if Chloe grew up in an environment that didn't make her take sides against either."

"I think that's a very rational reason," Robert said.

"That makes total sense to me, that she'd want to keep her daughter from all that negativity."

Susanna nodded. "Me, too."

"Did she appear shady in some way? Inexperienced? Incompetent?" Kevin asked.

"Not at all," Mallory admitted. "We even discussed one of the cases that had been submitted—strictly as a hypothetical, of course—and I have to admit she had some really impressive ideas about how to approach the investigation. I don't think she's afraid to think independently."

"I'm assuming you checked her references?" Kevin asked.

"She's only worked with one department, and the chief of police gave her a glowing reference."

"So she's an experienced, competent, well-qualified applicant with sterling references who can't wait to go to work for us." Kevin nodded his head thoughtfully. "I can see where she'd seem like a risk, Mal."

"When you put it like that, it does seem a bit silly." Mallory sighed.

Kevin turned to Robert.

"What did you think of her?"

"I only saw her for a minute." Robert shrugged. "She looked okay. Looked like a cop."

"What's that supposed to mean?" Mallory, a nine-year veteran of the local police force, narrowed her eyes.

"You know. She walked with purpose, head up, long stride." Robert took a bite from a cookie. "Like Trula said, she looks you in the eye when she talks to you. That's all I noticed, though, because I didn't talk to her for more than twenty seconds. Susanna?"

"I thought she was okay, too. I mean, nice, pleasant enough. It's Mallory's call on the qualifications, though," Susanna said. "Mal's call on the hire. That was the deal."

Kevin looked at Trula. "You're not going to toss in your two cents?"

"I already did. I said I liked her."

"Trula liked Emme's little girl," Susanna confided. "She liked having a kid to boss around in the kitchen."

"So our applicant is married? Divorced?" Kevin asked.

"Neither. She adopted Chloe as a single mother," Mallory explained.

"Would calling her back for a second interview be helpful?" Trula asked.

"Maybe." Mallory pondered the question. "Although I don't know what else I'd ask her. She's willing to apply for a private investigators license, so eventually she'll need some other reference besides the police chief."

"It's up to you, Mal," Robert replied. "She'll be working for you."

"She'll be working for—and with—all of us," Mallory reminded him. "This is not the Mallory Russo Foundation."

"Look, we haven't taken on our first case yet, right?" Kevin pointed out. "So do we have to make a final decision right this minute?"

"I guess not this minute, no. But now that you've brought it up"—Mallory reached down to the briefcase that sat open next to her on the bench seat— "here are copies of the three cases I sent to each of you earlier in the week. I'm assuming you read through them and have some opinion on which one we should choose, since that is the purpose of this meeting."

She passed the copies around.

"So who wants to start things off?" Mallory looked around the table. She passed the extra copy of the file to Trula, telling the older woman, "I'd like your input as well."

Obviously pleased to be included in the decision, Trula opened the file and began to read. Robert met Mallory's eyes from across the table and winked his approval.

"Anyone?" Mallory asked.

"They're all worthy cases," Robert said. "All three have merit. Missing daughter; missing brother; missing niece."

"I agree." Kevin placed his open file on the table. "I don't know how we choose one over the other, unless we flip a coin."

"Would one of these cases be more likely to be resolved than the others?" Susanna wondered aloud.

"I think they'd each have their challenges," Mallory said, "so I'd have to say probably not."

"This one about the college girl." Trula waved the sheet of paper. "How can a girl just disappear from a busy place like a college on a Saturday morning? How could it be that no one saw her?"

"If the police could have answered that, they'd have been well on their way to finding out what happened to her," Mallory told her. "I'm sure they asked around."

"Maybe they didn't ask the right people," Trula grumbled. "She wasn't invisible, was she?"

"Good point." Robert closed his file. "I vote for that case."

"I don't know how you pick one over the other, so yeah, I'm okay with that one," Kevin agreed.

"No argument from me." Susanna rested her forearms on the tabletop. "Mal? You all right with that?"

"Sure." Mallory shrugged. "I was intrigued with that one, too. And besides, geographically, it's within driving range. Not that that's going to be the criteria, but since right now we'll only have one investigator, maybe it's not a bad idea to have it somewhat close by. We'll be able to sit down and discuss the case as it plays out. So yes, let's do it."

"So what happens now? You're going to notify the uncle—this Nicolas Perone who submitted the case—and let him know you're going to be working his case?" Kevin asked.

"I'd love to work this case." Mallory frowned. "Unfortunately, there are a number of other applicants to interview and about another hundred cases to wade through."

"How can so many people just disappear into thin air like that? Where do they all *go*?" Kevin wondered. Realizing what he'd said, he turned to Robert. "Hey, Rob, I'm sorry. I wasn't thinking. . . ."

His cousin shrugged it off. "It's a fair enough question. The number of people who go missing every year is staggering. Beth, Ian . . . just two among many. All these others—they're missed, loved, too. Let's do our best to see if we can find a few of them."

The group fell silent for a moment, acknowledging

Robert's pain. His loss had been the seed from which the foundation had sprouted. Mallory knew that he was hoping to do for others what he'd been unable to do for himself.

"So maybe you should call Emme back for another interview and decide. If you want to get this thing up and moving, you don't have time to dither," Trula told her.

"I'm not dithering, I'm just being cautious." Mallory looked around the table at her companions, an odd collection of loners who, in a very short period of time, had become a family of sorts. She understood that whomever they hired would become part of that family: she would have to consider personalities as well as qualifications in filling every position for the foundation. She took the responsibility very seriously.

"Here's an idea," Kevin said as he poured a second cup of coffee for himself. He held up the pot, offering to pour for the others. Only Susanna pushed her cup forward. "Hire this person on a trial basis. Tell her she has six weeks or till the end of the case—whichever comes first—to prove herself. In the meantime, you'll be interviewing other applicants. If she doesn't pan out, at least you'll have some others in the queue."

Mallory nodded. "All right. I'll call her and see if she can come in tomorrow morning to go over the case with me. I think the first step would be to talk to the cops who handled the case originally, and maybe meet with the uncle and get his take on things."

"She's been a cop for seven years," Trula noted dryly, "she can probably figure out where to start. But she may need a little help figuring out what to do with that girl of hers."

"You're not going to offer to babysit, are you?" Robert raised an eyebrow.

"Not that I wouldn't if need be. Chloe's a bright, cheerful little thing. Well-mannered, polite. Seems like a happy little girl," Trula told him. "But she was saying this afternoon that she missed her friends at school, so I'm thinking Emme might need a hand finding a good preschool for Chloe in a hurry."

"We have a wonderful preschool program at Our Lady of Angels," Kevin said. "And—what a stroke of luck—you have an in with the guy who ultimately is responsible for the place."

"That's exactly what I was thinking." Trula smiled.

"Emme might want to make that decision on her own," Mallory pointed out, "but it's certainly a terrific option and one I'd be happy to pass on to her."

Mallory closed her briefcase and snapped it shut. "I'll give her a call from the car. So if there's nothing else . . . ?"

"Hot date tonight?" Susanna asked.

"You betcha." Mallory grinned. "The Conroy PD and Fire Company combined softball team is playing West Lincoln under the lights at the park out on Old-field Road. I might even be able to catch the first pitch."

"I suppose Detective Wanamaker is in the lineup?" Kevin asked.

"Charlie's pitching." Mallory stood and stretched. "He's been working a case for the past week so we haven't had much time together. And with everything we have going on here, this might be as good as it gets for a while."

She grabbed her bag and the briefcase and headed for the door. "I'll see you all in the morning, with or without Emme Caldwell."

Emme glanced out the window at the perfectly manicured grounds of the Magellan estate and fought an urge to pinch herself. The view was beautiful, the gardens spacious and gloriously in bloom. Beyond the garden was a cattail-ringed pond where fat ducks dove beneath the water only to resurface to float in the sun. It was so much more like a dream than any dream she'd ever had, it was hard to believe it was real. Had she really been chosen as the first hire of the Mercy Street Foundation?

Okay, provisional hire, she reminded herself, but she knew she could do this job. She'd been reading over the file on the case Mallory had handed her when she arrived that morning, and already she'd made some notes on how she wanted to proceed. She would discuss it with Mallory, of course, Mallory being her immediate boss, or so it appeared. She wasn't sure just what everyone else's role was in this, but she'd figure it out.

She sat back in the new leather chair and took stock of her office, with its wide wooden desk and walls lined with handsome walnut bookcases and matching file cabinets—all empty, of course. She hoped she'd be around to fill them. Robert Magellan was obviously a man who didn't hesitate to spend money, the fact borne out by the generous starting salary they'd offered. If she made the cut, the benefits would be great, every bit as good as what she'd had in California. But what had made Emme happiest was the consideration that had been given to her daughter.

"Chloe mentioned to Trula that she missed being in school," Mallory said when she'd called with the offer the night before. "Father Kevin wanted us to let you know that Our Lady of Angels, his parish school, has an excellent all-day preschool program that runs year-round. If you'd like, she can start as early as tomorrow. Of course, if you've made other arrangements, or if you'd prefer a secular school, or you'd like to look around on your own—"

"No, no, I haven't had time to make any arrangements," a stunned Emme had replied. She was still getting over the surprise of having the job offered to her so soon. "Chloe was in a full-day school back in California, and she really loved it, which was a blessing to a working mom. I'd sure she'd love to check out Our Lady of Angels. How nice of Father Kevin to think of it."

"I'll give you his number so you can call him and let him know what time you'll be in with Chloe. If you decide not to start her until Monday, she can stay with Trula today and Friday while you work. Unless you have other babysitting arrangements . . ."

"No, I . . ." Emme's throat constricted with emotion. "I can't thank you all enough, but Trula doesn't have to watch her. I'm sure that babysitting isn't in her job description."

"Trula's job description is whatever Trula feels like doing on any given day." Mallory laughed. "You'll find that she rules the roost here, with Robert's blessing. If she didn't enjoy your daughter's company, believe me, she'd never volunteer. So if she says bring Chloe in when you need to, I say bring her in."

"That's so kind of her."

"She definitely has her moments."

"I'll call Father Kevin and find out what time school starts in the morning. I'm sure Chloe is going to want to go. She's been lonely without her friends."

Chloe had been so excited at the prospect of going to school she was barely able to sleep and was up with the sun, urging Emme out of bed and chatting about what she should wear—"Do you think I should take my smock? Do you think there will be painting today?"—and whether she should bring her own crayons.

"Maybe I'll make new friends," Chloe whispered hopefully as she dropped out of the backseat and landed on her sneakered feet in the church parking lot.

"I'm sure you'll make lots of new friends," Emme had assured her. She took Chloe's hand and followed the concrete walk to the side door of the parish hall, just as Father Kevin had told her to do. She'd been about to ring the bell when the door opened and a tall, dark-haired woman greeted her warmly.

"I'm Mary Corcoran," the smiling woman said. "Father Kevin is a little tied up right now, so he asked me to welcome you and to walk you over to the classroom. What do you think, Chloe, does that sound like a good idea to you?"

"It sounds like a *very* good idea," Chloe had responded thoughtfully.

Mary handed Emme an envelope. "All the enrollment forms, the requests for medical records, that sort of thing, are in here. Just get them back as soon as possible. Now, Chloe, shall we go?"

Before Emme knew it, Chloe was settled for the day. The classroom in the church basement was in a long, narrow, bright room with a carpeted floor and lots of books and play areas. The teacher, Mrs. McHugh, appeared to be running a structured ship, which was what Chloe was accustomed to, and she welcomed the Caldwells with a wide smile.

"Chloe, we're so happy that you're joining us today. Victoria, would you like to show Chloe where to put her things?"

Not hesitating even for a kiss good-bye, Chloe skipped off, her little backpack over her shoulder.

"She'll be fine," Mrs. McHugh had assured Emme, who merely smiled and said, "Apparently."

Emme itched to take a quick run over to Our Lady of Angels at lunchtime to check on Chloe, but knew better than to actually go. If there were a problem, someone would have called her, she was sure. But knowing Chloe, there'd be no problems. She was a very social little girl and was never happier than when she was with her friends. The fact that Chloe had taken off without a backward glance that morning had reassured Emme that her daughter would be fine and would indeed be making new friends before the day was out. Knowing that Chloe was in a good place was all Emme needed to be able to turn her attention to the file on her desk.

She read for several hours before Susanna had tapped on her office door.

"We're going to lunch," she told her. "You're welcome to join us."

"Oh." Emme glanced at her watch. "I didn't realize it was so late." She reached for her bag. "Do you generally call out for lunch? Is there a place that delivers?"

"Yes, it's called Trula's kitchen."

"Trula makes lunch for everyone?"

"Every day. And if you work late, you get dinner as well."

"Isn't that a bit of an imposition on her?"

Susanna laughed. "Let me know when you're going to have that conversation with her, would you? I'd like to listen at the door."

They met up with Mallory in the hall, and Robert in the kitchen where Trula was ladling soup into white bowls.

They enjoyed a chatty, informal, intimate meal for a full hour before Robert excused himself and left the house by the back door. Susanna looked over at Trula, who said, "Golf with Kevin and a couple of his parishioners."

"Have you made any headway with that file?" Mallory asked as they returned to the wing of the house Robert had turned over for offices.

"I think so," Emme replied. "At least, I have a plan in mind, if you have a few minutes to go over it with me. I'm sure you have ideas on how you'd like to proceed."

"One of the good things about this being our first case is that there is no precedent." Mallory snapped on the switch for the overhead light in her office, then paused in the doorway. "Why not get your notes and come in and we'll talk it over."

Their ideas for working the case had been eerily similar, right down to the notes they'd made. By the end of the workday, Emme had her game plan ready, and had made several calls, the first to Nick Perone, the uncle of the missing girl. The second was to Edward Dietrich, chief of police in Eastwind, Maryland, the home of Chestertown College and, until five months ago, Belinda Hudson. She'd meet with both of them tomorrow, as well as, hopefully, Belinda's roommate, though she knew that might be a stretch. Emme had left a message for Debra Newhouse, and with luck, that call would be returned by the end of the day.

She pulled up a map of Maryland on her laptop, and charted her drive. If she left Conroy immediately after dropping off Chloe at school, she'd be able to make it to Nick Perone's by ten in the morning. Giving herself an hour there, she could be in Eastwind by one. If her meetings with both Chief Dietrich and the roommate went well and were conducted in a timely fashion, she'd be back in Conroy before five to pick Chloe up at school.

She typed up her notes and printed them out after forwarding a copy to the main file, which would be accessible by all the members of the team. Emme didn't mind sharing her thoughts with the others—as far as she was concerned, if anyone had a better idea than she did, she'd want to hear it. At ten till five she lifted the pages from the printer's tray and clipped them together. Tucking the pages first into a plain folder, then into her bag, she turned off the desk lamp and looked around the office that would be, for a while anyway, her daytime home. It was all so much more than she'd expected, more than she dared hope for. Over the weekend, she'd begin the search for a place for her and Chloe to live, and while she knew that Mallory had stressed the provisional nature of her position, Emme knew that if her luck held as it had so far that week, she and Chloe would be hanging their hats in Conroy, Pennsylvania, for a good long time to come.

FIVE

Nick Perone's auto-repair shop in Khoury's Ford, Maryland, near the mouth of the Susquehanna River, was a fancier affair than Emme had expected. Set at the back of a wide parking lot, the building was red brick, the windows shuttered and the front door painted shiny black, and looked more like a Colonial-style home than a place where cars were fixed. She parked in the shade of a tall maple to the right of the door, and gathered her bag and notebook. She wasn't sure that Nick Perone would have something to say that wasn't reflected in the file he'd submitted to the foundation, but if he did, she wanted it committed to paper rather than memory.

A brass sign on the door welcomed her to Perone Automobilia and invited her in. She found herself in a well-decorated reception room complete with cushy sofas and chairs and a large flat-screen TV. A counter with a granite top separated the room from the receptionist's desk. Emme glanced over the counter but the desk was unattended. She leaned on the cool stone and looked around, thinking perhaps she'd misunderstood what Nick Perone had told her on the phone the day before. When he'd given her an address and driving directions, she'd asked if they'd be meeting at his home.

"No," he'd replied, "I have an auto restoration business. I get in early, so whenever you arrive, I'll be available."

A door on the left opened and a man in a light blue button-down shirt entered the reception area.

"Mr. Perone?" Emme asked.

"No," he replied. "Can I help you?"

"I have a meeting with Mr. Perone this morning."

"Oh, you're the investigator from the Mercy place."

"Mercy Street Foundation. Is Mr. Perone here?"

"He's in the back, said to send you on in when you got here." He opened the door and held it for her. She stepped into a large warehouse-type garage—so well camouflaged from the exterior—where several old cars were parked here and there in various stages of disassembly.

"Where? . . ." she asked.

"Last bay there on the right."

Emme walked the length of the garage, ignored by the mechanics she passed, who appeared oblivious to her presence. The air smelled of grease and heated metal and something that reminded her of glue. The last bay held the chassis of a white car up on concrete blocks, the hood of which was open. The back of a pair of worn jeans appeared to be draped over the grill. As she drew closer, Emme could see the jeans were worn by a dark-haired man who was leaning as far into the car as one could without actually being part of the engine.

"Mr. Perone?" she called over the sound of a saw that seemed to echo through the high-ceilinged space.

"Yeah," he replied without raising his head.

"I'm Emme Caldwell. We spoke yesterday on the phone."

"Oh. Right. You're here about Belinda." He withdrew from under the hood and turned. There were dark streaks on his chin and over one very blue eye. Emme extended a hand but he held up a dark-stained cloth. "Sorry. I'd shake but I don't think you want to be wearing this for the rest of the day."

"It's nice to meet you all the same," she replied, feeling a bit awkward. "Is there a place where we can talk?"

"We can go in my office." He draped the cloth over the hood of the car and headed toward the office.

"I didn't realize there were still this many old cars on the road." She tried to lengthen her stride to keep up with him.

"What?" He stopped and turned and for a moment she felt trapped and held by those deep blue eyes.

"All these old cars." She averted her gaze and gestured toward the lot of them. "Do you think more people are keeping their older models rather than buying newer ones because of the economy?"

He looked at her as if she had two heads. Then, with studied patience, he said, "These are classic automobiles. Collectors items."

"Sorry. They just look . . . well, *old* to me."

"Yeah, well, that 'old car' I'm working on will be worth about a quarter of a million dollars when I'm finished with it." He opened the door and held it for her.

She stopped and turned back to look at the car in the last bay.

"You're kidding."

"Nope."

"Why?"

He paused in the doorway. "That's a 1956 Porsche 356. Back in 1969, the original owner parked it in one of several garages on his property and dropped dead the next day. The family kept the property as a rental all these years but no one bothered to look in those locked-up garages until they decided to sell the whole parcel. When they finally opened the doors, they found that"—he nodded toward the Porsche—"and a 1955 Thunderbird. Mint."

Emme looked blank.

"Never mind," he said, holding the door for her. "You're here to talk about my niece."

"Right. Belinda." She followed him into an office that was as comfortably furnished as the reception area.

He gestured for her to sit at one of the club chairs that faced his desk. He held up his hands and said, "Give me just a second to clean up a bit."

He ducked out of the room, and Emme settled into the chair, grateful for a moment to be alone. Nick Perone was nothing like she'd expected. There was a vibration of sorts that seemed to emanate from him and it unsettled her. That he was really good-looking was obvious, but she'd met a lot of really good-looking guys. It was this other thing—this vibe—that set her on edge.

She looked around the room, taking in the décor. On the walls were rows of photographs of—what else? she thought wryly—cars. Lots and lots of cars. Old cars, mostly, as best she could tell. She wondered if any of them had passed through his garage.

"Sorry," he said as he returned and took his place behind his desk. "Now. About Belinda . . ."

"I've read through the file you sent to the foundation, of course, but I wanted to get some facts nailed down. You're Belinda's legal guardian—"

"Until she turns twenty-one, yes," he nodded.

"She'll be twenty-one in . . . ?" She looked through her notes to avoid making eye contact.

"In two years. And while I appreciate you speaking of her in the present tense, I understand the odds of finding her alive."

"Well, I think we both realize the odds, Mr. Perone. I'm not going to try to build up your hopes. Your niece has been missing for five months and there's been no word from her. Could she still be alive? Possibly. Is it likely? No, but stranger things have happened."

"I just want to know the truth. If she is alive, let's find her. If she isn't, let's find out what happened."

"I promise we'll do our best to find the truth."

She acknowledged his "Thank you" with a nod, then continued. "So Belinda is your sister's daughter. . . ."

Emme had read all the reports, but she wanted to hear what Nick Perone had to say about his relationship with his niece in his own words. Sometimes the depth of information depended on the manner in which the questions were asked, and she preferred to ask her own questions.

"My sister, Wendy, was her mother, yes."

"And she's deceased."

"Wendy died in a car accident five years ago."

"I noticed there was no information in any of the reports about Belinda's father." Emme flipped over her notebook as if she were reading.

"I have no idea who her father was."

"You don't know who fathered your sister's child?" Emme raised an eyebrow as if learning this for the first time, too, though of course she was well aware of what he'd previously told the police.

"No. She never told me, and since it wasn't something she wanted to talk about, I never pressed her on it."

"Did she ever marry?"

"Once, very briefly, right out of college. I think it lasted maybe three months. Once they were divorced, she never mentioned his name again."

"But you weren't curious? Not even a little?"

"Sure. But when someone makes it clear that they don't want to discuss something, you leave it alone."

"So no hints, no clues?"

"The only thing Wendy ever said about Belinda's father is that he would never be a factor in her life. Look, we weren't particularly close. And we were half-siblings. Same dad, different mothers. Wendy was twelve years older than me. I was eighteen, just starting college, when Belinda was born. My contact with Wendy was usually limited to Christmas and birthdays. Frankly, I was surprised when I got the call from Wendy's lawyer telling me that she'd been in an accident and wasn't expected to survive, and that I should come right away because I was soon to be the guardian of a fourteen-year-old girl."

"She never told you she'd made you Belinda's guardian?"

"Nope." He leaned back in his chair. "Not that I'm complaining. Belinda is a great kid. It wasn't always easy, not by a long shot. The first eighteen months she was with me were pretty rocky, frankly, but we've done okay these past few years. We managed to become a family in spite of ourselves."

He handed her a framed photograph from his desk. In it, he had his arm over the shoulders of a tiny, confident-looking young woman in a cap and gown.

"Belinda's high school graduation. Just two years ago, almost to the day."

"She's beautiful." Emme had seen other photographs of the missing girl in the file. When Nick submitted his application, he'd sent several pictures in an attached file. Belinda Hudson had been petite and perfectly proportioned, with dark blond hair and a pretty smile. Had some unknown someone been dazzled by that smile, drawn to that beautiful face, with dark intentions? She'd seen all too many times what could happen to pretty young girls when they'd unwittingly attracted the attention of the wrong person.

"Let's go back to the weekend your niece went missing. You were out of town?"

He nodded. "I was in Los Angeles at a car show, had been there since Tuesday of that week. When I got home on Monday night, there was a call from her roommate on my answering machine, asking if Belinda had come home for the weekend. Said she'd left their sorority house on Saturday morning, that they had tickets for a concert on Sunday night, but Belinda never showed up. I called the police in Eastwind and when they tried to ignore me, I drove there and made them take a report. I'm sure you've seen the police reports. I sent in everything I had with my application."

"Why did they ignore you?"

"They said she'd probably gone off for the weekend and forgot to tell anyone."

"And you didn't think that was likely?"

"No. If she was going away for an entire weekend, she'd have told someone. Deb, maybe, or me, if she was going to be away for more than a day or two. She wouldn't just go and stay away and not let me or Deb know."

"So you told the police this and they made a report. Then what?" She gestured for him to continue.

"Then they interviewed the girls in the house, and they looked around her room hoping to find something that might give them a clue, where she might have gone. But there wasn't anything." He looked at the ground. "I looked too, when they were finished, in case they missed something."

Emme tapped her pen on the top of her notebook. "I know it's been asked before, but can you think of any reason why Belinda would want to walk away from her life?"

"That's a nice way of saying run away," he observed dryly. "No, no reason I know of. Her roommate told me she wasn't dating anyone in particular, that she hadn't mentioned anyone stalking her or paying undue attention to her, or following her. Deb—that's her roommate, Debra Newhouse—said Belinda was just enjoying her sophomore year. She was into all the activities at her sorority house, but she was also focusing a lot on her grades. She spent a lot of time in the library, Deb said. Beyond that, I don't know what else I can tell you."

Emme pulled a folder from her bag and opened it. She removed a sheet of paper and slid it across the desk to him. "This is from the police file you sent us. It's a copy of the page from Belinda's datebook for Saturday, January twenty-fourth."

"The day she disappeared," he noted as he reached for the copy.

"She has initials circled there." Emme pointed.

"D.S., yes. The police asked me if I knew whose initials they are." He shook his head from side to side. "Like I told them, I have no idea. I'm afraid I really don't know any of her friends, except for Deb."

"Maybe by now, she or one of the other girls in the sorority house has thought of someone." Emme reached across the desk and dragged the sheet of paper back toward her with one finger. She slid it back into the folder.

"I'm guessing you'll be contacting her?"

"I'll be meeting with her this afternoon."

"You'll let me know if there's anything new?" he asked.

"Of course. Is there anything you can add . . . maybe something that's occurred to you since you sent in the application?"

"No. I wish there were, but no. There's nothing. She's just . . . gone."

"By the way, what happened to your niece's things from her room at school?"

"The housemother boxed everything up and sent it to me. It didn't occur to me to clean out her room when I was there, but when the semester ended and she wasn't there, they thought it was best to send it home."

"Have you gone through her things? Maybe there's something there—a note, a letter, something that the police might have missed."

"I didn't really go through the boxes. Like I said, I looked through her desk and all when I was there." He paused. "Do you think there might be something there?"

Emme shrugged. "It's possible. Maybe you could take a little time over the weekend to find out."

"I'll drive out to the house later and take a look. Would you want to come along?"

"I really would, but tonight's out. I'm pretty much tied up until Monday." She and Chloe had some house hunting to do tomorrow and she wanted to get an early start.

Emme tucked the file back into her bag and stood. "Thanks for seeing me on such short notice."

"You're kidding, right?" He stood as well. "This is my niece we're talking about here. I appreciate your organization taking on her case, more than I can say. I had hired a private investigation firm, but didn't feel overly confident in them. Plus, let's not talk about the expense. They told me up front it could take months. I'd have had to mortgage my business to have kept them on. After six weeks they had nothing for me except a whopping bill."

"Well, the foundation was set up to take on cases like this. Ones the police haven't been able to move off dead center. We'll give it our best, Mr. Perone."

"Nick," he told her. "Call me Nick."

She removed a card from her bag. "I don't have any cards of my own yet, but this one has the numbers of the foundation on it, and I added my new cell number as well." She glanced at the card as she passed it to him, then said, "Oh, give it back and I'll add my name to it."

"No need." He tucked the card into his back pocket and smiled for the first time since she'd arrived. "I'll remember your name. Emme Caldwell, right?"

"Right." She nodded, wondering how long it would take for the name to stop sounding strange to her ear, how long before she'd stop feeling like a total fraud. "Emme Caldwell."

The drive from Khoury's Ford to Eastwind on the opposite side of the Chesapeake took just over an hour. Emme found the police station housed in the newly constructed municipal building right past a sign that read WELCOME TO EASTWIND, MARYLAND, HOME OF THE EASTWIND HURRICANES. Chief of Police Edward Dietrich was standing in the lobby talking to the receptionist when Emme entered through the automatic glass doors.

"I just came out here to tell Kate I was expecting you," he told Emme as he extended a beefy hand in her direction. "Come on back to my office."

He led the way to the first office off the hall.

"Have a seat there next to the desk, Ms. Caldwell." He sat on one end of his desk and stared down at her. "So you're here about the girl that went missing from the college back a few months."

"Yes. Belinda Hudson."

"You been on the job?" He narrowed his eyes to study her. "You have that look about you."

"Seven years," she told him. "In California."

"Well, then you'll understand what I mean when I say that I'm happy to turn it over to you. That case has been a pain in my ass since day one." He paused before adding, "We charge ten cents a page for copying, by the way. I explained that to the lady who called."

"I'm sure that's not a problem."

"Yeah, this was just one of those cases that started out bad, right out of the gate, you ever have one of them?"

Emme nodded. "I don't know a cop who hasn't."

He shook his head, and a strand of white hair flipped onto his forehead. "I've been a cop for almost forty years, and I never had a case where there were no clues. Nothing. That girl just walked out of that house on College Avenue and disappeared into the mist, just like you see on TV. You know those shows about missing people, how they just sort of evaporate? That's what this girl did. She just evaporated."

"Well, there's the datebook with the initials—" Emme pointed out.

He kept on going as if he'd not heard. "No one saw her leave the house that day, no one saw her on campus, no one saw her—period. We interviewed damn near everyone who was on campus that weekend, and spent two days making the rounds of the shops on Main Street. Nothing. A lot of folks knew her, but no one had seen her on Saturday morning. Now, that could be due to the early hour she left the house."

"She left a little before seven, I think the report said."

"That's what the roommate told us. Said she was half asleep but she knows that the Hudson girl was there because she borrowed some money from her. The roommate figured she was going to grab a coffee somewhere there on campus, then go on to the library, the way she usually did."

"Chief, do you have her datebook?"

He nodded. "I do. Did you want to look at it?"

"I would, thank you."

"Just a second, and I'll have that brought out for you. We have several boxes of interviews—you're welcome to go through them, too, if you like."

Emme turned her wrist to look at her watch. She had a few hours before she had to meet with Belinda's roommate. "I'd like that, yes."

"We can set you up in the office next door—we're waiting for the town council to approve a new hire for us. Built us this nice new space but didn't give us the money to put any more officers on board. Though with the college complaining to the mayor every week that the girl is still missing, you'd think someone would think it would be a good idea to put a few more uniforms on the street."

He shoved himself off the desk and disappeared into the hall, then returned a few minutes later, telling her, "They're going to bring the files down for you in a few, along with the evidence box."

"Chief, I appreciate you being so cooperative," she said. As a cop, she'd found most departments to be highly territorial, but Chief Dietrich didn't appear to be holding anything back.

"Hey, the sooner it becomes your problem, the sooner it's no longer mine," he told her bluntly. "I got enough problems in other areas without having the mayor, the council members, the college, parents of kids at the college, all on my back. If you can find this girl, that'll be great. But in the meantime, people call me, I tell them to call you, far as I'm concerned."

"That will be fine, Chief," she said evenly.

"You think you'll do a better job than we did?"

"This is my only case right now, Chief. If your guys had the luxury of devoting all their time to one case, I imagine by now we'd have some idea of what happened to Belinda Hudson," she answered, as diplomatically as she could. "I know how hard it is to work a complex case like this, to watch it grow cold, and meanwhile the new cases are stacking up on the desk. So no, to answer your question, I don't think I'll do a better job than your people did. I just think I'll have more time to do it."

He nodded, satisfied with her response.

"Hey, just think of me as that extra set of hands you always wish you had around here." She tried to sound chipper.

A uniformed cop stuck his bald head through the door. "Chief, the files are on the desk, like you asked."

"Thanks, Feldman. Take Ms. Caldwell next door and see that she gets what she needs." The chief turned to Emme. "There's a copier at the end of the hall there, if you need it. Just keep track of how many you run. Council's been driving us crazy down here, keeping track of every damned thing."

"I'll be sure to do that, thanks. And thanks for everything. We appreciate it."

"Good luck with the case. You'll keep us in the loop?"

"Of course. It's still your case."

"Right. You're just 'the extra set of hands,'" he said as she walked past. "But if you settle the case, I guess the press is going to be real good for your organization."

"Mine and yours." She smiled. "Like I said, it's still your case. If there's an arrest to be made in Eastwind, it's going to be your collar."

He stared at her. "You crack it here, you're turning it back over to us?"

"That's right. You're the law here." She'd already figured out that everything the foundation did was going to be scrutinized, that word in the law enforcement community traveled fast, and that she had to make nice with the cops into whose cases she'd be interjecting herself. She might as well start now, with the first case. Besides, other than making a citizen's arrest, what jurisdiction did she really have here?

The smile still plastered on her face, she followed the officer to the next room and dropped her bag next to the desk. There were seven boxes piled on top, in no particular order. She only had a few hours to go through them.

"Oh, Chief?" she called back to him. When he appeared in her doorway, she asked, "What about Belinda's computer? Has it been found?"

He shook his head, "No. She must have taken it with her. Sorry. No computer, no phone."

"The records from the phone company?"

"Should be in one of those boxes. We didn't get a whole lot of information from them, though. As often as kids use those things, you'd have thought we'd come up with more than some calls home and a couple of wrong numbers. . . ."

SIX

The Theta Phi Sigma sorority house at Chestertown College was set on a slight rise directly across College Avenue from the library, and bore its name on a banner that stretched across the front porch from one end to the other. The house itself was light gray, well-maintained stucco with a narrow drive that ran along one side and ended in a tiny parking lot out back. Emme hadn't realized just how tiny until she attempted to park there. Exasperated after several attempts to fit her car into any available space, she backed out of the lot onto the busy street, cursing under her breath all the way, just as classes were changing. She drove around the corner and parked in a metered spot. Finding that she lacked the proper change did nothing to improve her mood. She decided to leave the car next to the expired meter and take her chances with the meter maids.

A young woman seated in a rocking chair on the far end of the porch called to her as she walked toward the sorority house.

"Ms. Caldwell?"

"Yes. Are you Debra Newhouse?"

The girl nodded.

Emme joined her on the porch and took a seat in the rocker next to hers.

"Has anyone found out anything about Belle?" Debra asked.

"Belle . . . you mean Belinda?"

"Everyone called her Belle." Debra's voice was thin, her eyes red rimmed as if she'd been crying. "When you called, I was hoping that you'd have some good news to tell us. We've all been so upset about her. But you go along and after a while, you don't think about it all day every day like you do at first. I felt so guilty after you called, because I hadn't thought about her yesterday." Deb's eyes filled with tears.

"Did you ever hear the expression, time heals all wounds?"

Debra nodded. "But I don't feel healed."

"And you won't, not completely, maybe, until Belinda—Belle—is found. But I think what the expression really means is that each day it gets a little easier to cope."

"We were talking the other night about all the things that could have happened to her." She shivered.

"I don't think that imagining things that may not have happened is the best thing to do right now." Emme shuddered at the thought of what the unfettered imaginations of a roomful of college girls might have come up with. "Just try to remain hopeful, Debra. We'll do everything we can to find her."

"Tell me what I can do to help."

"Let's start with Belle's attitude that Saturday morning. How did she seem?"

"Like I told the police, she was upbeat . . . well, she was always pretty upbeat, that's the type of person she was, you know? Happy-go-lucky, positive, full of fun. But that morning"—Debra paused as if remembering, and wanting to get it right—"she was maybe a little more . . . I guess the word is *buoyant*. Like, she was singing while she was getting dressed."

"Did she give you any indication why?"

"Not really." Debra's eyes filled again. "I'd been out really late the night before, so I didn't have a whole lot to say to her. She asked me if I had twenty dollars she could borrow and I told her to look in my wallet. I was too tired to get up and look for it myself. I'm embarrassed to say it, but the truth is, I just wanted her to shut up and go away so I could get back to sleep." Debra's lips were quivering. "Some friend, huh?"

"You wouldn't have had any way of knowing what was going to happen, Debra," Emme tried to console her.

"It's bothered me every single day, you know? That I didn't pay more attention to her. Maybe she'd have told me something that could have helped find her."

"She didn't give you any hint of where she might have been going?"

"I just thought she was going to the library, since she'd taken her backpack."

"Were you able to tell if any of her clothes were missing?"

Debra nodded. "It was hard to tell, because I didn't really notice what she was wearing. Jeans, I'm sure, and I thought maybe she had on a brown tee. I didn't actually see her go out, though. She probably had her red jacket on. The way we all borrow stuff around here, though, I couldn't say what she might have taken. Her raincoat was gone, I did notice that, though. But if the police hadn't asked me to look, I wouldn't have thought to look for it, because it was sunny on Saturday morning, but they were calling for rain later in the day into Sunday."

"So she might have been planning on getting in late that night or staying over wherever she was going."

"Honestly, she could have been saying something about getting in late or not coming back but I wasn't paying attention." Debra began to cry.

Emme reached out and took one of the girl's hands.

"Debra, I know the police asked you these questions, but I have to ask you again. Was Belle involved with anyone?"

Debra shook her head.

"Are you sure? Maybe she'd met someone—"

"She'd have told me. She told me everything."

Everything, Emme thought, *except where she was going.*

"Did she ever mention her father?"

Debra reached for a tissue. "Only to say she didn't have one. We figured that meant he'd left her and her mom, or that he was dead or something, so no one asked about it again."

"The police asked you if you knew anyone with the initials D.S."

"I don't. I mean, I do, but no one who'd have been with Belle that morning."

"Who are you referring to?" Emme didn't recall seeing the name of anyone in particular in the file.

"Danielle Singletary is one of our sisters, but she left Friday night on the bus to St. Ansel's for a lacrosse tournament over the weekend."

"Do you know for sure she went?"

"She was the tournament's high scorer." Debra picked at a loose thread on the cuff of her shorts. "The bus didn't get back until late Sunday. It was a two-day thing."

"Maybe the library can give me a list of all the students and faculty members whose initials are D.S.," Emme thought aloud.

"I can print them off my computer," Debra offered.

"That would be great, thanks. Debra, who else was Belle friendly with?"

"Everyone here in the house is friendly with one another." Debra shrugged. "It's a pretty small school, so you know just about everyone. I don't think there was anyone outside of the sorority that she hung out with. There were four of us who were in the same dorm last year and got close and pledged together."

"Can you give me the names of the other two girls?"

"Patti Sullivan and Kendall Long. Did you want to speak with them?"

"If they're available, sure."

Debra stopped rocking and stood. "I'm pretty sure they're both here. We all signed up for summer session this year. I can check while I print out that list for you. I'll just be a minute."

The girl got to the door, then turned around and said, "I'd invite you in but the place is really a mess.

We had a little party last night, and we're still cleaning up."

"I'll wait," Emme told her, and while she waited, she rummaged in her bag for the notebook she knew she'd brought with her and the pen she was positive she'd picked up on her way out of the hotel room that morning. Moments later, the door opened and the two girls Debra mentioned joined Emme. She'd hoped that one of them would have thought of something that would shed some light on Belle's disappearance, but neither had.

Debra returned with three sheets of paper that she handed to Emme.

"I ran a search for all the students, faculty, and former students back three years whose initials are D.S.," Debra told her. "There are twenty-two names."

Emme scanned the lists.

"Debra, this is perfect." She smiled at the girl. "You'd make a good cop."

"Thanks." The girl beamed, evidently pleased at having done something that might help find her roommate. "I wish I could do more."

"I wish she'd have left something behind to guide us. Her computer would have been nice. I wish she hadn't taken it with her."

"Uh-uh, she didn't take it."

"Chief Dietrich thinks she did."

"Nope." Debra shook her head.

"Are you positive?"

"It was on her desk when I got up. That was around ten thirty. The cover was open, but the screen was dark, like it had gone into suspend mode? She used to do that all the time, turn it on and then forget and leave. I always told her she was lucky I wasn't a nosy person because I could read her email when she wasn't looking. Didn't seem to bother her, though"—Debra shrugged—"because she did it all the time."

"The police are under the impression that she took it. Why would they think that?"

"When they asked me if I knew where it was, I said no. It had been on her desk earlier in the morning but it wasn't there later. I guess they just assumed that I meant she'd taken it. Maybe she did come back later and pick it up—who knows?"

"What do you think the chances of that are?"

"Probably not so good," Debra admitted.

"So if it was still there after she left, and she didn't come back for it, what happened to it? Where is it?"

Debra shook her head. "I have no idea."

"Did you notice anyone in the house that day . . . someone who didn't belong here?"

"I was out all afternoon. There was a big basketball game and a bunch of us walked down to the gym together. After the game, we stopped in town for dinner so we didn't get back here till around eight thirty or so. Then we all got changed and went to a party, so I wasn't around much."

"Did you notice if the laptop was there when you came back after dinner?"

"I didn't. I'm sorry."

"I guess it's too much to hope you lock your doors when you leave?"

Debra blushed. "I didn't think about it. We almost never lock the door unless we're both leaving for the entire weekend." Her voice dropped to almost a whisper. "Do you think someone came in and stole it?"

"I'd say that's as good a guess as any." *Unless it sprouted legs and walked out on its own.* "How many ways in and out of the house are there?"

"There's the front door here, and the terrace door around the corner." Debra pointed to the left side of the house. "There's a door out back that goes into the kitchen, and one of those outside doors that go down to the basement."

"Are any of the doors left unlocked during the day?"

"The front door, but I don't know about the others. I guess it depends on what's going on."

"How about that Saturday? Anything going on that might have made it necessary to leave the doors unlocked?"

Debra thought it over for a moment. "I don't know."

Emme stood. "Debra, if you think of anything— anything at all, doesn't matter how small or silly it might seem to you—get in touch, all right?"

"I will." Debra stood also, and when Emme began to walk toward the steps, she followed along. "Do you think you'll find her, Ms. Caldwell? Do you think she's still alive?"

"I hope so."

"So do I." Debra corrected herself. "So do we . . . all of us. We all miss her, and we worry about her. We pray for her every night."

"You just keep on doing that," Emme told her as she turned to leave. "Every night until we find her. . . ."

SEVEN

Nick had remained standing on the walk while Emme backed out of the parking spot. He'd walked her outside mostly to satisfy his curiosity about her ride.

He'd figured her for a turn-of-the-century smallish sedan that had good gas mileage but not much under the hood. He permitted himself a smug smile as he watched her drive off in her 2001 Honda. That had been way too easy a call.

A pity. A woman that beautiful should be behind the wheel of something with more style, something small and zippy—maybe a Z or a Saab convertible. Then again, she hadn't seemed too interested in cars. Didn't know a classic Porsche when she saw one, but then again, to be fair, how many people did?

The understated sedan fit her to a T in some ways. She'd been pretty understated herself—rich, reddish hair pulled back in a simple elastic, and not much makeup, even on her eyes, which seemed to be where most women wore the most color. Her eyes had been the first thing he'd noticed about her. They were green—not almost green, but green-green—and flecked with gold. She had skin fair enough to burn if too long unprotected from the sun, he'd noticed that, too, and small hands that seemed to be moving all the time. An image flashed across his mind, Emme handing him the photocopy from Belinda's datebook. No rings on either hand. He was surprised that he hadn't picked up on that at the time. His fingers toyed with her business card. He knew he'd be calling her.

After she'd left, Nick had gone back to work and tried to keep his focus on the Porsche, but he was distracted thinking about the boxes of Belinda's belongings that had arrived at the farmhouse in Liberty Creek when the new semester had started. Back in February, the housemother had called with concern, but the bottom line was that she felt it would be better for everyone—especially Belinda's roommate—if his niece's things were removed from the sorority house. If he trusted her to pack for him, she would be happy to do that, and would she like him to ship them directly to his house. Her way of making sure it was done and done soon, he'd thought at the time. He'd opted to have everything sent to the farmhouse, since his place was small and he had no intention of unpacking her things and putting them away. The cartons could sit out there until she came back for them . . . or not. He'd given little thought to the call until Herb Sanders, whose property bordered the old Perone farm, left him a message saying that a whole lot of boxes had been delivered to the back porch and he'd put them in the barn for safekeeping. That had been sometime in March, Nick recalled. He'd kept telling himself that Belinda would be back and she could see to her own things, but that had proven to be just so much wishful thinking.

Nick rubbed a smear of grease from the back of his hand and turned off the spotlight he'd trained on the engine. It had been months since he'd been to Liberty Creek. Today was as good a day as any to go back.

The drive through the Maryland countryside was an uneven one, here an acre-sized lot sporting a trailer, there a breeding farm of thoroughbred horses or a herd of bison, then suddenly, a small town would appear as if by magic, like Brigadoon. It was only a forty-five-minute drive, but Liberty Creek was worlds away from Khoury's Ford.

He couldn't remember the last time he'd gone there without Belinda. Upon her mother's death, the property had passed to her. It suddenly occurred to him that if the worst had happened to his niece—he could not bring himself to even think the words *If Belinda was dead*—the farm would be his.

That was a sobering thought.

Not that Nick hadn't wanted it—he had. Still did, if he were to be honest with himself. He'd spent the happiest days of his life there when his grandparents were alive. There were a lot of surprised faces around Liberty Creek when it became known that Wendy, not Nick, had inherited the property. Back then—ten years ago, now—Nick hadn't minded. All he'd really wanted was his grandfather's garages and what they held. As long as he had those—and he did—Wendy and Belinda were welcome to the house and all the property that went with it.

He turned onto Evergreen Road without even realizing he'd done so. A quarter mile more and he made a second right, this time onto the long drive his grandfather had had paved almost twenty years earlier. Nick never drove up that lane without hearing his grandmother, Angela, bending her husband Dominic's ear over having spent so much money on the macadam.

"What, are you crazy?" She'd been incredulous when she found the entry in the checkbook. "For a *driveway?*"

He'd responded calmly, but from behind the safety of his newspaper. "I haven't spent all those hours and all that money on my cars to have them bottom out on a pothole, not to mention all the dust."

The only other time she'd mentioned it, he'd silenced her with a softly said, "Gotta protect my investment, Angie," and that was the end of that.

The house came into view before the row of cinderblock garages did. Since the passing of both grandparents, Nick had never driven up that lane without feeling his heart pinch just a little. He missed them both, and probably always would. More, maybe, even than he missed his parents.

He parked near the back porch where his grandmother's roses stretched up and over onto the roof and got out of his car, listening to the stillness there. No traffic noise, no human sounds. It was the quietest place he knew. He fingered the old key ring in his pocket, debating. House first or barn or garages? He opted for none of those, and instead, made his way down to the pond.

The air smelled clean, of new grass and the late spring flowers that grew wild. He knew the names of some—marsh marigolds, violets, cornflowers—but he'd forgotten more than he'd remembered. As a boy, learning the names of flowers hadn't been a priority. He knew roses, of course, and dandelions, and Queen Anne's lace, but it was too early still for them. He had a sudden memory of seeing a picture in one of his grandmother's magazines of a woman identified as Princess Anne, and wondering aloud if she was the lady the flower was named for, and if so, what she'd done to have been demoted from queen to princess. Wendy had laughed at him and called him a cute kid. It was the last summer they'd both spent time at the farm together. The following year, Wendy had gone off to Princeton and Nick had the farm and his grandparents to himself.

The cattails were thicker than he'd seen them in past years, and as he walked the slope down to the water, a great blue heron rose on wide wings from the reeds and took off abruptly, as much spooked by Nick as Nick had been by the bird. Geese nested amidst the grass that had grown long, and weeds grew unchecked on the bank. He put *Clean around pond* on his mental checklist.

The playhouse his grandfather had built on the bank still stood, but it looked as if it had taken a beating during that last winter storm. Nick pushed the door open and stepped inside. The smell of musk and dry rot hung in the air, and he added another mental note to ask Herb if he knew a good carpenter who could come out and take a look at it, see if it could be salvaged. He hated the thought of having to take it down. Wendy had moved most of the furniture up to the house at the end of the summer before she died. Belinda was too old for a playhouse, she'd told Nick, but a glance at the contents of an old bookshelf made him wonder. *Pippi Longstocking. Nancy Drew. Anne of Green Gables.* He picked one from the shelf and opened it, recognized the *BH* written in the fancy, curly script Belinda had affected when she was younger. He replaced the book on the shelf and went back outside, noting that the doorframe was rotting and the door itself loose on the hinges.

Better make that *Call Herb today.*

He checked the barn on his way to the house, the old door squealing like mad on its rusty hinges. Belinda's boxes were still stacked inside the door, and he carried them, one by one, up to the house where he placed them in the front hall. As he carried out the last of the cartons, he saw that the barn, too, could use some repair. He placed the box on the ground and walked back inside, taking note of the work that needed to be done. By the back door, he spied his grandfather's old John Deere tractor, the one he'd had for as long as Nick could remember. He'd retired it when Nick was in his teens, having decided that renting out his fields and having someone else plow and plant and harvest gave him more time for the things that really mattered to him.

The things that had mattered most to Dominic Perone—after his family, of course—were housed in the sturdy block garages he'd built, one after another, to accommodate them. By the time Nick was five years old, he could rattle off the names of every one of the occupants of those garages.

The 1955 Chevy. The 1959 Cadillac. The 1957 Studebaker Golden Hawk. The 1953 Oldsmobile Fiesta.

"These are the modern classics," his grandfather would tell Nick as he cleaned a spark plug. "Yes, sir, these and the American muscle cars, they're going to bring in big bucks one day. You mark my words, Nicky."

He'd point to the cars, ten years old or so, that he'd bought for cheap.

"GTO, Camaro, Charger, Mustang," he'd prophesized. "These babies breathe fire."

And then he'd open the garage that held his two very special loves. "Sixty-three Corvette Stingray split-window coupe, Nick. Instant classic. Only produced one year. Damn, but she's a beauty, isn't she?"

The other—"Sixty-eight Shelby Cobra GT 350 fastback. This little sweetheart could shake the ground under your feet and rattle the teeth in the back of your mouth"—he'd worked on restoring only when Nick was available. It had taken two full summers to complete. Nick had never had a better time in his life. Every minute he spent working on that car had been golden, magic.

Hell, that whole summer he'd been seventeen—the summer of '89—had been magic. There'd been the hot August night he and his granddad had been glued to the TV to watch the replay of Nolan Ryan of the Texas Rangers pitching that mystical five thousandth strikeout to the Oakland A's Rickey Henderson. Five thousand strikeouts! The thought of it had made Nick's head spin. His grandmother had been sitting in her favorite chair reading *The Joy Luck Club* and had paused to watch the replay and peered over the top of her glasses to murmur, "I'm not sure I understand what all the fuss is about."

The next year, Dominic sold the Shelby Cobra to pay Nick's college expenses after his mother died and his father had gone off to look for wife number three. Nick would never forget the sense of loss he felt when he found out that prized car soon would be parked in someone else's garage.

"You did *what*?" Nick had come very close to shouting at Dominic, something he'd never done.

"Sold it," his granddad replied with more nonchalance than he'd probably felt. "Got a great price for it."

"We spent two whole years on that car." He was close to going into shock. "How could you sell it?"

"It was an investment, Nick. It was always meant to be an investment. Nothing more."

Nothing more? As young as he'd been at the time, Nick had known rationalization when he heard it.

Even now though, almost twenty years later, the car and his grandfather both long gone, Nick almost believed he could open that garage bay and he'd see that blue car—Acapulco blue, to be precise—up on the lifts, his grandfather underneath it, a small part in one hand, the other hand gesturing for Nick to come see, to watch and to learn.

Magical days, indeed.

But if he had that car back now, what would it be worth? The last one he'd seen go at auction topped $110,000 and hadn't been in as good condition as theirs had been. But what was the point in looking back?

Try as he might to keep his focus on the present, sometimes looking back was unavoidable.

He entered the house from the side porch and

noted two of the steps were sagging. Just something else for the list to go over with Herb. Once inside, he got himself a glass of water and a kitchen knife and went into the front hall where he'd stacked Belinda's boxes. He opened the front door and the side windows to let the stiff, settled air escape and hopefully allow some fresh, dust-free air in.

His eyes went from one box to the next and wondered where to start. He didn't really want to start at all, he realized. If she were to come back, would she be annoyed that he'd rifled through her belongings? And if she wasn't coming back, it seemed macabre to him to go through the clothes she wore and the books she read and the things that mattered to her. The thought that she might not come back at all was one he'd avoided as much as possible, because it was too sad to think about.

Buck up, Perone.

With the knife, he cut through the tape on the top of the first box and peeled back the cardboard. Determining that the box held only clothes, Nick put it aside and turned his attention to the next one. Same thing: clothes. The third and fourth boxes were filled with more clothes.

"How many times a day did this kid change?" he muttered as he moved the unopened boxes to the living room.

Ah, this was more like it—books, papers, tests, more papers, notebooks. Nick took out a stack and shuffled through them, but he found no reference to anyone named D.S. nor anything that would give him a sense of where she was going on January twenty-fourth.

"Come on, Belinda. Help me out here," he muttered.

On to the next box. More textbooks—had he known she'd been taking a class in genetics?—and a blizzard of index cards scattered throughout. He reached into the box and pulled out the one thing he could see that had color. The orange folder held some printed sheets, which proved to be Belinda's cellphone bills. He recalled that the police had requested copies from the carrier, but they hadn't been much help in identifying D.S. He put the file back in the box, stood and stretched, thinking about where he might go to grab some food. His stomach had begun to loudly remind him that he'd skipped lunch and it was well past the time when he usually ate. There was the Friendly Diner down on Wilkins Road; they were always good for a decent meal.

He was out the door and behind the wheel of his car, about to make a K-turn, when he hesitated. Something nagged at him, something about the phone bills. Nick turned off the ignition and returned to the house, to the foyer, to the box he'd just closed up. The orange folder was visible through the crack made by the top flaps, and he stuck his hand in and pulled it out. The most recent bill was on top, and he scanned it for the date.

July, 2008. Then he remembered that she'd gotten a new phone, a new plan, a new carrier—and a new number that summer. What had she said at the time? Something about an old boyfriend who wouldn't stop calling. Deb would know.

He flipped through the pages, taking note of all the out-of-state calls Belinda had made over the 2007–08 school year and into the summer of 2008. Maybe Deb knew something about those as well.

He tucked the bill back into the folder with the others and took the whole thing with him. Back in the car, he plugged his phone into the charger to give it a little more juice. He had a feeling he'd need every one of those bars before the night was over.

EIGHT

So how'd your first day go?" Mallory said, as she stopped in Emme's office on her way home for the night.

"Good. Really good, actually." Emme ticked off her accomplishments on the fingers of one hand. "I met with Nick Perone, Chief Dietrich, Debra Newhouse, and got back in time to pick Chloe up from school, though just barely."

"I'd say that qualifies as damned good." Mallory dropped her briefcase near the door and came partway into the room. "What's the uncle like?"

Emme thought it over for a moment, considering how best to answer. *Tall, dark, and oh-my-goodness* first came to mind, but this being her first case, she went for something a little more professional.

"Seems smart. Smart enough to run a profitable business. He's what a cop I used to know would call a gearhead."

"A what?"

"A gearhead. Really into cars. He repairs—excuse me, he *restores* old ones. Excuse me twice, that would be classic automobiles. He has this spiffy garage that doesn't look anything remotely like a garage from the outside. It's brick, Federal looking. Very nice." She paused before adding, "I'd say he cares a lot about his niece. I think he suspects she might be dead, but he needs to know for sure. I don't think he's deluding himself, where she's concerned. He pretty much reiterated everything in the report he had submitted, but I did learn something very interesting. I asked about getting in touch with the girl's father, you know, thinking maybe she took off with him, but according to Nick, he's never known who the father was. That had been in the report, but I thought it had been mis-written or something. I mean, you'd know who your niece's father was, wouldn't you?"

"The girl's mother is his sister, right?" Mallory frowned. "How could he not know?"

"That was my reaction, too, but he said that his sister never told him, and when he hinted around about it, she shut down the conversation. So he let it go, figuring it was just something she didn't want to talk about."

"Like maybe a relationship that didn't work out?"

Emme nodded. "I suppose. He said the only thing she ever told him about Belinda's father was that he would never be a factor in her life."

"So maybe she never told the guy she was pregnant, and decided to raise her baby on her own."

"That's what it sounds like to me." Emme rested her head against the back of her chair.

"Any chance the father might have found out somehow, and came looking for her?"

"There's no way of knowing. Wendy—the mother of the missing girl—died in a car accident five years ago. Who knows who she might have been in touch with before she died?" Emme swiveled the chair slowly, side to side. "Now, the roommate did say that Belle—Belinda—once said that she didn't have a father, but she assumed that meant the father was dead or was AWOL."

"Did the roommate have anything else to say?"

"Only that while the police report reflects that Belinda took her laptop with her, Debra says that isn't so. She claims that the laptop was still on Belinda's desk when she woke up, hours after Belinda left the room. It was gone later that day, but she can't pinpoint when it disappeared."

"Did she report that to the police?"

"No, but I called the chief on my way back and told him. He was going to speak with the reporting officer about that. Debra thinks he merely misunderstood what she said."

"Any other little gems surface?"

"Not that I can think of offhand."

The sound of two small feet running drew their attention to the hall. Seconds later, Chloe and Susanna appeared in the doorway.

"In case you were wondering, I've commandeered your adorable child," Susanna told Emme. "She's been a great help to me, separating colored index cards."

"I made . . ." Chloe paused to count. "Four piles. Blue ones, yellow ones, white ones, and pink ones."

"Four very neat piles, I might add," Susanna noted.

"Maybe one day next week you can help me organize my pencils."

Chloe draped herself across her mother's lap and nodded solemnly.

"Really, Susanna, you don't have to—" Emme began.

"It's a pleasure to have her company," Susanna told her as she stepped backward toward the hall. "Chloe, unless I misunderstood, I think Trula has something in the kitchen she wanted you to see."

"What is it?" Chloe's head shot up.

"Let's go find out." Susanna beckoned to her, and Chloe was out the door in a flash. "I'll see you both on Monday. Have a good weekend."

"Have anything special planned, Susanna?" Mallory asked.

"Not much." Susanna smiled and followed Chloe. "You, know, just the usual."

"What's the usual?" Emme asked as Susanna's footsteps faded down the hall.

"No one knows. She leaves at the same time almost every Friday and isn't seen or heard from until Monday morning, but she never says where she goes or what she does."

"Maybe she doesn't do anything. Maybe she stays home and reads. Or paints. Or . . . something."

"Uh-uh." Mallory shook her head. "She goes *somewhere*. Charlie and I were on our way to Gettysburg one weekend and we were behind her in traffic all the way to the cutoff for the turnpike entrance."

"Maybe she was visiting family."

"She says she doesn't have any."

"That could be true. A lot of people have no family." *Like me,* she could have added.

"We—Trula and I—think she's seeing someone."

Emme looked confused. "But I thought she and Robert—"

"I thought that at first, too. There's just some sort of buzz—some sort of electricity—between them."

"Definitely. I assumed they were an item."

"Trula says no. That Robert will never look at another woman as long as he doesn't know whether Beth is dead or alive."

"Wouldn't she have contacted him by now if she was alive?" Emme's brows knit into a frown.

"One would think." Mallory nodded. "But I think Robert still needs to believe she's out there somewhere and there's a reason why she can't contact him. Amnesia, something like that, maybe. I think it's easier than facing the probability that she and Ian are dead. I think he could accept the truth. He just doesn't know what the truth is."

"Meanwhile, there's Susanna," Emme said thoughtfully.

"Yeah. There's Susanna, and that buzz. . . ."

.

Over her morning coffee, served with a smile from the same waitress who waited on her many a Saturday morning at the old-fashioned diner just east of Pittsburgh, Susanna studied the state map. Roads she'd already traveled were highlighted in green. It was somewhat disheartening to acknowledge that the green lines transversed half of western Pennsylvania and wove through the mountains like the twisted web of an enormous spider. Her challenge this weekend was to travel the next few miles that Beth Magellan could have taken. There were many possibilities to choose from, many roads through, over, or around the mountains.

Where did you go, Beth? Where did you turn off the highway? Where did your detour take you?

Questions she'd been asking for two years. Where were Beth and Ian?

Until she knew—until Robert knew—Susanna's life would remain trapped in the same limbo as his.

Law enforcement from many agencies—the local and state police along with the FBI—had searched the entire width of the state, from Gibson Springs, where Beth had attended a baby shower at the home of her sister, to Conroy, without success. Search parties had scoured the mountains and valleys of western Pennsylvania for weeks following the disappearance of Robert's wife and child, Susanna reminded herself. Did she really think she, alone and unassisted, could find what they had failed to find? She wasn't sure.

All she knew for certain was that Robert would never move on until he knew Beth wasn't coming back. And while Susanna could admire that sort of loyalty—if she were the missing wife, she'd surely cherish such devotion—the simple fact remained that she'd been in love with Robert Magellan since she met him all those years ago and he'd hired her as his administrative assistant.

They'd worked closely together, and Susanna had come to know him well—his faults as well as his virtues. She held out the hope that someday he'd look at her in *that* way, even after he'd met the beautiful

Beth Tillotson and it became apparent that he was falling in love. Somehow, even after Beth and Robert had married, Susanna hadn't been able to sever herself from him. She was one of his best friends, he'd told her one day when she'd tried to hand in her resignation. He and a partner, Colin Bressler, were starting up a new company—an Internet search engine they were calling Magellan Express—and he needed her to help set up the company. No one had better organizational skills than she did, and there was no one he'd trust more to get the new venture up and running. So she'd stayed through the years, through his marriage and the birth of his son, through the nightmare of the past two years.

She couldn't remember the exact moment when it occurred to her that if they were ever to be together, she was going to have to take matters into her own hands. She knew that in the months following the disappearance of his family, Robert had contemplated taking his own life many times. She knew, too, that only the possibility that they might be found kept him from going through with it. She'd been the one who'd pointed out to him how furious Beth would be if she came back and found out that he'd given up.

The only way to save him—and maybe herself as well—was to find Beth and Ian.

Susanna had studied every topographic map she could get her hands on, and was by now familiar with the terrain. The Appalachian Mountains ran through Pennsylvania in a series of highs and lows that stretched in every direction, and the turnpike was built over, through, and around the mountains. It had been established that upon leaving her sister Pam's home

late Sunday morning, Beth had gotten on the turnpike. Right after the first exit she came to, however, a
tractor-trailer had jackknifed on ice, and the state police had shut down the road. As a consequence, all
traffic was diverted off the turnpike to one of the
feeder roads. It was suspected that all of the detour
signs had not been in place when Beth pulled off the
toll road, and she might have had to depend on her
own sense of direction to get around the accident site
and back to the turnpike. The police had combed the
hills and mountains and ravines closest to the main
road for miles, but there'd been no sign of the car
Beth had been driving that day.

In one of those odd twists of fate, Beth's new car,
with its GPS system, had been blocked in her sister's
driveway by her brother-in-law—he'd left with a
friend early that morning to play golf. Impatient to
get home, Beth had borrowed an old Jeep from Pam,
one without a tracking system. In her haste, Beth had
left her cell phone hooked up to the charger in her
own car. At the time, the newspapers had made much
of the fact that Robert Magellan's wife may very well
have been found had she had the benefit of any of the
modern technology through which her husband had
made his fortune.

With a pencil, Susanna traced the route she would
take today. Satisfied with her agenda, she wondered if
this would be the day she'd come across that shred of
evidence that others had missed, if today would be
the day she'd help to set Robert free. Not that she
wished Beth and Ian harm, but she was clearheaded
enough to have analyzed the situation objectively and
had come to the only rational conclusion. If Beth had

run away—left her husband for another man, say—
surely she would have accessed her own bank accounts, or used her credit cards. If Beth and Ian had
been kidnapped, there'd have been ransom demands.
If they'd merely gotten lost, Beth eventually would
have stopped somewhere along the way and called
for help. If they'd been in a nonfatal accident, they'd
have ended up in a hospital.

Susanna had known Beth well enough to know
she'd have slit her wrists before she'd leave Robert
without first securing a very comfortable financial
cushion, but none of her accounts had been touched.
There'd been no contact from kidnappers, and no
calls for help. Hospitals from Pittsburgh to Philadelphia had been contacted, but there'd been no patients
with amnesia matching Beth's description.

To Susanna's mind, absent any of the alternatives,
there was one explanation for their disappearance.
Having traveled many of the mountain roads, she
could see how easily a Jeep could go off one of those
hairpin curves and straight down the mountainside
into a ravine without being noticed. There'd been
many times when she'd been the only car on the road
for several miles. On a Sunday, there was even less
traffic. If Beth had become confused, it would have
been easy enough for her to get lost. As the roads
wound around the mountain, one into the next, she
could have gotten turned around in any one of a
number of places. Beth had been impatient and im-
petuous and had unflagging confidence in her own
ability to do anything. It was no stretch for Susanna
to imagine Beth's certainty that she'd find her way on
her own. Add that to unfamiliar roads that had re-

portedly been icy that morning, and you had the very real possibility that the Jeep had gone over the side at some point, and was still waiting to be found.

Susanna was determined to be the one to find that Jeep, and when she did, Robert would finally be free to move on with his life. Whether he chose to take Susanna with him, well, that remained to be seen. But at least he'd have the truth, and Susanna would be the one who'd found it for him, regardless of what it might cost her in the long run.

She paid for her breakfast and set off on her journey.

NINE

We're going to find a new house today," Chloe sang as she climbed onto the bench seat at the restaurant in the lobby of the hotel where they'd been staying since their arrival in Conroy earlier in the week.

"I don't know if we'll find one, but we are going to look." Emme turned to the waitress who approached with a coffeepot in one hand and a booster seat in the other. "Good morning, Marjorie. I think we're going with the same old, same old this morning. Unless Chloe wants pancakes instead of waffles."

"Waffles." Chloe nodded as Marjorie slid the booster across the seat for her. "And bacon. And juice."

"Okeydokey." Marjorie poured coffee into Emme's cup then wrote the order down. "Mom?"

"Just coffee for me, thanks."

"I'll be back in a jif."

"She always says that, every day." Chloe wiggled into the seat. " 'I'll be back in a jif.' "

"She means she'll be back very soon." Emme fixed her coffee and took a sip. "Jif is short for *jiffy*."

"I thought that." Chloe nodded and rested her elbows on the table. "Will our new house be big?"

"I don't know. I don't think so. I don't think we need a very big house just for the two of us, do you?"

"But we would for us and a dog."

"We don't have a dog, sweet pea."

"We could have a dog if we had a house. With a yard."

"We'll see what houses the Realtor has to show us today. It may take us a while to find something we like, you know."

"But we *could* find something we like today."

"Yes, we could. And in the meantime, we have our nice room upstairs here, and we have Marjorie to be our waitress every morning for breakfast."

"We're going to look for a new house today," Chloe told Marjorie as their juice was served.

"You are?" Marjorie wiped up a tiny spill. "Well, I'd certainly miss seeing you every morning, Miss Chloe."

Inside Emme's bag, her phone began to ring. She retrieved it and held it to one ear and used one hand to cover the other ear to block out the ongoing conversation between her daughter and the waitress.

"Emme? Nick Perone." Without giving her a chance to return the greeting, he plowed on. "As you suggested, I went through those boxes of Belinda's that the sorority housemother sent a few months ago."

Emme sat up straight, her interest immediately piqued.

"I'm going to go out on a limb and guess you found something you thought I should know about."

"If you think the call records from Belinda's old cell phone are something you'd like to know about, then, yeah, I did."

"I thought the police already had the records for her cell phone."

"They have the records for the phone she'd been using this year. But she'd gotten a new one last summer. Different model, different carrier."

"But they transfer the call records when you get a new phone, right?"

"If you keep the same number with the same company. Belinda wanted a new number because she'd been getting calls from a guy she used to go out with who didn't seem to understand what 'Stop calling me' means."

"Wait a minute. Who's this guy? Where is he? Why didn't the chief know about him?"

"The guy is in school in Montana, and she hadn't heard from him since she switched phones, according to Belinda's roommate from last year. She said that the guy wasn't threatening, wasn't abusive, he was just a pain in the butt."

"Had she told the police about this?"

"The police never contacted her. She opted not to join a sorority, and she and Belinda just drifted apart this year. But she did give me the name of the kid who'd been calling, Clifford Steck."

"Had she ever mentioned him to you?"

"No. This is the first I've heard of him."

"I need to call him."

"I already did. He says he hasn't spoken with Belinda since last June, there's been no contact there at all. Offered to send me copies of his phone bills. And

I went one better than just calling Steck. Between last night and this morning, I called every one of the numbers Belinda called or received calls from over the past two years."

"That's a lot of calls."

"You're telling me. A lot of the numbers were repeats, some were to college friends, a couple were to old friends from high school, that sort of thing. At first the number of long distance calls seemed odd, but then I remembered that most kids brought cell phones to school that have their home area codes. There were calls to me, to my home, my business, my cell. Several of the numbers had been disconnected. A few may have been wrong numbers. I say may have been because after I dialed and the calls were picked up, I got several versions of the same story. The person who answered the phone insisted they'd never heard of Belinda Hudson. Or they just hung up. Odd, since each of those numbers appeared more than once, and the calls lasted as much as an hour."

"Maybe someone other than the person who answered had used the phone."

"I thought of that. Or they were outright lying. Or it could have been someone who'd gotten spooked when the police called the number right after Belinda disappeared."

"Meaning those numbers were on the phone records for Belinda's new phone as well as the old one. People she contacted last year and was still in contact with up until the time she disappeared."

"Yeah. Seems like an inordinate number of misdialed calls, but we'll let that go for now. There was one number that appeared several times over a two-week period in April of last year, then not again. I called it last night and got a recording. I called again this morning because I wasn't sure I'd heard the recorded message correctly."

"What was the message?"

"Thank you for calling Heaven's Gate Fertility Clinic. Our hours are nine AM to six PM. . . .'"

"Huh?"

"Yeah. That was my reaction, too. A fertility clinic outside of Reading. I looked it up on the map. It looks as if it's about twenty or thirty miles from where you are. Does that sound right?"

"I don't know. I'm new to the area. But why would Belinda be calling a fertility clinic?" Emme poked her fork into the waffle Marjorie had just served. "Maybe she needed money. I've read that some girls are selling their eggs to clinics to help pay for college. They're worth a lot of money to infertile couples. Maybe Belinda thought that was a good way to pick up some extra money to help pay her tuition?"

"Wendy left Belinda very well off. Money was not an issue."

"On the day she disappeared, she borrowed twenty dollars from Deb."

"I'm sure she just hadn't gotten to the ATM. I've seen her bank statements. She gets an automatic deposit monthly." He added, "And yes, I've checked the recent statements. The deposits are still being made, but nothing's been withdrawn."

"So she wasn't selling her eggs for the money, but maybe she thought it was a humanitarian thing to do, you know, to help out some infertile couples who wanted children."

"Belinda was a great kid, but I just don't see it."

"Then what's the connection?"

"That's what I'm going to find out on Monday morning. Are you in?"

"Yes. Yes, of course I'm in. I'm the investigator, re-member? As a matter of fact, I think I should proba-bly go by myself. I can call you and—"

"Uh-uh. I'm Belinda's legal guardian. Wendy was my sister. It's likely they won't tell you anything."

She signed heavily. "All right. Give me the address. I'll meet you there."

"Give me your address, I'll pick you up. No point in us both driving out there. Besides, you're on my way."

Emme hesitated. She didn't know how Robert would feel about one of their clients being directed to his home. She gave Nick the address of the hotel in-stead.

"I'll see you at nine on Monday," she said before hanging up.

Having finished her breakfast, Chloe had patiently passed the time until her mother finished her call by making lemonade in her water glass.

"How many packets of sugar have you put in there?" Emme asked.

After counting the empty paper packs with an index finger, Chloe announced, "Six."

"You think that might be enough?"

"Lemons are very sour," Chloe told her solemnly. Then without missing a beat, she asked, "Mommy, what's an infertile clinic?"

Emme searched for an age-appropriate response.

"It's a place where people go when they need help having a baby."

"Like the hospital when you got me?"

"No, it's—" Emme paused. Chloe never brought up the fact of her adoption. She'd been told but had never wanted to talk about it. "What made you think about being adopted?"

"My friend Lily at school said I must be adopted because we don't look alike. 'Cause I'm very dark and you are very light," Chloe related matter-of-factly. Before Emme could respond, Chloe had already moved on. "Isn't Lily a pretty name? I think I would like to be called Lily, too."

"Wouldn't that be a bit confusing for your teacher with two Lilys in the class?"

"Uh-uh. There are two Madisons," she held up two fingers on her right hand, then two fingers on her left, "and two Ryans."

"Maybe you ought to ask Lily how she'd feel about sharing her name." Emme smiled and handed Marjorie the check and its payment. "No change needed. Thanks, Marjorie."

"We'll see you tomorrow." Chloe extracted herself from the booster chair.

"And you can tell me if you found yourself a new place to live." The waitress patted Chloe on the head as the child bounced past.

"I will," Chloe said, and headed for the door.

"Chloe, wait up," Emme called to her.

"I'm not Chloe," Chloe said over her shoulder. "I'm Lily."

"Got yourself a live one there," Marjorie told Emme.

"You're telling me."

She caught up with her daughter at the door. "Wait for me, please."

"Lily." Chloe turned to her. "Wait for me, please, *Lily.*"

Emme sighed and took her hand. After having convinced her daughter that it was okay for them to change their names, she couldn't very well lecture her now.

"I'm Lily," the little girl insisted.

And Lily she remained, through the seven houses they looked at that day, and nine the next, all of which were unsuitable or unappealing or unaffordable.

"We'll look again next week," Emme assured her as they headed back to the hotel after leaving the Realtor's office. "Maybe we'll find something then, Chloe. Er, Lily."

"Olivia." Her daughter strapped herself into her car seat.

"What?" In the process of closing the back door, Emme paused.

"Olivia. Like the Realtor." Chloe smiled. "I think I'll be Olivia."

This too shall pass, Emme reminded herself. And it did. By Monday morning, her daughter was Chloe again. But only because she couldn't decide between Olivia and Chelsea, a name she'd heard on television the night before.

Emme dropped Chloe off at school and stopped by her office to bring Mallory up to date.

"You could have had him pick you up here," Mallory told her.

"I wasn't sure if Robert would object."

Mallory shrugged. "It's not like this is some undisclosed location. Robert even held his press conference here, if you recall."

"I'd forgotten." Emme swung her bag over her shoulder. "I'll let you know what we find today."

"It's certainly intriguing." Mallory's phone rang and she turned to answer it. "What do you suppose Belinda Hudson wanted with a fertility clinic?"

"With any luck, we'll have the answer to that in a few hours." Emme waved before leaving the office.

Ten minutes later, she had parked her car in the lot at the motel, and was walking toward the lobby, when she heard her name called. It always took her a split second to respond to Emme, to forget that she was Ann. Then again, she reminded herself, she wasn't even sure that Ann was the name she'd been given at birth, if her mother had bothered to name her before abandoning her in St. Ann's.

Move past it. You're Emme Caldwell now. That's the only name you need to know from here on out.

Nick Perone had pulled up to the entry to the motel lobby, opened the door of a red Firebird, and stood beside it.

"It's been a while since I saw one of these." She approached the passenger's side.

"Ah, you recognize it, then." He smiled and raised one eyebrow.

"I know it's a Pontiac Firebird." She rested one forearm on the roof on her side. "No clue on the year, but I know the make and model. Do I get points for that?"

"A few." He opened the driver's side door and got in. "It's an '87."

She got in and slammed her door, and took a long look at the interior.

"What, no four on the floor?"

"This particular engine only came with automatic trans." He turned the key in the ignition. "It was the only carbureted V8 used in an F-body."

"Too much information."

Nick laughed and drove from the lot, making a right into traffic.

"So where in your background would we find an '87 Firebird?"

"A year or two ago, I arrested a pimp who drove a car exactly like this one."

"Ouch."

It was her turn to laugh.

"So is this machine yours, or does it belong to one of your customers?" She settled into the bucket seat.

"You can adjust the seat," he told her.

Her hand under the seat, she nodded. "Found it. Thanks."

"The car's mine, to answer your question. I always say she was my first love. I worked on every inch of her. Replaced every part."

"Well, I'm sure she appreciates it."

"Purrs like a kitten every time I turn her on." He patted the console.

"Have you always been interested in cars?"

"For as long as I can remember. My granddad was a farmer but his big love was classic cars, collecting them, restoring them. I used to spend my summers with him and my grandmother. We'd do farm work from six in the morning till around three or four in the afternoon, then we'd head to the garage and work on his latest project till dinner. We'd stop and eat, then head back to the garage again."

"I'll bet you wrote some interesting 'how I spent my summer vacation' papers when school rolled around."

"Hey, I was the envy of every guy in my class. The other kids would talk about two weeks at the beach, or a week in the mountains, but I'd had the entire summer to play mechanic with some very cool automobiles." He glanced at her again and added, "Best years of my life."

"Are they still farming? Your grandparents?"

"They both died years ago. They left the farm to Wendy and the cars to me. When Wendy died, the farm passed to Belinda."

"Did she live there when she wasn't in school?"

"No. She stayed at my place in Khoury's Ford when she was on break. The farm's too far off the beaten track for a kid. You know, nothing to do, no one to see. There's another farm nearby, and the couple who own it keep an eye on the place for us. In return, we let them plant the fields."

"What do they plant?"

"Mostly corn. Some years soybeans, some years potatoes, but mostly it's always been a corn farm. There's a small orchard there, a pond. It's a great place."

"Any chance Belinda's been hiding there all this time?"

"None. For one thing, the neighbors would have seen her, they'd have let me know. For another, she didn't really like to be there by herself. She said the place was creepy and haunted."

He reached in his shirt pocket and pulled out a folded sheet of paper.

"Here's the map I printed off the Internet." He handed her the paper. "See if you can figure out where we get off the highway."

She unfolded the paper and skimmed the directions. "It's the next exit. You'll go left at the stop sign and then straight for another 3.3 miles."

"Thanks. Would you mind navigating from here? I seem to remember there are a few more turns between the interstate and the clinic, but I'm not sure of the names of the roads."

"Sure. According to this, you're good for another few miles before we get to the exit."

"You know, if you hadn't asked about Belinda's stuff from school, I don't know how long it would have been before it occurred to me to look in those boxes."

"Well, I'm sure that sooner or later . . ."

"Later might have been too much later."

"Was there anything else in the boxes that gave you a clue to what Belinda might have been thinking back then?"

"There was a lot of stuff there. Honestly, I don't know if I'd recognize a clue unless it was pretty obvious. Like the phone bill. Other than that, all I can tell you after going through those boxes is that that girl had a hell of a lot of clothes." He ran long fingers through his hair and she watched them glide, front to back. "I don't know how nineteen-year-old girls think. I don't know what's meaningful to them, or what she might have had in her possession that might have led me to something else." He paused and turned to her. "Am I making any sense?"

"You're not sure if any of her belongings have any relevance to her disappearance or to the investigation."

"Yeah. That's what I mean."

"Would you mind if I took a look through the boxes?"

"Not at all. You just say when."

"Oh, our exit's coming up on the right."

He made the turn. "Left at the stop sign?"

She nodded. "Then straight for 3.3 miles, at which time you will"—she referred to the directions—"make a right onto Howard Road. The clinic will be on the right, about five miles down the road."

They drove in silence for a mile or so. Emme watched Nick fidget, first tapping his fingers on the side of the steering wheel, then on the shift.

"Are you concerned about what we might learn at the clinic?" she asked.

"I'm more concerned that they won't tell us anything. If she was treated there or . . . whatever it is they actually do there, they're not going to tell us without a release signed by Belinda, right? There's a law about confidentiality, isn't there?"

"There is."

"That's what bothers me. What if the key to the whole thing is here, and we can't get to it?"

"Well, if I was still a cop, and I believed there was information in the records that could help find a missing person, I'd ask a judge for a subpoena. But in this case . . ." That's exactly what she'd do. If she was still a cop. "Oh, there's Howard Road."

He made the turn.

"Mallory Russo at the foundation has a friend who's a detective. Maybe we could get him to help us." There were jurisdictional issues and issues of probable cause, but there was no reason to go into all that now. "Let's take it one step at a time."

She watched the scenery change from hilly farmland to strip malls. "Did you make an appointment with anyone?"

He shook his head. "I didn't bother to leave a number, so I didn't get a call back. I figured we'd play it by ear when we got here."

Moments later, the clinic—unmistakable with its monster-sized sign—came into view. Nick parked in the nearly-empty lot and turned off the engine. They got out of the car and followed the walk to the front of the building.

"There you go." Nick touched her elbow and pointed to the sign just inside the door. "Heaven's Gate Fertility Clinic. Dorothea G. Drake, PhD., Executive Director."

He held the door for her. "That's who we ask to see."

"And if she isn't here? Or she's booked up?"

He gestured in the direction of the parking lot. "There were four cars out there besides mine. I'm thinking she's free. Think positively."

The receptionist sat at a half-round desk twenty feet back from the front door. At the sound of Nick's voice, she looked up and looked them both over.

"Good morning. Mr. and Mrs. Fields? You're early." The woman smiled brightly.

"Ah, no. We're here to see Dr. Drake." Nick began.

The receptionist looked at the appointment book that lay open on her desk and frowned.

"You are? . . ."

"Nicolas Perone and Emme Caldwell."

"You don't seem to have an appointment." She made a point of turning to the next page, ostensibly to check the next day's listings.

"No, we don't."

"May I ask what this is regarding?"

"It's personal."

"Mr. Perone, everything that happens here is personal."

"Tell her it's extremely important that we speak with her today about my niece, Belinda Hudson," Nick told her.

"I'll see if she has time to see you. In the meantime, if you wouldn't mind waiting." She gestured in the direction of a sofa and some chairs on the opposite side of the room.

The receptionist waited until Nick and Emme had taken seats before disappearing through a doorway behind her desk. Nick sat on the edge of the sofa cushion, his elbows on his thighs, his hands clasped between his knees, and stared at the floor. Emme sat in a club chair opposite him, her bag on the floor next to her feet. She picked up a copy of a travel magazine that sat on the dark wood coffee table and flipped through it absently before tossing it back. It landed atop another publication and she reached for the second magazine.

Emme scanned the cover, which had a picture of a sort of crazy quilt comprised of photographs of children. *Donor Siblings Reach Out to Connect* was written across the sea of faces. Curious, she paged through the magazine searching for the lead article, but was interrupted when the receptionist opened the door and called to them.

"Dr. Drake will see you now."

"Thanks." Nick smiled at the receptionist when he and Emme passed her, and she closed the door behind them softly.

"Dr. Drake." Nick said, as he crossed the carpeted floor, his hand extended to the woman who stood next to a wide wooden desk. "Thank you so much for seeing us. I really appreciate it."

"You said it was extremely important." The woman was all business. Tall, in her midsixties, and blond going gray, Dorothea Drake motioned to them to sit before she leaned against the side of her desk. "Your names again?"

"Nicolas Perone. This is Emme Caldwell. I apologize for not calling for an appointment first, but we needed to see you today."

"The extremely important part?" she asked impatiently.

"My niece, Belinda Hudson, has been missing for five months. I've gone through her phone records, and it seems she made a number of calls to this clinic last April. I was wondering if you could tell me the nature of her business with Heaven's Gate."

Dr. Drake stared at Nick for a long moment, but before she could speak, he said, "If she had business with your clinic, as her legal guardian, I'd like to know what that business was."

He stood and reached in his pocket. "Here. I have a picture of my niece. Maybe if you looked at it, it would refresh your memory."

"No need, Mr. Perone. I remember your niece. She was here last spring."

"Can you tell me why?"

"Since she wasn't seeking medical advice from one of our fertility specialists, and she wasn't undergoing any procedures, I don't see why not." Dr. Drake moved behind her desk and sat, her arms resting on the desktop. "She was hoping we could give her some information, but unfortunately, in her case my hands were tied. I could not give her what she wanted. I don't think she really expected me to turn over the file."

"What file?"

"Her mother's file." Dr. Drake tilted her head to one side.

"Her mother's file?" Nick repeated.

"Yes." Dr. Drake appeared to Emme to be slightly confused. "She came here hoping to find out who her donor was, but of course, I could not give her that information. Our donors are guaranteed anonymity unless they choose otherwise, and the name would not have been in the file, so access to it would not have helped her."

"Wendy was the patient, not Belinda," he said, as the truth became apparent.

"Yes. She bought several vials of sperm from us twenty or so years ago, as I recall." She stared at Nick. "You were not aware of this?"

"I never knew how my sister conceived Belinda. I assumed it was a relationship that hadn't worked out."

"I'm sorry. I assumed you knew." Dr. Drake appeared flustered.

Emme's attention was drawn to a small booklet on the corner of the desk. *FAQ: What if my child asks if he/she has siblings?*

"Donor siblings," she murmured, recalling the magazine in the reception area.

She touched Nick's arm.

"D.S.," she said softly. "Donor siblings."

Dr. Drake nodded. "Belinda said she was the spokesperson for her siblings. They were trying to track down their father and were curious about any—"

"Wait a minute." Nick leaned forward. "What are donor siblings?"

"Children who were conceived using sperm from the same donor," Dr. Drake explained.

"How many of these . . . donor siblings did she have?"

"I can't really say."

"Is that privileged information?" he asked.

"I can't say because I don't know for certain. I know how many live births attributed to that particular donor were reported back to us, but you have to understand, not every woman who successfully conceived and gave birth reported that birth."

"So you could have had fifty women receive sperm from the same donor, and maybe all fifty of them conceived and had a child, but maybe only thirty of them told you of their success." Emme thought aloud.

"There would be twenty more children out there who were half-siblings to the other thirty. Theoretically."

Dr. Drake nodded. "Exactly. And keep in mind, some women bought more than one vial of sperm. They may have kept the extras in the freezer until such time as they wanted a second—or third—child." She stood and began to pace. "It's not unheard of that a woman might give her 'leftovers' to a friend. Those children would not be in our network."

"Is that legal?" Nick asked.

"I don't know of any law against it," Dr. Drake replied.

"How would Belinda have discovered that she had these donor siblings?"

"The Internet holds a wealth of information, Mr. Perone. It's all in knowing where to look." Dr. Drake picked up a pen and wrote something on a Post-it note. "Try this website. I think you'll be able to find what you're looking for there."

She handed the note to Nick. "It's a website where children go to find their half-siblings."

"Half-siblings?" Nick frowned.

"Certainly. These children may have had different mothers, but they had the same fathers." Dr. Drake sat back in her chair. "What would you call them?"

"I don't know."

"If the same man had fathered children by five different wives, what would you call the children?"

"Confused, most likely."

Dr. Drake smiled weakly.

"Of course they'd be half-siblings," Nick said.

"Because they had the same father but different mothers," Dr. Drake pointed out the obvious. "The same applies to these kids. Same father, different mothers. Therefore, half-siblings. Donor siblings." She tapped the pen on the palm of her hand. "Keep in mind that most of these children will never know who their father is. That one entire half of them is missing. Half of their history is unknown. They know their mother's side of the family, they can see what traits they've inherited from her. But at the same time, there's this great void that may never be filled, this great unknown about that other part of them. By connecting with their half-siblings—other kids just like them, who were conceived with sperm from the same father—perhaps they can fill in some of those blanks."

"All of their mom's family is tall and blond, but they're short and dark haired," Emme thought aloud. "They'd want to know where that dark hair came from."

"Exactly." Dr. Drake nodded. "They see certain traits that they all share, possibly, and by knowing each other—"

"They'd know a little something about their father. A means to fill in some of the blanks. To understand where they came from, who they are," Emme said thoughtfully. She understood exactly what questions Belinda and the other donor siblings might have, because her entire life, she'd been asking the same ones. In her case, however, there was no website she could go to, no half-siblings she could locate, to help fill in the blanks of her own story. They simply simmered and bubbled under the surface.

"Right again, Miss Caldwell."

"So Belinda went on this website, and she asked—"

Nick still appeared puzzled. "What would she have asked? How would she know her half-siblings from kids who were conceived from another donor's sperm?"

"You'd have to know the sperm donor's number," Dr. Drake told him. "In this case, it would be Donor 1735."

"How would they know the donor's number?" Emme asked.

"The number is no secret. The mothers would have had those. That's the only way the donors are identified. It's a number assigned by the clinic so we know which vial to give the clients. As a matter of fact, it's written right on the vial. The potential mothers choose their prospective donors by the traits they'd like passed on to their children. Dark hair or light, blue eyes or brown, tall or short. Some women want the donor to have a similar ethnic background, some are looking for athletes with high IQs."

"So you sort of pick through the available data until you find a donor who has what you're looking for," Emme said. "You want blond hair and blue eyes and a propensity for higher mathematics and when you find a donor on the list who has those traits, you say, I'd like donor number twelve?"

"That's right." Dr. Drake nodded.

"So with just her donor number, and that Web address, Belinda could locate these other kids." Nick pondered the possibilities.

"She could find her donor siblings, yes, Mr. Perone. There are almost twelve thousand donor offspring registered on that one website alone. I've been told that almost five thousand donor siblings have been matched already."

"Five thousand?" Nick frowned. "How many of these donor kids are there?"

"The estimate is between thirty and forty thousand born every year. But again, because there are no regulations, no one really knows for certain."

"And any one of those kids could be related to Belinda?"

Dr. Drake shrugged. "The sky's the limit, Mr. Perone. Donor 1735 was a popular guy. We sold a lot of his sperm."

"Like how much?"

"Over fifty vials. That was back in the day before we starting limiting the number of reported births to eight from any one donor. But remember, every vial did not result in a birth. Some resulted in multiple births. Some vials were frozen and never used. Some were passed on to friends."

"I get the picture," Nick nodded.

"As I said"—Dr. Drake took a few steps toward the door to indicate, Emme assumed, that their time was up—"the sky's the limit."

TEN

"So the first thing we need to do is find a computer."
Nick said as they passed through the front door of
Heaven's Gate.

"I've got that covered," Emme told him. "My laptop is in your car in my briefcase. What we need is a
coffee shop that has Wi-Fi."

"That shouldn't be too hard to find." They arrived
at the car and got in. Nick started the engine impatiently. "Though maybe we should look for a town.
We're more likely to find a coffee shop there than on
the interstate."

He gunned the engine on the way out of the parking lot and bolted into traffic. They followed the main
road over a series of hills, past wooded areas and old
farms. Finally, Emme touched his arm, then pointed
to a small strip mall.

"There, on the left. Starbucks."

"Hey, it's even a drive-through." Nick made the
turn and parked out front. "They don't look very
busy."

"As long as the coffee is hot and the wireless connections are good, that's all we need." Emme grabbed

her briefcase from the floor next to her feet and got out of the car. "You get the coffee, I'll get the table and get this going."

"Fair enough. What would you like?"

"Decaf grande latte. One sweetener. Whole milk."

"Got it."

Emme took a table near the back wall and set up her laptop. By the time Nick returned with two coffees and a package of cookies, she was ready to roll. He took the chair nearest to hers and moved it as close as he could in order to see the computer screen. She tried to ignore the fact that they were thigh to thigh in the small space.

"You have the Web address of that site Dr. Drake told us about?" she asked.

He handed her the slip of paper and she copied the URL into her browser, and waited for the website to pull up.

"Here we go," she said as the home page opened on her screen. "Started by a woman in L.A. who has three kids from three different donors. Wanted to see if they could find other kids from each of their donors, yada yada yada.

"Apparently they did . . . big picnic three years ago, everyone invited. Has reunion every summer, kids and their parents, grows in number every year as more siblings are identified, blah blah blah."

"Be careful what you wish for," he muttered.

"It says here that last summer not all the invitees attended but there were still over sixty people." She glanced up at him. "Can you imagine?"

"No. Get to the part where it tells you how you find someone."

She read silently while he sipped his coffee. Every time he moved, his thigh rubbed against hers. She stole a glance at him but he didn't appear to have noticed. She tried to scoot over but there was nowhere to move her chair.

"You have to go to the message board and look for other kids who have the same donor number. In our case, we're looking for donor number . . ."

"Number 1735."

"Right, 1735," she repeated and pulled up the message board. "Let's see if anyone is talking about Donor 1735 and his offspring."

She scanned the messages for several moments.

"Oh! Here we go." She sat up a little straighter. "Look at this folder. Donor Sibs 1735."

She clicked on the icon, Nick leaning over her shoulder.

"We can't read the posts." She read the heading. "You have to send the group a message and ask to be approved as a member before they'll open the messages to you. But you can post a message."

She slid the laptop from its position in front of her to the space in front of Nick.

"Go ahead. Send them a message," she said. "Tell them who you are, that you're trying to find Belinda."

She paused. "Deb said everyone called her Belle. Use that instead of Belinda."

"Just, Hi, I'm Nick, I'm Belle's uncle. She's been missing for five months and I'm desperate to find her?"

"That's a good start." She nodded, and he began to type. "You might say something like, she's my only relative and I'm trying to find her. That's important, I think, because these kids come to sites like this because many of them feel they have no one except their mothers, so they should relate to your situation."

"Good point." He typed for a few minutes, then turned the laptop in her direction and asked, "How's that?"

Emme leaned in and read to herself.

"It's a good start. But I think you need to go further. Say you're trying to find her but you've run out of possibilities, that you've spoken with all her friends from school but no one's been able to help. Ask if she's been in contact with anyone on the list, if anyone knows where she is or has any ideas of someplace she might have gone. Had she mentioned taking a trip? Anything at all that might lead you in the right direction."

"Hold up." Nick frowned. "I can't type as fast as you talk."

He continued to type. Finally he tilted the screen again so that she could read his message.

"That's excellent. Now just add your home number, your cell number, the number at the garage, your email address, and ask anyone who's heard from her since January to contact you ASAP. Oh, and ask for permission to join the list so you can access Belle's old posts. Maybe we'll pick up something from those."

When he was finished, he hit *send,* then turned to look at Emme. "Now what?" he asked.

"Now we wait."

·

He read the new post with great interest. He thought about shooting off a quick reply, but then thought better of it. Why insert himself into this now? If this post really was from an uncle of Belle's, and he was really looking for her, he'd post again.

But what would the others do?

He paused, thinking it through. Always best to avoid that shoot-from-the-hip thing. Didn't he always get into trouble when he did that?

In the end, he decided that he was going to have to toss in his two cents. Someone was going to have to guide this crew, and it was going to have to be him.

It took him almost twenty minutes to come up with the right thing, but finally, he thought he'd nailed it.

Hey, everyone. You see the post from Belle's "uncle"? How do we know that this really is a relative of hers? I'm thinking maybe we should ignore him. Maybe he'll go away.

A few minutes later, the first reply arrived.

Who else would be asking? I don't see the harm in contacting him.

Annoyed, he wrote back.

I think we should respect Belle's privacy. If she's hiding from this guy, she has a reason.

The response was almost immediate.

What makes you think she's hiding from him?

His fingers struck the keys like hammers on an anvil.

Maybe this guy's a perv. Maybe she's run away because he abused her. Maybe she's staying with a friend. Whatever. The bottom line is, if she wanted him to know where she was, she'd tell him.

Ewwww. I'd understand her not getting in touch with him if that's true, but what about us? Why hasn't she contacted one of us? I haven't heard from her in a really long time. No calls, no emails, no texts.

Her choice. No one is obligated to stay here.

He reminded her in terms more civil than he wanted to. It was all he could do to keep his fingers from flooding the post with obscenities.

We come and go as we please. Apparently right now it pleases Belle not to post or call anyone. Her choice, right? Maybe she's really busy doing other things. When she wants to contact us, she will. So I say we need to respect that. And without her okay, I say we shouldn't let him join the list. How do we know who this guy really is? Anyone?

He sat back and waited for the replies. When everyone had checked in, and the consensus was to ignore the post, he smiled and turned off his computer.

He went to his desk and unlocked the bottom drawer with a key from the chain he kept in his pocket. He opened a large manila envelope and slid his hand inside gently, his fingers stroking the silk within. He closed his eyes and wound the soft loveliness around his fingers. Removing his hand from the envelope, he raised it to his face. He breathed deeply, filling his nostrils with that singular scent of pine and lavender. He rubbed the silken strands across his cheek, his lips, and he remembered. He felt himself harden, and he moaned softly.

"Belle," he whispered as he lowered the zipper of his jeans. "Oh, Belle. . . ."

ELEVEN

No one's responded." Nick was on the phone to Emme by noon the next day. "No one's called any of my numbers, there's been no email. . . ."

"Be patient. It hasn't even been twenty-four hours since you posted."

"Patience isn't my strong suit."

"Clearly."

"I want to post something again."

"Go ahead."

"I'll get back to you." He hung up, and she shook her head.

"Impatient" might be an understatement.

Emme returned to her computer screen and continued her search. There was much more information on donor siblings than she'd realized. She was partway through a long magazine article on the subject when her phone rang again.

"Okay, this is what I said." Nick began without bothering to identify himself. "Does anyone know what happened to Belle? Doesn't anyone care?"

"That's it? That's your post?"

"Yeah. Well, I put in my information again, phone, email—" He paused. "You think it's too curt?"

"No, I think it's probably just right. Just enough drama to catch the attention of a teenager." She thought for a moment before adding, "Though I probably shouldn't assume everyone on that board is a teenager. We don't know how old these people are or how many of them there might be. I'm guessing at least as old as Belinda, since Dr. Drake did say this guy's goods were pretty popular, but there could be some much older. According to the information I've been reading, women have been using donated sperm to achieve conception for over a hundred years. Traditionally, the recipients were women married to infertile men, but more and more single women and lesbian couples are using sperm donors to conceive."

"So Belinda's donor siblings could be anywhere from toddler to fifty- or sixty-year-olds?"

"Conceivably. No pun."

"That could put a whole new spin on this," he said. "Thinking of her getting involved with a bunch of kids her own age doesn't seem as odd as some of these people being middle-aged. Which to my suspicious mind seems a bit creepy somehow."

"Kids can do creepy things, too, believe me."

"I guess." He was quiet for a moment. "What if I still don't hear from anyone? Where do we go from here?"

"I'm working on that."

"What?"

"I'll get back to you."

"Get back to me now. What are you working on?"

Persistent SOB, she thought. Aloud, she said, "I

told you that Mallory Russo's boyfriend is a detective. We asked him to run a quick search of the phone numbers on Belinda's bill to see if any of the incoming calls are from landlines, and if so, to do a reverse search."

"Enter the phone number in some sort of database to get the name and address?"

"Exactly. As soon as I hear from him, you'll hear from me."

"How long do you think it will take?"

"Not long. He said he'll get to it as soon as he can. That's the best I can tell you."

"But you'll get back to me. . . ."

"The second I hear from him. Promise."

She glanced at her watch. It was twelve thirty. She'd bet her first paycheck that Nick would call back by three and he'd more likely than not ask her to follow up with the detective, something she'd rather not do. Doing everything you needed to do on your own cases was hard enough for a cop without someone leaning on you for a favor.

Fortunately, it never came to that. Mallory buzzed her office phone just before two.

"Charlie just called. I sent you all the info in an email," Mallory told her.

Emme swiveled back to her desk and opened her mail. Mallory's was the one on top.

"Got it," Emme said. "Thanks. And thank Charlie for me. Please tell him I appreciate it."

"Consider it done. I hope it helps."

"Me, too. Right now, this is all we've got. Thanks, Mal."

Emme read the email, then printed it out and read

it again. One name. One address. She reached for the phone and dialed Nick's number.

"This is good news, right?" he said by way of a greeting.

"How'd you know?"

"You wouldn't be calling just to tell me you still hadn't heard anything. What have you got?"

"Almost all of the numbers on Belinda's cell-phone bill were other cell numbers. Which makes sense, since that's how most kids communicate. Other than the calls to your house and your office, a couple of calls to a dentist's office, a drugstore, and a bookstore near the college, there was only one number attached to a landline."

She heard him sigh through the phone and could almost hear his silent thought. *Get on with it.*

"The number we're interested in is listed as Nash Children."

"Where?"

"Princeton, New Jersey."

He fell silent again, planning, no doubt, what he'd say when he called. Time to nip that in the bud.

"I'll let you know what I find out after I get in touch with someone there," she told him.

"Well, actually, I'm thinking I should be the one to call. You know, since I'm Belinda's uncle, and the posts on the message board were from me."

"Now might be a good time to remind you that you contacted us and asked us to take on this case for you." Before he could protest, she added, "And the fact that you posted the messages on that board is one of the prime reasons I'm going to be making the phone call. If this kid saw your post and chose not to contact you, there has to be a reason why. I'm the investigator, Nick. Let me do my job."

"You'll make the call and you'll let me know what you find out?"

"Of course. But I'm asking you not to make any attempts to contact these people on your own."

After a moment's consideration, he replied, "All right."

Surprised that Nick conceded with no further protest, Emme began to dial the Princeton number, then realized that whomever the Nash child was she was seeking, he or she would probably still be in school at this hour. She'd wait until four to call. She redialed Nick to let him know she'd wait.

" 'Preciate it," he told her. "I'd have been wondering."

"Who are you kidding? You'd have been calling."

"You catch on fast."

At 4:10 P.M., Emme dialed the number, which rang five times before voice mail activated. She hung up without leaving a message. When she tried again thirty minutes later, a young girl answered.

"Hello?"

"Hello, may I ask who's speaking, please?"

"This is Hayley. Who's this?"

"Hayley, my name is Emme Caldwell. I'm a private investigator. I work for the Mercy Street Foundation. I'm looking for Belinda—Belle Hudson—on behalf of her family."

Silence. Then, "I don't know anyone with that name."

"Of course you do, Hayley," Emme's voice

dropped to a soothing tone. "She's one of your donor siblings."

"How do you know that?"

"I'm a really good investigator."

"What do you want?"

"I want to talk to you about Belle."

"Why?"

"Because she's been missing for a long time, and she went missing on a day when her calendar indicated she'd had something planned with her donor siblings."

Again, silence.

"Hayley, do you have ideas about what might have happened to Belle, where she might be?"

"I . . . I didn't know she was really missing. Everyone just thought she got involved at school or something and was just taking a break from the board."

"Have others done that? Taken a break?"

"Sure. Sometimes things get pretty intense."

"Why's that?"

"Oh, you know. Some people are more into the whole sibling thing than others."

"Look, Hayley, I'd like to meet with you and talk about—"

"I don't think I—"

"Hayley, this is a very serious situation." Emme's tone became more authoritative. "Belle could be in great danger."

She didn't think adding "if she's still alive" would have been best under the circumstances.

"I don't know where she is," Hayley protested. "I don't know anything."

"I'm sorry you feel that way. I'm sure your mother will appreciate how serious this is, even if you don't."

"No, no, don't call my mother." Hayley began to cry. "She'll be so mad. She doesn't know about the boards. About the others. She'll freak out. She didn't want me to look for my sibs, but I did it anyway. If she finds out, she'll ground me. Like, forever."

"I'm sorry about that. I really am. But we're talking about a missing girl here."

"All right." Hayley sniffed and blew her nose. Emme held the phone from her ear until the blowing stopped. "I'll meet you. It will have to be after school, though, on one of the days when I'm in town late."

"You tell me where and when and I'll be there."

"How do I know you're not a white slaver or something? How do I know you're really a detective?"

"You look up the Mercy Street Foundation on your computer. You'll find my name on the website."

"Is there a picture of you there?"

"No." No picture of me anywhere, Emme could have told her. God knows who might see it, and recognize her for who she really was.

"Then how will I know?" the girl persisted.

"Look up the number and ask for me and when I get on the phone, you ask me for a code word. No one would know that but me."

"Okay, cool. The code word is . . . Bonkers."

"Bonkers?"

"That's my cat."

"All right. I'll expect to hear from you within the next fifteen minutes. No later."

Kids do enjoy a bit of intrigue, Emme thought as

she hung up. She supposed she had when she was younger, too. For years she'd waited for her real parents to show up at whatever foster home she was in at the time and take her to her real home. Every night before she fell asleep, she'd play the scene over in her head like a scene from *Growing Pains* or *Family Ties*, the shows she watched on TV every week. There'd be a tearful reunion and she'd be swept from her tiny bed in her foster home into a long white limousine and transported to a beautiful house on a hill where every moment of her previously meager existence would be forgotten.

Emme smiled ruefully. Those were the days . . .

Her phone rang and she answered, "Emme Caldwell."

"Okay, so what's the code word?" Hayley asked.

"That would be Bonkers."

"Okay, so it's really you. I guess that's cool."

"So what day this week looks good to you?" Emme pressed her.

"I have a music lesson on Thursday, but I usually have to wait until six for my mom to pick me up on her way home from work."

"Where and what time?"

"There's a pancake house on Nassau Street, right near the theater. I can meet you there at four o'clock." Hayley paused. "How will I know you?"

"Well, we could—"

"I know, I'll wear a red scarf. You wear something red, too."

"All right. I'll see you on Thursday at four. Red accessory mandatory."

"No, no, a red rose," Hayley said excitedly.

"There's a flower shop down the street. You can buy one there."

"Fine." Emme couldn't help but smile. "One red rose it is."

Intrigue, indeed.

She punched in the number of Nick's cell phone.

"I have a sit-down with Hayley Nash on Thursday at four. I'm assuming you want to come along." She was typing the pertinent information into her computer. "I'm estimating it will take three hours to get there, so you need to be here no later than one, in case we hit traffic."

"Where will you be?"

"I'll meet you in the parking lot at the hotel. And oh, yeah—this time, I'm driving."

·

"So, this whole donor sibling thing, it's like a movement now?" Nick asked. They were driving over the Scudder Falls Bridge connecting Pennsylvania to New Jersey in light midafternoon traffic. "Not that it isn't understandable. Dr. Drake said there were tens of thousands of these kids born every year. That's a lot of kids who know only half their story, so I guess it's natural to want to know the rest of it. I mean, everyone wants to know who they are, where they came from, right?"

"Not necessarily."

"Spoken like a woman who knows who she is."

Emme forced a smile.

"Hey, not everyone is as secure as you are, you know?" he told her. "I think it would be really hard to only know one half of your family. You know your mother, but your father—nada. It's normal to want to be able to get a feel for him. To be able to reach out to all the members of your family."

He paused, as if expecting her to say something. When she did not, he continued. "Take my grandparents, for example. They were real important to me. Shaped my whole life. I don't know where I'd be or what I'd be doing if it hadn't been for my granddad."

"Have you ever thought of doing something else?"

He shook his head without hesitation. "Why would I want to do that? I have my own business. I'm doing something that I love. I look forward to going to my garage every single day."

"There are a lot of people into this car thing, I take it?"

"A lot, yes."

"And a lot of them come to you to fix their cars?"

Nick smiled. "I *restore* the cars, not fix them. Big difference. And yes, a lot of people bring their babies to me."

"I take it you're good at what you do."

"There's a waiting list," he said.

"Really? How do people know about you?"

"Car shows. Magazine and newspaper articles. Word of mouth." He grinned. "And I've written a few books on the subject."

"They have car shows? Like dog shows? Horse shows?"

"Close enough, yes. I started going with my granddad when I was twelve or thirteen. Damn, those were the days."

"How many cars did he fix? Er, restore?"

"Seventeen."

"So he'd buy the car, restore it, then take it to a show and sell it?"

"He didn't restore his cars to sell them, and he went to the shows because he liked to look at automobiles, liked to see what other people had, what they were doing. Sometimes, he did show his. Some he loaned out for special occasions, like the local Fourth of July parade or the Founders Day parade, but he only sold one while he was alive." His voice dropped. "He kept the rest for me."

"You still have them? You own seventeen cars?" Emme frowned. "What do you do with seventeen cars?"

"I don't have them all now. I had to sell most of them to start up my business, which is what my granddad had in mind all along. He figured they'd be a good investment, that they'd appreciate as the years went by, and they did." He smiled. "Better than the stock market."

"How many do you have now?"

"Originally, I kept four and sold the rest for my business. Now I only have the Firebird and a Corvette."

"What happened to the other two?"

"I sold them to hire the private investigators to find Belinda after the police told me they had no leads. When they found nothing, I realized I was wasting the money. Until I saw Robert Magellan on TV that day a few weeks ago, I wasn't sure what my next move was going to be."

"You're lucky you responded as quickly as you did. I understand there's been a flood of applications since that press conference."

"There are that many people missing in this country?"

"More than you could ever imagine."

She followed the signs off the interstate to Lawrenceville Road. The GPS assured her it would lead her straight into the heart of Princeton. Nick let her know when they'd arrived.

"That's Nassau Hall." He rolled the passenger window down to gaze at the venerable brownstone building that sat back off the street behind tall gates, its entrance flanked by bronze tigers. "At one time, the capital of the United States."

He turned to Emme. "That would have been in 1783. The Congress of the Confederation met on the second floor."

"History buff?"

"Revolutionary War, yes." He nodded, then added, "And also my sister went to school here."

"You knew how to get here all along?"

"No. I've never been here before, never visited her when she was in college." His expression was somewhat regretful. "Like I said, Wendy and I were never really close. When she was an eighteen-year-old freshman, I was six. I sort of understand why Belinda searched for her donor siblings. It's occurred to me that she's as connected to them, in a way, as Wendy and I were. Same sperm donor. Different mothers."

"You think of your father as a sperm donor?"

"He never seemed to stick with any of his wives after they'd had a child. Neither Wendy nor I really knew him."

"How many wives has he had?"

"I think four."

"You have other half-siblings then?"

"I only know about Wendy, but I suppose anything is possible."

"Is he still alive?"

"Last I heard. We're not particularly close." Nick stared straight ahead, his jaw squared. It was clear this was not a subject he wished to discuss. She could respect that. There were some things she didn't like to talk about, too.

Emme craned her neck to look over the traffic that blocked the lanes in each direction. "We have to find Nassau Street."

"You're on it." He pointed across the street to the sign on the corner. "Where are we supposed to meet Hayley?"

"At a pancake place near the theater." Traffic crawled toward the light. Several times she had to brake to avoid the pedestrians who crossed the street without apparent regard to the cars. They approached the next light slowly.

"This is Witherspoon Street," she told him. "According to the map I looked at online, there should be some public parking down here somewhere. The pancake house is at the far end of this block of Nassau Street. We'll park and look for the florist."

"What florist?"

"Hayley wants me to carry a red rose so she'll know me." Emme smiled.

"Kid watches too many old spy movies."

"My thoughts exactly."

She made the turn, and searched for a parking spot. She found one in front of a small café, and fed the meter before heading up toward Nassau Street. At the flower shop, they stepped inside for the requisite red rose.

"This one's on me." Nick paid the clerk and handed the flower to Emme. "It's the least I can do to thank you for letting me tag along."

"Thanks." She took the rose and they walked toward the corner, sidestepping the students who walked in pairs or in clusters. Nick took her arm as they navigated through the throng.

"There." Emme pointed ahead at the two-story building with the striped awning. "Pancake House."

They stepped through the red double doors, and once inside, she scanned the tables and booths for a teenaged girl wearing a red scarf.

"Hold the rose up a little higher." Nick stood behind her, whispering in her ear.

"How stupid do I look twirling this thing around?" She gave the stem a twist as she glanced from one crowded table to the next.

"Well, I'm not sure that stupid is the word I'd use." He took several steps away and pretended to be scrutinizing her. "Silly might work. Amusing is better. But not stupid."

"Very funny. I'll try to remember not to ask rhetorical questions around you."

Emme looked around the room. It seemed every kid in town and half of the students from the university had stopped in for a snack after class.

"Her red scarf should be easy enough to pick out. Oh, there, on the right. . . ."

Emme took a few steps forward, holding the gaze of the young girl who sat alone at a booth against the wall, a bright red scarf tied jauntily around her neck.

She had dark blond hair and round tortoiseshell glasses. She smiled uncertainly when Emme waved, and raised her hand to wave back. When she realized that Nick was headed her way as well, she froze.

"Who's that?" Hayley asked suspiciously.

Emme slid into the booth next to Hayley. "This is Nick Perone. Belinda . . . Belle's uncle."

"The perv?" Hayley's expression was one of disgust.

"What?" Nick stared across the table. "What did you call me?"

"You're the perv who's looking for Belle." She turned to Emme. "You didn't tell me you were bringing him." Hayley shook her head. "I wouldn't tell you where Belle was even if I knew."

"Go back to the part where you called me a perv." Nick's frown creased his forehead and drew his eyebrows close together. "Where did that come from?"

Hayley shifted uncomfortably on the bench.

"Hayley, why would you say such a thing?" Emme asked.

The girl shrugged. "They were saying on the loop that maybe the reason why she ran away was because her uncle . . . the one who posted on the loop . . . maybe he, you know, *hurt* her."

"Did Belle ever give you or any of the others any reason to think that her uncle—or anyone else—had been abusing her?" Emme asked. "Or had hurt her in any way at all?"

Hayley thought it over before shaking her head, "No."

"Then maybe you shouldn't put any stock in some

idle comment that someone"—*some thoughtless jack-ass kid*—"tossed out without any regard to the truth."

"Listen, Hayley." Nick lowered his voice and leaned his body closer to the table. "I am not now and never have been a 'perv.' I'm looking for my niece because she's been missing for five months—five months when anything could have happened to her. She's all the family I have, Hayley. I need to find her. You may be the only person who can help us to do that."

"I'm sorry. You're right. It was just something stupid someone said." Hayley turned to Emme. "Everyone knows I'm meeting with you. If anything happens to me, they have your name and your phone number. I posted it on the message board."

"That was very smart of you, Hayley," Emme assured her. "Good thinking on your part. Nick and I are only interested in finding out what happened to Belle, but you were right to take some precautions, just in case."

The girl seemed to relax slightly.

"Are you hungry?" Emme asked.

"The food's pretty good here," Hayley said, hopefully. "I usually get the peanut-butter-and-chocolate-chip pancakes, but the raspberry ones are good, too."

"I'm sold. Raspberry for me." Emme looked across the table at Nick. "You need a menu?"

"Are you kidding? They have peanut-butter-and-chocolate-chip pancakes and you have to ask?"

He gestured for the waitress and gave her their order. When she'd turned away from the table, he said, "So you told your donor siblings that you were getting together with Emme."

"Not really everyone." She appeared to Emme to be debating with herself. "Well, really just Ava."

"Ava's one of your sisters?"

Hayley nodded. "She's the oldest. I always go to her when I have a problem or anything. You know."

"Because every girl wants to have a big sister. I do understand," Emme said, because she did, although her wanting had stopped long ago. "Hayley, how old are you?"

"I'm sixteen. I know, I look younger, but I was sixteen on my last birthday."

"How old is Ava?" Nick asked.

"She's old. Like, twenty-four. Everyone says we look the most alike."

"And that makes you happy." Emme could tell that it did.

Hayley nodded again.

"Where does Ava live? What's her last name?"

"She lives in Boston. She's in graduate school. And we don't do last names. Just first names."

"Why no last names?" Nick asked.

"Because they don't matter," Hayley said simply. "We all have different last names, so we decided none of us would use them."

"Because you're bonding as siblings, and you want to stress what you have in common, not what's different," Emme noted. "I get it."

Their beverages were served, coffee for Emme and Nick, soda for Hayley.

"How many are you, all together?" Emme asked.

"There are ten on the message board. We know there are others, but for whatever reasons, they're not into it."

"Maybe you could tell me about the ones who are," suggested Emme.

"There's Ali—she's eighteen. She lives in Pittsburgh. She's going to college at Bryn Mawr next year, so I'm going to apply there, too, when I'm a senior. We thought it would be fun to go to the same school and see each other more often."

Emme took a small notebook from her bag. "I have to write this down. I'll never remember everyone."

"I thought you just wanted to know about Belle." Hayley frowned.

"I do want to know about Belle. But I need to know the people she cared about, if I'm going to be able to understand where she might have gone."

"Hayley, you don't think she would have gone to stay with one of the other kids, do you?" Nick asked as if the thought had just occurred to him.

Hayley shook her head. "Uh-uh. Someone would have said."

"So we have you, Belle, Ava and Ali—who are the others?" Emme tapped her pencil on the tabletop.

"There's Henry—he's twenty-two and he lives in Connecticut. He just graduated from college. Lori is his sister—they're from the same donor and the same mother so they're, like, full siblings. She's twenty and goes to Yale. Jessie—she's nineteen—she used to live in Florida but last year her dad moved them to France. She used to be on the board a lot, but now, not so much." She thought that over for a moment before amending, "Not ever anymore. Wayne and Will, they live in North Carolina. They're seventeen and they're twins. No one's met them except for Belle."

"When did Belle meet them?" Nick asked.

"She drove down to meet them one time last year. She said they're both really sweet guys but their mom doesn't want any part of the donor-sib thing, so they don't get to come to any of the get-togethers."

"Why would Belle drive all the way down there just to meet them?" Emme wondered aloud.

"Because they never got to meet anyone and they were both feeling left out, I guess." Hayley shrugged. "Belle didn't make a big deal out of it, she just went. The rest of us probably wouldn't have even known if the guys hadn't posted a picture of the three of them on the board. That was Belle, though. She'd do something nice but never talk about it."

"So that makes nine, if I counted correctly," Nick said.

"There's Justin, he's twenty-one and lives in Virginia. He's in college so we don't hear from him very often."

"Where does he go to school?" Emme looked up from her notes.

"I don't know. He transferred someplace but didn't say where. He's pretty much dropped out."

She rested an elbow on the table and planted her chin in the palm of one hand and looked wistful. "That happens sometimes. People drop out, they drop in, they drop out again, depending on what's going on in their lives. They get busy."

She smiled ruefully and added, "Sometimes they get grounded. That's sort of what we thought about Belle, that something was going on and she didn't have time for us for a while. We—me and Ava and Ali—figured she'd be back when it suited her."

"So it's really not unusual to not hear from some-one on the list for a while." Nick said. "But you wouldn't have thought it odd that someone dropped out for several months?"

"No." Hayley shook her head. "Sometimes you just get overwhelmed with work. Plus, Belle said she was getting really busy with sorority rush coming up. We all thought she'd be back at the end of the school year."

"Have you met, face-to-face, with everyone on the board?"

"No. Just Ali, Ava, Henry, Lori, and Belle. We've gotten together a few times. Well, Ava only once, 'cause she's in grad school and is real busy."

"How about last January?" Nick asked.

Hayley turned to Emme. "That's the day you said she had on her calendar? The day she disappeared?"

"Yes. Did you get together that day?"

"We met in Philadelphia, me, Ali—she was in the area to visit Bryn Mawr—Belle, Henry, and Lori. I told my parents I had to go to the Philadelphia Art Museum for a school project, and that's where we all met. We went through the museum together and then we had lunch there. It was so much fun." Hayley rested her elbow on the scarred tabletop, her fingers absently tracing a heart that someone had carved long ago, the inscription *AS & MR* still visible. Emme noticed the entire top of the table was one mass of carvings, as if people had been leaving their mark for generations.

"Did anything unusual happen?" Nick asked.

Emme kicked him under the table. *My job.*

He sat back against the seat. *I got the message. She's all yours.*

"I can't think of anything," Hayley told him.

Emme sat back to permit the waitress to serve their pancakes. The aroma reminded her that she hadn't eaten since six thirty that morning. By the way Nick was eyeing his plate, she suspected that he'd had an early breakfast as well.

"Anyone following you? Or maybe paying too much attention to your group, or to Belle?" Emme waited for Hayley to finish with the syrup.

"No." Hayley shook her head, then a moment later, her eyes widened slightly. "Oh. Well, there was this guy in the restaurant when we went downstairs to have lunch who was kind of flirting with her."

"What did he look like?"

"Tall, kind of thin. Real, real light blond hair." Hayley shrugged. "I didn't pay much attention to him. I just remember that much because she sat across the table from me, and Henry said something like, 'Hey, Belle, your boyfriend's back,' and I turned around and saw him sit down at a table behind us."

"What did he mean, he's back? Had he been hanging around her, following her?"

"I don't know. I hadn't noticed if he did." She bit her bottom lip. "I guess I should have been more observant. I should have noticed—"

"No, no," Emme assured her. "It's probably nothing. But just for the record, after lunch, where did you go? Did you go back to the exhibits?"

"Lori, Henry, and I went upstairs to the second floor, because he wanted to see the arms and armor display. He's all into that Knights of the Round Table thing. Ali and Belle wanted to look at the photography exhibit on the ground floor. We all met up later outside, on the front steps. Then everyone sort of went their own way."

"How did everyone travel that day, do you know?" Emme continued to make notes.

"Lori, Henry, and I all came in by train, so we shared a cab back to Thirtieth Street Station. My train was already there, so I left as soon as we got there. Ali and Belle both had cars."

"Do you know where Ali and Belle parked?"

"Ali got to park in the museum parking lot because she was early, but Belle was parked on some street somewhere." Hayley nodded. "I remember that because Ali said she'd drive Belle to her car but Belle said it was okay, she'd walk, 'cause it was such a nice day."

"Have you heard from Belle since the day at the museum, Hayley?"

Hayley stared into space, as if trying to recall.

"Maybe . . . but I'm not really sure. Maybe I did . . . but maybe not. I don't know when I last heard from her. I didn't really pay attention." She shook her head. "I . . . I don't remember. But you said that was the day she disappeared, right?"

Emme nodded.

"So whatever happened to her, it must have happened to her there, right?" Horrified, Hayley looked up at Emme. "Something bad happened to her right there, that day, and none of us even knew."

"There's no way you could have known." Emme put her arm around Hayley in an attempt to comfort her. "And there's no way to prove that whatever happened, happened there and then. Something could have happened on her way back to school, or once she got there."

"Or someone could have kidnapped her after she left us!" she sobbed softly.

"Hayley, I'd like to have the email addresses and phone numbers of the other donor siblings," Emme told her, while making a mental note to find out if the art museum has surveillance cameras in the restaurant. "Can you give me those? I think it's time we spoke directly with them."

"They might not like it."

Tough.

Aloud, Emme said, "I think they'd like it far less if they knew that something really bad could have happened to Belle, and that any one of them might know something that could lead us to her."

"All right." Hayley found a tissue in her bag and wiped her face. "I have the list at home. I can email it to you."

"That would be great. Can you do it tonight?"

Clearly reluctant, Hayley nodded, and Emme suspected she might be worried what the others were going to say when they found out she was the one who gave out their information.

"Hayley, did Belle get along with all of the others?" Emme asked, an attempt to find out if all was well among the siblings.

Hayley nodded. "Everyone liked Belle. She's the best."

"We spoke with Dr. Drake at the fertility clinic," Nick told her. "She mentioned that Belle had been there, hoping to find some information on Donor

1735. She said Belle had described herself as the spokesperson for the group."

"When we started talking about maybe trying to find a way to figure out who Donor 1735 is—maybe even meet him—Belle volunteered to go to the clinic and see if they'd let her look at her mother's file." Hayley smiled weakly. "Which we all figured they wouldn't let her do, but she wanted to give it a shot."

"There was interest in finding Donor 1735?" Emme asked.

"Sure. There's a kid, Aaron? He actually did it, and he started out with only the little bit of description the clinic gave his mother, and the donor number," Hayley replied. "There was a whole magazine article about him. It was pretty cool."

"How complete was the description?" Emme asked.

"I don't know, but my mom said they told her that our donor was tall, blond, of Slovak and Irish background, athletic build, and that he was born in Philly. Just that kind of stuff."

"Someone was able to trace a donor with nothing more than that type of information?" Nick appeared impressed. "This Aaron must be one determined kid. How did he do it?"

Hayley shrugged. "I don't know. He did almost all of it on the Internet, but we all talked about how cool it would be if we could find 1735. Have a big reunion, you know?" She played with a strand of her hair. "Of course, it wouldn't really be a reunion, you know, 'cause we'd never met him before."

"Hayley, do you remember when this discussion took place?" Emme asked.

The girl thought for a moment. "I'm pretty sure it was sometime last year." She paused as if trying to remember. "Yeah, it would have been. Because Jessie said she was going to do what Aaron did, but then her dad got transferred, like I said, and she pretty much forgot about it, I guess. Then it all came up again in the fall, and we were all still talking about it when we got together."

"You talked about this when you were at the museum?" Emme asked.

"Yeah. Someone said how cool it was that we were in Philly and that he had been born in Philly, you know, back then. And how maybe he could even have been there, at the museum, right then. And then someone else said that maybe he'd been going out when we were coming in and we'd walked right past him and didn't know him and he didn't know us. Stuff like that."

"Was anyone in your group thinking about tracking down Donor 1735, besides Jessie?" Nick's fingers closed around his coffee cup.

"Belle was. She'd already gotten in touch with this kid, Aaron, the one who found his donor? She said he told her what he did, and how he did it, and she was pretty sure she could do it, so we were all pretty psyched about that."

"Do you know how far she got? Was she able to identify him?" Emme asked.

"I don't know, but I kinda think she might have been getting close." Hayley sucked the rest of her drink through her straw in a loud whoosh. "When we asked her about it, she just smiled and said 'Stay tuned.' "

"Stay tuned." Nick repeated flatly.

"Yeah."

"Hayley, was Belle particularly close to any one of your siblings? Someone she might have confided in?"

"Ali, maybe. But she was pretty friendly with all of us."

"So everyone knew she was looking for Donor 1735."

Hayley nodded. "Sure. It wasn't a secret. And Belle was scary smart. If she said she'd find him, we all knew it was only a matter of time until she did."

TWELVE

Well, so much for Belle's father not being a factor in her life," Nick said after they'd exchanged email addresses with Hayley and headed back to Emme's car. "Wendy got that wrong."

"Maybe Belle never showed any interest in her father while your sister was still alive. Maybe losing her mother when she did made her curious about her other parent. Once she realized she had all these half-siblings, her curiosity might have been fueled by theirs." Emme had to stretch to keep up with Nick's long stride. "Did she ever say anything at all to you about her father, or wanting to know more about him?"

"Never." He shook his head. "Belinda never gave any hint that she knew how she was conceived or that she'd found she had half-siblings. I've been looking back over conversations we've had these past few years, thinking maybe she'd tossed out a sign or two and I just missed it. But I can't recall that she'd even hinted at any of this."

"I wonder how long she knew, how old she was when Wendy told her."

"I have no idea. I'm still trying to figure out why Wendy never mentioned it to me. She never mentioned wanting to be a single mother. I had no idea why she made that decision, or when." He appeared thoughtful. "Or why Belinda never said anything. Wendy I can maybe understand. She was so much older than I was, maybe she thought I was too young to have that conversation with. But Belinda . . . well, I guess I thought we were closer than that."

"Maybe she assumed you knew and that you didn't want to discuss it. Maybe she thought her mother had told you and that you'd disapproved."

"Maybe."

"I wonder how far Belinda got in her search for her donor."

"I was wondering that myself." They reached the corner of Witherspoon Street and turned right.

"Suppose, just suppose, Belle had been able to figure out who Donor 1735 was. Suppose she even tried to contact him. How happy would this guy be to hear from a kid he didn't know existed, who maybe wants to call him Daddy? Oh, and to find out he had ten other kids who want to call him Daddy, too." Emme dug in her pocket for her car keys.

"Probably not so much. There might be some guys who'd take it in stride but they'd be in the minority." He thought for a moment. "Yeah, mostly I don't think these guys would be too happy. They were promised anonymity; they don't expect that to ever be violated."

"And let's face it, this would be a huge invasion of their privacy."

"Do you think that would stop a bunch of kids from trying?"

"No. Nick, if Belle had gotten that close to finding him, would she have told the others?"

"I don't know. Belinda—I have a hard time calling her Belle. It's tough to keep a name straight like that when you've always known someone by another name."

Tell me about it.

They arrived at her car, and she unlocked both doors with the remote. She started the engine and pulled away from the curb, her mind racing.

"Okay, how about this?" Emme was thinking aloud, playing with different scenarios. "Suppose she had figured it out. Would she have contacted the guy her research led her to and asked him if he'd been a donor, *before* she told the others she'd found him?"

"You mean, instead of telling them first?" Nick thought it over. "Yeah, I could see her doing that. Rather than get everyone tuned up that she'd found him, she might go that one extra step and make sure."

"Are you sure there were no notes about this in any of those boxes you went through?"

"No, I'm not sure. I didn't really know what I was looking for. Maybe you should take a look."

"I'm going to do that." She drove thoughtfully for a few minutes, watching for the signs for I-95. "Damn, I wish we had her computer. You know it was all in there."

"You're probably right."

"No *probably*. You heard Hayley. This kid, Aaron, found his donor by using the Internet. If Belinda had contacted him, and followed his lead, she'd have done the same."

"I wish we knew for sure what happened to her laptop."

"I think we do know what happened. I think whoever is responsible for her disappearance has it."

Emme signaled to turn onto the interstate and noted that rush hour traffic was in full swing.

"So where do we go from here?" Nick asked.

"We contact each one of the kids on that board, and we ask them to talk to us. I want to get a feel for the rest of the kids involved in this, get a better idea of how they all felt about Belle, how they felt about searching for their donor. Some of them might not have been as cozy with the idea as Hayley thinks they were."

"Why wouldn't they be?"

"Some of these kids were born to single mothers, some to lesbian couples, some to married couples. In cases involving the latter, there may be a bit of touchiness on the part of the dads, if their infertility was the reason the moms went the donor route in the first place. The kids might be sensitive to that, might be afraid that their dads could be hurt if they knew the kid was looking for the sperm donor."

"But those kids might not want to seem like the wet blanket when their donor siblings were all stoked about the possibility of finding Donor 1735."

"Exactly."

"You think one of these kids could be involved in Belinda's disappearance?" he asked.

"I think there's a very good chance that Belinda's disappearance is connected to her involvement with her donor siblings. It's premature to say how it's related, but I definitely think there's a connection. I just have to figure out what that connection is."

"We," he corrected. "We have to figure it out."

"And you went on the foundation's payroll, when?" She raised an eyebrow.

"You're going to want me along when you talk to these kids, right?"

"Hadn't planned on it." Emme frowned. "But for the record, why would I want to do that?"

"Because I'm the uncle. Her legal guardian. It gives the whole questioning-the-kids thing credibility."

"I'm not seeing that connection. And besides," she added, her eyes on the road straight ahead. "They think you're a perv."

"Yeah, well, we're going to get to the bottom of that real fast." Nick looked justifiably annoyed. "I'd sure love to know which of them started that nasty little rumor."

"I'm sure it was just speculation, like Hayley said. They were just looking for a reason why she might have run away."

"Why would they have assumed that she'd run away, I wonder?"

"Because it's easier for them to think she'd gone off on her own, than for them to think that she was abducted by someone who meant her harm. Especially if it was someone connected to them."

"What do you think, Emme?" Nick asked quietly. "What do you really think happened to her?"

She hesitated. "I honestly don't know. I don't think she's a runaway, if that's what you're asking. I do believe she was taken against her will."

"Do you think she's alive?"

"I don't know." She owed him an honest answer. "The odds are against it, though. I know you understand that."

He nodded slowly. "I know that after five months it's not looking too good."

"I'm sorry, Nick. I hate to assume the worst has happened, but . . ."

"Yeah, I know. I still want to find her. I still want to know what happened to her."

She was about to assure him that they'd do their best to make that happen when her phone rang. She glanced at the number before she answered, then looked at the clock. It was well after six.

Shit. Chloe.

"This is Emme," she said with a sigh.

"Emme, it's Trula. I just wanted to know if it's okay with you if Chloe has dinner with us here at the house."

"Oh, God, I am so sorry, Trula." Emme blew out a long breath. "I didn't think we'd be quite this long."

"Now, don't be sorry. You have a job to do. And I appreciate you letting me borrow this girl for a few hours. We've had a dandy time this afternoon . . . wait a second there, Chloe would like to say something."

"*Hola,* Mommy!" Chloe sang into the phone. "That means 'Hello, Mommy,' in Spanish."

"Where did you learn that, sweetie?"

"At school today. And know what else I can say? *Tu eres muy linda.* That means 'You are very pretty,' " Chloe said proudly.

"Well, that's certainly a lot for one day." Emme

couldn't help but notice how perfect Chloe's accent was. If she said it pleased her that her nursery school teacher was teaching the kids a little Spanish, she'd be lying. Anything remotely connected to Chloe's father would be objectionable. Then again, Spanish was a great language to know. Emme was fairly fluent herself. And to be fair to Chloe, she would someday need to know about her own heritage.

"Mommy? Are you there?"

"I'm here, sweetie."

"Me and Trula made muffins with walnuts in them. Robert ate one and said it was his favorite muffin *ever.*"

"You mean Mr. Magellan," Emme corrected her.

"No, I mean *Robert.* He said to call him Robert."

There was no arguing with the boss.

"Okay. Robert, then. Chloe, please put Trula back on the phone."

"Okay, bye." Chloe giggled and passed the phone to Trula.

"Again, I apologize for being so late, Trula. And judging from this traffic, it will be another hour at the very least before I get back to pick her up."

"No rush, dear. We're all going to have a nice dinner and then we're going to practice printing our C's."

"Trula, you don't have to do that."

"Nonsense. My C's could use a little spiffing up. We'll see you when you get here and we'll have some dinner saved for you."

"Bless you, Trula. When I asked if you'd mind picking her up today, I had no idea I'd be so late,"

Emme said before she realized that Trula had already moved on.

"A problem?" Nick asked after Emme slipped her phone back into her pocket.

"I guess not. Robert Magellan's housekeeper— I say housekeeper because I don't know what else to call her—is entertaining my daughter until I get back to pick her up. Or maybe Chloe is entertaining Trula, I'm not sure." She smiled in spite of her discomfiture at being late.

"How old is your daughter?"

"She's four."

"One of the women who works for me has a four-year-old. That seems to be a fun age. At least, this kid is fun. She likes to help polish the chrome before the cars get picked up."

"You let a four-year-old touch those valuable classic automobiles you restore?"

"Sure. She's very careful not to smudge. Better than some of the guys sometimes." He smiled. "They're always in a hurry, but this kid, never. She takes it very seriously."

"Well, four seems to be the age of earnestness. Chloe is very much into helping and doing things just right."

After a few minutes had passed, Nick asked, "So, are you divorced from her dad?"

"I've never been married."

"Oh."

"Chloe is adopted," she told him. "I've had her since she was only a few days old. She was born on a Friday, and on Monday morning I walked out the front door of the hospital with her in my arms." She smiled across the console. "Long story. The short version is, it was love at first sight."

"I guess it's hard sometimes, raising a child by yourself."

"Only on days like this when work runs over. Thank God for Trula."

"It's always good to have a backup," he agreed. "Who backed you up where you used to live?" Before she could answer, he added, "You have to be new to the area or you wouldn't be living in a hotel, right? Unless your house burned down or something like that."

"We are new to the area, and we haven't found a permanent place to live yet, so yes, that's why we're still in the hotel." She nodded. "It isn't too bad, other than the fact that it's Chloe and me in one and a half rooms, not counting the bathroom. There's a pretty good fitness center, which I haven't been able to use as much as I'd thought I would, and an indoor pool, which Chloe and I have used several times. And they do have a pretty good restaurant, so we're able to eat well. Though I'm afraid Chloe is getting spoiled. The chance of me making waffles or pancakes for breakfast every day once we're in a place of our own? Slim to none."

"Not a cook?"

"Not really. I do okay, but—truthfully—not my thing. Before Chloe, I ate most of my meals on the run. Now I have to make sure we eat healthy and watch the sugar, which means my days of having leftover cake or brownies for breakfast are over."

"You eat brownies for breakfast?"

"Doesn't everyone?"

He laughed, and she found herself liking the sound of it.

They drove a few miles in silence. Finally, Nick asked, "Are you going to be talking to the parents of the donor kids?"

"I haven't decided yet," she admitted. "On the one hand, most of these kids are over eighteen, so it's not a legal issue. On the other, if there is something else going on here, the parents should know about it. I'm just not sure they should hear about it from me."

"That's why I think you need me to set up these appointments, take the lead on contacting these kids."

"I seem to have missed that connection."

"Because my niece is the one who's missing. It's a great cover. Besides, I'm starting to grow on you. You like me."

"Why do I need a cover?" She ignored his attempt at humor.

"Because otherwise you, being an official investigator—a private investigator—could create a panic amongst these kids, who are then unlikely to talk to either of us."

"Panic might be too strong a word," she said, "but I suppose some of the kids might feel uneasy if they knew there was a full-scale investigation going on."

"You said you thought that some of these kids were contacted by the police when they were checking the phone numbers on Belinda's cell phone. As I recall, they all denied knowing her, or said the calls were wrong numbers," he reminded her. "Which tells me they didn't want to be part of any investigation."

"Possibly. On the other hand, at least one of these kids thinks you're the reason Belinda is missing."

When he started to protest, she said, "And remember that you've already contacted these kids via the message board, and no one responded. So I think we're just going to play this by ear. Sometimes I'll take the lead, sometimes you will, but when you make the contacts, I tell you what to say. And I tell you what to type in your emails and I'm on the line when you make those calls. I want to hear exactly what's said and the manner in which they say it. I want to hear the pauses—what's not said as well as what is said."

"Fair enough."

"You won't mind working from a script if it comes to that?"

"Hey, I did theater when I was in high school."

"Really? What plays were you in?"

"I had the title role in *Harvey*," he said loftily.

"The title role in *Harvey* was an invisible rabbit." She worked unsuccessfully to control the smile that tilted the corners of her mouth. "And had no lines."

"None that you could hear."

Emme laughed. "All right. We'll try it your way and see what happens. But if I think we're getting off track, or I don't like the way things are going, I call you off and you don't argue with me."

"Okay."

"Okay what?"

"Okay, if you don't like the way it goes, you get to shut it down."

"And shut you out."

"Right. You get to shut me out."

"And you don't argue if that time comes."

"Right." His sigh was loaded with reluctance. "I won't argue with you."

"I call the shots."

"Sure. You call the shots."

She smiled in the darkness. Somewhere she'd read the line, "Promises made in haste are the first to be broken." She didn't believe for a minute that Nick would keep his word.

"So when do we start? And where?" he asked.

"*We* start with the email addresses and phone numbers I expect to get from Hayley tonight." She checked her rearview mirror before taking the exit that would lead them from I-95 back to Conroy. "In the morning, I'll call the chief in Eastwind to see if we can get our hands on the surveillance tapes from the museum, see if we can get a picture of this guy who was stalking Belinda. It could mean something, or nothing."

"Why don't you just call the museum and ask to see them?"

"That would constitute a huge security breach for them. The firm that handles the security isn't going to want anyone to know where their cameras are or what measures they take, and I certainly don't blame them. The only way we can hope to get a look is by subpoena, and the museum and the security company will probably want to fight that—again, not that I blame them. My guess is that the case will be solved before the legal issues are resolved, but since you never know for sure how things will play out, we'll get that ball rolling anyway."

"All right. I can start calling some of these kids. Maybe I can arrange to meet with—"

Emme shot him a loaded glance, and he caught it.

"What?" he asked.

"Did we not just agree that I call the shots?"

"Well, yes, but . . ." He held up one hand in surrender. "Right. Sorry. When you've run your own business for as long as I have, you're used to being in charge. It can make you bossy and impatient at times." Nick took a deep breath. "Just tell me what you want me to do."

"I think I'm going to like this new Nick."

"You like men who do whatever you tell them to do?" He frowned as if the idea was foreign to him.

"There are times when it works for me."

"I'll keep that in mind."

"I'm counting on it."

He raised an eyebrow, but did not comment further.

"In the meantime, we need a game plan. There are too many questions, too few answers right now. For starters, I think we want to approach the kids who were at the art museum on January twenty-fourth. Maybe one of them will have a better description of the guy Hayley says was flirting with Belle."

"Hayley said that after lunch, Belinda and one of the other girls went in one direction, the others went somewhere else," Nick recalled. "Maybe she'll be able to tell us if the guy followed them, and if Belinda spoke with him."

"That was Ali, I think. So we'll put her near the top of the list. And then Henry and Lori. Maybe Ali can shed some light on just how far your niece had gotten on her search for their donor, and where Belinda went after they left the group. After that, we go on to the others on the message board, see if anyone knows anything or has heard anything from our missing girl."

Emme thought for a moment, then added, "And we need to find this kid, Aaron, to find out exactly what he told Belinda to do that would help her find her donor. I'm pretty sure I saw a reference to him when I was reading through some articles online. I think we need to know, step-by-step, what formula he followed to find his donor, and if he gave those same instructions to your niece."

"The next obvious question being, if he did, did Belinda follow them?"

"And if she followed, where did they lead?"

THIRTEEN

It took a great deal of patience to sit through the dinner Trula had kept warm. As thoughtful and as much appreciated as that dinner was, and as congenial as the company may have been, Emme was eager to get back to the hotel, settle Chloe for bed, and get to work on her laptop.

Settling Chloe wasn't easy even after they'd returned to their room. She was wound up from her afternoon with Trula and overtired after having been out a little later than she should have been. It was almost nine before the bedtime storybook had been selected and the story read a sufficient number of times. Finally, Emme tucked Chloe in and turned off the light next to the bed. She retreated quietly to their tiny sitting room and set up her laptop on the desk. Moments later she was skimming her mail.

There, as promised, was the email from Hayley.

Emme opened it and quickly read its contents, pleased to see email addresses for all other eight members of the Donor 1735 message board. Several, however, had no phone listings. She dashed off a reply to Hayley, thanking her for the information and asking about the missing phone numbers. She busied herself on the website of the Philadelphia Museum of Art and awaited a reply. It was forthcoming in minutes.

> Will and Wayne don't have cell phones, their mom doesn't like them. Go figure. I never had a number for Justin, just email, but I wouldn't have called him anyway. Jessie must have gotten a new phone when she moved to France 'cause the old number doesn't work anymore and no one has a new one for her. No one's heard from her since she moved.

Emme studied the list, then forwarded the email to her work computer so she could print it out in the morning before Nick showed up. She'd called the house and tried to gauge Robert's feelings on having Nick come to the house to work with her, but he seemed ambivalent. Finally he said, "Oh, for heaven's sake, this is not Fort Knox. If you need to work here, there's a conference room on the second floor. Someone should use it once in a while."

Having that settled, Emme shot off an email to Nick, giving him directions to the Magellan estate. Five minutes later, the cell phone Mallory had given her on the first day began to ring.

"What time tomorrow?" Nick asked.

"I'm usually there by eight, but you don't have to be that early," she whispered.

"I want to get an early start." She noticed he'd lowered his voice.

"I don't know how early we want to start making phone calls."

"If kids are still in school, they're probably up,

right? Unless they had a late night of partying the night before. Is Thursday night a big party night?"

"I don't know. Listen—"

"Why are we whispering?"

"My daughter is sleeping about fifteen feet away and I don't want to wake her. She had a big day at preschool."

"What do kids learn in preschool these days?"

"Letters. Numbers. Colors." Emme thought back to her earlier conversation with Chloe. "And apparently foreign languages. Chloe hit me with a little *Español* this afternoon."

"Good for her. It's a very useful language to know."

"Agreed. Listen, while I'm thinking of it, what kind of car did Belinda drive? And where is it now?"

"She had a white BMW sedan, the smallest model. And as for its whereabouts, I have no idea what happened to it. All I know for certain is that the Philadelphia police did not have it in their impound lot, and it hadn't been towed from where she parked it."

"Which means it was driven from where she'd parked it."

"It was reported missing but it's never been recovered—as far as I know, anyway."

"Not to cut you short, but—"

"But you're going to cut me short."

"I don't want to wake Chloe."

"And just when I was getting used to whispering. It makes for a kind of intimate conversation, don't you think? Anyone ever tell you that you have a very sexy voice?"

She laughed softly.

"I'll see you in the morning, Nick."

She was still smiling when she slid her phone back into her bag, turned off the laptop and the light, and made her way into the bedroom for the night.

Emme had just finished printing out two copies of the phone and email list the next morning when she heard Trula in the hall.

"This is Emme's office," Emme heard her say. "Right on through the door here. Come for a coffee refill anytime."

"Thanks, Trula." Nick was smiling pleasantly as he strolled into the office. To Emme he said, "You didn't tell me your job came complete with a fairy godmother."

Emme laughed. "That's as good a description of Trula as I've heard since I got here." She pointed to the chair that stood next to her desk. "Make yourself comfortable for a moment while I finish this."

"Seriously, that woman is something else. If she was thirty years younger, I'd ask her to marry me." He moved a pad of paper closer to the edge of her desk and set his coffee cup on it. "I'd *beg* her to marry me."

"You must have gotten a whiff of those muffins she bakes every morning."

"I got more than a whiff," he smiled.

"She gave you a muffin?"

"Where do you think I've been since eight fifteen?"

"She must think you're here for a job interview."

"Nope. She knows why I'm here. She just couldn't resist the old Perone charm."

Emme coughed into her hand.

"Think you can drag that charm up to the conference room so we can get started?"

"Sure. Lead the way."

Emme gathered up her files. When she struggled to pick up her laptop, Nick grabbed it for her. Halfway up the stairs they met Robert, who was on his way down. Emme made the introductions.

"I'm really glad to meet you," Nick told him. "I think what you're doing here is amazing. If I'm lucky enough to see my niece again, I'll have you to thank."

"You'll have Emme to thank," Robert corrected him. "She's doing the work."

Robert went down two more steps, then stopped and turned around. Looking up, he said, "Do I know you from somewhere?"

Nick shrugged. "I don't think so."

"You look familiar." He continued down a few more steps. "Nick Perone. Even your name is familiar."

"Your name is familiar to me, too," Nick said, "but you're Robert Magellan. Everyone knows who you are."

Robert was at the bottom step, looking over his shoulder. "If we've met before, it'll come to me. I never forget a face."

"Could you have met him somewhere?" Emme opened the door to the conference room and turned on the light.

"I think I'd remember if I had. I doubt we travel in the same circles." Nick followed her into the room. "Wow. Looks like an old-fashioned library."

"The library is downstairs. And that's pretty much off-limits to the rest of us, one of the few places in the

house off-limits to us. That's Robert's private do-
main. Invitation only." She placed her files on the
table and looked around for a coaster for Nick's coffee. Not finding one, she handed him a file. "You'll
have to use this."

"Have you ever been invited?" he asked, and when
she looked blank, he added to clarify, "To the private
library."

"Are you kidding? That's family only. Robert.
Kevin—his cousin, Father Kevin Burch, but no one
around here seems to remember he's clergy half the
time. And of course, Trula."

She glanced around for the phones, and found
them at the far end of the table.

"Let's move down to that end," she told Nick. "It's
easier than moving the phones."

They repositioned themselves, the laptop between
them flanked by a phone on each side.

"I spoke with the Eastwind police this morning.
The chief is going to start working on those surveillance tapes. I think he was happy to be kept in the
loop. Oh, and here"—she handed him a piece of
paper—"I printed out Hayley's email so we'd have
clean copies to work from. I also printed out what I
think the order of things should be."

Nick glanced over the list.

"You want to start with Ali, then move on to
Henry, then Lori," he read.

"I'm thinking Ali might be home. She's a high
school senior so she's probably finished with her
exams. Depending on the school system she's in,
she might have already graduated. Hayley said that
Henry just graduated from college, but that he wasn't

living at home right now. Lori's still in college but she has an apartment with a few other girls and she's staying in New Haven for the summer."

"You know what you're going to say?"

"I can do this in my sleep. Seven years on the police force, remember."

Nick pointed to the phone. "Dial away."

While she dialed, he asked, "Did you like it?"

"Did I like what?"

"Being a cop."

"Loved it."

"Why'd you leave?"

"I love my daughter more." She flushed pink and mentally kicked herself. She was grateful that the call was answered on the third ring, saving her from an explanation she didn't want to give.

"Hello, is this Ali?" she asked.

"Yes. Who's this?" The young girl yawned blatantly.

"My name is Emme Caldwell." She hit the speaker button but kept the volume low. "I'm an investigator with the Mercy Street Foundation. I'm calling about Belle Hudson."

"Belle?" She yawned again. "I haven't heard from her in a couple of months."

"She's been missing for a couple of months, Ali. We're trying to find her."

"Belle's really missing? She's not just AWOL from the board?"

"I'm afraid so."

The yawning stopped and Ali was suddenly fully awake.

"Are you sure about this? Who'd you say you were again?"

Emme reintroduced herself. "And yes, we're positive she's missing. Actually, no one's seen or heard from her since January." Emme paused for effect. "January twenty-fourth, to be precise. The day you spent in Philadelphia at the art museum with several of your donor siblings."

"Oh my God." Ali's voice cracked. "She's really been gone all this time?"

"I'm afraid so. Weren't you contacted by the police a few months ago about this?"

"Someone called and asked if I knew her—months ago, this was—but I didn't really understand what the call was about, so I hung up," she said sheepishly. "When they called back, they said they were checking numbers on a cell phone, so I said I didn't know her. They didn't tell me she was missing."

"Why would you have said that, Ali?"

"Look, some of the kids' parents are real nervous about us getting together. You have to understand the whole donor-sibling thing, what it means to some kids to find out they have brothers and sisters, that they're not alone."

"I think I have a pretty good idea what that might mean, Ali." Emme, who'd been alone all her life—until Chloe—had a damned good idea of what it might feel like to discover a connection. Any connection.

"Some of the parents don't. They feel threatened by it, like they think because their kid finds some family somewhere outside of them, that it means they don't love their own family or their mom, or their dad, if they have one." She sighed. "Some of us only have a mom. Or in Henry and Lori's case, two moms. They don't really understand why we'd want to know who fathered us or what that side of our gene pool might be like or why we'd want to have contact with them, why it matters whether or not we connect with these other kids who—as far as the parents are concerned— are only connected to us by a biological event. Because to some moms—that would be moms like mine—the only side of the family that's supposed to count is hers."

The words all came out in a rush, and Emme sat quietly, listening.

"So when a stranger calls and says, I'm calling numbers on a cell phone, do you know—fill in the blank, any one of my donor sibs would do—the answer is going to be no. Even if they said they were the police, how would I know if they were lying or not?"

"But didn't you think it odd that you didn't hear from her after the trip to Philadelphia?"

"I did hear from her."

"You did?" Emme almost lifted off her chair in surprise. Nick opened his mouth but Emme clamped a hand over it and shook her head. "When?"

"I got an email from her a day or so later."

"What did she say? Did she say where she was?"

"No. All she said was that it was fun to get together with everyone on Saturday, and that she was really busy with school and was taking a break."

"That's all she said?"

"In the email, yes, I think so. Which didn't surprise me, since on Saturday, she'd been talking about how she was going to be really busy with rush at her sorority once the new semester started. Besides, she was trying to find—" Ali stopped in what seemed to be midsentence.

"Trying to find out who Donor 1735 was," Emme finished the sentence for her. "I know."

There was silence on the other end of the line, and for a minute, Emme was afraid the girl had hung up.

"Ali?" she asked.

"I'm here."

"I know that she thought she was close to finding him. Did she tell you how close?"

"No. She just sort of hinted." Ali started to cry. "All I know for certain is that Aaron, this kid who found his donor mostly through the Internet, was helping her."

"Do you know how to get in touch with Aaron?"

"I have his email address somewhere."

"Would you mind looking for it? I'd like to contact him."

"Why?"

"I'm calling anyone who Belle had been in touch with. We're trying to figure out where and when she was last heard from."

"Like I said, the day in Philly was the last I saw her."

"At the art museum," Emme said, just to be sure.

"Right."

"I understand there was a young man in the museum restaurant who was paying a lot of attention to Belle that day."

"Yeah. The jerk."

"He was a jerk?"

"He looked like a jerk. Acted like a jerk. I mean, he

was totally cute, don't get me wrong, but there was something about him that was just . . . not cool."

"Why do you say that?"

"Okay, this guy was just totally focused on Belle. And like, because he was so hot, and knew he was hot, he took it for granted that she was focused on him, too. Not cool."

"What did Belle think of him?"

"Same. Totally not cool. She turned her back on him at lunch and acted like he wasn't there."

"Was that the end of it?"

"Are you kidding? I wish. He followed us into the photography exhibit. Which was the main thing I was interested in seeing that day."

"Do you know if he spoke to her?"

"He tried to, but she just ignored him. Belle is totally cool. Way too cool for a guy like that."

"Did she say anything at all about him?"

"At first she thought she might know him, but then realized she didn't."

"He looked familiar to her?"

"I guess sort of, but then she said no, he wasn't and we just finished looking at the photographs."

"Did you notice if he followed her outside?"

"No, I didn't. We all met up out on the steps so I could take a picture and I really wasn't paying attention."

"You have a picture from that day?"

"I have a couple of them, yeah."

"Can you scan them and send them to me?"

"Why?" Ali seemed wary at the request.

"For one thing, so I can see what Belle was wearing that day. Can you do that now, while we're on the phone, so you can identify everyone in the picture for me?"

"Tell me again why you're looking for Belle?"

"Her uncle, Nick Perone, with whom she lived, is her only relative." Emme paused, then hastened to add, "On her mother's side. He's been looking for her since January, Ali. He's asked us to help find her, because the police have pretty much given up."

"Belle told me all about her uncle Nick."

"What did she say?" Emme and Nick were both all ears.

Nick whispered, "If she calls me a pervert—"

"She said he was her mom's younger brother and he was a really good guy. That he took her in after her mother died and that she went through this stage where she did everything she could to make him angry and make him not like her, but he kept her anyway. She said she didn't know what made her do the things she did and she was sorry, and that after a while she just cut it out and they got to be good friends. She said she cared a lot about him, that he was, like, her best bud. Oh, and she said he was really into cars and had the coolest Vette on the planet."

Emme glanced over at Nick. He made no attempt to hide that his eyes brimmed with tears. She reached over and gave his hand a squeeze, telling herself that years of comforting victims had made such gestures come naturally. He held on to her, and she let him.

"So you wouldn't think she'd run away?"

"Belle? Uh-uh. She was a really happy, sweet, fun girl. Probably my favorite out of all the sibs, but don't tell the rest of them that."

"Your secret is safe with me."

"What do you think happened to her?" Ali's voice dropped.

"We don't know. We're trying to track her movements after she left the museum that day. We'll be speaking with all the kids, by the way, to see if anyone's heard from her."

"Some of them might not talk to you."

"I guess they'll just have to tell me that themselves. I'm going to try anyway."

"Give me your email address," Ali said, "and I'll scan these photos in."

Emme did as she'd been requested.

"You have the photos handy?"

"They're right here on my desk. Hold on . . . this will just take a couple of minutes. Don't go away."

"I'll be here," Emme assured her. "Good of her to do this," Emme said, putting her hand over the speaker.

Nick nodded. Clearly, he was still slightly shaken after having heard how much Belle thought of him. Had she never told him? Emme wondered. Probably not. Kids sometimes don't think to tell the adults in their lives how they feel about them.

Chloe, on the other hand, at four, never hesitated to speak her mind about who she loved and how much. Just last evening, after Emme had finished the meal Trula had saved for her and they were leaving for the hotel for the night, Chloe had thrown her arms around Trula's neck, hugged her, and declared, "I love you, Trula. I wish you were my grandma." Trula had been *this close* to puddling up—there'd been no mistaking that look.

Would the day come when Chloe's heart would no longer be as open? Emme hoped not. . . .

"Okay, the pictures should be there any minute now." Ali was back on the line.

"Hold on, let me check." Emme turned the laptop in her direction and hit a few keys to access her mail. "Yes, they're here."

She opened the email.

"Tell me who's who," she said.

Nick pushed back his chair and stood behind Emme's, leaning over her shoulder to get a closer look at the photos.

"On the top one, from left to right, there's Hayley, me, Lori, Henry, and Belle."

Hayley, clearly the youngest, wore an orange stadium coat with fur around the hood. Ali was tall and had very short blond hair and looked nothing like any of the other kids in the photo. Lori and Henry favored Hayley slightly, and bore a strong resemblance to each other. Belle wore a red peacoat over jeans and had a paper bag tucked under one arm. All five faced the camera with happy-go-lucky smiles.

Emme twisted in her seat to look up at Nick. He touched the back of her neck ever so slightly, the gesture catching her off guard. She looked back at the screen and kept her attention focused there. Or tried to.

"Who took the pictures?"

"A really nice lady who was taking some pictures out front offered to take them for me."

"It looks like Belle has a bag under one arm," Emme observed.

"Yeah, she bought some stuff in the museum

store," Ali told her. "Some postcards and a scarf. It had, like, some Renoir painting on it. Flowers."

"What time was that, do you remember?"

"Ummm . . . maybe around two?"

Emme studied the photos for a long moment, then reached over and enlarged the image to fill the screen.

"Ali, who's that in the background on that last photo?"

"I don't know, just someone who was in front of the building when we were, I guess. I hadn't noticed."

"Looks like the same person is here, in this one," Nick said. He leaned closer and touched the screen. "Here, near the door."

"Who's there?" Ali asked suspiciously.

"Ali, I'm sorry. Belle's uncle Nick is here with me. I apologize for not mentioning it."

"It's okay, Ms. Caldwell." To Emme's surprise, Ali didn't sound the least bit annoyed. "Hi, Belle's uncle Nick. I've heard a lot about you. Nice things. Or maybe you heard."

"I didn't mean to eavesdrop, but I'd be lying if I said I'm sorry I overhead you, Ali. Thanks so much for what you said about Belinda . . . Belle. I appreciate it."

"No big."

Emme assumed she meant no big deal, but knew it would be too uncool to ask.

"You were saying something about the door." Emme got closer to the screen. "This person here? Is that a male or a female?"

"I can't tell." Nick said. "I can't really see the face or the clothes that well. It's just sort of a form there, maybe a reflection off the glass. Could even be some-one on the other side, maybe."

"I can't tell either," Ali said, reminding them she was still on the line.

"Ali, this uncool guy who was hanging around you and Belle—" Nick began, but Ali cut him off.

"Belle," she corrected him. "He was hanging around Belle."

"Do you remember what he looked like?"

"Kinda tall, blond hair. Buff. Like I said, really cute."

"What was he wearing?" Emme asked.

"He had on a dark green sweater and jeans. And a brown suede jacket. I remember that, because it was really good suede. The real expensive kind."

"How could you tell just by looking at it?" Nick asked.

"He was carrying it over his arm and it brushed against me when Belle and I were leaving the photography exhibit. He got way too close but his jacket was the bomb."

"Sounds like a bold little bugger," Nick said.

"Way bold," Ali agreed.

"Did he get close again?" Emme asked.

"No. We left after that and went outside."

"Hayley said she and Henry and Lori shared a cab back to the train station but that you and Belle had both driven that day. So were you still with Belle after the others left?"

"Uh-huh. There's some limited parking behind the building and I was lucky enough to get a spot there when I arrived that morning. Belle was late and had to park on another street. I offered to drive her, but she said since it was the first somewhat warm day of the winter, she wanted to walk."

"Where did you part company?"

"Out front."

"Did you happen to see which way she went when she left you?"

"She went straight down the steps. You know, where they did the Rocky thing? There's that big oval drive out in front of the building so I figured she was parked down there someplace."

"She didn't say how far she had to go to get her car?"

"I don't remember if she did."

"Ali, do you still have the email you got from Belle after the museum trip?"

"I'm sure I deleted it. I'm sorry."

"One more thing," Nick said. "Did you see Mr. Uncool again that day?"

"No. I guess he just gave up." Ali paused, then added, "You don't think he followed her or something creepy like that, do you? Because if something happened to her because I let her walk to her car alone, and he followed her and—"

"Whoa, Ali, back up. First of all, you didn't *let* her walk to her car. That was her idea. She's a big girl. And regardless of what happened to her and where, it wasn't your fault, so please don't even start down that path. The only person responsible for what happened to Belle, is the person who actually did . . . whatever might have been done."

When it seemed Ali had been too quiet for too long, Emme said, "Ali?"

"You're right. It's just that . . ."

"I know. It's always easy to second guess yourself, but in this case, I don't think anything you could have done would have made any difference."

"Why not?"

"If someone—this guy or someone else—was determined to get to Belle, he'd have found a way."

"But why would someone be after Belle?" Ali began to cry.

Emme sighed. "That's what we're trying to figure out."

FOURTEEN

"So now we're on to Henry and Lori, right?" Nick put his notes aside once they'd hung up with Ali. "I see they have separate numbers. Which one do you want to call first?"

"Let's start with Henry." Emme dialed the number, then handed Nick the phone. "He might respond better to you, being a guy."

When no one answered, he left a message that he thought was vague enough to spark some interest, but not so specific as to scare Henry away. The call to Lori resulted in Emme leaving a message as well.

"I hope they call back," she said as she hung up.

"You think there's a chance they won't? They were with Belinda that last day. I'd think they'd be interested."

"You never know with kids." Emme added, "Especially this group. I think they're a bit more suspicious than others might be because of their situation. Like Ali said, some of the families aren't happy about the kids connecting, so maybe it's tough to know who to trust when you don't know who you're dealing with."

"Ali was okay with you."

"I guess I hit the right note with her. You never know how it's going to go when you interview witnesses." She thought for a moment. "Maybe we should do another email to the group. And I'm thinking that this time, the email should be from me, since I am an investigator—so the others understand that Belle really is missing."

"Good idea."

Emme pulled up the website and located the Donor 1735 message board.

"What are you going to say?" Nick asked.

"I think I'm just going to shoot from the hip. Lay it all out there."

Deep in thought, she began to type. A few minutes later, she turned to Nick and said, "How does this sound?" and began to read:

My name is Emme Caldwell. I'm a private investigator with the Mercy Street Foundation, which is an organization that specializes in finding missing persons. Our services were requested by Nick Perone, the uncle of your donor sibling, Belinda Hudson—you know her as Belle—who was last seen on January twenty-fourth, 2009. It's been determined that she spent most of that day with several members of this board. Over the next several days, I will be contacting each of you to talk about Belle. I hope I can count on all of you for total cooperation and honesty. If you'd like to contact me, please call me at the number below. If you'd prefer to contact Belle's uncle directly, you can reach him at . . ."

She finished and looked up at Nick. "Does that sound okay?"

"It sounds great. Thanks for including me. At least now they'll know my earlier attempts to contact them wasn't a joke. Or the attempt of some perverted guy trying to—"

"Stop it. I realize that upset you—justifiably so— but I think we need to just chalk that up to some wiseass kid being, well, being a wiseass."

"Agreed."

Emme hit post and leaned back.

"I guess that will take a while to generate any activity. Let's move on to the next item on the agenda." She picked up her list. "Aaron. First thing this morning, I reread the article about him in a magazine. I printed it out—it's here somewhere. . . ." She thumbed through a folder that had been sitting to her left. "Here it is. Take a look at this. The kid's a genius. How he figured this out step-by-step and made it all work out is just beyond me."

Nick took the file and began to read to himself.

"I'm running downstairs for coffee." Emme stood and stretched. "Can I bring you a refill?"

"That would be great, thanks." Engrossed in his reading, Nick handed her his mug without looking up. "You're right, this kid is really sharp."

She returned some minutes later, a mug in each hand.

"Trula is feeling philosophical today," she said as she placed both mugs on the table.

"What do you mean?" Nick asked.

Emme pointed to his mug. " '*Define the moment or*

the moment will define you,' " she read. "Walt Whitman."

She turned hers around. " *'Reality leaves a lot to the imagination.'* John Lennon. Trula has a penchant for coffee mugs that have messages printed on them. She has dozens of them."

"They all have famous quotes on them?"

"Some do. Those run from Nietzsche to quotes like, *'Talk is cheap because the supply exceeds the demand.'* Others are just plain silly. Like, *'I see dumb people.'* Or, *'You say bitch like it's a bad thing.'* That sort of thing." Emme smiled. "You just never know what you're going to get."

He took a sip and sighed. "Who cares what the coffee's in when it's this good?"

"That's pretty much my feeling, too." She sat down. "Did you finish the article?"

"I did. You're right. This kid is beyond clever. Swabs his own DNA, sends it off to have it tested at one of those online genealogy DNA-testing services, has it matched up to anyone in the same paternal line whose DNA is on file. Apparently, there are a hell of a lot of people who have supplied their DNA to these genealogy websites. There's a place called ShakeYourFamilyTree.com that has been running a project to collect DNA samples for the past three years, and now has a huge database available, and they're not the only place on the Internet you can go to find DNA registries. For less than three hundred dollars, you can find out if anyone matching your DNA is on record there. Anyway, this kid gets a couple of names back—their Y chromosomes were close enough to suggest they had the same very close male relative."

"Well, father, grandfather, great-grandfather. A brother or a cousin wouldn't have done it."

"Right. So he gets four names back, all with the same last name. So he takes that name, and the information his mother got from the clinic where she purchased the sperm, and he puts two and two and two together and gets his donor."

"Just by knowing his donor's place and date of birth and what degree he earned in college, he found the guy. Talk about looking for a needle in a haystack. He goes to one of those online search sites, buys the names of every man who was born on that day in that place, and bingo—there's one with the name he's looking for."

"It sounds as if his donor wasn't too upset about being found. More like he was as impressed as we are by this kid's smarts. Enough that he and Aaron have actually been able to develop a real relationship." Nick handed the article back to Emme. "Nice to see there was a happy ending there."

"It makes me wonder how far Belle really got with this. I'd love to know if she was successful in getting a name," Emme said. "And if she did, did she tell any of the other kids?"

"You think they'd admit it to you, if she did?"

"I like to think someone would."

"Maybe they're afraid you'll hassle the guy if you know who he is. Or maybe they want to contact this guy themselves and are afraid you'll scare him off. Or there could be reasons only a kid would think up."

"So if no one admits to knowing, it could be that she didn't tell anyone. Or it could be that she didn't find him." Emme took another sip of coffee, and found it had cooled. She drank it absently. "Supposing she did find him, but he was one of the donors who really didn't want to be found."

"I've thought about that." Nick leaned an elbow on the table and rubbed his chin. "Of course, that would mean that this kid at the museum was just a coincidence, right? Just some kid who thought she was cute and wanted to get a little closer. That sort of thing happens all the time."

"I don't know how he fits in," she admitted, "or, as you suggest, if he fits in to the rest of this at all. Generally speaking, I don't like coincidences—most cops don't—but that doesn't mean they don't occur."

They heard a clicking sound coming from her computer.

She turned the screen slightly to eliminate the glare. "A message from Will and Wayne."

She read it aloud.

"Belle is really missing? Are you sure? This isn't a joke?"

Her fingers flew across the keyboard.

No joke, guys. She's really missing. When did you last hear from her?

A minute later, the reply.

We think probably around Christmas?
We never got to go to the get-togethers because they were too far away. We only met her one time, she came to see us last fall.

She's really pretty. All our sisters are pretty—Ali sent us some pictures from a get-together they had. We wish we had something to tell you but we don't.

Emme turned to Nick. "That's pretty much what I expected from those two. Ali said they weren't real active on the message board and they didn't even have cell phones."

Another click. Another message, this one a private email.

Miss Caldwell—Lori and I are shocked to learn that Belle has been missing all this time! We have both been away at school and haven't been on the board too much recently because of exams. We both are willing to meet with you whenever, wherever you want. Are you near CT? If you're close by, maybe we can meet partway? Henry Carroll-Wilson

"His name is Henry Carroll-Wilson?" Nick frowned. "For real? Wasn't Henry Wilson the name of Dennis the Menace's cranky old neighbor?"

Emme laughed. "Could be."

She typed a reply email and hit send. "Just to let him know where we are and that we can meet him halfway or drive up there, whatever it takes. Every one of these kids we talk to could conceivably bring us one step closer to finding out what happened that day."

Henry's reply was immediate.

Lori and I can drive to Philadelphia this weekend and meet you there. Is tomorrow okay with you?

When Emme hesitated, Nick asked, "Something wrong?"

"I'm kind of tied up this weekend."

"Heavy date?"

"Yeah. With a Realtor and a four-year-old. We're still looking for a house to rent." She thought for a moment. "Even if I schedule the Realtor for one day instead of both, I still have Chloe. I don't really have anyone to watch her, except Trula, and I don't want her to think I'm taking advantage of her. It's enough she has her company after school until I finish up in my office."

"Why don't you bring her along?"

"I don't want her hearing the kind of stuff we'll be talking about."

"We can all meet at the zoo, then I can take Chloe to see some of the animals while you talk to Lori and Henry."

"I can't impose on you like that. She's a great kid, don't get me wrong, but she'll talk your ears off. You'll be deaf for a week."

"She's that loud?"

"Not loud, just constant."

"It's okay. I won't mind. My life's been kind of quiet for a while now." He smiled weakly. "It's been a really long time since I've been to a zoo."

"Nick, are you certain?"

"Absolutely. You do the investigating, I'll do the zoo with Chloe."

She nodded, more pleased than she was willing to show, and she typed her reply to Henry. He called her cell phone in response, and together they viewed a map of the zoo online to locate the main gate.

"He sounds like a really nice guy," Emme told Nick after she hung up from Henry's call. "He and his sister are both really upset that they didn't realize something was amiss sooner. We'll meet them tomorrow at one, right inside the zoo gate."

"Great. Tell Chloe to wear her walking shoes. I hear it's a really big zoo." He moved closer to the table, his fingers on her keyboard. "May I?"

"Sure. What are you? . . ."

He pointed to the website for the Philadelphia Zoo that was still on her screen.

"Look here, America's first zoo. Check out all the habitats." Nick pointed to the screen. "African plains. Australian animals. Bear country. Big cats. Rare animals. Which of those do you think Chloe would like?"

"All of them. She loves animals and is ridiculously curious." Emme grabbed the mouse and clicked on Prairie dogs.

"She'll love these. But you're going to have to watch her like a hawk, Nick. She'll be trying to get right in there with them."

"We'll set the rules with her before we get there, and we'll set an itinerary so that she'll be able to see you. I'm assuming you can walk and talk to Henry and Lori at the same time."

"We might end up lagging behind at times, but having an itinerary is a really good idea. Then if it's crowded and we get separated, we'll know where the other is headed for next." She clicked again on the screen and brought up a list of exhibits. "Let's do that now while we're thinking about it."

An hour later, they had their Saturday afternoon mapped out, and Emme had her Realtor switch all of their appointments to Sunday. When they'd finished, Emme sent the command to the wireless printer in the room to print out two copies. She retrieved them just as the computer signaled incoming mail.

"Let's see who this is," she said. "Oh, it's Hayley."

I called Ava. She's very upset about Belle. I went on the message board and asked everyone to call or email you as soon as possible and tell you when they last heard from Belle. I told everyone that you're trying to help. And I emailed all the others who don't go on the board very often or who stopped going on at all. Everyone needs to know about this. Is there anything else you want me to do?

"Sweet girl," Emme murmured as she began to type. "Since we can't read the messages that are posted on the board, except for the ones we write, I'm hoping Hayley will tell me if there's any rumbles going on about this on the message board."

Hayley, you've been a huge help—we can't thank you enough. Please keep in touch, and let us know what's posted on the message board by the others.

"So now we go on to Aaron." She began to compose the email. "Do we want this one from me, or from you?"

"Maybe from me. Getting an email from a private investigator might make him nervous."

"Good point." She nodded. "We'll send this one from Uncle Nick. . . ."

They worked on the email for almost twenty minutes before they were satisfied with its contents.

"Let's send it before we change our minds again," Nick said, his fingers poised.

"I agree. There's not much more we can say other than what we already have." Emme ticked off the high points of the text. "We read the article, admire his creative mind. We know Belle was in contact with him, here's the situation with Belle. When did he last hear from her? How far had she gotten in her quest? Does he know if she completed her search? And more specifically, if she located Donor 1735, did she contact him?"

"That's it." He hit send. "We're done. What else today?"

"That's it for now," she said. "We're not going to know anything more until we hear from the others, and that could be anytime between now and never."

"I think I'll head on back to the garage then." Nick looked at his watch. "I have a '65 Mustang coming in this afternoon for an evaluation and I need to be there when the owner arrives. I'll let you know if I hear anything from Aaron."

"So I'll meet you at the zoo tomorrow at one, then." Emme closed her laptop.

"Maybe we should make it a little earlier, so Chloe and I can get to know each other a little," Nick said thoughtfully. "Let's make it eleven thirty at the gate, and we can walk over to the Tiger Terrace and have lunch. I saw it on the map, it's near the middle of the zoo. That way, Chloe and I won't be total strangers when I walk her off to look at the animals. She might think it's strange that you let her walk away with someone she doesn't know."

"Chloe believes that strangers are merely friends she hasn't met yet. She's entirely too trusting. But you're right. She needs to understand that I wouldn't let her walk away with just anyone. She should know that we're . . ." She fished for the right word. "Acquaintances."

"Acquaintances?" He raised an eyebrow. "Is that the best we can do? After all, we've been spending a lot of time in each other's company. I'd like to think at this point, we're at least friends."

"Friends." Emme nodded. "Friends works."

"Okay, then. I'll see you and Chloe tomorrow morning."

"Great." She walked him to the door. "Eleven thirty. At the front gate."

"And if you hear anything noteworthy from any of the siblings—"

"I'll contact you."

"Good. Well, then." They reached her office door. "I guess I'll see you there."

"Right." She smiled and hugged her laptop to her chest. She stayed in the doorway and watched as Nick headed for the front of the house.

"Whoa," someone whispered in her ear. "That was the uncle?"

"Yeah." Emme turned to find Mallory enjoying the view as Nick disappeared around the slight bend in the hall.

"Nice jeans." Mallory smiled and returned to her own office.

"Yeah." Emme nodded in agreement. "Not bad."

He stared at the screen, not quite believing what he was seeing. When it became apparent that he was not imagining the message he'd received, he smacked his fist on the desktop.

"Stupid bitch," he growled. "Stupid, stupid bitch!"

He went on to the next message, which did little to improve his state of mind. Nor did the emails, which had been copied to all of the members of the group.

"God damn it."

He rose, hoping to walk off the rage that was building inside him. It wasn't working.

"Why can't people mind their own fucking business?" he muttered as he paced the length of the room and back.

He returned to the screen, making mental notes of the wheres and the whens. Satisfied that he had all he needed to know, he turned off the computer. He just couldn't take anymore.

He left the house by the back door and walked out to the yard. A swim might help, he told himself as he passed the pool. The sun was high in the sky and the humidity was building by the hour. A swim, yes, a swim would help. He went to the pool house and changed into a suit he kept there. He grabbed a clean towel off the stack by the door and tossed it onto a lounge as he passed by. Walking directly to the deep end, he dove deeply, his fingers tracing along the bottom of the pool until he reached the shallow end. He surfaced quickly, the water sliding smoothly off his skin. He floated on his back for a moment, the itching inside him only growing more intense.

He began to do laps, hoping to wear down the feeling, but after nearly an hour, close to exhaustion, he realized exercise would not help. Not today, when he was so agitated.

Pulling himself up onto the diving board, he leaned back and rested on his elbows and stared down at the water, and wondered how things had gotten so messed up in his life. As if it mattered at this point, he reflected. There was no turning back now.

And in truth, did he really want to turn back? Would he really wish away the one thing in his life that brought him true satisfaction, true ecstasy, true bliss?

He tried to remember when he first realized that he was actually going to take a life. It had seemed necessary at the time but he couldn't remember when that had become clear, that the killing wasn't an option, but, like it or not, something he had to do. He'd come to accept that sometimes there were certain things that simply had to be done. Killing was one of them. It was something he'd sort of grown into, something he found he had a surprising talent for, and that he'd liked. A lot.

That had been the biggest surprise—that he enjoyed it as much as he did, liked the high like nothing else he'd ever experienced. He dove into the water again when he felt the first stirring of the desire that came over him every time he thought about taking a life. The knowledge surged through him that he'd be feeding that desire, and soon—much sooner than he'd expected. This time would present a greater challenge, would require more planning, but that was okay. He enjoyed the process, though not quite as much as he enjoyed the execution.

He smiled, realizing his pun. *Ha! The execution. Good one!*

He got out of the pool, dried off, and walked back to the house, whistling all the way.

FIFTEEN

The steam rose off the asphalt in waves. Emme pulled the elastic from her ponytail and reworked it to raise her hair off the back of her neck, then did the same for Chloe.

Leave it to me to pick the hottest day of the year for a trip into the city. Way to go, she grumbled to herself.

"Where's your friend, Mommy?" Chloe asked.

"He'll be here soon, I'm sure." Emme and Chloe stood well inside the zoo gate, holding hands and watching the crowd filter in. It was nearly eleven thirty, but already the temperature was rising toward ninety, the humidity keeping pace. "I called him on my cell phone before we left to tell him we'd meet him here, instead of the Tiger Terrace."

"What's the Tiger Terrace?" Chloe kicked a little pebble with her foot, then followed it to where it lay, and kicked it again. Emme grabbed her by the shoulder before she could kick it out into the stream of tourists coming through the zoo gates.

"It's a place where you can buy food and eat. At least I think it is. Like a restaurant."

"The place where Trula didn't want us to eat?"

Emme looked up and saw Nick walking toward them. She couldn't help but smile. He looked happy to see her, and in spite of the heat, looked cool as the proverbial cucumber. She wondered how he did that.

"Trula was afraid we'd eat hot dogs," Emme said, her eyes still on Nick.

"Why is she afraid of hot dogs?" Chloe asked.

"Because sometimes they have things in them that might not be good for you." Nick said as he joined them. "Hi, Chloe. I'm Nick, your mom's friend."

"I know what's in hot dogs, do you?" Chloe asked solemnly, looking up at him.

"Nitrates?" he replied.

"No, beef." She turned to her mother. "Why doesn't Trula like beef?"

"Trula does like beef. What Nick said—nitrates— aren't good for people and some hot dogs have them." Emme looked from Chloe to Nick. "Why are we having this conversation?"

"Because someone is curious. But for the record, I'm betting the Tiger Terrace has other things besides hot dogs," Nick said.

"But we have a picnic," Chloe pointed to the cooler on wheels that stood next to her mother's feet. "Trula made it."

"So your mom told me on the phone." Nick nodded in the direction of the cooler.

"Trula only likes special food," Chloe told him.

"So what's in the special picnic basket?" he asked.

"Turkey sandwiches. Salad. Grapes. Cookies. Water." Chloe counted off the contents on her fingers.

"That does sound special," he agreed.

"That's cause the turkey is free grown," Chloe confided.

"Free range," Emme corrected.

"Right." Chloe nodded. "That."

"There are some tables over here under the trees," Emme said, pointing. "I suggest we take one of those while there's still one to be had. In this heat, I'm thinking the tables in the shade will be the first to go."

Nick grabbed the cooler. "You lead, I'll follow."

"Trula was mad because she didn't know we were going on a picnic and she didn't have time to make us more food," Chloe said as they began to unload the basket.

"Judging by the weight of this cooler, I'd say she did just fine," Nick observed.

"Trula dotes on Chloe," Emme explained. "Actually, she dotes on all of us there at the foundation."

Nick placed the cooler on the designated table and opened the lid. Chloe dove in.

"But mostly on me, 'cause I'm special." Chloe handed Nick a bottle of water. "She said to make sure we remember to drink a lot of water today because it's going to be a scorcher."

Nick bit back a laugh and took the bottle. "Well, she's right about that. It's already hot."

"Maybe too hot to be at the zoo," Emme said.

"No, it's not," Chloe held up her bottle and her mother twisted off the top for her. "It's going to be just right."

"The animals might be a bit mopey," Emme told her. "Some of them don't like the heat."

"But some do, right?"

"I suppose some do," Emme nodded and passed out the sandwiches, hers and Nick's on rolls, Chloe's on a biscuit, just the right size for a four-year-old appetite.

They chatted through lunch, and after they finished and cleaned up the table, Nick found an information stand that had a map of the zoo and several brochures.

"Here, Chloe, let's decide where we'll go first," he said.

Emme checked her watch. Lori and Henry should be arriving any minute. She stood for a better view of the gate.

"Do you have the photo that Ali sent you?" Nick asked.

"No, but I remember what they look like," she assured him.

"Look, Nick, giraffes." Chloe pointed excitedly to the brochure. "I never saw a real giraffe."

"Yes, you did," Emme reminded her, never taking her eyes off the gate. "In San Diego, remember?"

"I was too little then." Chloe shook her head. "I don't remember."

Chloe turned her attention back to the brochure and the map, chatting happily about the animals they'd see.

"No sign of them yet?" Nick asked after another ten minutes had gone by.

Emme shook her head.

"How much longer before we can see the animals, Mommy?" Chloe tugged on her arm.

"Soon, sweetie. Just be patient for a little longer."

"I have been very patient." Chloe pulled on Emme's arm until her mother was bent at the waist and they were face to face.

"Yes, you have." Emme smoothed back Chloe's hair. "But I think we have to wait a little longer. I don't know why they're so late."

"You always say it's rude to be late."

"And it is. Unless you're stuck in traffic, which they might be."

"Then they should call you. You always say—"

"Chloe, how 'bout you and I go take a look at the Rare Animal Conservation Center." Nick held up the brochure. "Look, here are some of the animals we might see there."

He squatted down, the brochure open, and Chloe leaned over his shoulder. "What's that one?"

"That is a blue-eyed black lemur," he read.

"Its eyes are very big." She pointed to the animal. "Are they really blue?"

"How 'bout we go find out?"

"Mommy, can we go to see the . . . what was it again?"

"The blue-eyed black lemur."

"That. Can we go see it?" Chloe asked excitedly.

"You and Nick go on. I'll wait here." Emme crossed her arms over her chest. Chloe wasn't the only one feeling impatient. "But you must stay with Nick. Promise."

"I will." Chloe grabbed his hand. "Which way?"

Emme watched as her daughter disappeared into the crowd with Nick and felt just the slightest bit of unease. She could count on the fingers of one hand the number of people she'd let Chloe go off with alone. Steffie, of course, and recently Trula. Other than that . . . had there been anyone else she'd trusted enough? She didn't think so.

She checked her watch again. Lori and Henry were now thirty minutes late. Of course there could be traffic—after all, they were driving down from Connecticut, and it was a Saturday in the summer. Lots of people on the road, heading off on vacation. They'd turn up sooner or later. She returned to the bench where they'd had their lunch and sat on the edge of the table.

After another twenty minutes had passed, she dialed first Lori's phone number, then Henry's, leaving a message for each and hoping that one of them would be listening to it before much longer. She was getting hotter and more annoyed with each passing minute. She took a bottle of water from the cooler and placed it on the back of her neck, cursing the heat and the fact that the website for Conroy, Pennsylvania, had neglected to mention anything about humidity.

To pass the time, she put in a call to Steffie. It had been several days since they'd spoken, and she wanted to keep an eye on what was being said in Silver Hill. The last she'd heard, everyone in the department was still buzzing about her abrupt departure. Steffie'd made up some story about Ann being very ill and staying with some friends.

"So does everyone think I'm still dying?" she asked when her friend answered.

"Pretty much, yeah, I'm afraid they do," Steffie admitted. "At least if you die, they'll stop asking."

"I guess that's one way of looking at it," she muttered, still not sold on the idea. "But I'm not dead yet, right?"

"Right," Stef cheerfully told her. "So we still have a little wiggle room as far as your story is concerned. I just want everyone to eventually stop asking me. I'm not real comfortable lying all the time but it was the first thing that came out of my mouth. I wish I could take it back, but it's too late now."

"Stef, I'm so sorry. I don't know what I was thinking. I should have thought this all through so much more thoroughly. I was just in such a panic. . . ."

"Hey, don't worry about it. Given the alternative, well, the lies are a very small price to pay for your safety, and for Chloe's." Stef had assured her. "Really. It's okay."

Emme was just about to apologize again when her phone announced that she had a text message.

"Stef, I'll try to get back to you later. I need to check on something."

"Okay. Just keep in touch. And give my girl a big hug for me," Steffie said before she hung up.

Emme pulled up the text message:

Having car trouble and had to turn back. Sorry won't be able to make it today. Will get in touch when we have wheels. Henry

"Well, could you maybe have waited a little longer to let me know?" she grumbled aloud, and shoved the phone back into her pocket. She was just about to hoist the cooler when she saw Nick and a very animated Chloe coming toward her through the crowd.

"We've been stood up," she told Nick. "I just got a

text message from Henry. Car trouble. They had to go back. He said they'd be in touch."

"Funny he didn't call and talk to you," Nick said, "but at least he let you know they weren't going to show."

"He probably was embarrassed to speak with me after making us wait so long. Besides, it seems kids would rather text than talk anyway."

"At least we're getting an afternoon at the zoo out of it," he pointed out. "How about I take that cooler out to my car and then we head off to the African plains? Chloe and I have been reading about it."

"I think they have giraffes," Chloe said hopefully. "I'm pretty sure they do."

"All right." Emme opened the water bottle and took a drink. "If you don't mind hauling the cooler, we don't mind waiting here until you get back. And Chloe can tell me all about the rare animals she saw."

He smiled, lifted the cooler, and winked at Chloe. "Five more minutes, kiddo," he told her, "and we'll be on our way to the African plains."

·

It had been so much easier than he'd imagined.

"What do you think?" he'd said, in his most concerned voice. "Do you think Belle really is missing, like this investigator says?"

"Yeah, I do," Henry had replied. "We do. Did you see Lori's post on the message board? Lori and I are going to drive down to meet her and Belle's uncle today in Philadelphia."

"Yeah, and it got me thinking, you know, about Belle trying to find Donor 1735 and her talking to

Aaron and stuff. I hadn't said anything on the message board, 'cause Belle had asked me not to, but she thought she'd found him, and—"

"She did? She told you that?"

"Yeah. Do you think I should tell the investigator?"

"Absolutely. That's the stuff she needs to know. Tell me what Belle told you, and I'll be happy to pass it on to her and Belle's uncle."

"Actually, I'd feel better talking to her myself, you know, in case she has some questions or something." He tried to sound tentative. "Do you think I could hook up with you guys somewhere and tag along?"

"Sure. Definitely. Hey, man, it'll be great to finally meet you. I can't wait to tell Lori. She'll be so excited."

"I'm excited about meeting her, too."

He'd picked a rest stop that was almost always deserted—"It'll be easier for us to find each other if there are fewer people around. Not so easy in a crowd."—and had been delighted to find no one when he arrived. He parked at the back of the lot, near the trees, and waited. He set the stage—his car door open, his feet sticking out as if he was taking a nap. When he heard the car approach, his fingers closed around the handle of the gun he'd borrowed from the bottom drawer of his father's desk. Henry had appeared first, as he'd hoped. He couldn't have written the scene better if it had been for a movie.

"Hey, buddy, wake up." Henry had grabbed his right foot and given it a friendly shake.

Had the flash from the barrel of the handgun even registered before the first round struck him in the chest? Had he heard the crack, understood what was happening?

Confused, Lori had seemed frozen, half in, half out of their car, as she watched her brother collapse like a balloon losing air.

"Henry?" Finally, she got out of the car and got a good look at the heap on the ground. She opened her mouth to scream, but nothing came out. She probably hadn't even felt the crack to the back of her head with the butt end of the gun.

He tidily placed Henry in the Dumpster behind the restroom area, and Lori, still out cold, in the front seat of the car that would before long carry her to her destiny. Their long lost brother hesitated over the license plate of Henry's car. If he was going to remove it, he'd have to be fast. It was getting late and he could no longer count on no one needing the rest stop. He pulled on thin rubber gloves and removed the plate, then opened the glove box and took out the insurance card and the registration. He threw them into the trunk of his car along with the wallet he'd already lifted from Henry's back pocket, Henry's cell phone, Lori's handbag and laptop.

He closed up Henry's car and locked it before stripping off his gloves and tucking them under the front seat of his car.

"That oughta do it," he said to Lori, who was just beginning to moan slightly as she started to come to.

He duct taped her wrists together and put a strip over her mouth, then strapped her in with the seat belt and closed and locked her door. Whistling, he got in behind the wheel and started the engine. Driving north, he thanked his lucky stars that he was having such a good day.

He opened the sunroof to let in light and fresh air, and turned on the radio just in time to hear the beginning of one of his favorite songs. Damn, but it was a fine day.

Lori stirred beside him, and he smiled. The day was about to get even better.

SIXTEEN

"Where should I put her?" Nick turned in the doorway of Emme's hotel room, Chloe in his arms.

Emme gestured for him to follow her into the next room, then pointed to the far side of the bed.

"Thanks," she whispered as he laid the child gently on the bed.

"I'll be out there." Nick tilted his head in the direction of the small sitting room they'd first passed through.

She nodded and proceeded to remove Chloe's shoes. She lightly pulled the blanket up and tiptoed from the room.

"That was fast," Nick said from his seat in the room's sole chair.

"There's no point in trying to undress her, it would only wake her. Though she's pretty well out right now."

"She had a big day."

"That's an understatement." Emme sat on the edge of the small love seat, her knees touching his in the narrow space between the two pieces of furniture. "I don't know how to thank you for everything. You really didn't have to drive all the way back here. It's so far out of your way. I can't even offer you a cup of coffee. Though we could call room service." She stole a peek at the clock on the television. "The kitchen stays open until ten. I usually call down for coffee around now."

"I wasn't ready to say good-bye after the zoo, and I wasn't ready to say good night after dinner. And I didn't come for the coffee."

Emme's eyes darted toward the sleeping area where her daughter lay.

"Relax." He reached across the short span between them and took her hand and gave it a squeeze. "I just meant after spending the day together, I wasn't ready to have it end. On the drive over here, I was trying to remember the last time I enjoyed a day more . . . other than maybe at a car show. But if you're tired . . ."

"No, no," she said. The last thing she wanted right now would be for him to leave. She knew that much. What she didn't know was what she'd want if he stayed.

"Good." He smiled. "Now that we've got that out of the way, let's take a look at what we learned today."

"Right." She nodded. "What we learned." She cleared her throat. "Well, we learned that . . . not so much about the case."

"I wasn't talking about the case."

"Oh." She shifted slightly on the love seat. He was still holding her hand. "Well, then. I guess I learned that Trula's picnics pack a better selection than the kiosks at the zoo, and that my daughter has an infinite capacity when it comes to learning the names of new animals."

"And I learned that when you're with your daughter, you're a completely different woman. You drop your guard and you smile a lot more. Laugh a lot more, too," Nick said. She opened her mouth to say something, but he continued. "But I understand that. I found myself smiling and laughing more than usual, too. It's hard not to when you have the opportunity to see the animal world through the eyes of a four-year-old."

"I told you she'd talk you near to deafness."

"What's that you say?" He cupped his ear with his hand like an old man who was hard of hearing, and laughed.

His laugh was sexy, low and deep in the back of his throat, and she wondered if she'd been trying to ignore that fact all day. Nah, she'd noticed. It would have been impossible not to.

"Chloe's very entertaining, and very smart, and very much fun to be around. She's lively and quick and doesn't miss a damned thing." With both his hands holding hers, he tugged on them until their faces were less than a foot apart. "You've done a remarkable job with her. I'm sure it hasn't always been easy, raising her alone."

"I haven't minded. I wouldn't trade a day with her—even the worst ones, and there have been some dicey times. Chloe slid face first into her terrible twos at about eighteen months and life was not so sweet there for a while. Fortunately, it passed in time for her to go to preschool."

"She talked a lot today about school," he recalled. "She must really like it."

"It was so hard on her when we left California. It just killed me to take her away like that." She bit back the words.

"Why did you?"

"I thought it would be better for her in the long run." She repeated the story she'd given Mallory about the feuding factions in and around Silver Hill.

"Were you afraid her birth mother might change her mind and want to see her?"

"Her birth mother is dead."

"How about her father?"

"He should be," she snapped.

"Whoa, Emme." His eyes narrowed at her outburst. "Tell me how you really feel."

"Let's just say her birth father is not a good person, not a nice person. Not a man you would ever want your child to find out she was related to."

"I think I stepped too close to the line," he said. "I apologize."

"It's okay, Nick." For a moment, she was tempted to tell him the truth, but she forced that moment to pass. There was no point in spilling her secrets to him. The case she was working for him would end sooner or later, and he'd go back to his life and she'd get on with hers. There'd been times in her life when she'd regretted sharing a secret, but she couldn't recall a time when she'd been sorry she'd kept her mouth shut. "I don't dwell on it. Chloe and I came east because I had the opportunity to work for Robert Magellan. The Mercy Street Foundation is an exciting concept—not quite law enforcement, but . . ."

He leaned forward so smoothly, covering the space so easily, that she didn't see the kiss coming. One moment she was focused on steering the conversation into safer waters, the next she was focused on his mouth. Tentatively he'd drawn her closer, and when her hand rose to touch the side of his face, he'd pulled her even closer, deepening the kiss and kissing her in a way she hadn't been kissed since . . . she wasn't sure she'd ever been kissed like that. She felt a sudden heat flare up inside her and for a moment she thought of backing away from the flame, but her instincts took over and she kissed him back. When he finally broke away, it was a slow withdrawal of his lips, which lingered just slightly before making its way to the edge of her chin.

"I've been wanting to do that since the day you walked into my garage."

"What took you so long?" she heard herself say.

"I was afraid you'd think I was like every other guy, and I didn't want you to think that." His thumb traced a lazy outline of her lips.

"Like every other guy?"

"Every guy you meet must hit on you. I'm sure it gets old after a while." He added, "I didn't want to seem like a cliché."

"A cliché," she repeated, and shook her head. "That's about the last word I'd use to describe you. And as for guys hitting on me . . . I can't remember the last time someone did."

"You've gotta be joking."

"I was a cop for seven years. I won the marksman award every time we went out to qualify on the range." She grinned. "It's amazing what a few rounds of target shooting will do for your reputation in a small town."

"So are you packing now?"

"I don't have a license to carry concealed in Pennsylvania yet," she told him. "I've applied though."

"That isn't what I asked. Slick answer, though."

"I bought one of my handguns from the department before I left California. Right now it's in the trunk of my car. I can't take the chance of Chloe finding it, but at the same time, I can't take the chance of . . ." She paused again. "The chance of needing to protect us and not being able to. What can I say?" She tried to make light of it. "I guess it's a cop thing."

He looked as if he were about to comment when her phone rang. She pulled it from her pocket quickly before it rang again.

"Hello?" She waited a moment, then said again, "Hello?"

There was no response, but it was clear someone was on the line. "Who is this?"

For a moment before the line went dead, she thought she heard music in the background. Then . . . click. The line went dead.

Frowning, she scrolled up the number on her caller ID list. Henry Carroll-Wilson's name came up.

"What's wrong?" Nick asked. "Who was that?"

"Henry." She hit redial, but the phone rang and rang. When the call went to voice mail, she left a message. "Henry, it's Emme Caldwell. Your call was apparently dropped. I'm trying to get back to you but seem to be having a problem. I'm sorry we missed meeting up today but hopefully you're calling to reschedule. Please call me back so we can set something up."

She was still frowning when she ended the call.

"What?"

"It didn't sound like a dropped call. There was someone on the line, I'd swear to it."

"Maybe it was just one of those screwy connections you get sometimes."

"Mommy?" Chloe called from the bedroom.

"I'm right here, honey." Emme put the phone down on the table and excused herself to Nick. "I'll be right back."

"Who are you talking to?" Chloe mumbled and rubbed her eyes, her feet sticking out from the blankets on one side of the bed.

"Nick." Emme pulled the covers back over her and leaned over to kiss the top of Chloe's head.

"Nick didn't say good night to me." Chloe's eyes were opening.

"Nick," Emme called to him. "Would you mind saying good night to Chloe?"

"Good night, Chloe," he said from the doorway.

" 'Member you said we could go to an amusement park?"

"Sure. As soon as your mom and I can arrange the time, we'll go."

"Yippee! Can we go to one that has—" she began to sit up.

"Back to sleep, Chloe." Emme gently coaxed her back down. "We can talk about that some other time. It's late now, and we have to meet the Realtor in the morning, remember?"

"Are you going to sleep now, too?"

"In a minute," Emme told her.

"I was just leaving," Nick said. "I can let myself out. I'll talk to you tomorrow, Emme. Let me know if you hear from Henry or Lori."

Before she could protest, Nick had turned his back and she heard the door open and close softly.

"Who are Henry and Lori?" Chloe asked sleepily.

"The people we were supposed to meet at the zoo today." Emme curled up next to Chloe.

"I'm glad they didn't come." Chloe yawned and snuggled closer to her mother. "We got to be with Nick."

Well, there was that.

"I like Nick," Chloe murmured as sleep reclaimed her.

"So do I, sweetie," Emme whispered. "Now go to sleep."

When Chloe's breathing slowed, Emme climbed off the bed carefully and locked the door. She turned off her computer and turned out the lights, then changed into a nightshirt. She slid back into bed and lay in the dark, her hands clasped at the back of her head, staring at the thin outline of the window drawn by the lights in the parking lot, her mind bouncing from one thing to another. She could hear car doors slamming and engines starting up and wondered if one of them was Nick.

Her tired mind settled on him for a moment, then warned her that this was not safe territory. She concentrated on finding something objectionable about him, but she was having a hard time coming up with anything. The fact that he was a client could have been enough to deter her, but she reminded herself this wasn't a criminal case she was handling and she was no longer a cop. Did the same rules apply in this situation?

It was hard to overlook the fact that they'd had a perfect day. There'd been no strangeness and no awkwardness. He and Chloe had taken to each other like the oldest of friends. They'd laughed and strolled around the zoo, looking like any of the families that strolled along with them.

She shook herself out of that thought in a hurry.

She'd never had much luck at relationships. It wasn't hard to figure out why. Success in interpersonal relations depended largely on the ability to trust, and that was one thing she'd never learned how to do. She'd taken her share of psychology courses at the community college and she understood that her unsettled childhood, where no one had ever claimed her and no one had ever asked her to stay, made it difficult for her to believe that anyone would ever want to keep her around for more than a little while. Until Chloe, no one had ever been a constant in her daily life. She looked back on her decision to take Tameka up on her offer to sign over the parental rights to her child as the luckiest day of her life.

When Tameka Jackson had asked Emme to take her child, Emme'd been stunned. She'd never thought of having a child, and her first instinct was to brush her off and pretend the offer had never been made. But Tameka had already gotten it into her head that the cop who'd tried so hard to help her get off the streets and get her life together would give her baby a better life than anyone else she knew, and she wasn't about to give up. With the assistance of a social worker, and a lawyer Emme knew to make it legal, Tameka's baby girl left the hospital as Chloe Nolan. And whatever premonition Tameka had had become reality. Ten days after the birth of her baby, Tameka had been stabbed to death in the shower in the county prison. No one had ever been charged with her murder.

Like *that* was some big mystery. Her trial for the sale and distribution of cocaine was drawing closer, and word on the street was that Anthony Navarro wasn't taking any chances that Tameka would talk. At the time, he hadn't shown the least bit of concern for his baby. Now he was willing to pay thousands to get her back.

"Over my dead body," Emme whispered.

Chloe was hers now, and no one was going to take her.

Not for the first time, she wondered at the wisdom of having begun to play such a precarious game. If anyone came for Chloe, who would have her back?

Her fingers followed the path Nick's thumb had traced along her bottom lip, and thought that maybe—just maybe—there might be one person she might be able to count on.

"What are you doing here so late on a Sunday afternoon?" Having stopped at Robert's to return Trula's cooler on her way back from looking at houses, Emme had made a quick run to her office to pick up the file she'd left on her desk. On her way down the hall, she'd been surprised to find Mallory's door open, and even more surprised to find Mallory at her desk.

"I can't keep up with all the applications," Mallory sighed. "They're coming in faster than I can field them."

"Anything I can do to help?" Emme stepped into the room.

"You are helping. You're investigating our first case." Mallory rubbed her eyes. "How's it going?"

"Two steps forward, three steps back." Emme brought her up-to-date on everything she'd learned that week, right up to the Carroll-Wilson kids not showing the day before. The only thing she left out was the part about Nick following her back to the hotel.

"This is crazy stuff." Mallory shook her head. "Who'd have seen all this coming when we decided to take this case on?"

"Hey, you were a cop, too. You know you have to always expect the unexpected."

"Yeah, but this should be different. This should be . . . saner."

Emme laughed. "How do you figure? We're doing the same work." She thought that over for a moment, then amended it. "Actually, we're doing work that, for whatever reason, the cops were unable to do."

"Which should make this job harder." Mallory rubbed her eyes again. "I think I need to stop. I'm getting loopy."

"Go home to Charlie. Go out to dinner. Go to the movies. Do something fun," Emme said.

"Don't I wish. Charlie's working a case. I probably won't see him for days."

"Get one of your girlfriends."

Mallory shook her head. "Don't have any."

"Everyone has friends." It was Emme's turn to frown. "Why don't you have friends?"

"Long story. Too tired to tell it."

"Okay, then, how 'bout family?"

"Don't have any of them, either."

"You're kidding." Emme sat on the arm of one of the chairs in Mallory's office. "No family at all?"

"Nope." Mallory leaned back, as if in deep thought. "Well, there is someone who *claims* she's my sister, but she could be lying."

"How is she your sister?"

"I don't know. I don't know that she really is, and I don't really care."

"Didn't you ask her why she thinks . . ."

"I didn't answer her letter. Didn't I just say that I don't really care?"

"Wait a minute. Are you saying you got a letter out of the blue from someone who says she's your sister and you just tossed the letter without answering it?"

"I didn't toss it." Mallory averted her eyes. "I have it at home. Some place."

"But you didn't bother to find out if she's really related to you?"

"Why should I?"

"Because if she's your sister, then it means you do have family. You do have someone."

"I don't need anyone."

"We all need someone."

Mallory stood. "I think I'm done for the day. I think I'll take these files and—"

"Mallory, I'm sorry. I shouldn't have brought my feelings into your situation. It's just that, well, I'd just about die if someone came along and said she was my sister. It's been one of my fantasies for most of my life."

It was Mallory's turn to stare. For a long moment, she appeared to be debating with herself. "If my mother had another child and she decided to keep that one, well, good for her. It has nothing to do with me."

"Am I not hearing right? Didn't you just say you had no family? But now you're saying you have a mother *and* a sister?"

"I haven't seen my mother in thirty-five years. Not since she dumped me on her sister and split."

Emme was only vaguely aware that her mouth had dropped open.

"Sorry," Mallory mumbled, and waved a hand as if to dismiss the conversation.

"I'm the one who's sorry," Emme told her. "I'm the one who's gaping."

"Yeah, I know. It's not a pretty story."

"It's not that. It's just that, well, I always thought I was the only one."

"The only one who what?" Mallory looked puzzled.

"The only one whose mother dumped her and took off."

"You're kidding. You too?"

"On the day I was born. She left me in a church. The nuns found me when they came in for mass at five in the morning. They named me—" Emme caught herself. She'd almost said, *They named me Ann, after St. Ann, for whom the church was named.* "I didn't have a name, so they named me."

"Seriously?"

Emme nodded.

"Were you adopted?" Mallory asked.

Emme shook her head. "No. I spent eighteen years in foster care. I've never known who my parents were, either of them. I don't know if they're dead or alive, why they left me, if I have a brother or sister somewhere . . . cousins . . . aunts . . . uncles. . . ." She shrugged. "I've never had anyone. Until Chloe, that is."

"We're quite a pair—two girls without any family."

"But you said your mother left you with her sister. That means you did have someone."

"It wasn't quite like that. When I say my mother left me there, I mean she made like we were only visiting. Then she left in the middle of the night. She didn't bother to take me with her. My aunt did the right thing by keeping me, but she never for a minute let me forget that it was only through the goodness of her heart that I had a home. I never felt welcome there, I never felt loved."

"Did you ever ask your mother—"

"No, and I probably never will."

"Why not?"

"My mother was a hooker in the casinos in Atlantic City. My aunt always said she'd left her burden behind so that she could go back to work. That she couldn't give up the glitz and all that high life she enjoyed to take care of a baby she hadn't wanted." Mallory's facial muscles drew taut.

"Wow." Emme shook her head slowly. She simply couldn't think of anything else to say. "Just . . . wow."

"So you can see why I don't have any interest in contacting my mother. I've never known who my father is, never even knew his name."

"Well, we certainly have a lot in common, don't we?" Emme said softly. "But maybe your sister—aren't you at least curious about her?"

"No. Why should I be?"

Emme stared at her. "All my life I've waited for someone to appear and tell me that we share the same blood, the same background. That we have a connection that goes beyond friendship or anything else."

"Some of us don't need that connection."

"Don't kid yourself," Emme heard herself say. "Everyone needs that connection."

"Not everyone." Mallory cleared her throat and stuffed the papers she'd been holding into her briefcase. "I'll see you tomorrow."

"Right." Emme backed toward the door, knowing she'd overstepped. "I'll see you then."

"Look, I'm sorry I was short. I just don't like to talk about . . . all that."

"I understand. I should have kept my two cents to myself. I'm just going to say good night to Susanna and head out."

Emme was already into the hallway when Mallory called to her, "Susanna's not here. She took off again this weekend. Charlie said he saw her headed toward the turnpike on Friday night."

"Still won't say where she's going?"

Mallory shook her head. "Just one more little mystery for the Mercy Street Foundation to work on. See you Monday."

*   *   *

Robert stood at the kitchen window overlooking the vast grounds that spread out behind his house. He watched Trula's face light up as Chloe ran across the yard to the pool where Trula floated in an inflatable chair. Cleopatra's barge, he'd dubbed it when Kevin presented it to her on Memorial Day, which happened to be her birthday. It had an airtight pocket that zipped up, big enough to hold one of those paperback novels she was always reading when she thought no one was looking, and a special inflatable cup holder made to hold a can of soda—which Trula wouldn't be caught dead drinking—or a bottle of water, which she had with her at all times.

Chloe danced along the side of the pool, excitedly telling the older woman something. Trula threw back her head and laughed out loud at something the little girl said, and the sheer joy on her face tugged tightly at Robert's heart. Trula had never married, had never had a child of her own—though she probably should have, he reflected. She'd have been one hell of a mom. As it was, she'd spent most of her life living under other people's roofs, first his grandmother's—who'd been Trula's best friend since grade school—then his own, where she'd spent the last several years bullying him and Kevin and loving every minute of it. He'd loved it, too.

The scene was almost painful for him to watch. He hadn't seen that much pleasure on the woman's face since she'd held his son in her arms. Ian had brought her—had brought all of them—great joy.

He rested his forehead against the glass and squeezed his eyes shut even as the vise inside squeezed his heart. Lately he'd been trying to convince himself that he'd need to face the facts sooner or later. In his heart he knew that Beth was gone from this world, but he could not bring himself to speak it aloud. No woman would stay away from her home this long . . . especially a woman like Beth, who had loved everything about her life, loved being the wife of one of the wealthiest men in the country. He hated thinking of her like that, but there it was. Not that she hadn't loved him—he believed with all his heart that she had, that they'd loved each other. It was just that, well, she loved being the wife of a mogul and all that entitled her to. She'd loved the big house, the magnificent grounds, the cars, the jewelry, the trips, the designer clothes. He couldn't blame her for that. It was just a part of who she is.

Who she had been, he corrected himself. She wasn't anymore. He was pretty sure of that.

Over the past few months, even her memory had become more and more distant, her voice not so clear or so often in his head, her face harder and harder to pull up in the dead of night. Some days he couldn't remember what her laugh had sounded like, and it saddened him. It saddened him, too, to know that one day he might even move on. One day, maybe there'd be someone else. . . .

But Ian . . . Robert would never get over losing his son. Not ever. Not if he had ten sons—a hundred sons—would he forget his firstborn. Ian would remain an open wound on his heart for as long as he drew breath.

Funny, he had trouble recalling things about Beth, but he could remember every smile, every baby laugh, every giggle, every one of Ian's firsts. None of that had dimmed in the least for him. He could even feel the way those tiny fingers had gripped on to his.

He opened his eyes to see Trula emerge from the pool, and smiled in spite of himself at Chloe's rush to bring her a towel. It made him happy to see Trula happy, to see her enjoy this child so, to know that her love for that little girl was so freely, so openly returned. He gave silent thanks to Emme Caldwell for having answered the Mercy Street Foundation's call for investigators as quickly as she had. Without realizing it, she'd brought life back into Robert's world, which Kevin had once referred to as the Dead Zone, and he, Robert, would always be grateful.

SEVENTEEN

"Well, you hardly look rested." Trula watched Emme come in through the back door and head for the coffeemaker. "Did you forget that weekends are for taking it easy?"

"I took it easy." Emme yawned and reached for a red mug that had *Commit Random Acts of Kindness* printed in white letters on one side.

"How did your house-hunt go this weekend?" Susanna blew into the kitchen the way she always did, smiling and light as a summer breeze. "Any luck?"

She looked over the selection of mugs Trula had set out that morning and settled on *Send lawyers, guns, and money.*

"I did see one place I liked, but it didn't have much of a yard," Emme said. "How 'bout you? How was your weekend?"

"Oh, you know. same old, same old." She poured her coffee carefully into the tall, narrow mug. "Not nearly as exciting as looking for a new home."

"We spent all day yesterday going from house to house. Chloe's thinking she might need to have a dog one of these days, and a swing set. The one place I liked didn't have much room for either."

"So you're going to keep on looking?" Susanna asked, as she opened the refrigerator looking for the half-and-half.

"Already out," Trula told her. "Over on the counter."

"Any closer and it would have bitten me," Susanna muttered. To Emme she said, "So I'm assuming you find Conroy to your liking and you plan to stick around for a while."

Before Emme could answer, Trula interjected, "Of course, she's staying in Conroy."

"I do want to stay here. I thought I'd start looking now for a house because maybe I'll have found a place by the time my probationary period is over, and if I make the cut, I'll be in a position to buy something." Emme added sweetener to her cup. "I really do like the area, and Chloe is so happy in her new school with her new friends."

"Mrs. McHugh is an excellent teacher," Trula agreed. "And there are a lot of really nice families in Kevin's parish."

"It's a godsend to working mothers like me that the school runs all year round, and I think it's really cool that Mrs. McHugh is teaching the kids Spanish. It's a really useful language."

"I agree, but Mrs. McHugh isn't teaching the kids Spanish," Trula said.

Emme frowned. "I thought Chloe said she was learning all those Spanish words and phrases at school."

"*At* school, maybe, but not *in* school." Trula began

to rinse off her breakfast dishes. "She told me that the lady on the playground has been teaching her."

"What lady on the playground?" Emme blanched and set her cup unsteadily on the counter. "What lady on the playground?"

Surprised at the alarm in Emme's voice, Trula turned around to face her. "She said there's a woman who talks to her on the playground. I'm thinking it may be one of Kevin's Hispanic parishioners, because Chloe said the woman was dark, like her, and that she comes everyday and that she—"

Emme grabbed her bag and left the kitchen almost at a sprint, her car keys in her hand. Through the window, Trula and Susanna watched as she ran to her car, passing Mallory without greeting. Within seconds, the small sedan was making a squealing turn in the driveway and headed out the gate.

Mallory came through the back door, which Emme had left open, with a puzzled look on her face.

"What was that all about?" she asked. "Emme acted as if she didn't even see me."

Trula shrugged. "We were talking about Chloe learning some Spanish words and phrases from a woman who shows up at the playground at school, and next thing we know, Emme's out of here on two wheels."

She went to the wall phone and lifted the receiver. "I think I'd better give Kevin a heads up. I'd bet my last dime she's headed for Our Lady of Angels."

Her heart pounding, Emme drove to the school in half the time it normally took.

Had she been found out? Had her movements since she left California somehow been traced? The combination of a mother's fear and an overactive imagination had her assuming the worst by the time she pulled up in front of the church and school. She all but ran to the playground—empty of children this time of the morning, but there, there at the fence . . .

A woman stood gazing into the playground as if waiting for someone.

Emme broke into a run.

She was halfway across the playground when she heard someone calling her name.

"Emme! Emme, wait!"

Without slowing down, she looked back over her shoulder to see Father Kevin running after her. *Thank God*, she thought. He'd help her. . . .

"Emme, hold up," he called.

"Kevin, I'm so happy to see you, you have no idea." She leaned forward slightly, her hands resting on her thighs, her breath coming in gulps. She'd been unaware of how out of shape she was after a few weeks of inactivity.

He took her gently by the arm and led her in the direction of the fence. "There's someone I want you to meet."

"Kevin, this woman . . ." Emme grasped his arm. "She's . . ."

"Maria Clemente. She's been a member of Our Lady of Angels parish for more years than I have." He continued to walk at an even pace, forcing Emme to slow down as well. "Mrs. Clemente, I'd like you to meet Emme Caldwell. She's the mother of your new friend, Chloe. I believe she's come to thank you for teaching her daughter and the other children a few words and phrases in Spanish."

His hand still lightly on Emme's arm, he added, "Mrs. Clemente—*mamacita* to the children—knows every child in the parish. She's sort of our unofficial guardian angel."

Maria Clemente smiled broadly. "Your daughter is a quick study. She catches on like that." She snapped her fingers. "Smart as a whip, that one is. And a real charmer."

Emme was speechless, her brain scrambling for words.

"Mrs. Clemente brings flowers from her garden to church every morning and stays after mass to dust the altar. She noticed Chloe in the playground and asked if perhaps she was of Hispanic origins, thinking perhaps a new family had moved into the neighborhood, that maybe she could assist them in some way to get settled."

His words swirled around in Emme's brain and she struggled to follow him.

"I told her about you and Chloe."

"I'd called *hola* to her one day, thinking perhaps she knew the language. She did not, but she asked what the word meant. The next day, when I was coming from the church, she called to me. '*Hola, mamacita.*' " The woman beamed. "Such a smart cookie. She wanted to learn more, to surprise you, she said."

"Yes," Emme found her voice. "Yes, I was surprised."

The smile began to fade from Maria Clemente's face. "Was that all right? Did I presume—"

"No, no, it's fine." Relief washed over Emme and with it came a deep sense of embarrassment. "Thank you so much, Mrs. Clemente. I appreciate you taking the time to teach her."

"It's nothing." The smile returned to the woman's face. "She's a joy to be around."

"Thank you." Emme could have cried. "Thank you so much."

"I'll see you in the morning, Mrs. Clemente," Kevin told her.

"You will. And you let me know if the Chastians will need flowers for the altar for the funeral on Thursday," Mrs. Clemente replied. "I have some dahlias that should be open by midweek that are the size of dinner plates. Maybe we can make some arrangements, save the family some money."

"You're kind to think of others, as always."

"Goodbye, Chloe's mother. God bless."

"Goodbye, Mrs. Clemente. It was nice meeting you."

After she'd walked away, Emme turned to the priest and said, "She seems so . . . nice."

"Pillar of the community." Father Kevin nodded. "Don't know what I'd do without her."

"Trula called you, didn't she?" Emme's face burned. If Father Kevin hadn't been around, what might she have said to that good woman?

"She did."

"She told you—"

He nodded. "Pretty much everything. Everything except why the thought of someone teaching your daughter a few harmless phrases in Spanish caused such panic."

"It wasn't the phrases," Emme said, torn between telling him the truth and fearing the consequences. "It's . . . it's okay, Kevin. I apologize for . . ."

She was clearly struggling.

"Emme, I don't know what made you feel so threatened, or what you are afraid of, but I'm here for you if you want to talk about it."

"Thank you," she said, wishing she could unburden herself, but knowing she could not.

He walked her to her car in silence. As she slid behind the wheel, he told her, "If you're in some kind of trouble, maybe we can help."

She shook her head. "Thank you, but it's something I'm going to have to deal with on my own."

"You know, there's Robert . . . he'd be there for you, too." Before she could speak, he added, "We're an odd little group, Emme, at the Mercy Street Foundation. But we're a family, and from what I can see, you and Chloe are ours now. Families stick together, you know, so if you need . . ." He sighed. "Whatever you need, we'll all be here if you change your mind."

Too choked up to even say thank you, Emme merely nodded, and then drove off. When she reached the stop sign at the end of the street, she looked in her rearview mirror. Kevin was still standing in front of the church, watching.

You and Chloe are ours now . . . His words rang in her ears. *Families stick together . . .*

She turned the corner, pulled the car to the curb, covered her face, and wept.

*   *   *

It took her almost an hour to pull herself together. So much had happened over the past few weeks, and she'd had no outlet. She missed Steffie more at that moment than she had since she'd left California. They'd agreed to keep contact to a minimum for a while, knowing that there was a good chance Navarro's people would be watching Steffie, maybe even tapping into her phones or watching her mail. Emme missed her friend's counsel, missed her levelheaded advice, her sense of humor . . . hell, she missed having a friend. There was no one she could talk to about the mess her life was in at that moment. Trula, maybe, but her loyalties lay with Robert; Mallory, too. Father Kevin's offer of friendship had been genuine, she knew that, but she knew, too, that he had no idea of the secrets she was keeping from everyone. Of course, he was a priest. He could probably handle the shock of finding out that everything she'd told them about herself was a lie. He must have heard a lot worse than even that over the years.

The only honest part of her life right now was the work she was doing for the foundation. She was giving the search for Belinda Hudson her best efforts. She was getting closer to the heart of it—the answer was with Donor 1735, she knew that much—but he was still clouded in mist.

And then there was Nick. He was the one complication she hadn't planned on. All her professional life, she'd made a point of not getting involved with people connected in any way with any case she worked. She'd spent the past four years devoting her time and energy and total focus on Chloe. For most of that time, she'd convinced herself that at this time of her life, she didn't need anyone else. Work and her daughter had been more than enough for her. Now she wasn't so sure.

She wiped her wet face with a tissue she found in her bag and blew her nose.

"No time to feel sorry for *you*," she chided herself. "A girl is still missing. There's work to be done."

She drove through the gates somewhat sheepishly, waving to the security hut without really looking at the man who was stationed there this morning. Having practically blown through the gates on her way out earlier, she was too embarrassed to meet his eyes now. She parked near the side of the house and entered through the front, hoping to slip in without being seen.

She should have known better.

"Are you all right?" Trula was just coming through the front hall when Emme opened the door. "Dear lord, child, the way you fled this morning, you'd have thought demons were at your heels."

"I'm okay. And I'm sorry." She could have added, *And yes, there were demons at my heels,* but that would have required more explanation than she was prepared to give. "I didn't mean to upset anyone. There was just . . . just something I had to do."

"Honey, if something is bothering you—oh, hell, clearly something is. Maybe there's something we can do to help."

Emme started down the hall, not wanting to look back on that kind face. She'd be tempted to spill it all, everything about Chloe's father and about her own deceit. Once they knew—Trula and Robert and Mallory and Kevin—they'd be showing her the door. Falsifying her résumé, getting Steffie to lie and cover for her . . . what would happen to Steffie if the truth came out? She'd be bounced from her job in a heartbeat. Emme flushed scarlet just thinking of the terrible position she'd put her friend in.

I had to save Chloe, she reminded herself.

"Emme?" Trula stood in the hallway, a worried look on her face. "You know I'd—we'd—help you in any way we could."

Emme nodded. "I know, Trula. And I appreciate it more than you could know."

She continued down the hall and quietly went into her room. The kindness of everyone around her had been so unexpected, it had overwhelmed her. Last night she'd been thinking that in a pinch, it would be her, Trula, and Nick. Now she found herself for the first time ever feeling part of something larger than herself. It was more than she could think about and still function the way she needed to. She pushed away the events of the morning and stuffed her emotions back into that place where she kept things she didn't want to think about, and got to work.

First things first. She dialed Henry Carroll-Wilson's cell phone. Forced to leave another message when voice mail picked up, she tried Lori's number. No answer there, either, so she left basically the same message she'd left for her brother.

Next on the list: Aaron.

She turned on her computer and searched her email. There was still no response from him. She called Nick

and was disappointed to have to leave a voice mail
for him as well. She couldn't think of much to say
other than "Please let me know if you've heard from
Aaron."

When she hadn't heard back from anyone by noon,
she decided she was losing too much time waiting.
She hunted through her file for the article about
Aaron. Skimming, she made notes on an index card.
His last name was Sparks. His hometown was Gettys-
burg and his father was from Rising Sun, Maryland.
She went online and found a phone listing for A.
Sparks in Gettysburg and dialed the number. The call
was forwarded to another line, and she was expecting
voice mail to pick up when the call was answered.

"Hello?"

"Is this Aaron Sparks?"

"Yeah. I mean, yes. Who's this?"

Emme introduced herself and explained that she
was following up on the email he received from Nick
Perone.

"Oh. Right. Belle's uncle." He stifled a yawn. "I
didn't get around to answering that yet."

"Well, since I have you on the phone, I can save
you the trouble. I'll ask you a few quick questions,
you can give me a few quick answers, and hopefully
that will take care of it."

"Is Belle really missing?" he asked softly.

"Yes, Aaron. She really is missing."

"You swear?"

"I swear. Why would I make that up?"

"Because she . . ." he hesitated.

"Because she what, Aaron?"

"Because it's just weird timing, that's all," he mumbled.

"Because she was looking for Donor 1735?"

"No. Because she found him."

"She found—" Emme took a deep breath. She hadn't expected this.

"Well, she thought she did, anyway."

"Did she give you a name?"

"Uh-uh. She just sent me an email one time that said *bingo,* all in capital letters. I wrote back and asked if she'd gotten lucky and she wrote back that she was pretty sure she had, that she'd keep me posted but I didn't hear from her again."

"That was your last contact from her? Do you remember when you got that email?"

"I think it was after Christmas break from school."

Emme thought for a moment before asking, "How did she track her donor, Aaron?"

"Same way I tracked mine. I walked her through the process, but she was pretty much doing it on her own. Belle was one smart chick."

"Can you walk me through it? I'm guessing she contacted you first via email and told you she wanted to search for her donor the way you had."

"Right."

"Then what?"

"Mostly, at first, she asked pretty general questions. Like, what lab did I use and how did I find it. Stuff like that."

"How did you find the lab?"

"Online. That was the easy part."

"So then she asked you to help her and you said yes. What steps did—"

"Well, actually, no. I told her I couldn't help her."

"Why wouldn't you help someone who was trying to do the same thing you did?"

"I said I couldn't help her, not that I wouldn't."

"I'm not following you, Aaron."

"Belle wanted to find her donor the same way I found mine, but that wasn't possible. I tracked my donor through my Y chromosome DNA." He paused to let that sink in.

"Which Belle, being a female, wouldn't have." Emme gave herself a mental slap on the forehead. "The Y chromosome is passed male to male, father to son."

"Right. It's sort of like the way the last name is passed on, you know? Boys get the X chromosome from their mom, and the Y from their dad. Girls get two X chromosomes, one from each parent. No Y chromosome, no Y chromosome-DNA test. No way to find the donor using the method I used."

"But you just said that Belle later told you she found her donor." Emme frowned. "How did she do that without the right DNA?"

"I didn't ask her who she got it from. But she came back a few weeks later and told me she had the DNA goods. I walked her through it from there."

"She didn't say where the DNA came from?"

"Nope."

One of the brothers, Emme thought. It had to have come from one of the brothers. Henry? The twins? Justin?

"Can you take me through the steps you went through with her?"

"Oh, sure. But . . ."

"But what?"

"But I might not have the information she sent me about 1735 anymore. I don't know if I kept all that."

"What information?" Emme frowned.

"Where he was born and when. Where he went to college. What his ethnic background was. All the stuff the clinic would have given to Belle's mom." He paused. "You know how I found my donor, right? I knew where he was born and the date and his ethnic background, which was Italian. After I had the DNA markers run through the online genealogy databases, I found a couple of guys with the same Italian last name. I went online and found one person who was born on the right date in the right city with that last name. So even if you had the DNA from the donor, without the rest of the information, you're not going to find him."

"Can you check to see if you still have Belle's info and get back to me?"

"Sure. I'll do that right now. Can you hold on?"

"I've got all day."

It only took six minutes.

"Sorry," he told her. "I must have deleted those emails."

"And there's no way to get them back?"

"I don't think so." He grew quiet. "Maybe . . . I don't know. I can ask my buddy. He's like a super tech whiz."

"Would you do that, Aaron? Please."

He hesitated. "I'm wondering if this is a cool thing to do or not."

"What do you mean?"

"It was one thing to help Belle find her donor, but I

don't know about this. How do I know who you really are? How do I know this is really, like, kosher?"

She gave him the website address for the Mercy Street Foundation. "Check it out. Check out Robert Magellan. Belle has been missing since January, Aaron. Her uncle came to us to help find her because the police had no luck. There's a real good possibility that maybe she found her donor, maybe he knows where she is." She felt herself losing patience. "And besides all that, we have no other leads."

"I guess it's okay," he said. "I'll call my friend and see what he can do."

"Thank you, Aaron. If we find her—if she's still alive—we'll have you to thank."

There was a long silence on the phone. "You think maybe she's not alive?" he asked, his voice quivering.

She could have kicked herself for that slip.

"There's always that chance when someone's been missing for so long."

"Shit."

"That pretty much sums it up," she agreed. "Call me after you talk to your buddy. I'll be waiting to hear from you."

She hung up and pondered her next step. She had the names of four of the male-donor siblings. Which one would Belle have contacted for a DNA swab?

Henry was the most likely. She tried calling him again, but had to leave another message. She didn't have phone numbers for Justin or the twins. She went to the donor-sibling website and posted a general message.

It seems that Belle was pretty close to finding Donor 1735, but apparently she had help from one of you. The Y chromosome-DNA test that could provide information about the male line would have had to come from one of you guys—because girls don't have Y chromosomes. You can email me privately if you like, but I'd like to confirm which one of you gave Belle your DNA.

Thanks—Emme Caldwell

She sat back and rubbed her temples, berating herself. She certainly was no DNA expert, but she certainly should have figured out that you couldn't trace Y chromosomes through a female offspring.

She got up and walked to the window and looked out on a perfect summer day. *Which of your brothers came through for you, Belle, and what did you do with the results of his test?*

What would I have done? Emme asked herself.

I'd have found the lab, just like Aaron said, and I would have sent the swab in. Then when I got the results back, I would have sent them in to the databases, just like Aaron did. But first, before I sent the report anywhere, I would have made a copy. Several copies. I would have kept at least one—maybe more than one, in different places, just for safety's sake, since I wouldn't take chances with something that precious. And I would have sent a copy to the brother who'd given me his DNA.

She walked back to her computer and checked her mail. Nothing yet. She wondered how long she'd have to wait before one of the boys owned up—if he'd own up at all. She sent out one more email to the four boys, an addendum, telling them it was okay if they didn't want to own up to having given Belle their

DNA, but in the alternative, a copy of the DNA profile Belle had sent back to them would be just fine. She typed the address of the foundation on the bottom of the email and hit send. There was nothing she could do now except wait.

EIGHTEEN

For the third time that day, he sat at his desk, checking her new emails. It had become almost an obsession. At first, he'd only wanted to know what she knew, who she corresponded with on a regular basis, whom she'd told what. Once he had the answers to those questions, he wanted to know more, and so the game had begun. He'd studied the emails for her style, and thought he'd been doing a pretty damned good job mimicking her. He was clearly winning this round: He knew who, and he knew what. Now he had to figure out how best to resolve this particular mess.

This latest one was a bit of a mystery to him.

> OMG, Lori, where the hell are you? Answer your phone! Call ASAP!!! Phone home and all that! Seriously, L, I'm worried.

The email wasn't signed and he was certain it wasn't anyone he knew. Lori's roommate, maybe? He debated the wisdom of replying to a message from someone who might pick up right away that he wasn't Lori. As much as he'd love to play with

Pammiegirl22's head right now, he really shouldn't. He'd put that one on ice for a while and see what happened.

He reopened and reclosed emails that were months old. She and Belle had been busy little bees, hadn't they? And so eager to share with their donor siblings.

He lingered over the photos that Belle had sent Lori of Belle, Will, and Wayne on a Georgia beach the year before. Once again he enlarged the photo to fill the screen. Belle was so perfect, with her pretty skin and that long beautiful hair. And her smile . . . she really did have a beautiful smile. It made him happy just to look at her face and remember when one of her smiles had been for him.

The twins, well, they were a different story. It had been a source of irritation to find that they had the same hairline that he had. The same shape of the face. The same eyes. The resemblance, while not overly strong, was definitely there.

He heard a ping and returned to the screen. Ah, he'd been waiting for this one. He opened it quickly.

I appreciate your advice but I don't know that I totally agree. I still don't know what to do about the stuff Belle gave me. If I should tell EC or if maybe I should talk to my mom. On the one hand, my mom won't be happy about me looking for Donor 1735—we've had that discussion before and she thinks it's a bad idea, that the clinic gave him a guarantee of anonymity and that we should respect that. On the other hand, Belle worked really hard to find him—I hate to see all her work be for nothing. And she did trust me with the information. Why would she have done that if she hadn't wanted me to finish what she started? Ali.

He growled deep in his throat. Sometimes it seemed he spent the majority of his time dealing with stupid people. Could she really be serious? Turn over Belle's notes to the fucking investigator? Jesus give me strength. He began to type furiously.

I understand your dilemma totally. It is a hard decision to make. But I did have an idea. I might have told you that I was going to be working in a forensic lab over the summer, right? I start next week—I am so looking forward to it. Anyway, maybe I can get someone in the lab to help me run the DNA results through that website so we can see if 1735's profile is on record somewhere. I think it would be so cool if we could find him—but I think we should be the ones to be looking. It isn't any of that investigator's business, you know? It's ours. Are you still planning on driving to Bryn Mawr on Wednesday? I can maybe meet you someplace and you can give me the stuff and I'll take it with me to work next week. Lori

He waited a few minutes. The sound of Lori's cell phone ringing startled him and made him jump. He opened the bottom drawer of his desk and checked the caller. Of course, *she'd* want to talk. Well, she was just going to have to go back to her laptop and start typing, because no one was going to answer that phone, probably ever again. He only kept it to monitor who was missing Lori and Henry, to see which fires he could put out via email or text messages. The longer he could keep others from looking for them, the better off he'd be. He knew from his phone call with Henry that their mom had left after his graduation to spend some time in California, so he figured that gave him some time. He frowned, hoping Pammiegirl22 didn't turn out to be the spoiler.

He watched, and within minutes, another email appeared.

Just tried to call but you didn't pick up. Yes, I am still planning on driving to Bryn Mawr but I'm leaving in about an hour. My field hockey workshop starts at eight tomorrow morning so I have to go today. I really want to play this fall! I can meet you on campus or off. Any idea of the time? It's going to be hot so we might have a late afternoon or early evening practice. Ali

What time were you figuring on arriving today? We're going to be driving to—here he had to stop and consult a map—Harrisburg for our cousin's wedding—*God, how lame was that?*—so we'll be leaving sometime today too! We could stop to see you on our way through the Philly area! Lori

Oh, wow—that would be so cool to see you both again! I should be there around seven if the traffic through the turnpike tunnels isn't too bad. By the time I check in and everything, I guess I can get away by around eight. Is that too late? Ali

No, that would be perfect. How about eight thirty? Maybe we can find a coffeehouse or something and visit for a while. Lori

Oh, yay! I can't wait! Ali

Neither can I! See you soon! Lori

He added, P.S. Don't forget to bring Belle's notes!

He sighed as he hit send. Dear God, this girl was such a loose cannon. To think she'd come *this close* to handing over all of Belle's notes to the PI. Clearly, she had to go, and go soon.

He returned to the screen with the pictures and pulled up the ones Ali had sent Lori from the front of the art museum. Those were the ones that bothered him the most. He enlarged one of the frames and cursed under his breath. Granted, no one looking at the pictures would know it was him there in the background—why would anyone even notice?—but still, it was a mistake that should not have happened. This girl was clearly going to be the death of him.

Or actually, he reminded himself as he turned off Lori's computer, it would be the other way around.

NINETEEN

Emme had always considered herself a patient woman, but by three in the afternoon, when she hadn't heard from any of the boys, she'd just about exhausted what patience she had. She dialed Nick's cell phone again and was prepared to leave a message when he picked up.

"Hey," he said. "I was just about to call you. My client just left—finally. I say finally because he's been here since eight fifteen this morning. And I say that with all fondness and gratitude, because he brought me one hell of a car."

"What kind of car?"

"A very sweet 1949 Cadillac. There were less than eight thousand of this model made, less than fifty are registered." He sighed happily. "Like I said. It's one sweet car."

"Well, good luck with it." She wasn't exactly sure what one said under the circumstances, but figured that would suffice.

Nick laughed. "So what good news did today bring? Aaron cough up the name of Donor 1735?"

"I wish it was going to be that easy." She related the gist of her conversation with Aaron that morning.

"So whatever DNA Belle used had to have come from one of her male donor siblings?"

"Right. I emailed the four of them but no one's gotten back to me yet. Of course, there could be a lot of reasons for that. It's summer, they could all be working today. Or the one who gave her the DNA could be reluctant to speak up."

"Why?"

"I don't know. I don't know how kids that age think. But I do think there's a high probability that Belle sent a copy of the DNA profile to whomever gave her their DNA. I did ask, but so far, nada."

"Aaron is still going to try to retrieve Belle's emails, though, right?"

"He's going to consult with a buddy who apparently knows a lot about computers."

"I thought you could retrieve just about anything from a hard drive."

"I don't think it's quite that cut and dried. And Aaron didn't know if email, once deleted, could be retrieved. But he said he'd do his best and I have to trust him to do that. In the meantime, though, I think we need to be prepared in case we can't get the information from him."

"So your thoughts for plan B would be . . ."

"I think we need to go through all those boxes of Belinda's. The more I think about it, the more I'm sure she'd have printed out copies of whatever information she had on her computer. She'd have wanted a hard copy. And besides, if she was successful in getting a DNA profile, she'd have sent it to one of these genealogy services that tracks DNA, right? She'd have kept a record of that, too."

"You're right. We need to go through her stuff. What are you doing tomorrow?"

"Well, I was hoping to start on that, but if you have this car to work on . . ."

"The Caddy can wait. How early do you think you can get there?"

"I can drop Chloe off at eight."

"It'll take you about two hours to get to the farm. Get a pen and paper and I'll give you directions."

•

"I guess I didn't put things back too neatly last time." Nick and Emme stood in the farmhouse's foyer, surveying the pile of boxes, some half-opened, some with articles of clothing draped over the sides.

"Well, we'll start with those, then, the ones that are already opened." She poked into the nearest carton, which appeared to contain mostly sweaters. "We'll go through every single item and when we're done, we'll pack the box up again and move it into the living room."

"Okay."

He'd already opened all the windows to let in some cool morning air. Now he opened the front door. "It's going to get pretty hot in here," he told her. "By one, the sun is going to be coming right through those windows."

"Maybe we'll get lucky before we have to worry about the heat." She dove into the box and began removing things item by item. She held every sweater by the shoulders and shook each piece vigorously.

"Just in case Belinda hid something inside," she told him when she found him watching her, one eyebrow raised. "And check every pocket. You never know what you're going to find."

She straightened up, a red hooded sweater over her arm. "You can start any time now, you know."

"I just like watching you."

"Watch me later. We are going to get through all these boxes today."

He pulled one of the cartons closer and pushed the lid all the way open. "This one had a bunch of skirts and pants and jackets."

"All things with pockets."

"Right." He stuffed his hand into the pocket of the pair of black pants he'd drawn out of the box. When he was convinced that it held no hidden treasure, he folded it and set it aside.

"She sure had a lot of stuff," he muttered.

"Girls that age do," she smiled. "Clothes . . . can there be too many clothes? Shoes. Oh, and bags . . . I'm still fighting my addiction to good bags."

"Bags? You mean, like handbags?"

She nodded and shook out another sweater.

"One of these boxes only contained handbags."

"A girl after my own heart."

"What's with that?" He frowned. "You can only use one at a time, right?"

"This from a guy who thought nothing of having nineteen cars? Dare I say you can only drive one at a time?"

"Hey, it was only seventeen. And I sold most of them."

A knock on the back door was followed by a voice calling for Nick.

"That sounds like my neighbor, Herb," he told Emme. "In here, Herb. Front hall."

"Nick, I've got the estimates for the repairs to the . . . oh, hello." Herb Sanders stopped midway through the door. "I didn't know you had company."

"This is Emme Caldwell. Emme, meet Herb." To Herb, Nick said, "Emme's helping me look for Belinda."

"You a cop or something?"

Yes was on the tip of her tongue, and then she remembered. "No, I'm a private investigator with a firm working with Nick."

"Well, it's nice to meet you." Herb nodded. "I hope you find that girl. Seems she's been missing a long time."

"We're doing our best."

Herb waved a fat envelope at Nick and said, "I have some estimates here for you to look at. Three for each of the projects you asked about. I'd have a fourth, but Greg Burton, he said he wanted to take another look at that back wall in the barn, so he'll be stopping out. Want me to just leave these on the kitchen table? You can give me a call when you're free, and we can go over them."

Nick glanced at Emme hesitantly.

"I can go through this stuff by myself," she told him. "Go do what you have to do."

"It shouldn't take too long."

"It's okay." She turned back to the box she was working on and resumed sorting. When she was finished, she repacked the sweaters and dragged the box into the living room, then started on the next box, this one filled with books. She dragged it over to the stairs where she sat and began to search through every book and notebook.

"Find anything?" Nick came back into the foyer with two bottles of water. He handed one to Emme and put the other down on the top of an old desk that sat to one side of the front door.

"Not yet."

"It's getting stuffy in here. There's no breeze outside." He stood at the window. "I'm sorry we don't have any fans. And obviously, no AC. I keep thinking I might do that, one of these days. But someone would have to be living here full-time to justify that kind of expense, and as long as the property stays in the family, that isn't likely to happen."

"It's a charming house," she said, looking up from the book she was holding upside down. She fanned through the pages, then closed it and set it next to her on the step. "I love the old woodwork in these places, the high ceilings, the big rooms with the big windows and the fireplaces."

"Yeah," he agreed. "The entire property has a lot of charm. There's a pond and what's left of my granddad's peach orchard. They sold off most of that parcel a long time ago."

"How many acres did they have?"

"When my granddad was farming, they had over two hundred. Wendy sold some to Herb after she inherited it. Now, we're down to about sixty, and Herb uses most of that for his corn. I guess we have about a dozen acres that we use, between the garages and the pond."

"I noticed an old cemetery on the road as I drove up. Is that your family's?" She shook out another book but nothing fell out.

"It's on the property, but there aren't any Perones buried there. The family my grandparents bought this place from had owned it for almost two hundred years. Their name was Sawyer. They're all buried down there."

"None of their descendants wanted to keep the farm?"

"I don't think they had any children. My granddad showed me where the folks he bought from were buried—Mary Alice and Henry Sawyer—and he was careful to keep the graveyard respectfully mowed and the weeds out."

"That was nice of him. It looked pretty tidy when I drove past," she said.

"Herb kind of took that over after my granddad died. Wendy would never have thought to do it, and I wasn't here."

"Herb sounds like the ideal neighbor."

"He is. He and his wife are the best. They keep an eye on the place for me. Last time I was out here, I noticed that we're in need of a lot of repairs. Herb lined up some contractors to come out and look things over and write up some estimates. That's what he was dropping off. The barn needs work, the pond house my granddad built for Wendy and me—remind me to show you that before we leave—that needs a new—"

"Oh," Emme exclaimed as several sheets of folded paper fluttered from a book she'd turned upside down. She bent over to pick them up and straightened them out. She looked them over quickly before handing them off to Nick. "Emails from Blondebelle to aspark1010." She looked up at Nick. "Belle to Aaron."

He read through them. "This is stuff we already knew. Donor 1735 was of Scandinavian and Irish descent. Oh, here's stuff Hayley hadn't told us. He was born in Philadelphia on August first, 1961, and he's a lawyer."

Emme leaned around him to read for herself, and he put his arm around her to bring her closer.

"So all we have to do is find a lawyer who was born in Philly on August first, 1961. Hey—piece of cake," he said dryly.

"Right. It'll be a snap." She pointed at the box that sat at his feet. "Keep looking."

"Here's the box with the bags in it." Nick pulled out a black leather clutch and looked inside. "It seems to have a lot of pockets in it. Maybe you should look through these."

"Because I said I liked bags?"

"No. Because you'll know where to look for the pockets." He opened another box. "Looks like . . . stuff girls wear that guys don't. Sorry—this creeps me out a little. This one's yours."

"Okay. You finish up on this box of books and I'll do the bags and the girly stuff." Emme pushed a carton aside to make room to walk. She peered inside the box Nick had relinquished to her. She was through it in less than five minutes. "No place to hide stuff in any of these things."

She moved that box into the living room and moved on to the box of handbags.

"Wow. Belinda really did have a lot of bags."

She began to sort through them, finding sticks of gum in some, pink packets of sweetener in others, pens in most, but no papers that would bring them closer to finding Donor 1735.

When he finished with the box of books, Nick said, "Want to take a break? It's getting hot in here."

"No, I'm good."

"Maybe there's a fan in the attic." Nick wiped sweat from his forehead. "I'll be right back."

Emme glanced up to see him take the stairs two at a time. Overhead, she heard first his footsteps, then the creak of a door being opened, followed by the sound of footsteps on the stairs. A few minutes later, he came back down.

"Nothing. I don't know how anyone lived in this house in the summer without even a damned fan."

"We only have four more boxes to go." Emme pointed out. "I think we'll survive."

"Not without cold drinks," he grumbled and went into the kitchen. The refrigerator door opened, then closed.

"The cupboard is really bare," he told her. "I have an idea. Let's drive into town and pick up some lunch."

"You go," she said. "I'll keep working here."

"You sure? You're not dying from the heat?"

"No, I'm fine."

"Sandwich, all right?"

"Whatever. I'm not fussy. Just get me whatever you get for yourself."

"That's easy enough. I'll be back in twenty, thirty minutes."

"Fine." She looked up and smiled. "I'll be here."

He left through the back door and she heard the Firebird rumble softly as it passed the window to her left. The house grew very still, and she became aware of a clock ticking in one of the other rooms. She wished there was music, a radio, an iPod, anything to cut through the silence. It was just too quiet.

She finished going through the bags—Belinda had excellent taste in bags, she'd give her that. There were several in that box that Emme had admired, but none of their zippered pockets had hidden secrets. She folded over the top and dragged the box into the living room with the others.

It was a nice room, a comfortable room. She could see a young Nick sitting on that sofa—now covered with a well-worn sheet—with his grandfather, watching TV. She peeked at the books gathering dust on the shelves that flanked the side windows. He'd mentioned his grandmother reading something . . . ah, here it is. *The Joy Luck Club.* She lifted the book from the shelf and opened it. *Angela Curcio Perone* was written in a beautiful script inside the front cover. She wondered which of the sheet-covered chairs his grandmother had sat in to read. The picture in her mind was a gentle one, one of two generations of a loving, happy family enjoying each other's company on a hot summer night. *It must have been nice to have that,* she thought with a tiny stab of envy.

Emme replaced the book and went back to work. She looked inside several boxes, and decided to go with the one containing books. Sliding the box on its side, she sat cross-legged on the floor and reached inside and pulled out the top book. Geometry. The only math course she ever did really well in. She thought if she were superstitious, she might take that as a sign, but she wasn't, and the book held no surprises. She pushed it to her right and tried again.

She heard the car before she saw it. Standing and stretching out the kinks, she went to the window and watched the Firebird slide past. Just below the windows on that side of the house, a bank of roses grew leggy and wild and covered with blooms. She went out the front door to get a better look.

"Em," Nick called to her as he got out of the car. "Is something wrong?"

"No, I just came out to get a better look at these rose bushes." She walked toward him.

"My grandmother planted them about a million years ago." He shifted the bag from the deli from one hip to the other. "Wendy tried to get them under control, but I'm sorry to say no one's tended to them since she died. There's always been something else that seems more important. I'm surprised old Angie— that was my gram—hasn't come back to haunt me over it. She really took a great deal of pride in them."

Don't offer to prune them, Emme commanded herself. *You have other things to do that are more important. Besides, you won't be back here again. Let it go. Tempting as it may be. . . .*

"You can cut some before we go, if you want, to take back to your room."

"Maybe a few for Trula for helping out so much. Thanks."

"Trula has her own rose garden," he reminded her as she came toward him. "I think Emme and Chloe could use something pretty to brighten up that hotel room."

"Thanks. I do love roses." She looked back over her shoulder and thought about which colors she'd pick. Definitely the light pink ones, and some of those lavender ones as well.

"Let's take our lunches down to the pond house and eat there," he suggested. "It'll be shady, and cooler than the house."

"Sounds good. Should we lock up the house?"

"There's no one around to break in. Let's just walk."

He held out a hand to her and she took it, matching him stride for stride. They walked through a field that sloped downward toward a large pond. A tiny cabin sat on its bank and a narrow dock jutted into the water.

"This is beautiful," she told him. "So quiet it's almost scary. How do people sleep out here?"

"Very soundly."

"I guess I've gotten used to hotel noise over the past few weeks. Our room overlooks the parking lot and the main road into Conroy, so there's always road noise. And there's always someone coming in around one or two who slams the door to their room. And the elevator pings when it hits our floor whether it stops or not. We're two rooms down from it, so I hear it all night long."

"Sound to me as if the whole hotel thing is wearing thin."

She braced herself for the slope, tugged at the hem of her short skirt, and tried not to lose her footing in her sandals.

"I'm not really dressed for this," she muttered when they reached the dock.

"I think you look great," he said, making no effort to pretend that he wasn't looking at her legs. "This is the pond house my granddad built for Wendy, but she'd outgrown it by the time I came along. It was the best playhouse you could imagine."

"Did you have playmates here?"

"Just my granddad." He smiled. "He made for one hell of a pirate."

He pushed the door open. "It needs a lot of work, as you can see. One of the estimates Herb dropped off was for this place."

"Are you going to go to the expense of renovating it? I mean, since no one's used it in a long time."

"It's not my first priority—that would be the house—but yeah, I'm going to take care of it. Some-day maybe there will be kids to play in it again." He backed out of the doorway and she followed. "Be-sides, my granddad built it himself."

He handed her the bag holding the food and said, "I'm going to run back to the house and get us a blan-ket to sit on. I'll be right back."

"Can't we sit on the dock?"

"Sure. If we want to spend the afternoon picking splinters out of each other's butts." He smiled. "Which, maybe on second thought, might not be so bad . . ."

"Go get a blanket."

He took off up the hill at a trot. Emme sat the bag on the wooden planks that formed the dock and watched a duck and her ducklings bob and weave be-tween the reeds.

"I didn't realize how much of Gramma's stuff Wendy kept," Nick said, making his way down the slope. "For some reason, I assumed she'd gotten rid of most of the old stuff and replaced it with new things of her own." He held up a mostly blue quilt. "I found this at the foot of one of the beds. I remember it from when I was a kid."

"Why would you assume your sister would have gotten rid of it?" She helped him spread the blanket on the dock.

"I guess because everything else about her was very hip, very contemporary. It surprises me that the second floor looks just the way I remember it."

He knelt down and reached for the bag and opened it. "I hope this is okay. I figured burgers would be good, since everyone likes burgers, but then I thought they'd get cold on the way out here. So I went with cold sandwiches."

"I'm sure whatever it is will be fine. Thanks." Emme sat opposite him on the blanket and opened the foil packet. She stared at the contents for a moment, then asked, "Ah . . . just for the record, what is this?"

"Chicken, avocado, field greens, and sprouts on whole grain." He stared at her. "What's it look like?"

"That, what you said." A tiny smile played at the corners of her mouth and she peered into the bag as if searching for something. "Did you get chips, by any chance?"

"That's them, in that foil bag." He held it up, then tore it open.

"Let's see that. Oh. Sweet potato and beet chips. Yum."

"Don't knock 'em till you try them." He laughed and twisted the top of his water bottle.

"What, no soda?" she asked innocently.

"Soda is the invention of the devil." He spoke solemnly, but his eyes gave him away. "It's loaded with high fructose corn syrup." He handed her a bottle of water.

"You and Trula would get along just fine," she told him. "She is militant about what goes on in that kitchen of hers. Everything's organic, and comes from local farms. She's totally indoctrinating Chloe, who asked the waitress this morning which local farm her eggs came from. She'll be really proud when I tell her what I had for lunch today."

"You can let her think it was your choice. I won't give you away."

A pair of dragonflies danced on the air between them before chasing each other across the pond.

"All kidding about the quiet aside, it is very peaceful here," she noted.

"I don't come back as often as I should, but it's where my heart is." He took a bite of his sandwich, chewed thoughtfully, then asked, "Where's your heart, Emme?"

"In terms of a place?" She shook her head. "There's no place I have any attachment to."

"How 'bout the house you grew up in?"

"There were way too many of them, and none of them particularly memorable for anything I'd want to hold on to."

"Your family moved around a lot?"

"Actually I had no family." She hesitated for a moment, debating with herself before telling him her story—selectively edited—in the most nonchalant manner she could muster. When she finished, it occurred to her that she'd told that story more in the past few weeks than she had in the past ten years. The thought was both comforting and unsettling.

"So you really never had a home."

She could tell by the look on his face that this disturbed him, so she said, "It's okay. I turned out okay."

"You turned out just fine, from everything I can see. But that doesn't make it okay."

"It's one of those things you don't get to change, you know?" She tried to make light of it, but feared her attempts were falling flat, so she added, "The only thing I can do to make the past not matter so much is to try to make the future better. To make Chloe's childhood better than mine was, to give her the security and love I didn't have."

"She's one of the most confident and self-assured kids I've ever met, so I'd say you were doing a great job."

"Actually, I am doing a hell of a job." She thought then about telling him everything, about Anthony Navarro and the reward he'd put on his child's head, about changing one false name for another, but he reached out for her, one of his big hands wrapping around her forearm and sending a current through her entire body.

"I'm glad you recognize that," he said, just before pulling her closer and covering her mouth with his own.

The buzz was back, filling her head and flowing through her like live current. His tongue teased the corners of her mouth and she took his head in both her hands and urged him to explore more. He tasted salty like the chips and smelled like the summer day, and when he eased her back onto the quilt, she drifted down willingly. His hands made fists in her hair for a moment, then slid along her sides, one elbow coming to rest on the dock to take his weight, the other hand seeking her breast with a light caress.

She hadn't expected that heat could overtake so quickly, or that want could swell like the tide, without control and without limits, but the feel of his hand on her skin set her senses into overdrive. When his lips led a hot trail from her mouth to the side of her face, to the warm spot under her ear, to her neck, her throat, she arched her body to encourage him to keep going. When he reached the place where her shirt impeded his progress, she slid a hand between them and unbuttoned it, his eager mouth following each inch of skin as each button came undone until his mouth closed over the thin lace that covered her breast. He eased the strap over her shoulder and feasted on her flesh, his tongue's sure flickering stoking the flame right to her core. He covered her body with his and she moved against him, wanting him closer. The only thought resounding inside her was *More*.

"Do you want to go up to the house and . . ." His breath was ragged and he seemed to be struggling for control.

"No," she whispered. "Here. Now."

He tugged her skirt up over her hips and his fingers were inside her, stroking her nearly to insanity.

"Nick." She gasped, tugging at his waistband and finding his zipper, pulling it down as far as she could.

"Right." He swallowed hard. "Here. Now."

She parted her legs wider to welcome him, and

sighed with pleasure when he entered her. Her hips rocked in rhythm with his, together gathering speed and intensity like a runaway train. When the crash came, it was mighty and swift and overwhelming.

"I think the top of my head just blew off," Emme said when she could find her voice.

"I'm sorry," he murmured. "I usually take a little more time than—"

"If you apologize, I'm going to have to hurt you," she told him, her breath still uneven.

He laughed and started to say something, but as he rose up on one elbow, his attention was drawn to the top of the slope.

"Uh-oh," he said. "We have company."

"What?" She bolted upright, closing the front of her shirt and pulling down her skirt.

From somewhere behind them she heard the barking of a dog.

"Shit." Nick grumbled and pulled his cutoffs up, zipped the zipper and pulled on his T-shirt. "When Herb said one of the carpenters would be stopping over, I didn't think he meant *today*."

He looked down at her with concern. "Are you all right?"

"Other than the fact that I'm half-undressed and there's a stranger about to slide down that embankment, yeah, I'm fine."

"I'll head him off," he told her, pausing to lightly kiss the side of her face before standing and taking off up the slope.

What in the name of God has gotten into you? her inner voice demanded as she gathered their partially eaten lunch.

She began to smile, cutting off the voice and offering no explanation for her uncharacteristic behavior. Every decision she'd made over the past four years had been strictly for Chloe. Today she'd made one strictly for herself. She'd be damned if she was going to make excuses for it.

She folded the quilt and slipped her feet back into her sandals and started up the hill. She was whistling when she arrived at the drive, where a big, brown lab sat next to a pickup truck, and a tall, thin man stood talking to Nick.

"Emme, this is Greg. He's going to take a look at the barn," Nick told her. When Greg turned to greet her, behind him, Nick rolled his eyes. "He thought since he was out this way, he'd stop and take a look at that back wall."

"Great." She smiled and offered her hand to the dog to sniff before patting him on the head. "Good timing."

"That's what I was just thinking," Nick agreed.

"Oh, yeah," the carpenter nodded. "You got a weak back wall there, no telling when it's going to come down."

"I'll be in the front hall," she told Nick. "Nice to meet you, Greg."

"Likewise."

She left the grocery bag on the kitchen table and went upstairs to find a bathroom. On her way back down, she paused at the landing overlooking the driveway. Nick and the carpenter were nowhere to be seen, so she assumed they'd gone into the barn. Well, it spared them from having to come up with after-sex talk, she reasoned. She'd never been real good at that.

It was just one of any number of reasons she hadn't been good at relationships.

She poked into the remaining boxes and decided to finish up the clothes to get those all out of the way. She sorted through a half-dozen pair of jeans and found the bottom of the box contained notebooks. She flipped through several, reading the subjects on the colored tabs.

"Genealogy," she read aloud with a laugh. "Now, if I were going to . . ."

The packet of folded papers, held together with a small black and chrome clip, fell into her lap. She opened them flat on the floor and let out a yelp.

She took them into the kitchen and sat at the table, ironing out the folds with her hands, and began to read. A few minutes later, Nick came in through the back door.

"Em?" he called.

"In the kitchen," she told him. When he came into the room, she smiled and said, "This is your lucky day."

"Boy howdy, is it ever." He leaned over to kiss her neck.

"No," she laughed. "I found the paperwork we've been looking for."

"You're kidding," he paused, his lips still at her throat.

"Here, take a look." She handed him the stack.

"Where?"

"In her genealogy notebook."

"Of course. Where else?" He breezed through them, shaking his head. "I have no idea what any of this means, all these columns of lines and letters."

"Neither do I. But we can find someone who knows what to do with it all, and with luck, they're going to lead us to Donor 1735. And hopefully—eventually—we'll find your niece."

"You still think we will?"

"I think we will find the answer to what happened to her," she replied, choosing her words carefully. "For better or for worse."

"But I should probably prepare for the worst."

She nodded slowly. "It's always good to be prepared, Nick."

"Right." He straightened up and handed her the sheaf of papers. "So let's get on with it. For better or for worse, let's see where this leads. . . ."

TWENTY

He lay back against the grass and watched the sun come up. He couldn't remember when he'd felt more alive.

Ali had been a joy, a treasure, from the moment she realized that he wasn't her good friend and her brother, Henry, and that her dear sister, Lori, wasn't there to save her. Too late, she'd recognized him, and only the chloroform had subdued her. He really hated to have to resort to that, but she'd been winding up for a good long scream, and in that neighborhood, screaming was bound to bring someone running.

He'd arrived at the college early to scout out the best location—that is, the location where he could remain in the shadows for the longest period of time without appearing to be trying to hide. It was, he reasoned, a very fine line. He found the perfect spot on Yarrow Street, just past a building that had a very gothic air—it looked like some type of theater—across the street from a prep school that looked deserted now that classes were over for the summer. There was a wooded area right past the main building that would give him a buffer, in case someone was about, and the gothic structure sat by itself near the road and was obviously closed. Just beyond it the road dipped down nicely, and as a bonus, a wide grass stretch surrounded it. He parked well past the streetlight and dialed her cell phone.

"Hey, we're here," he told her when she answered.

"Where's here?" She sounded out of breath, as if she'd been walking fast.

He described the surroundings.

"Oh, you're all the way over there. I should have told you to stay straight on Morris for a bit." She paused as if debating. "I think it would be easier for me to find you than for you to drive around trying to find me."

He smiled to himself. "Are you sure? Because if it's too far for you—"

"No, no. It's fine. It'll just take a couple of minutes. Is Lori with you?"

"Yes, she's here. She just took a little walk down the street to look around."

"Yeah, it's a nice neighborhood over near the theater. I'll be there soon."

He got the towel ready, then stepped out of the car and leaned back against the driver's door, his heart pounding. He tried to remain cool and calm, but really, how could one when anticipating such pleasure? Deep inside him, the beast pawed impatiently.

He saw her step into the light from the one streetlamp at the end of the walk near the theater. She appeared to pause, her steps hesitant. He stepped into the street and waved to her. Seconds later, his phone rang.

"Yes, it's me," he said, trying to inject a lightness into his voice.

"Why are you parked all the way down there?"

"Lori wanted to get a better look at this old house down the street and I didn't want to park in front of it 'cause I didn't want the owners to think we were casing the place. Keep walking, Ali. I'll call Lori and tell her to come back to the car."

"Oh, okay. I just wanted to make sure it's really you."

"It's really me."

"I'll be there in a minute."

He kept the phone close to his head as if speaking to someone while he opened the car door. In one hand he held the towel he'd prepared, and he kept his back to her until the last possible minute.

She was a few feet from the car when she called out, "Henry, you didn't tell me you got a new car." and he spun around in a flash, like a dancer.

It took several seconds for her to realize that he was not Henry, but by then he had the towel to her face and was dragging her quickly to the passenger side where he taped her hands, feet, and mouth, and strapped her in to the seat.

He talked to her as he drove through the night, explaining to her what he was going to do to her and why, then turned on the radio and sang to her for the last few miles before turning off the main road and heading for his special place. He'd had no trouble hiding the car behind a stand of trees, nor had it been a problem for him to carry her through the field. The moon was high and bright and he knew the way. He'd laid her on the ground and stared into her eyes, drinking in her fear and panic until the beast swelled within him. He was invincible then, and knew that nothing could stop him from having her.

Nothing had.

TWENTY-ONE

Mallory sat in her office, nervously tapping a pen on a file that sat open on the desk. She'd been bothered since the day Emme had blasted out of the drive, then later came slinking back, slipping into her office as if she didn't want anyone to know she was there.

Something was just not right with that woman.

Something had been nagging her since their conversation on Sunday afternoon. A quick look at the documents she'd received from Silver Hill and it hadn't been hard to spot.

Why was Emme lying about her background? Why had she gone on about having been abandoned at birth—in a church, no less, where she'd be found by nuns!—when her file clearly indicated that she'd come from a long line of law enforcement personnel? One of the recommendations that had been submitted to the Silver Hill department when she applied for the job was from a member of the California legislature who wrote about her family's "fine tradition of public service, from her great-grandfather all the way to her younger brother, who was a decorated member of the California Highway Patrol."

What the hell? Mallory thought.

She lifted the phone and dialed the number for the Silver Hills PD, then asked to speak with Chief Jenkins when the call was answered.

"I'm sorry, Chief Jenkins is out of the office," she was told. "This is Sergeant Whitaker. Would you like to leave a message?"

"My name is Mallory Russo. I'm with the Mercy Street Foundation in Conroy, Pennsylvania. I spoke with Chief Jenkins a few weeks ago about Emme Caldwell. I have a few more questions."

"Oh." He sounded surprised. "Anything I can help you with? I was Emme's partner on the street for a few years, when we first started. I knew her real well. Still miss her."

"I'm sure she'd be happy to know that, Sergeant." She knew better than to get into a discussion about Emme with anyone other than the chief. "Please let Chief Jenkins know that I need to speak with her as soon as possible."

"Sure thing."

Mallory gave her cell and office numbers, then said good-bye.

Still miss her. It struck Mallory as an odd thing to say. She returned the phone to the base. Emme only left Silver Hill a few weeks ago, hadn't she?

•

Carl Whittaker finished writing the note for the chief and left it on her phone where she'd be sure to see it when she returned from vacation. He went back to his desk and closed the right-hand drawer, the one where he kept his crossword-puzzle books. It was another relatively slow morning in Silver Hill, and the chief wasn't expected back until Monday. He was working on a particularly vexing puzzle when the phone had rung. He'd been planning on going right back to it, but now there was something more pressing on his mind. He went to his favorite search engine and typed in *Mercy Street Foundation*.

In seconds the site's home page filled his screen. He'd seen the press conference that had run over and over again on the TV news stations for almost a week after Robert Magellan had made his announcement. He'd even heard about an officer from L.A. and another from San Diego who'd applied, and several more who were thinking about it.

Why would someone from the Mercy Street Foundation be asking about a dead cop from Silver Hill?

He clicked on the sidebar and waited while the Staff page loaded. There was a picture of Mallory Russo . . . she's the one who called. Pretty girl. He smiled to himself. Course, you couldn't use "girl" anymore. It's un-PC. But pretty woman didn't have the same ring. Besides, that was that movie about a—

Hello.

Under Mallory Russo's picture was an empty square captioned "Check back later for a photo of our newest hire, our first full-time investigator, Emme Caldwell, who comes to us with seven years of law-enforcement experience."

He stared at the screen, his eyes narrowing. Maybe there was another Emme Caldwell who'd been a cop somewhere else for seven years. Could be a really weird coincidence. It's a big world.

But Russo said she'd already spoken to Chief Jenkins about Emme. Wouldn't Steffie have told her that *their* Emme was deceased?

A very odd picture began to form in his mind, but he was having a real hard time getting it to focus.

Steffie. Ann.

Emme Caldwell.

The thought came like lightning. His mouth went dry and his fingers began to shake. He didn't like what he was thinking. He got up and walked outside, past the cars parked behind the building and across the street to the deli. He went in and ordered a large fountain soda in a take-out cup.

"Hey, Sarge," the woman behind the counter greeted him. "What's the count down to now?"

"Sixty-two days, Elsie." He met her at the cash register and paid for his drink. "Sixty-two more days."

"You'll have to let me know how retirement feels." She counted out his change from a five. "God knows I'll never get to experience it. I swear, if it isn't one thing, it's another."

"Those kids of yours still giving you grief, Els?"

She rested one elbow on the counter. "My daughter Regina blows in last week with both her kids in tow. Says she got evicted from her place and had no where else to go. Tell it to their father, I tell her." She shook her head. "But no. So here I am, at my age, the son moved back home last year, now the daughter with her kids. . . ." She blew out a breath laden with exasperation. "So I figure the only way I'll be able to experience retirement is vicariously, through my friends."

"I were you, I'd be moving to a smaller place. No room for anyone to move in, take advantage of you."

"Don't think I haven't thought of it, Sarge, but hey,

your kids are your kids, right? What are you gonna do? Pray for a windfall, is all."

The bell over the door rang as another customer came in, and she slapped her hand on the counter. "Good seeing you, Sarge."

"You too, Elsie." He took his drink and walked to the small park at the corner, found a bench and took a seat and thought about his retirement. His pension wasn't going to go as far as he'd hoped it would. He couldn't say he wasn't worried about that. Thirty-three years as a cop and he'd be leaving without a whole lot to show for it.

Windfall.

That's what was really on his mind.

He'd heard the rumors on the street, he'd even been slipped a phone number in the bar the other night, just in case he heard something. He suspected that most of the members of the force had been given the same number. Would anyone hesitate to use it? Anyone other than Steffie, that is?

The whole thing had been odd, Ann disappearing like that, just taking off. Steffie's explanation that she'd quit and left without notice because she was sick. Well, that just wasn't credible. Steffie and Ann had been best friends. Steffie was the godmother to Ann's daughter. He could buy the part about Ann quitting and not giving notice once the story about Navarro started circulating, but not that Steffie didn't know where she'd gone. And Steffie didn't even seem that upset. All she ever said was that Ann did what Ann thought was best for her. If she wanted anyone to know where she was, she'd let them know.

Then out of the blue, there's this call about Emme Caldwell.

No, not out of the blue. Mallory Russo said she spoke with Steffie a few weeks ago. What had that been about?

He thought he might know.

He went back to his office and closed the door behind him, then went through his top drawer until he found the crumpled piece of paper. He smoothed it out and before he could change his mind, he dialed the number. It rang four times before a man answered.

"This is Carl Whittaker. Tell Mr. Navarro I might know where he can find his daughter. . . ."

TWENTY-TWO

Susanna will be here in a minute," Mallory told Emme as she came into the conference room. "She's on the phone but she's wrapping up the call now."

Emme nodded and went over the mental notes she'd made on her way back to Conroy. She'd called Mallory from the car and brought her up-to-date, but Mal thought everyone should know where things stood. Nick had insisted on following her back and had wanted to sit in on the meeting. Since no one had objected, he'd taken a place at the table and now waited for Emme to begin.

"I figured out where I knew you from." Robert slapped Nick on the back as he came into the room. "Six years ago, you had a 1970 Aston Martin for sale at an auto show in New York."

Nick thought for a moment, then nodded. "I was selling it for a client. You were at that show?"

"Yeah, I wanted that car in the worst way." Robert made his way around the table and seated himself across from Nick. "I couldn't afford it then. Now, when I can, I can't find one."

"That year's tough to find," Nick agreed, "but they

do come on the market from time to time. I can ask around for you if you want."

"I want." Robert nodded enthusiastically. "As soon as I saw that Firebird out there, it jogged my memory. You deal in classics, right?"

"Mostly, yes."

"I checked you out at the time. You had a good reputation."

"I like to believe I still do."

"Okay, boys, continue the man talk later." Susanna, the last arrival, seated herself. "It's getting late."

To Emme she said, "Father Kevin is on his way over but he said to start without him. He said to tell you he'll bring Chloe here so not to rush things thinking you have to get to school."

"Thanks, Susanna. And thanks, Father Kevin." Emme looked around. "Where's Trula?"

"She wasn't sure she was supposed to be included," Susanna told her.

"Can we get her up here?" Emme glanced from one face to the next.

"Yes, she should be here. She always has good insights." Mallory left the room. "I'll be right back."

"So, Nick, about the car . . ." Robert tapped on the tabletop.

Mallory came back into the room and Trula followed moments later. Trula rested a hand on Emme's shoulder and leaned over to tell her, "I put those roses you brought back with you in a vase. They're on the counter in the kitchen. Make sure you take them with you when you go."

"Thanks, Trula." Emme patted Trula's hand before the woman took her seat.

Mallory sat at the head of the table at one end, Emme the other. "Okay, everyone, Emme's going to bring us up-to-date on the progress of our first case. Nick Perone, who sent the application in to us, is here. He's been working with Emme because of the number of young people associated with the case, some of whom might be put off by being questioned by a PI, but are okay talking to Belinda's uncle. Emme?"

Emme walked them through the case, from finding Heaven's Gate and discovering that Nick's sister had used a sperm donor to conceive Belinda, through finding the donor siblings, to finding the DNA report from the lab Belinda had used.

"I have a question," Trula asked. "How many of these donor siblings did Belinda have?"

"Nine."

"Of those nine, how many have you met or spoken with?"

Emme paused to think. "We've only met Hayley in person. But we spoke with Ali on the phone, and we spoke with Henry. We—Nick and I—were supposed to meet Lori and Henry at the zoo on Saturday, but they had car trouble and never showed."

"So did you set another meeting with them?"

"Actually," Emme said uneasily, "I haven't heard from them at all. I've called and emailed, but neither of them have responded."

"Odd, wouldn't you say?" Trula asked.

"Very. As far as the others are concerned, I've

emailed every one of them, and have posted on their message board."

"How many of them answered you?"

"All except Ava, Jessica, and Justin." Emme frowned and looked at Nick. "That's right, isn't it?"

He nodded. "Hayley said Ava is in Boston in grad school—I'm guessing she isn't real active right now on the message board, and maybe she doesn't keep up with the email from the kids."

"The kids?" Susanna raised an eyebrow.

"Hayley said that Ava was twenty-four. Most of the others are in their late teens or early twenties. At sixteen, Hayley is the youngest, but Ava seems to respond to her via personal email. The impression I have is that she's busy with school and she doesn't really want to be bothered by the group."

"What about Jessica?" Susanna asked. "Does she not want to be bothered either?"

"Hayley said her father was transferred to France last year, and the family relocated. They haven't heard from her since she left."

"They do have the Internet in France, right?" Trula said dryly. "And what about this kid, Justin, why hasn't he checked in? Did he respond to your email about the DNA swab?"

"No one did," Emme told her.

Trula frowned. "Where are all these kids?"

"I've been wondering that myself," Emme admitted.

"Maybe they decided they don't like outsiders interfering with their lives," Mallory suggested. "Right now, the important thing is that we have the DNA profile."

"What are you going to do with it?" Susanna asked.

"We're going to do what this sixteen-year-old, Aaron, did," Emme told her. "We're going to send it to every one of the online genealogy services until we find one that can give us a match."

"What are these genealogy services?" Trula asked.

"They're online search services," Emme explained. "You can search for relatives—living ones or your ancestors—in a number of ways. You could have them search by surname, or you can have them search for DNA matches. You provide your DNA, and they compare it to DNA that's been submitted by other people."

"The world is becoming a complicated place." Trula shook her head. "Imagine finding your relatives that way."

"A lot of people are doing it, apparently. There are several of these services available. We're going to hit all of them at the same time. Then if we're lucky, we'll find matches, and we'll try to locate those persons using the Internet."

"To what end?" Susanna persisted.

"To locate Donor 1735," Emme told her. "Who may or may not be involved in Belinda's disappearance."

"You mean, maybe she figured out who he was, and he was someone who didn't want to be found and maybe . . ." Trula left the thought unfinished.

"That's certainly a very real possibility." Emme nodded.

"Have you considered that if he didn't want her to

find him, he isn't going to want you to find him, either?"

"It's possible, Trula, but I'm not a starry-eyed nineteen-year-old girl looking for her daddy," Emme replied. "I think I can take care of myself."

"So it's a matter of running those"—Robert pointed to the papers on the table in front of Emme—"through some databases?"

"Databases on specific websites that contain DNA profiles."

"Oh, I can do that," Robert said.

Five pairs of eyes stared at him. Robert stared back.

"Excuse me," he said, with no small amount of sarcasm, "you're talking to the man who developed the most sophisticated search engine on the planet. I think I can handle this part."

"Seriously?" Emme asked. "How would you?"

"I still have some pretty mad computer skills," he said, as if amused. "Besides, my former partner designed a computer that will never see the retail market. That sucker can . . . well, never mind what it can do. I'm going to fax your report to Colin and see what he can do for us. If the database exists that has a match to that profile, he'll find it. Then we'll see what we can do about tracking down the matches." He waved a hand impatiently in Emme's direction for the papers.

"Okay, then, Robert's on the DNA." She passed him the report.

He looked it over. "Was there anything else for today?"

"No," Emme said. "That should do it for now."

"I'll be in my office." Smiling, Robert left the room.

"Well, he looked happy," Mallory said.

"He has a project." Susanna's eyes were still on the door Robert had just exited. "He hasn't had work to do in a long time. I think he's missed it."

"I didn't want to appear rude, but this partner of his—"

"Colin Bressler." Susanna stood and pushed in her chair. "He's the ultimate computer geek. He'll have that DNA traced through every database that exists."

"How can he do that?" Emme frowned. "Without subscribing, that is?"

"I trust he'll find a way." Susannah appeared amused.

"Is he going to hack his way in?"

"Emme, 'hack' is such a harsh word." Susanna drained her coffee cup. "And besides, hacking is for amateurs."

"Robert did seem pretty confident," Nick noted.

"Seriously. If there is a database out there that contains those sequences, believe me, Colin will find it," Susanna said as she left the room. "And way faster than anyone else could."

Childish giggles echoed from the hall.

"That sounds like Chloe," Trula said. "I'll take her down for a snack while you fill Kevin in. I know he'll want to be kept up-to-date."

By noon the following day, Emme was a believer.

"Robert wants you to go straight to his office as soon as you get your coffee," Trula told her when she entered the house.

"Good news or bad news?" Emme frowned as she read through the selection of coffee mugs. She'd had practically no sleep the night before, having relived and rethought and reconsidered her relationship with Nick—did they even *have* a relationship or had they just had sex?—and wasn't in the mood for any of what Susanna called Trula's smart-ass mugs. She settled on *Never judge a book by its movie.*

"What's the difference? He's the boss and he wants to see you pronto," Trula reminded her.

"Good point."

Emme fixed her coffee and went directly to Robert's office. She tapped lightly on the half-opened door.

"You wanted to see me?" she said.

"Come on in." He had his back to the door, his attention focused on a very large screen that sat on the sideboard next to his desk.

"Is that a TV or a computer?" she asked.

"Yes." He looked up and smiled. "Both. Either. Whichever I need it to be."

"I never saw one like that."

"And it will be awhile before you do. This is one of Colin's toys," he explained. "Now, here's your list of names. Note that the spelling of . . ."

Her jaw dropped. "Are you serious?"

"Sure. I told you, Colin is quite brilliant when it comes to finding things. He apologized for not having it to us sooner but he was out last night."

"I'm stunned. I thought it would take a few days."

"Get unstunned, ye of little faith." Robert was clearly enjoying this. "We have quite a few names. Where do we go from here to narrow them down?"

She stared over his shoulder at the screen.

"All of those men share the same Y chromosome as Donor 1735?"

"So say the databases."

"Gardner. Gardener. Gartnor. Gartner." She read the long list of surnames aloud. "I guess we'll start with those who were born in Philadelphia."

He hit a few keys, then looked up. "It wants to know which Philadelphia. I'm assuming you mean the one in Pennsylvania and not the one in Mississippi?"

Emme nodded and he selected the entry.

"That took out quite a few. Next?"

"Birth date. August first, 1961."

He entered the date and sat back and waited. After a moment, he leaned back, smiled broadly, and said, "I believe this could be your man."

Emme exhaled, barely believing it. Donor 1735 had a name.

John Jennings Gardner.

"Now, we'll see where our Mr. Gardner is these days. . . ." Robert tapped into the search engine that bore his name. Data flickered onto the screen. "Uh-oh."

"What?" Emme drew closer. "Couldn't you find him?"

"Oh, we found him all right." Robert moved away from the screen so she could read for herself.

John Jennings Gardner, state congressman from the state of Maryland.

"Wait, didn't he just—" Wide-eyed, Emme pointed at the screen.

"Announce that he was running for the U.S. Senate?" Robert nodded. "Yeah. That would be him."

"Let's see what else we can find out about him." A few more strokes of the keys and Robert had pulled up Gardner's bio.

"He went to Mount Penn law school," Emme read over her boss's shoulder. "That fits like a glove."

"Mount Penn's about an hour from here," Robert noted.

"And it's about twenty minutes from Heaven's Gate, the fertility clinic," she told him. "Looks like we have our man."

"Damn good reason not to want a passel of children coming out of the woodwork to claim your DNA." Emme called Nick's shop to give him the news. "I imagine it could prove embarrassing if the press got hold of that story."

"Yeah, puts him in an awkward position," Nick had snapped angrily. "Do I acknowledge them? Do I try to ignore them? Seems to me whatever he does, it's going to prove to be a distraction during his campaign." He paused, then added, "Unless, of course, he got rid of the distraction. Permanently."

"Don't jump to conclusions, Nick. We don't know if Belinda ever contacted him, or that he even knew about any of these kids."

"So let's go ask him. Point blank."

"Let's find out where he is first, then we'll make an appointment, then we'll—"

"No. First we find out where he is, then we show up."

"Let me give some thought to the right way to go about this. I'll get back to you."

She was still holding the phone in her hand, debating the best way to approach John Gardner, when Robert strolled into her office.

"You get in touch with Gardner yet?" he asked.

She shook her head. "I have the numbers of his local office and his office in Annapolis."

"Forget the Annapolis office," he told her. "It's summer. No one's going to be there now."

"Good call."

"I'm trying to decide the best way to go about this, the best way to get in touch with him."

Robert reached past her for her desk phone and hit two numbers. "Suse, call Maryland state congressman John Gardner and tell him I'd like him to meet with a few of my people as soon as possible. No, don't give any reason. Just that I'd appreciate it if he could clear his schedule, as soon as he can swing it." He hung up the phone and sat in one of the wing chairs facing her desk. "She'll let us know. So, Emme, how do you like Conroy so far?"

"I . . . it's fine. Great." She nodded, surprised at his intervention. From what she'd seen so far, except for putting his computer skills to work, he hadn't seemed too engaged in the foundation.

"Chloe seems like a really happy kid," he went on. "She's really something. You never know what she's going to say."

Dear God, what has she said? Emme went cold inside.

She must have gone white because Robert immediately said, "Oh, nothing bad. Just funny stuff. And we all know that Trula adores her. I haven't seen her have this much fun since . . . well, not in a long time."

A shadow crossed his face and Emme suspected

that he was thinking of the joy his own child must have brought Trula.

Her phone rang and he answered it. "Great. I'll tell Emme. I'm sure she can make it. Thanks, Suse."

He handed her the phone to hang up, and said, "One of the good things about having an easily recognizable name is that when you call people, they usually respond."

"She found him?"

"He's at his summer home on the Eastern shore. He'll see you at ten tomorrow morning. Stop by Susanna's office and get his address and the directions." He slapped a hand on her desktop before rising from the chair, a smile on his face. "Good luck. I hope this leads to the break you've been looking for."

"So do you know what you're going to ask Congressman Gardner?" Nick asked.

"I'm working on it." Curled up on the love seat in the sitting area of her hotel room, Emme juggled the phone with the remote for the TV. "I know what I want to ask. I just want to be sure to approach him in a way that will give us the answers we need."

She channel surfed through the cable news stations and settled on her favorite talking head. It was the top of the hour, and the day's headlines were being read.

"On the one hand, I think we need to go slow and easy and build into it, and on the other, I'm thinking we need to go the direct route, hit him with it right up front. Then we—" She stopped, her attention drawn to the newscast. Uncertain of what she'd just heard, she increased the volume.

"Then we what?" Nick was asking. When she didn't answer, he repeated, "Emme, then we what—"

"Oh, dear God in heaven." In a flash, she was on her feet, standing directly in front of the TV screen. "Dear God, no."

"Emme, what's wrong?" She heard the alarm in his voice, but was powerless to respond. "What's happening, baby? What's wrong? Is it Chloe?"

"It's . . ." She felt as if she were underwater, struggling to breath. "Turn on your television. Carolyn Craft's show."

". . . investigators say they have no suspects in the shooting death of Henry Carroll-Wilson, whose body was found in a dumpster in a rest area off Route 213, and the disappearance of his sister, Lori Carroll-Wilson. Anyone having any information is asked to call . . ."

"Henry." She gasped. "Henry's dead. And Lori . . . dear lord . . ."

"Are they saying when they think this happened?" Nick was asking. "Emme, come on. Get a grip. Did they say when this happened?"

"They're saying that they haven't been seen since Saturday morning." She repeated to him what the newscaster was saying. "Henry lived with his girlfriend in Hartford . . . Lori staying in New Haven with a roommate over the summer, working at a restaurant . . . the roommate said Henry picked up his sister very early on Saturday morning . . . she's saying it was around 6 A.M. The roommate was leaving for a weekend at the Cape, so she isn't aware of when—or if—Lori ever came back to the apartment. The investigation is continuing."

"Did they say if this is a suspected carjacking, some random shooting, what?"

"They don't know. They did find blood on the ground near a car that matches the description that Henry's girlfriend gave the police, but the tags are off it. And now they've moved on to another story." Emme sat on the sofa and opened her laptop. "Let me see what's on the wires."

"Are you still there?" Nick asked after a few quiet moments passed.

"Yes, I thought maybe I could find some more detailed information online but there really isn't much yet." She closed her laptop and blew out a long breath. "This is just crazy. Henry dead and Lori gone. First Belinda, now these two . . . I don't like what I'm thinking, Nick."

"I don't like what I'm thinking, either. What are we going to do about it?"

"Let's take this one step at a time. The first thing I'm going to do is call the detective who's investigating Henry's murder. I'll tell him about the meeting we were supposed to have on Saturday and I'm going to tell him why. I'm also going to tell him about Belinda. Then tomorrow, we're going to keep our appointment with Congressman Gardner. After that, well, we'll just have to see where it all takes us."

TWENTY-THREE

What's got you all pissy this morning?" Nick strapped himself into the passenger seat of Emme's car after having tried to plant one on her when he first got in.

"Detective Lou Stafford, that's what's got me pissy. Your door's not closed." She pointed to the light on her dash.

Nick opened and reclosed the door. "So what's his problem?"

"I called him and told him everything." She pulled into traffic and headed for the highway. "I mean everything. From Belinda trying to find Donor 1735, then going missing in January, to our planning a meeting with Henry and Lori on Saturday and their unexpected car trouble and their canceling out on us."

"Okay, and he said—"

"He said he thought it was highly unlikely that the two cases were related because there was so much time between them. That it's probably a coincidence that Belinda disappeared and then months later one of her donor siblings was murdered and another—also a young girl—has gone missing. And besides, he said they're looking at the case in two ways. One, Lori could have killed Henry for some as yet unknown reason. . . ." She glanced over and saw the look of skepticism cross his face. "Yeah, that's what I thought, too. I asked him how she would have made her getaway, if the car was there at the scene. His answer for that was theory number two, which involves a guy Lori recently broke up with."

"A recent ex is usually the first person you look for, right?"

"True."

"So this thing with Belinda, with the donor sibs, that could just be a coincidence," Nick pointed out. "Stranger things have happened."

"I'm not feeling it that way."

"You psychic?"

"No. Just . . . smart. Yes, there is a possibility that this ex of Lori's shot and killed Henry and abducted her. As far as this whole other scenario is concerned, well, let's just say that I was a cop for too long to put much stock in coincidences. Do they happen sometimes?" She nodded. "Yeah. Sometimes. This just doesn't seem like one of those times."

"But if you were handling the case, you'd look at the ex-boyfriend."

"Yes, I would certainly want to know where he was all weekend," she conceded.

"Okay, so like you said last night, we're going to take this one step at a time. You did what you had to do, you gave the detective the information that you had. If he doesn't know what to do with it, or thinks it isn't worth following up, that's out of your hands."

Nick played with the radio dial, looking for music he liked.

"I guess," she grumbled, and Nick laughed in spite of the topic. "I just want to get to the bottom of this before something else happens."

He leaned to his left as far as the seat belt would permit, and rested his elbow on the top of her seat. "And then what?"

She glanced at him sideways.

"Then what happens, Em? You're staying in Conroy, right?"

"As long as I pass the probationary period, yes." She kept her eyes on the road, not wanting to meet his.

"I'll still be in Maryland."

"And?"

"And . . . just saying, we'll still be close enough to see each other." He hastened to add, "If you still want to see me, that is."

"What brought this up?" She stopped at a red light and turned to study his face. His expression was unreadable.

"I was just thinking, as tough as it's been losing Belinda, meeting you has been . . . well, it's been a really good thing." His fingers touched her shoulder and lingered on the collar of her white shirt. "I'm glad you left California. I'm glad you came east. I'm glad you were the one who took Belinda's case."

"I'm glad too, Nick."

"Good." He smiled and pointed to the light that had turned green. "Drive."

They crossed the bridge to the Eastern shore of Maryland and sped onto the highway toward

Ballard, home of the congressman who would be senator—and possibly the biological father of an unknown number of offspring.

"So I'm just saying that when this is over, I still want to see you." He put it out there like a summation.

"I would still want to see you, too."

"Of course, you're going to see me, anyway. I'm going to find your boss that Aston-Martin if it's the last thing I do."

Before she could respond, her phone rang.

"Caldwell," she said, realizing that for once she hadn't been tempted to identify herself as Nolan.

"Whoa, calm down, Hayley. I can't understand what you're saying . . . yes, I heard about Henry and Lori. I spoke with the detective who—"

She fell silent, and in the next second, she felt the color drain from her face. She flicked on her right-turn signal and pulled over onto the shoulder of the road.

"Say that again . . . when did this happen? Are you sure? Her mother is certain? Hayley, you have to tell your mother everything you've told me. Tell her about Belle, and tell her about Henry and Lori. She can call me if she needs to, but right now, she needs to know this. No, honey, I don't know what it means. But don't go anywhere alone until we figure it out."

She finished her call but did not put the car into gear. She merely sat, staring straight ahead.

When Nick asked, "What?" she swallowed hard and said, "Ali. She's supposed to be at a field hockey clinic in Bryn Mawr, but she's not there. Her car is there, on campus, but there's no sign of her. She's just gone. She hasn't been seen in two days."

Her heart nearly pounding out of her chest, she covered her face with her hands. Nick reached over and turned off the car.

"What exactly did Hayley tell you?" he asked.

"That Ali's mother called her this morning, that she'd seen the story about Henry and Lori on TV." She glanced up at Nick. "Apparently, after we spoke with her on the phone, Ali told her mother about meeting her donor siblings and looking for Donor 1735 and what it all meant to her. Her mother didn't like it so much, but she told Ali that if this was so important to her, it was okay for her to pursue her sibling relationships. Ali had even told her mother about the other kids. So when she couldn't get in touch with her daughter, Ali's mom went through the list of phone numbers Ali kept on a bulletin board in her room and recognized Hayley's name and called her to see if she'd heard from Ali."

"When was the last time anyone heard from Ali?"

"If I understood Hayley correctly, it's been since Tuesday."

"What are you going to do?"

Emme thought it over, then reached for her phone. "I'm going to have the same conversation with the Bryn Mawr police that I had with Detective Stafford this morning. And God help him if he blows me off."

She unhooked her seat belt and looked out her window before opening her car door and getting out.

"I need to pace." She left the door partially open. "I'll be back when I've finished my call, but right now, I have to move."

*   *   *

John Jennings Gardner's home was located on a wide swath of land that faced the Chesapeake Bay and was bordered by a long stretch of marsh on one side and woods on the other. The house was cedar, grayed by salt air and sunlight and wind over the years, and looked as if it belonged on a spare spit of Cape Cod beach. It had two stories and there were two additions built onto the original section. It looked charming and homey and had no trace of pretension, and was probably worth in the millions. Next to a five-car garage that was sided to match the house, three cars were parked: two Mercedes sedans and an SUV.

"You're going to have to promise to let me do the talking." Emme turned off the engine and glanced across the console at Nick. When he didn't respond, she said, "Seriously, Nick, I need you to cooperate."

"I didn't argue when you wanted to drive, did I?"

"Please don't make me the heavy here. I put a lot of thought into how I'm going to conduct this. I've spent a lot of time over the past few years interviewing people. I'm good at getting answers they otherwise might not have given."

"Why don't you just tell me to stay in the car?" The sarcasm was unmistakable. "Forget I said that. For all we know, this guy is a killer. I don't think you ought to just walk in there alone."

"I was a cop for seven years, Nick. I can take care of myself. This wouldn't be the first time I walked into a situation on my own."

"I'll bet you were armed then, though, right? You got a gun in that bag of yours?"

"No," she said. "It's still in the trunk. I'm not a cop anymore, Nick."

"Well, my point is, there's safety in numbers. But I promise to keep my mouth shut and let you do the talking."

"Right," she muttered. She checked her face in the mirror before opening the door. She didn't want the emotional effect of the morning's news to show. She wanted to go into this interview fresh, as if she hadn't just heard that one more donor sibling was missing. There was time enough to deal with that but it would not be her opening here.

"Ready?" Nick asked her, and she nodded. He got out of the car and waited for her before heading for the front door.

They rang the doorbell, and heard dogs barking somewhere in the house. The barking drew closer, and moments later, the door was opened by a man wearing khaki shorts and a Madras button-down collar shirt with the sleeves rolled to the elbows. On his feet he wore bright green flip-flops, and in his arms he held a Scottie dog. Another danced around at his feet.

"Miss Caldwell? Mr. Perone?" he asked.

"Yes." Emme nodded and the man stepped back into the foyer.

"Jack Gardner." He put the dog down on the carpet and shook their hands in turn. The dog wagged a greeting with his entire body. "Come on in. I was just having some coffee and scones. Join me, why don't you?"

They followed him to a bright room at the back of the house that overlooked lush gardens. He gestured to the table, which was already set. "Have a seat. Iced tea? Coffee?"

"Iced tea would be fine, thanks," Emme told him.

"Same for me, thanks," Nick said.

Jack Gardner poured and passed the glasses around, then raised a plate of pastries and asked, "Scones?"

When they both declined, he said, "I hope you don't mind if I do. I look forward to the mornings down here, when the house is quiet, the kids are who knows where, and the phone isn't ringing. I love my work, but I sure do love a little time off." He fixed himself a cup of coffee, then leaned back in his seat and said, "So what can I do for Robert Magellan?"

"Actually, we're here for the Mercy Street Foundation," Emme told him.

The congressman frowned. "I had a call from Robert Magellan's office yesterday. I was under the impression that I was to meet with two of his people."

"Robert set up the foundation," Emme explained, "and he funds it, so yes, we're his people."

"His foundation to look for missing persons or whatever." Jack Gardner nodded as if recalling. "It got a good deal of press not too long ago. Interesting concept. Of course, it helps to have that kind of money. Not so many people do anymore. But what does this have to do with me? I'm not missing anyone." He smiled as if he'd made a joke.

"Congressman Gardner, I don't know exactly how to ask you this," Emme began. Then she hesitated long enough for him to say, "Please. Whatever it is, it can't be worse than what I get thrown at me in my press conferences. Go ahead. Just ask."

"Sir, are you familiar with a fertility clinic called Heaven's Gate?"

He stared at her blankly for a long moment. "Is that the place near Mount Penn?"

"Yes."

He nodded. "I went to law school there, you know."

"We know."

Jack Gardner rubbed his chin. "What's all this about, Miss Caldwell?"

"Congressman Gardner, did you ever hear the term 'donor siblings'?"

He shook his head. "No, I don't believe I have. But I have a feeling you're going to explain it to me."

She did.

"Donor siblings, eh? That's a new one on me. What is it these kids want?"

"They know who their mothers are, they know their mothers' families. But for some of them, half the picture isn't enough. They want the other side of the picture filled in as well. They want to feel complete."

"They want to know who their father is."

"Yes, sir."

"So what you want to know is, am I your Donor 1735?" He touched his napkin to the corners of his mouth. "That's what you're asking me. Otherwise, you wouldn't be here."

"Yes. That's what I'm asking you, Congressman."

"I guess you can find out easily enough," he said, "so there's no point in me trying to deny it. Yes, I did in fact make several donations to Heaven's Gate back when I was in law school."

He took a pack of cigarettes from his shirt pocket. "I know, I know. Nasty business, this smoking. Can't seem to break the habit. I've cut way back, but I just can't seem to cut it out completely. Back when my wife was still alive, I wouldn't dare light up in the house, but since she passed away—cancer, three years ago—there doesn't seem much of a reason not to. The kids aren't here so much these days, so most of the time, there's no one around to nag me."

He struck a match and lit a cigarette, then rose and opened a drawer in the sideboard. He returned with a small ashtray, which he placed on the table.

"So where was I?" He inhaled, then blew the smoke out slowly.

"You were saying you'd been to Heaven's Gate. . . ." Emme reminded him.

"Right. Kathleen and I were married when we were sophomores in college. By the time I got to law school, I had two children and not very much in the way of income. Several of the guys I knew were steady donors, doing it for the cash, and of course, the clinic liked to be able to brag about all the lawyer-goods they had to sell. Christmas rolls around, and I'm thinking, hey, why not? So when one of my buddies went, I went along with him, and it turns out to be easier than I thought it would be. We had a pretty decent Christmas that year, as I recall, and the rent was paid on time."

"So you made a few more donations."

"Right. You could say I was a steady contributor there for a while." He took another drag on the cigarette, then stubbed it out. "Look, I don't know what you think of it, and frankly, I don't care. I needed the money, it wasn't illegal, and while I'm not an especially altruistic person, it did occur to me that what I was doing might lead to something good in someone else's life. So if you think this is going to cause some kind of kerfuffle in the press . . ."

"Congressman, my only interest is in the children who were conceived by way of your donations."

"I never thought about them," he said matter-of-factly. "Never gave a thought to what might develop from those test tubes I filled up, frankly, until you showed up here and told me there were . . . how many did you say?"

"Ten that we know about."

"Ten kids." He smiled warily. "That's a hell of a lot of college tuition."

"They're not looking for you to ask you for anything. They're just looking for some . . ." Emme tried to recall Hayley's words. "Some connection. They were just hoping to find out who you are, what kind of a man you are."

"I like to think I'm a good man, Miss Caldwell. I didn't mean to sound callous a moment ago. But I haven't thought about Heaven's Gate in twenty years. It never occurred to me to think about having fathered any children other than the two I had with my wife. That might sound silly to you. After all, you could say, 'What did you think they were going to do with all that sperm, Jack?' " He shook his head. "It was a long time ago, and I haven't had cause to think about it since I left law school. I got a job with a good firm in Baltimore, and I never had to moonlight, as it were, again. It just wasn't something I thought about." He paused. "But I seem to remember some promise—some guarantee, actually—of anonymity from Heaven's Gate."

"The clinic didn't give out any information," Emme assured him. "The kids found a way to figure it out themselves."

"Really? How'd they do that?"

Emme explained the process.

"Seriously?" he said, in a manner that was both guarded and oddly proud. "Smart kids."

"Very." Emme agreed. "Congressman, in January, one of these kids went missing. Since Saturday, three more of your offspring—for want of a better word— have disappeared, one of whom has been confirmed dead."

"Three this week!" He pressed against the back of the chair as if he'd been shot. "Three? You mean, four, in all . . . four out of ten are missing? And one dead?"

"That's correct."

"What are the chances that these kids are runaways, or are on vacation, or are . . ."

Emme shook her head. "Henry Carroll-Wilson was found shot to death on Sunday morning, and his sister, Lori, is still missing."

"Maybe she shot him, have you thought of that?" He rose, agitated.

"No, sir." Emme could have told him that the detective investigating the case had, however. "One of the other girls went missing two nights ago from a field hockey camp. These aren't runaways, and they aren't the kind of kids who'd shoot one another in cold blood, sir. Someone is targeting these kids, and the only connection between them appears to be you."

"If you're trying to connect me to all this somehow, I can give you the names of fifty people who will tell you I was at my yacht club on Saturday. Race during the day, dinner dance at night. This other girl disappeared when? Tuesday?"

When Emme nodded, he continued. "On Tuesday morning I took a small group of my colleagues on a fishing trip. We met at five in the morning and returned to the marina at four in the afternoon. We came back here and cooked up our catch. Several in the group stayed the night. The newspapers covered both events, by the way—the thing at the club and the fishing expedition."

He got up and left the room and returned within minutes with several newspapers under his arm. Wordlessly, he handed them to Emme and sat back while she skimmed the articles. When she was finished, she passed the papers off to Nick.

"Thank you," she said simply.

"I just thought I'd save you a little bit of time," he told her, "since I know you'd want to be seeing those photos for yourself."

"I appreciate it."

"Look, I don't know what happened to these kids. I won't say I don't care, because that wouldn't be completely true. You never like to hear stories like this. But I don't know them, I've never met them, never heard of them until just now, and at the risk of sounding cold, I don't need to meet them. They were the result of some biochemical reaction years ago, and despite whatever connection they might feel, I have to admit to feeling none whatsoever."

"I understand, sir. But I have to ask you to think back over the past few months. Are you sure no one contacted you, no one ever called alluding to being related to you in some way?"

"I'm positive. Believe me, I'd have remembered something like that. But there's been nothing. The first I've heard of any of this was when you showed up here today." He stood and pushed his chair back. "Now, if there's anything else I can do for you, I'm due on the golf course in about twenty minutes."

Clearly dismissed, Emme and Nick both stood.

"Should you hear from any of these kids . . ."

"You're the first person I'll call." He ushered them toward the door. "Actually, you'll be the only person I'll call."

One of the Scotties appeared out of nowhere and accompanied them to the front of the house. When they reached the door, Emme reached in her bag and pulled out one of her new business cards. She held it out to Gardner and he took it, and without looking at it, dropped it on a long table that held a crowd of photographs.

"Your children?" Emme noticed that most of the pictures were of a boy and a girl.

He nodded. "My daughter. My son."

"Your daughter's lovely," she said, leaning closer for a better look. "Look, Nick, how pretty the congressman's daughter is."

"Yes, she is." He agreed. "Very pretty."

They stepped out onto the shaded porch and down

the steps to the sand-and-shell drive, but Gardner did not follow. He stood on the top step and watched them, looking like a man who knew that something was about to change his life, something he wasn't going to like, and he was powerless to stop it.

TWENTY-FOUR

He heard her on the steps and in the hall, knew she was now standing in his doorway, but didn't bother to turn around.

"What?" he asked.

"You have a problem."

"Yeah? What?"

She crossed the carpeted floor to his desk and slid something under his nose. He glanced sideways, studying it, then raised his eyes to meet hers.

"Where did that come from?"

"It was on the table in the front hall." Hand on hip, she stood as if waiting for his response. When one didn't come, she poked him in the back and said, "You have a problem. What are you going to do about it?"

"*I* have a problem?" He snorted and spun around in his chair. "*We* have a problem. This is just as much me as it is you."

"You have got to be kidding." She scoffed and flipped her hair over her shoulders. "I haven't raised a finger. . . ."

"Who are you kidding? This was all your idea." He

stood and faced her down. "Who found the folder in his desk drawer? Who did all the research on this donor sibling stuff? Whose idea was it to go online and see if anyone was looking for Donor 1735?"

"Whose idea was it to eliminate the competition?" She lowered her voice. "What did you do with them, J.J.? Before you killed them, I mean? Did you play with them? Did you rape them?"

He turned away from her, feeling the hot flush rise up above his collar.

"You did, didn't you?" She smirked. "You had sex with your own half sisters. You're a disgusting, perverted—"

"They're not our half sisters." He grabbed her by the arm and squeezed it. "Do not dignify what they are."

"Did you tell them that while you were putting it to them?" She was still smirking, even though he knew his grip must be hurting her arm. "Did you make it clear to each of them that you were *not* fucking your sister?"

"Don't make me hurt you," he said. "And don't pretend that your hands are clean in all this. We have a legacy to protect, a name that used to mean something, and don't ever forget that. Besides, don't pretend for one minute that you'd be happy about having to share all geat-grandmother Gardner's china and silver with all your *half* sisters."

She yanked her arm away and took a step back. "So what do we do now?"

He shrugged and sat back in his chair at his desk. "You tell me. You're the idea person. I'm just the grunt who carries out your every whim."

"Stop it, J.J." She exhaled and looked almost defeated for a moment.

He knew better. His sister—his *real* sister—was never to be counted out.

"The investigator has been here. She talked to Dad."

"How do you know he talked to her?"

"I found that card on the table when he was leaving just now. When I asked him about it, he said she was someone who was looking for a missing person that she thought he might know something about." She sat on the edge of his bed. "He said it was a conversation for another time because he was in a hurry and didn't want to miss his tee time."

"You really think he's going to explain how he got his rocks off years ago for a little cash, and how all those chickens scattered up and down the east coast are coming home to roost?"

"I didn't press him. The important thing is that she knows that Dad is Donor 1735. How do you suppose she figured it out?"

"Easy. One of the donor-sibling boys gave Belle some of their DNA." With a few strokes on the keyboard, he pulled up Emme's email asking who the DNA donor was. "Read it and weep."

He turned the screen in her direction.

"Swell," she muttered after she'd finished reading. "That's just swell. Who do you think it was?"

"My first guess would have been Henry."

"Well, then, let's just email Henry and ask him . . . oh, right." She snapped her fingers. "We can't. You killed him. I guess we'll have to go to plan B."

"Very funny. He and Lori were going to meet

Emme Caldwell and Belle's uncle. They would have told them everything they knew."

"Who are you kidding?" The smirk was back. "You have no idea what they knew or what they didn't know. You just wanted to get your hands on Lori."

She leaned closer and whispered in his ear. "Was she worth it? Was she that good?"

"Actually," he whispered back, "she was."

She rolled her eyes. "So how many are left?"

"The twins and Hayley." He held up three fingers, then he added two more, and grinned. "And Ava and Justin."

"Leave Hayley alone." Her eyes went hard.

"We'll see."

"No, she's just a kid, J.J. You leave her out of this."

"And when she figures out she's the last man standing? Then what?"

"You leave that to me. But you give me your word, you don't touch her."

"Fine." He held up both hands as if in surrender. "Hayley's untouchable. Not that I would have. As you say, she's just a kid. I really do have some standards, you know."

"Right. I seem to recall those *standards* going right out the window when it came to Jessica. She wasn't much older than Hayley."

"Jessica looked like she was twenty." He waved her off.

"Yeah, well, that's what started this whole mess. You couldn't keep it in your pants, and the next thing I know, you're coming back from Florida with a dead girl in the trunk of your car."

"She was the one who insisted that we get together," he reminded her. "I wouldn't have thought of—"

"Spare me. You couldn't wait to get your hands on her once you saw her picture."

"She was pretty hot, you have to admit."

"I bailed you out of that one. Now I'm wondering if I should have."

He laughed out loud. "I have to admit, 'My dad just got transferred to France and we're moving to Paris' was a pretty good cover. Which of course would not have worked if I hadn't brought her laptop back with me so that she could occasionally check in with the group."

"That's quite a collection you've got, isn't it? Jessica's, Belle's, Lori's."

"And Ali's. Don't forget Ali's. You have to admit, they've come in real handy." He smiled. "It's sort of my version of keeping my friends close and my enemies closer."

She pushed at his chest and walked to the door. "When you get serious about figuring out what we do next, you let me know."

"I already have it figured out," he told her calmly. "Sit yourself back down and listen. I'm going to need you to set this up. . . ."

TWENTY-FIVE

"Okay, what was the first thing you noticed about that photograph of Gardner's daughter?" Emme turned to Nick as soon as they were in the car.

"That the silver frame it was in was probably worth more than your car?"

"Funny man." She turned the key in the ignition. "Who did she look like?"

He thought it over. "Like Belle. Hayley. And the picture Ali sent us of Lori."

"And the son. He reminded me of one of the other boys. The first thing I'm going to do when we get back to the office is pull up those photos on my laptop."

"Well, one thing you can say for the guy, his gene pool is pretty damn consistent. There is a resemblance among those kids. But what did you think of him? Do you think he was telling the truth?"

"I do. I think he was totally caught off guard about the whole thing. I think he really expected us to be envoys of some sort from Robert, and I think this was the first he's heard about these kids looking for him. I believed him when he said he did it for the money and then promptly forgot about it. I don't think he ever spent two seconds wondering what might come from all those donations he made way back then."

"So you don't think he's involved in Belle's disappearance?"

"No, I don't. I know you were hoping we'd find the answer in that house, but everything tells me the man knew nothing about all this until we told him."

"Did you think his reaction was strange? About the kids disappearing?"

"No, I think it was spot-on for a man in his position. Look, something he did twenty or so years ago, with little or no thought to its consequences beyond the obvious financial benefit—except maybe to do something good for someone else, someone like your sister, for example, who wanted a child—has just come back, big time, into his world. I'm sure he was shocked to hear about the kids getting together and trying to find him, and I'm sure he was shocked to hear that so many of them have disappeared. But he's a man of considerable means and stature. He's not going to open his doors to these kids. He's going to stay as removed as possible, and frankly, I don't know that I blame him."

She turned onto Route 50 and headed for the bridge.

"He has a lovely family and a high-profile career to protect. He's going to protect those things. But my gut tells me he didn't know about any of this until we told him."

"So where do we go from here?" Nick asked.

His phone rang before she could respond. "Hold that thought," he said as he answered it. A minute later, he hung up and asked, "What number should I call to get Robert on the phone?"

"You can use the same number you call for me, then when it asks you for an extension, just put in R-O-B."

"Give me the number again, please."

While he tapped in the number, she slanted a glance in his direction. He caught her eye and said, "I located a car that Robert might want to look at."

She smiled. If she knew Robert as well as she thought she'd come to know him, Robert would want to look *now*.

Listening to Nick's side of the conversation proved her right. Once he completed the call, he turned to her and said, "Robert wants to see the car first thing tomorrow. To say he sounded enthused would be an understatement." He put his phone back into his pocket and leaned back against the seat.

"Where's the car you're going to look at?"

"Indiana. Robert said he'd line up a plane if I can make the arrangements with the owner." He smiled. "It must be nice."

"I heard he has his own plane. No surprise. He can afford it. He doesn't seem to travel a whole lot, though. Mostly stays around the house or does things with Kevin. Father Kevin, his cousin. They golf and stuff like that."

"It must be tough, losing your wife and child. Not knowing."

"He may never know," she told him. "I think it's going on two years since they disappeared. That's not good. After a certain amount of time has passed, it's unlikely—"

She stopped, biting back the words before they could leave her mouth.

"It's all right, Emme. I know the odds about finding Belle. I just hope we can get to the bottom of it."

"Me, too. For both your sakes."

He glanced over at her and in response to his unasked question, she added, "Yours and Belle's."

.

"I can't remember when I last saw Robert so excited about anything." Trula wandered into Emme's office around lunchtime the following day. "He just called a few minutes ago; they're on their way home. He bought this car Nick found for him and he sounded so happy. He said that Nick is going to fix it for him."

Emme smiled. "Restore." She corrected Trula as Nick had corrected her. "Nick would tell you that he restores cars, he doesn't fix them."

"Whatever he's going to do to it, Robert is just so enthused. It's good to see him interested in something again. Even if it is just a car. He's been at such loose ends for so long now."

"It was nice of you to send them off with such a great breakfast this morning." Emme put her pen down and turned from her computer. "Even nicer of you to have made enough for the rest of us, too."

"Well, I couldn't very well have fed the three of them and not the three of you growing girls—Suse, Mal, and yourself." Trula draped herself over the back of one of the wing chairs near Emme's desk. "I know that Kevin likes bacon with his eggs, and I know that Robert likes pancakes, so it made sense to keep them both happy. Your Nick seemed to like everything."

"He's not my Nick." Emme averted her eyes and turned back to her laptop.

"Well, he's the Nick who's involved in that case of yours. He's what we used to call a handsome devil."

When Emme didn't respond in any way, Trula sat in the chair. "Don't you think he's a good-looking boy?"

"Very." Emme pretended to read her email.

"Nice, too. Polite. Chloe sure likes him a lot. She told me all about the trip to the zoo. I'll bet she didn't leave out one second of the day. Said he took you both out to dinner on the way back and promised to take her to one of those amusement parks where they have all the wild animals roaming around." Trula smiled. "She also said he came back to your room and—"

"He came back to the hotel with us so he could carry Chloe upstairs. She fell asleep over dinner."

"No need to be so defensive, Emme."

"I just wouldn't want you to think that . . ."

"Why? You're a lovely young woman, and he's . . . well, we've already established what he is. And Chloe likes him. What's the problem?"

"The problem is that Chloe likes him." Emme gave up. When Trula wanted to talk about something, damn it, you were going to *talk*. "Look, since I adopted Chloe, I've made it a point to not get involved with anyone."

"Are you telling me you haven't had a date in four years?" Both of Trula's eyebrows rose almost to her hairline.

"No, I'm not saying that. I'm saying I haven't gotten involved with anyone in particular because I didn't want her to get attached to someone who wasn't going to be around."

"Don't go so fast. You haven't met anyone you liked in four years?"

"I've met a couple of guys that I liked over the past few years, yes."

"But you didn't give any of them a chance because you were afraid your daughter might like them?"

"Not that she might like them, but that she might get used to having someone around, and then when they weren't, it would be hard for her."

"Why did you assume none of these men would care enough about you to stay?"

When Emme didn't answer, Trula said, "That's the real issue, kiddo. At least as I see it."

Emme's throat constricted, and she wanted nothing more than for Trula to leave, but the woman made no move toward the door. Choosing her words carefully, Emme said, "I didn't have a very stable childhood. I want better for Chloe."

"Understandable. Admirable, even. But don't assume that everyone is going to leave you, Emme." Trula stood and brushed a tiny bit of flour from her sleeve. "There are people in this world who will love you, who will care about you, who will stand by you and who will not let you down, no matter what. I think that's something Chloe already knows. It seems to me that you could learn a little something from her."

When Emme finally composed herself enough to

turn around, Trula was gone, and her phone was ringing.

"Oh, shit," she muttered as she wiped her eyes. Clearing her throat, she answered the call.

"Is this Miss Caldwell?" a young woman's voice asked.

"Yes. Who's this?"

"This is Ava, Miss Caldwell."

"Ava . . ."

"Yes. I've been away at school and really tied up with work at the end of the semester. I read your emails—I know you're looking for Belle. I was so sorry to hear that she's been missing."

"Unfortunately, she's not the only one."

"Hayley called me. She told me about Henry, Ali, and Lori disappearing. I know it has something to do with our donor, with Donor 1735. I know Belle figured out his identity," Ava said, her voice choked with emotion. "I never should have let her contact him on her own. I should have followed my instincts and—"

"Wait, Ava. Are you saying that Belle was in contact with Congressman Gardner?"

"You know it's him, then?"

"Yes. Are you telling me that Belle contacted him?"

"She did. And now she's missing. And Henry is dead and Lori and Ali are who knows where." She sobbed. "I can never forgive myself for not being more involved in this. I really didn't think these kids would be able to figure out who he was. If only I'd . . ."

"Why do you think you could have changed things?"

"Because I'm older, and supposed to be wiser. I

should have just taken this on myself. I would have approached him in a different way. I would have done a lot of things differently, and my sisters wouldn't be missing. Henry wouldn't be dead."

"You know, the police investigating Henry's death don't believe it's connected to any of this. They don't believe that Lori's disappearance has anything to do with Belle being gone."

"Really?" Ava paused. "I would have thought they'd want to investigate the similarities. Especially with Ali being gone now."

"It makes no sense to me, either."

"The reason I called is I'm going to go talk to Congressman Gardner. I was wondering if maybe you'd come with me."

"I already met with him, Ava. He denies knowing about the donor siblings and he made it quite clear he had very little interest in meeting any of you. I'm sorry, I know that isn't what you want to hear."

"I don't think it matters to me whether he's interested in meeting us or not. I need to see him. I need to ask him about Belle."

"Why are you so certain that she contacted him?"

"Because the night of that art museum get-together, she drove down to his house to talk to him."

"How do you know that?"

"She told me she was going. I wasn't able to make it to Philadelphia that day, so I called her later in the afternoon. She was in her car, on her way to Maryland. She told me she had his address and was going to his house to talk to him."

"Was he expecting her?"

"No, I think she was going to surprise him."

"So you don't know if she actually spoke with him."

"No, but I'm going to find out."

"Ava, if you've known this all this time, why didn't you tell someone?"

"Because, like I said, I was off the board most of this year because of school. I'm working on a doctorate in education, and most of the time, my head is spinning, there's so much work to do. I wasn't aware that Belle was missing until recently."

"If you knew Donor 1735's identity, why didn't you follow up with Belle to find out if she met with him?"

"For one thing, I didn't really care about him. I have a father, Miss Caldwell. I come from a very happy and secure home. I had no interest in this man just because he happened to donate sperm to my mother. I feel no connection to him whatsoever. I don't feel that I have any right to intrude in his life and I don't want him in mine."

"So why are you going to speak with him now?"

"Because three of my sisters are missing, and one of my brothers is dead."

"You feel a connection to them even though you feel no such connection to him."

"Yes," Ava said, after a moment's hesitation.

"Ava, Congressman Gardner has assured me that he knew nothing about the children who were born as a result of his sperm donation."

"I would like him to look me in the eye and tell me that."

"He's agreed to see you?"

"Yes."

Emme sighed. "When are you planning on meeting with him?"

"In about three hours. I'm on my way there now."

"That's about how long it would take me to get there." Emme looked at the clock. It was already one.

"I know it's an imposition, but I'd just feel safer if you were there. It would be more official, since you're investigating Belle's disappearance, and since you're a cop or something and you probably carry a gun."

"Ava, I'm a private investigator, not a cop. I don't carry a gun, and even if I did, I wouldn't go into the home of a state congressman with a concealed weapon. If you're worried about him, why not call the police?"

Ava laughed. "Miss Caldwell, he's a congressman, and I'm a grad student from Boston. Besides, what would I say that wouldn't backfire on the other kids if he really doesn't know anything about Belle, and the others really want to meet with him?"

When Emme didn't immediately respond, Ava added, "Besides, I need a little moral support. I've never grilled a congressman before."

"All right. I see your point. And I understand why you'd rather have someone with you, so yes, I'll be there. I should be able to get there by four if I leave now."

"Super. Thanks, Miss Caldwell. I really appreciate it."

Emme hung up the phone. She would have to leave within the next fifteen minutes. She slipped her feet back into the sandals she'd earlier kicked off and grabbed her bag and went directly to the kitchen.

"Trula," she called, as she came through the swinging door from the back hallway.

"She ran to the store," Susanna told her. "Are you joining me for lunch?"

"No, I have to run out for a few hours and I won't get back till later tonight. I was hoping to ask Trula if she'd pick up Chloe for me at school at five and let her hang out here until I get back."

"One of us will get Chloe, and I'm sure Trula will be delighted to spend some time with her."

Emme grabbed a banana from the fruit bowl Trula left on the counter for them and calculated how long she thought she'd be. If she left now and made good time, she could be there by four. She wouldn't stay more than an hour at the congressman's house—he made it pretty plain that he only has so much to say and when he's done, the conversation is over. She doubted he'd have much to say to Ava, so an hour would be generous. Traffic permitting, she shouldn't be too late. "I think I should be back between eight and nine. Chloe can curl up on one of the sofas in the family room if she gets sleepy."

"That one never gets sleepy when she's around Trula, haven't you noticed that? The two of them are like peas and carrots, as Forrest Gump would say."

"Tell Trula I'll give her a call when I'm on my way home."

"Sure. Don't worry about Chloe. We'll take good care of her," Susanna assured her.

"Thanks. I'll see you later, Suse." Emme hurried out the back door and headed for her car. Nick's Firebird was parked right next to hers and she paused, thinking maybe she should leave a note for him.

They'd talked about dinner tonight, and she didn't want him to think she was standing him up. She'd been looking forward to spending some time with him, but she knew he'd understand. She'd call him from the car and explain. Maybe he'd even wait for her.

She got into her car and took off. The last thing she felt like doing was driving to Ballard again, but if something happened to Ava while she was at Gardner's house, she'd never forgive herself. Besides, if Gardner had been lying to her, she wanted to know. Her instincts had told her he'd been truthful, but if she was losing her touch, she wanted to be the first to know about it.

Mallory rubbed her eyes and searched the pile of applications for her misplaced reading glasses. Had she had them on earlier when she went down to the kitchen? She couldn't remember. But they weren't on the desk and they weren't in her bag, and they had to be somewhere. Besides, it gave her an excuse to go down to the kitchen and see what was cooking. Literally. She'd bet on vegetable soup and lemon squares but she could be wrong.

"Oh, look who's here." Mallory smiled when she saw Chloe on a chair at the sink. "Are you helping Trula, Chloe?"

"Uh-huh. I'm helping Trula clean up. But I'm not Chloe."

"You aren't?"

Chloe shook her head, no.

"You look just like Chloe Caldwell, but if you're someone else, who are you?" Mallory asked.

"My name is Nancy Drew," Chloe said without turning around.

"Nancy Drew is the name of a famous girl detective." Mallory tried not to smile.

"I know. Like my mommy."

"I think Nancy Drew was a little older than you, though." Mallory helped herself to a lemon square and sat at the table.

"Trula told me. She's going to read one of the books for me 'cause I can't read yet."

"Well, they're certainly fun books. I read them all when I was younger. Maybe not quite as young as four, though."

"Chloe has very sophisticated tastes." Trula winked at Mal.

"*Nancy* does," Chloe corrected her. "*Nancy* has . . . what you said."

"Oh, to be four again. It must be fun to just change your name whenever you feel like it." Mal looked beyond the little girl to Trula.

"You don't have to be four," Chloe told her. "Grown-ups can change their names, too. My mommy changed her name."

"You mean, from Emily to Emme? That's sort of shortening her name, like a nickname." Mallory licked confectioners' sugar from her fingers.

"No, her name wasn't Emily. It was Ann." Chloe held up her soapy hands and squished them together.

"Ann Caldwell?" Mallory tried to remember if the application had shown Emily or Ann as a middle name.

"No, Ann Nolan."

"Ann Nolan?" Mallory looked across the room at Trula, who'd turned to stare at Chloe.

"Uh-huh. She changed it before we left California. She liked Emme Caldwell better and she said that sometimes you can change your name if you want to, if you find one you like better. I change mine all the time." She turned and grinned at Mallory. "So you could have a new name too, if you wanted."

"I think I'll go upstairs and . . . think about that." Mallory was still looking at Trula. "I'll be in my office . . . looking up names, Trula."

Trula nodded but appeared too confused to speak.

Mallory couldn't get to her computer quickly enough. She entered Ann Nolan into Magellan Express and waited for the information to be retrieved. She watched in horror as pictures of Silver Hill, California, police officer Ann Nolan came onto her screen. The woman she knew—the woman they all knew—as Emme Caldwell was identified in caption after caption as Ann Nolan.

She read every article, then sat with her head in her hands. Who was this woman really? What was she hiding? Why had she lied?

And what were they going to do about it?

TWENTY-SIX

Well, you boys look like you had a fun day," Trula said as Robert, Kevin, and Nick filed through the back door.

"We had a great day." Robert kissed her on the cheek as he passed by, causing her eyebrows to rise. "I found my car, Trula. The car I've been coveting for years."

"Well, that's nice." Trula turned back to the sink where she'd been cutting the stems off some flowers she'd just brought in.

"Hi, Mal," Robert said as Mallory came into the room.

"Hi. Um . . . Robert, could I have a word with you?" Mallory asked.

"Sure. What's up?" He went to the refrigerator and opened the door. To Nick and Kevin he said, "Iced tea, guys?"

"Yes, thanks." Kevin got out glasses. "Nick?"

"No, thanks," Nick said. All he really wanted was to see Emme.

"Privately." Mallory stood in the doorway, her arms crossed over her chest.

"What's going on, Mal? Problem?" Robert persisted.

"It's business, Robert."

"Sorry, Mal," Robert said as he poured tea into two glasses. "I'm just so stoked about this car. I'll be with you in a minute." He turned to Trula. "You know, Prince Charles has a car like this one, only he had his converted to running on bioethanol fuel. He has it specially made from surplus wine."

"Is that true?" Trula asked, and Robert assured her it was.

"I don't see Emme's car." Nick looked out the back window, feeling a bit awkward. There was obviously something going on that Mallory didn't want to discuss in front of him. "Did she go somewhere?"

"Actually, you just missed her," Trula told him. "She left about forty minutes ago."

"Do you know how long she'll be?" he asked. "I was hoping to say hi while I was here."

"She's planning on being awhile, wherever she went. Suse said she'd need one of us to pick up Chloe from school."

"Oh." He hadn't realized just how much he'd been looking forward to seeing her. "Well, I guess I'll be getting back to my shop. Robert, thanks for a fun day. My first time in a private plane. I could get used to it."

"Hey, anytime you get a lead on a car like that one, we're in." Robert slapped Nick on the back. "Seriously. That Aston-Martin is a dream come true for me."

"In its present condition, that might be a stretch,

Robert." Nick grinned. "But we'll see what we can do for you."

"I can't wait." Robert shook his hand, and Nick said his good-byes to Trula and Kevin.

Nick went out to his car and rolled down the windows, thinking how nice it might be to have a new car with all the most up-to-date features like automatic windows and air-conditioning that blew really cold. He might have to break down one of these days and look into picking up something with air bags and antilock brakes. There was something to be said about the latest safety features.

He turned the Firebird around and drove toward the gates, waving to the guard as he passed by. He drove slowly and dialed Emme's phone.

"Hey," he said when she answered.

"Hey, yourself. How'd the great car search go?" she asked.

"Today Robert joined the ranks of classic car owners. He's a very happy man. I'm thinking if you're going to ask for a raise or a day off, today might be a good day to do it," Nick replied.

"We'll see what kind of a mood he's in when I get back there. I'm on my way to meet Ava at Congressman Gardner's home."

"Wow. There's a pitch out of the blue. How'd that happen?"

"Ava called and said she wanted to talk to Gardner about his donor status, and asked me to be there with her. She said she thought my presence might make the meeting more official, and that she'd feel safer if I was there."

"Safer?" Nick frowned. "Safer from whom? Gardner? He didn't seem like much of a threat to me."

"I agree, but she told me an entirely different story than the one we got from him. According to Ava, Belle told her that she had identified Gardner as Donor 1735 and that she was on her way to meet with him when she left the art museum in January."

"What?"

"She said that she spoke with Belle while Belle was driving to Maryland, that Belle was going to Gardner's house to try to talk to him. When Ava didn't hear from Belle, she just figured Gardner wasn't home when she got there and that Belle just continued on back to school. Ava said she's been busy at school and figured that Belle was, too. Until she saw my emails, she wasn't aware that Belle's been missing all this time."

"She didn't try to contact Belinda at all?"

"It's the same thing we've heard from all these kids, Nick. They get busy with their own lives, they back off for a while, they resurface when things are less hectic for them. Ava said she hadn't heard from Belle, but on the other hand, she hadn't been in contact with any of the others during that time, either."

"So she doesn't know if Belinda ever spoke with Gardner."

"No, and it's my guess she did not. I really thought he was being up front with us the other day."

"So you said." Nick fell thoughtful for a moment. "Any chance you're wrong about that?"

"There's always a chance that I'm wrong. But I'm pretty good at reading people. I didn't believe he was lying at the time, and I still don't."

"Hey, you know, Ballard is only a little more than an hour away from me. Maybe we could meet somewhere and have dinner. I know a couple of really great seafood places on the bay."

"I'd love that. I don't expect to be with Gardner for too long. We both know the congressman doesn't have a problem pulling the plug when he's said what he has to say."

"True enough. So what do you think, maybe a half hour there?"

"I doubt he'd give Ava any more time than that," Emme said. "He made it pretty clear the other day that he doesn't have any interest in these kids."

"I know a great little place we can meet. It's maybe a half hour from Ballard."

"Perfect."

"Call me when you get to Gardner's, and I'll know how much time I have to get there."

"Will do. I should be there by four, so I should be leaving by about four thirty, probably no later than four forty-five. Do you think we should invite Ava to join us?"

"No. I want to see you, spend some time alone, public though it may be."

"Sounds good. I was just trying to be nice, anyway."

"You are being nice. You're driving three hours to keep her company. I'll see you later." Nick hung up, smiling. He knew it would be only dinner—she did have Chloe waiting for her—but even that was fine. He wanted to see her, wanted to be with her. They'd spent some time together since the day at the farm, but neither of them had spoken about what had happened between them. There'd been things he'd wanted to say, words that had just never made their way out of his mouth. He was hoping to do better tonight.

He turned on the radio hoping for inspiration. The best he could find was a station that played love ballads from the fifties and sixties. He sang along all the way to Khoury's Ford.

He stopped at Automobilia to look over the mail and to check on what the other mechanics had done while he was gone. He finished making his rounds in the garage and looked up at the large wall clock over the door into the office. It was four thirty. He checked his phone for missed calls but none showed on the screen. Frowning, he dialed her number. She should have been there by now. Actually, according to her timetable, she should be leaving Gardner's by now. Had she simply forgotten to call? Or had he misunderstood? Had she said she'd call when she was leaving Gardner's?

Emme didn't pick up his call, so he left a message that he was going to head over to the restaurant and gave her driving directions, then drove there himself. When he arrived at five fifteen and she still hadn't called, he called her again.

Once again, the call went to voice mail. He got out of his car and walked to the end of the parking lot and back again. He pulled out his cell phone, scrolled down his contact list until he found the main number for the foundation, and called. Then he waited while the directory went through the staff names and extensions. He punched in the number for Robert, and waited, not confident that the call would be picked up. When Robert answered, he was caught off guard.

"Robert, it's Nick. I really didn't expect to get through to you but I'm glad I did."

"I'm usually not in my office at this hour but something's come up." Robert sounded distracted.

"I'm sorry to bother you. I was just wondering if you'd heard from Emme." Nick explained the situation.

"No, but let me ask." He put his hand over the phone and spoke with someone in the background. "No, no one's heard from her."

"Maybe I should drive down there and see if she ever arrived." Nick thought aloud.

"I can tell you if she's there," Robert said, "if that would help."

"How can you do that? She isn't answering her phone."

"She doesn't have to for me to track it. The phones we had designed for the foundation have GPS in them."

"I thought most cell phones had GPS."

"A lot of them do. But ours have a system I can track on the computer myself. Hold on, Nick, let me see what I can do."

Moments later, Robert came back on the line. "I have her at 38 Pond Drive, Ballard, Maryland."

"That's it. So she is there."

"Is there a problem, Nick?"

"Probably not. Thanks, Robert. Sorry to have bothered you." Nick hung up and walked back to the car. He was feeling antsy, unsettled, and wasn't sure why.

Maybe things hadn't gone so smoothly with Congressman Gardner after all. Maybe he should drive down to Ballard and just see for himself what was keeping her. He debated. If all was well, Emme might not appreciate him inviting himself to the party.

But if all was well, why hadn't she called?

·

Mallory sat across the desk from Robert and studied his face. In the time she'd worked for him, she'd never seen him so confounded.

"You're telling me that Emme Caldwell isn't Emme Caldwell," he said, as if he had trouble understanding the words. "Emme isn't Emme, she's really someone named Ann Nolan?"

"Yes. That's what I'm telling you."

"And you are absolutely, 100 percent positive of this."

"I wouldn't have come to you if I wasn't certain, Robert."

"But she's still a cop, right?"

"Yes, she was a police officer in California."

"Have you spoken to her former department about this?"

"I tried to," Mallory told him, "but the chief of police is on vacation this week and I really didn't want to discuss this with anyone else there."

"Why would she lie about who she is?" He frowned. "And how could she get the chief of police to lie for her?"

"I've been asking myself those very questions."

"I guess you're going to have to ask her point blank," Robert told her. "I guess we'll both have some questions for her when she gets back tonight. I want to know why she wasn't honest with us."

"Well, as far as I'm concerned, the *why* is almost immaterial. She gave us a false application, Robert. The real question is, what are we going to do about it?"

Anthony Navarro leaned against the fence rail and brushed the dirt from his hands before answering his ringing phone. He'd been out for his afternoon ride on his favorite horse and had just dropped the gelding off at the stable for one of the hands to cool down. Some of his compadres fussed over him because he took off on his own every day for thirty or forty minutes, but he paid them little mind. What was the point in being who he was if he was to be locked in this house or that—he owned several—and could never leave? Besides, he knew he had little to fear. He owned everyone between here and the US border.

"Yes?" He wasn't wary of answering this most private of phones. Only those closest to him knew the number. He checked the caller ID. It was his brother, Jesus.

"We got a call that you might be interested in," his brother said. "We have a tip on the girl."

"We've had a lot of tips. She's in Detroit. She's in Florida. She's gone to Canada. Last week she was seen on a beach in Costa Rica. So where is she this week?"

"Pennsylvania."

"Of course she is. If I'm going to run with the daughter of a dangerous man, I'd run to Pennsylvania, too."

"Seriously, Anthony. One of our friends was contacted by a cop from Silver Hill."

"The department Nolan worked for?"

"Yeah. He says she's changed her name and she's working for this Mercy place."

"What is that?"

"It's some like, company, that finds missing persons for free."

"They work for free?"

"Yeah. This rich dude, Robert Magellan, runs it."

"Robert Magellan?" That was a name Navarro knew. "Rich dude, for sure. This cop says Nolan is working for him?"

"Yeah. He said he intercepted a phone call about it."

"Magellan is like, one of the richest dudes in the country." Navarro began to walk to the house. "He probably has mad security."

"At his workplace and his house, sure. But she has to live someplace else, right? And kids are kids. She has to play sometime, has to go to school somewhere."

Navarro went through his front door and directly to his office and sat at his desk.

"What's the name of this place again?" he asked.

"Mercy Street Foundation."

"Give me a minute." He typed in the name and waited for the website to pull up.

"Here we go. Let's see what they have here. Staff bios . . . Robert Magellan . . . Susanna Jones . . . Mallory Russo . . ." Navarro laughed. "He's even got a priest on his staff. Is that for real?" He clicked on the icon for Father Kevin Burch. "Pastor, Our Lady of Angels . . . there's a picture of the church."

He went back to the staff page.

"Interesting. Only one member of the staff doesn't have a picture on line. Emme Caldwell."

"That's her. That's Nolan."

"You're sure of this."

"This cop that called, Whittaker, says it's her."

"What do we know about him? Whittaker?"

"He's helped us out from time to time," Jesus told him. "What do you want me to do, Anthony?"

"Nothing, bro. I'll take care of this myself. Thanks."

He hung up the phone and leaned back in his chair, staring at the ceiling. His first instinct was to send a squadron of thugs to Conroy, Pennsylvania, grab his daughter and this woman, Ann, Emme, whatever she was calling herself. But that would be stupid. Anthony Navarro was a lot of things. Stupid wasn't one of them.

He got up and walked to the window, thinking it through. The woman didn't matter. As much as he'd love to punish her for taking his only child and trying to hide her away—make this Ann Nolan regret the day she was born—he didn't have to take her to hurt her. He would simply leave her to live in the hell of knowing that the girl was gone and was going to stay gone, that she'd never see her again.

He turned his attention back to the website and

read, then reread every page until inspiration struck. When it did, he found himself grinning from ear to ear, overwhelmed by his own brilliance.

He was pretty sure he knew where to find his child, and who to send to bring her to him.

TWENTY-SEVEN

All Emme knew when she opened her eyes was that it was much later in the afternoon than it had been, and she had one bitch of a headache. She could hear voices from somewhere close by but her head hadn't cleared quite enough to figure out what was being said or by whom. She lay awkwardly on the ground and hoped the fog would begin to clear soon. She tried to move but her wrists were taped behind her and her ankles were taped together. There was tape across her mouth, which forced her to breath through her nose.

It took several moments for it to dawn on her where she was, and why she'd gone there. She remembered the conversation with Ava on the phone, the drive to Ballard. She'd parked the car next to a black Mercedes sedan, reached for her phone to call Nick, and from there things began to get fuzzy. She'd gotten out of the car, hadn't she? A young woman had been walking toward her, a smile on her face.

"I'm Ava," she'd said, her hand stretched out to Emme.

Had there been a sound behind her, something

she'd not been able to place? A smack to the back of the head—that she was certain of. Something hard that had driven her to her knees, and had flooded her mind with darkness.

The voices came closer, and she tried to focus her eyes on the approaching figures. The young woman, Ava—yes, the same one who'd earlier greeted her. Funny, Emme thought, one would think she'd be upset that Emme had been knocked cold and still lay upon the ground. Shouldn't she have called for the police or for an ambulance?

Apparently not.

And the young man with her . . . he was familiar in a way, yet Emme was certain she'd never seen him before. It took several moments for her to place him. He bore a strong resemblance to the twins, Will and Wayne, in the photo Ali had sent her, and he matched the description of the boy who'd followed Belle in the museum. Tall, blond, buff. But who was he, and why was he here?

". . . done with it now. I got her here for you. You do whatever it is you're going to do, but I don't want to know about it. I am out of here as of right now," the girl was saying.

"Oh, for God's sake, you're such a fucking wimp," the young man sneered. "What would you do if you didn't have me to do your dirty work for you?"

"Who are you kidding?" Ava stood with her hands on her hips. "You've loved every minute of this."

"True enough, sister dear." He pushed a shock of light hair back from his forehead. "Well, if you don't want to stick around for what comes next, I suggest you get on your way."

Emme heard the sound of jiggling keys and footsteps that passed close by. She closed her eyes, not wanting it to become apparent that she was awake and alert.

"Hey, did you check to see if she's armed?" The boy called after her.

"No, but she isn't. I asked her on the phone if she had a gun, and she said she wasn't a cop and wouldn't come here carrying one anyway."

"Rule number one: trust no one." He squatted next to Emme and ran his hands over her body. It was all she could do not to flinch or cringe with disgust.

"Where are you taking her?" Ava was in the Mercedes, the motor running.

"Same place I took the others. Only this time, I think we'll go by sea rather than by land."

"Where?"

"I thought you didn't want to know."

"I'm just curious."

"Remember that old Indian burial ground at the other end of the woods?"

"Where we used to look for artifacts? That's where you took them?"

There was no answer, but she could see his shadow. He was nodding his head, and Ava began to laugh.

"That's so gross. What if you dig up some old Indian bones? Aren't you afraid the spirits would come after you?"

"Well, since we never found any artifacts, I'm thinking there probably aren't any old bones, either. But hey, you never know," he replied, and it occurred to Emme that he sounded amused by the prospect. She heard the car creep closer.

"What are you going to do if someone comes looking for her?" Ava asked.

"Looking for who? No one's been here all day except me and my sister."

"What are you going to do with her car?"

"I'll take care of the car later. Now go, if you're going. Otherwise, feel free to watch. Maybe you should. You might like it."

The car shot past where Emme lay on the ground, and a moment later, the boy Ava had called J.J. was leaning over her.

"No one's out that long from a little tap on the head," he said, "so you can stop pretending, Emme Caldwell. I know you can hear me."

When she didn't reply, he pushed a thumb in her eye and pulled the lid back. When she blinked several times to focus on him, he smiled.

"That's better. Now, come on, work with me here. Let's get you up on your feet." He pulled her up by lifting under her arms. She let herself go limp, a dead weight, and he dropped her, letting her hit the ground like a sack. "I said, work with me, Miss Emme, unless you want me to have a go at you right here and now. I promise you, you won't like it once I begin, and once I do, I won't be able to stop. Now, when I lift you, I expect you to take your weight on your legs and feet . . . there you go. That wasn't so hard, was it?"

He leaned her up against the side of her car and pressed himself against her, his breath coming more quickly.

"You're hot, you know that? For an older woman,

that is. Not quite what I'm used to, but beggers can't be choosers and all that."

His teeth toyed with the tape at the side of her mouth, not enough to rip it off, but just enough to excite him.

Dear God, she thought, *what will happen to Chloe if I don't make it home tonight? This cannot be the end of me.*

She let him tease himself while she assessed the situation. What were the odds she could get him to remove the tape from her mouth? And once unfettered, where might her teeth do the most damage?

She felt herself being lifted, then hoisted over his shoulder. He began to walk without effort, as if her hundred and twenty pounds were of no consequence.

She tried to push her feet apart to test the strength of the tape that bound her ankles, but there was no give. She forced herself to take a few deep breaths. She'd have to keep her wits about her, and pray that she could keep herself alive long enough to figure out how to get out of this mess, or until Nick came looking for her. And he would look for her, of that she was certain. He knew where she was going, and he'd expected her to call once she got there. When he didn't hear from her, he'd know where to go. She could only pray he'd get there in time.

"We're taking a little boat ride, Miss Emme," he told her, as they rounded the side of the house and headed toward the water. "I do hope you aren't one to get seasick."

So much for the posse riding into town in time, she thought as he lifted her over the side of the boat and placed her on a seat near the motor.

"Now, in case you're thinking of escaping by throwing yourself over the side, I'd like to remind you that you'd find it real tough to swim with your hands and feet tied. But if you want to give it a go, hey, it's your life." He laughed as if he'd made a great joke.

Swell, she thought. *He thinks he's a comedian.*

She watched him closely, hoping to find some sign of weakness, searching for some way to gain an advantage. She felt certain that his intention was to rape her before he killed her, which meant that at some point, he'd take the tape off her ankles and free her legs. Between now and then, she'd have to figure out the best way to use them.

He tried to start the motor, but it failed to turn over the first time. He cursed under his breath and tried again.

She searched the seating area for something she might be able to use to cut the tape binding her wrists, but there didn't seem to be anything useful. There was a metal strip along the line where the top of the hull met the inner liner of the boat. She studied it, inch by inch, hoping to find a spot where the strip might be raised up and the metal accessible, but the boat was well maintained and there was nothing loose nearby.

The motor coughed.

"Well, we know we have fuel," he told her.

A few short bursts followed, then he pulled back on the throttle and the motor idled for a minute or so. He walked back to where she sat, his feet just far enough apart to give him balance, and for a split second, she thought about jamming her feet up between his legs, but she hadn't reacted quickly enough. He stepped to the side of the boat to untie the line, and pushed off from the dock.

He leaned over so that they were face-to-face. "Usually I just tell my passengers to hold on while we pull away and accelerate, but I guess we'll just have to depend on your sense of balance to keep you on that seat. I'll go nice and slow until you get the hang of it."

She muttered behind the tape and he laughed. "I'll take that as a thank you."

"Mmmmmmmmmmm."

"No need to be so effusive in your thanks, Miss Emme." He started back to the wheel, then stopped and turned back to her.

"Once we get to where we're going, I'll take the tape off your mouth. As long as you promise not to scream." He studied her face, and for a moment, his eyes bored into hers. She did not like what she saw.

He eased out of the lane and seemed to almost drift toward the center of the river before he pushed the throttle forward and sped up.

"Hold on," he called back to her, laughing at her struggles to remain upright.

She scanned both sides of the river for signs of life, but there were none: no other boats, no houses on either side, just woods, for the most part. She sat upright, the roar of the motor in her ears, and silently pleaded for just one chance to take him down.

The black Mercedes shot out of the end of Gardner's drive like a ball from the mouth of a cannon. Nick slowed the Firebird to get a look at the driver, then craned his neck to try to catch the number on the plate, but the car was moving too fast. He made a left onto that same lane and drove through the pine-lined drive until the house came into view. Emme's car was parked to the right, and he pulled up behind it and came to a stop.

When he got out of the car, the first thing he noticed was the quiet. The only sound was that of the stones and crushed shells crunching beneath his feet. He opened Emme's driver's-side door and leaned into the Honda. Her bag was on the front seat, her phone next to it, as if she'd taken it out to make a call. *Hopefully to me,* he thought.

Where was she?

There were no other cars in sight, but he walked up to the front door, which stood ajar by only an inch or so.

"Hello?" he called, as he stepped inside. "Anyone here?"

He made his way through the entire first floor, but there was no sign of life. He ran up the steps and quickly went from room to room, calling out, but the only sound was his own echoing footsteps.

Something was really wrong here.

Suddenly he heard what sounded like the sputtering motor of a boat that didn't really want to start. He went to the landing on the stairwell and looked out through an arched window that faced the back of the house. A stone patio surrounded a pool, and beyond that stretched a river that flowed into the bay several miles to the west. A dock ran along the edge of the property, and several boats were tied up. One was bobbing farther from the dock, and Nick shielded his eyes with his hand and squinted to take a good look. A man stood at the wheel, and a figure sat stiffly upright at the back of the boat. When the late day sun came through the clouds and the light danced off the back of the passenger's head, her identity was plain.

Who was driving, and where was he headed?

Nick ran down the steps and out through the front door, his phone in his hand, dialing 911. He reported his location and his suspicions as ran back to Emme's car. On the console was a release for the trunk, and his fingers found it quickly. Hadn't she once said something about carrying a handgun, not on her person, but in the trunk of her car?

Throwing the lid up, he searched quickly, and found what he was looking for wrapped in a blanket at the very back of the trunk. He pulled the blanket all the way out of the car and shook it, hoping to find some ammunition. A clip fell to the ground, and he picked it up and shoved it into the base of the gun. Cuffs that had been hidden in the blanket's folds fell out with a clunk and he stuffed them in his back pocket. He grabbed the tire iron for good measure, and took off for the water.

He was almost to the dock when the motor caught. The boat began to take off slowly before picking up speed. He jumped into the first boat he came to, praying he'd be able to start it without a key. He could hotwire a car with his eyes closed, but he'd never tried it with an outboard motor.

He fumbled at the wheel. There was no key. Was it even possible to start a boat's motor without one? He didn't have time to figure it out. He jumped to the next boat, and smiled when he saw the name on its motor. "Yamaha" said speed to him, and when he found the key in the ignition, he knew he'd made the right choice. Whoever was driving the other boat had a head start on him, and with Emme at risk, he needed as much horsepower behind him as he could get.

He untied the lines, then studied the controls. The lever standing upright would be the throttle. He wiggled it slightly and heard it click. That would be neutral, he thought. He pushed in on the key, and the engine cranked for several seconds before catching. He figured there should be something to shift gears with, and something to feed fuel to the engine, but there was only one lever. Maybe the throttle and the shift controls were on the same handle. He experimented and found that appeared to be the case, so he pulled back on the lever and allowed the motor to idle for a moment before giving it enough to pull away from the dock. He continued to let the throttle out, slowly at first, to get a feel for it. When he felt he had control, he pushed it gradually. He sure wished this thing came with instructions written where he could see them. He'd lost precious time figuring out how to start the damned thing, but he knew better than to jam the engine too quickly. Motors were motors, and once this one flooded, who knew how long it would be before he could get it started again?

Nick headed upriver, speed building along with his anxiety until he heard the motor up ahead. He was used to asphalt under the wheels, not water under the hull. He held his breath until he closed the distance between them enough to know for certain this was the right boat. Within minutes, he was close enough to read the boat's name: *Follow Me*.

You bet your ass I will.

As he drew closer, the driver of the other boat sped up. Nick drew more from his engine, not knowing if he had enough fuel to keep up or what his strategy should be.

What would he do if he was behind the wheel of a Viper, hot on the heels of a Porsche that he absolutely, positively had to stop?

He'd run the Porsche off the road.

Nick pulled to the left of the *Follow Me* and yelled to Emme to get down. At first, he wasn't sure she heard him, but there was no mistaking that she understood his intent when he eased the boat closer. She slid to the deck, and Nick got his first look at the man who, if he won this race, would take Emme from him forever.

The man at the wheel wore dark glasses and a Ravens cap, brim backwards, a dark red sleeveless T-shirt, cutoff jeans, and a sickening smile. Nick pulled the gun from his waistband and yelled over, "Slow down and head for shore or I'll shoot."

The man at the wheel laughed out loud, and gave his boat more juice. Nick kept up, but could feel his engine struggling. If the *Follow Me* went much faster, he'd likely outrun him. The bay lay up ahead, and even Nick knew that the small boat he was in probably wouldn't be a good match for the choppy waves of the Chesapeake.

His index finger on the trigger, Nick aimed as

steadily as he could, thinking he'd need to hit something on the boat that would hinder its performance. The truth of it was that he didn't know enough about boats to know where to do the most damage, short of hitting the driver. But an out-of-control boat—one with Emme in it—could be deadly.

The gun probably was not the best idea right now.

He stuck it back into his waistband and edged the boat more to the right. The driver of the other craft was still laughing, as if having the time of his life. Nick swung closer still, until the bows were less than five feet apart. The *Follow Me* put on more speed, and Nick knew he'd lose him if he didn't act quickly. With a quick twist of the wheel, he smacked into the side of the larger boat, and both vessels careened from the impact. The *Follow Me* rocked unsteadily, but maintained its speed. Nick took a deep breath, and drove the bow of his boat into the side of the other, trying to force it toward shore. Two more whacks and speed propelled the bow partially out of the water and in the direction of the gravelly river bank. Nick waited for the man in the cap to pull back on the throttle, but he never did. With his heart in his mouth, Nick watched the *Follow Me* barrel toward the shore. Right before it hit, the driver of the boat bailed over the side and disappeared into the dark water.

The *Follow Me* slammed onto the bank bow first in a sickening crash, the motor screeching when it hit the sand. Nick pulled up on his motor and steered toward land. The driver could drown for all he cared. He just wanted to get to Emme. When he was ten feet from the shore, he cut the engine and dove into the water. Almost immediately, something grabbed his legs and pulled him under.

The driver of the *Follow Me* was younger and stronger than he'd looked while standing at the wheel, but Nick was taller and equally strong. The two men battled for advantage under the water. Twice they broke the surface to gulp air, and twice they went back below. Finally, Nick was able to get a grip around his opponent's neck, and swam to land with his arm locked tightly around his throat. Gasping for breath, Nick struggled to drag the man with him to where the *Follow Me* had landed on its side.

"Emme!" he called, but there was no answer. With his free hand and with one good push with his foot, he righted the boat, and saw Emme on the stony beach. She moved awkwardly, and he realized her limbs were constrained. He found his pocket knife and cut the tape from her hands.

"You okay, Em?" He was still holding on to her abductor and wasn't about to give the bastard a bit of slack.

Emme swallowed hard and nodded, then screamed as she ripped the tape from her mouth. "Damn, that hurts!"

"Are you all right?" he asked again.

"I don't think anything's broken, but I think I'm going to be damned sore. Everywhere."

He handed her the knife and she cut the tape that wound around her ankles. She rubbed at her wrists, then wiped the blood from her cheek where the skin had torn away.

"I see you met J.J. Gardner. My, my, won't daddy be proud." She took a moment to catch her breath before grabbing the side of the boat and pulling herself up unsteadily. "J.J., meet Nick Perone. Belle's uncle."

J.J. glared.

"Your cuffs are in my back pocket," Nick told her. "Fish them out and you can have the honors."

She reached into his pocket and tugged at the cuffs. Nick turned J.J. around so she could snap them on his wrists.

"Is that my Glock I saw you waving around?" she asked.

"It is."

"Thanks for not losing it." She pulled it from his waistband and pointed it at J.J.'s groin. "Now, J.J.— Justin to us folks on the message board, right? I'm not in the best of moods right now, so why don't you just tell us where you buried the girls so we can get on with the business of digging them up?"

He smirked at the Glock. "If you think that scares me, you're dumber than you look. That gun was under water. It isn't going to—"

She pulled the trigger and shot a round into the side of his boat.

"You were about to say something?"

He went white.

"Talk about being dumber than you look." She smiled at him and held up the handgun. "Here's something you may not have learned on TV. One of the beautiful things about the Glock is that it has all these plastic parts, see? And the ammo's in this nice, tight, dry clip. You can swim with this sucker and it's still going to shoot. So tell me, J.J., where are they? Where are your sisters?"

"They're not my sisters," he snarled.

"Right, technically, they're only half sisters."

"They're nothing to me. That whole donor sibling thing, that's such a stupid sham."

"Clever of you and your sister to climb on that bandwagon so you could see what was going on, though. How'd you find out about them, anyway?"

"Avery found some papers in my dad's desk and she showed them to me."

"Avery?" Nick asked.

"My sister. Ava." J.J. rolled his eyes. "She called herself 'Ava' on the board because she thought it was funny."

"Funny, how?"

"Our last name's Gardner, get it?" J.J. stared at Emme as if waiting for the light to dawn. "Hello? Ava Gardner?"

"Oh. Right. Funny girl." Emme wasn't finding anything about these two amusing. "Go on."

"We started looking around on the Internet for information about sperm donors and found this website and decided to pretend to be one of them just for fun. It was so lame, you know, this whole donor sibling thing. Like these kids really thought they were related somehow."

"They are related. They share the same paternal DNA that you have," Nick reminded him.

"That's just bullshit, don't you get it? They were accidents. Test-tube accidents. Me and Avery, we're his only kids. Those others . . . they were biological freaks."

"And what kind of freak are you, J.J.?" Emme asked quietly.

From downriver, they heard sirens. A moment later, three speeding boats were hurtling in their direction.

"Here comes the cavalry," a much relieved Nick told her. "Right on time."

TWENTY-EIGHT

It was almost four on the following afternoon when the Firebird pulled up to Robert's gate. Emme waved a weary hand to the guard and he waved back.

"I can't wait to see Chloe." Emme came to life after having slept for half of their drive time. "I can't remember the last time I wasn't home to tuck her into bed. I hope she's okay."

"Are you kidding? I've got a twenty in my wallet that says she barely knew you were gone."

She shot him a withering look.

"Okay, she knew you weren't here, but let's face it, she had Trula. And we both know what that means." He smiled as he parked the car behind the great house. "If anyone can make you forget what's bothering you for a while, it's got to be Trula."

"I knew she'd be in good hands, and you're right, she didn't seem at all upset when I called last night. Still . . ."

The back door opened and the little girl shot out.

"Mommy!" she cried as she ran to the car.

"See, she did miss me." Emme got out of the car and opened her arms to her child.

"Mommy, guess what? Trula and me got a kitty! Her name is Foxy and she's this big!" Chloe held her hands about eight inches apart, then grabbed her mother by the hand and tugged her toward the house. "Come see her."

"Chloe, don't I get a hug?" Emme knelt down.

"Sure." Chloe wrapped her arms around her mother's neck and squeezed for one second, which was apparently all she had time for. "Come see Foxy."

Nick walked past, whistling.

"Smug is not a good look for you," she told him, and he laughed.

"Nick, come see our kitty," Chloe ran past them both to open the door.

Trula greeted them in the kitchen. "Well, you two look like you had a rough night."

"A very rough night," Emme agreed, not wanting to go into detail in front of Chloe. "We'll talk about it as soon as we can get everyone together."

Trula nodded. She got the message: the story wasn't one for tender ears.

"Actually, everyone's here," Trula told her. "In the conference room."

"Is something going on?" Emme gave Trula a hug. "Thank you so much for letting Chloe stay with you. I appreciate it so much."

"We had a grand time." Trula patted Emme on the back. "I suppose you heard all about our trip to the small-animal-rescue shelter this morning."

"Not quite, but I'm sure I will very soon."

"I hope you don't mind, Emme. The cat will stay here, of course, but she's talked about nothing else for the past several days, and frankly, once she brought it up, it did seem like a good idea."

"I don't mind at all. I think it's wonderful of you to do this."

"Here she is, Mommy. Isn't she beautiful?" Chloe held up the little orange tabby kitten. "She is so soft. You can pet her but you must be very gentle because she's just a baby."

"She is very sweet." Emme took the kitten and held it up to take a good look. "Such pretty eyes."

"Let Nick hold her next." Chloe jumped up and down. "Then me again."

Emme passed the kitten off to Nick and he made a suitable fuss. Mallory came in through the swinging door and stopped in her tracks when she saw Emme.

"So. I hear you had a successful evening," she said. "Congratulations. We saw everything on the news this morning. Good job."

Surprised by her curtness, Emme nodded and replied, "If by successful you mean"—she glanced quickly at Chloe and found her totally wrapped up in her new pet—"we found what we were looking for on all counts, then yes, we had a very successful evening. I'll be happy to give you all the details. The story isn't a pretty one, but we did what we set out to do. We found Belinda."

"You have my condolences, Nick," Mallory told him. "I'm sorry there wasn't a happier ending for your niece and for you."

"It's what I expected, but thank you. And thanks for taking on the case. Otherwise, I'd still be wondering. . . ."

"Well, I guess the thanks all go to Emme." Mallory turned to her and added, "Or should I say, to Ann?"

Emme froze for a moment, her breath caught in her throat, the beating of her heart stopped inside her chest. She opened her mouth, but no words came out. She glanced at Nick, who was staring at her, a puzzled expression on his face.

"I think you owe us all an explanation," Mallory said coolly. "Actually, we've been waiting for you to get back."

Emme nodded slowly. "I suppose now is as good a time as any."

"Em?" Nick was still staring at her from across the room.

"Nick, would you mind staying with Chloe for a while?" Her voice quivering, she addressed Trula. "I think you should probably come, too."

"I don't mind staying with Chloe, but I would like to know what's going on."

"I'll explain everything later. Right now—" She shook her head.

Emme kissed the top of her daughter's head and told her with more enthusiasm than she felt, "I'll be in the conference room, sweetie."

"Okay, Mommy." Chloe's attention was on the length of string she was dangling in front of the kitten, which was batting at it wildly.

Mallory and Trula followed Emme from the room and up the steps. Her heart was in her mouth as she entered the conference room where Robert, Susanna, and Father Kevin awaited them.

"Before anything else is said, I do want to say congratulations," Robert told her. "I understand you had a bit of a rough time."

"I managed to get away with only bruises, which is more than any of his other victims managed to do," she said softly.

"How's the congressman taking it?"

"About as well as anyone who found out that his son was a serial murderer, and his daughter an accomplice. And all the victims were his incidental offspring." Emme took a seat and exhaled. "Gardner is going to withdraw from the senate race and is resigning from the state House of Representatives."

"It's a shame," Robert said somberly. "I understand he was a good man. Word was that he'd have been an asset in the U.S. Senate."

"How many victims were there?" Father Kevin asked.

"J.J. Gardner raped and murdered four of his half sisters. There may have been others. The FBI has been called in and will be handling the case from here on in. We know that he shot and killed one of the boys—Henry—but I'm pretty sure he would have gone after the other two—the twins—before too long."

"So how many of these kids are left?" Trula wanted to know.

"Just Hayley, the youngest of the girls, and the twin boys. I think his plan was to get rid of all of them."

"Didn't he think that someone would put this together?" Kevin wondered.

"They lived in different states, and so far no one had connected the disappearances. I actually called the department that was handling the Carroll-Wilson case, but they didn't think there was a connection because there was so much time—five months—separating the incidents."

"So these kids, Ava and J.J., were afraid the others coming out of the woodwork were going to ruin his father's chances to win the election?" Robert rested his forearms on the table. "You think that's the motive?"

"I think that's part of it. And Ava, by the way, is actually Avery. J.J. was Justin on the message board." Emme told him. "I think in the beginning, to her, it was a game. But right from the start, J.J. was protecting what he saw as his. His home, his name, his share of what would be quite a substantial inheritance someday. He wasn't about to share with these nobodies. And once he killed that first time, he found he liked it, pure and simple. He wanted to do it again. He'd convinced himself that these girls were no real relation to him, so he felt okay about raping them and strangling them afterward."

"So his first victim was one of the girls he met online?" Susanna asked.

"Yes. Jessica. He met her on the message board, but then he got together with her during a trip to Florida last year and talked her into going off with him. He killed her and drove back to Maryland with her in the trunk of his car, then he buried her at the far end of their property. There's a place the locals believe to be an Indian burial ground, and he buried her there. He stole her laptop and went onto the message board and posted as Jessica, said she was leaving for France because her father's job was transferred. End of Jessie, nice and neat."

"If his first victim had been one of the boys, do you

think he would have enjoyed it as much?" Mallory asked.

"Probably not. I don't think shooting Henry gave him the kind of thrill that strangling the girls did. I think the whole thing kind of got all twisted in his mind. He enjoyed the rapes—he must have, because he kept souvenirs of each of the girls. A necklace of Jessica's, a length of Belinda's hair, a ring of Lori's. They were still trying to figure out what he took from Ali, but he did keep all of their laptops. I'm only guessing, but I think he probably got a thrill from reading their emails, you know, like a way to know them better?"

"How did Nick take it?" Robert wanted to know.

"As well as anyone can. I think it was terribly painful for him to hear what had been done to Belinda. He showed an admirable amount of restraint."

"Emme—Ann—I'm not sure how to address you now," Mallory said. "Obviously, we're pleased that our first case was successful. But, you know, we have a real problem here. You lied to everyone at this table."

"I did. And I'm sorry . . . I cannot begin to tell you—each of you—how sorry I am that I had to do that."

"*Had* to?" Kevin asked. "Why did you feel you had to?"

"Father Burch, it's a long story," she told him, tears welling in her eyes.

"I'm still Kevin," he told her, reaching out to cover her hands with his. "Why don't you start from the beginning?"

She took a deep breath and tried to get her

thoughts and emotions under control. She kept her eyes cast down, unable to meet the gaze of anyone at the table. She had lied, she had let them down. Would she have eventually told them the truth? She didn't know. She'd like to think she would, someday, but she couldn't be sure of that.

"Mallory, we talked one day not too long ago, and I told you—"

"Some bullshit story about being found by nuns in a church as a newborn." Mallory rolled her eyes. "You probably could have done better than that."

"That bullshit story was the truth." Emme managed a weak smile. Even now, she didn't want to think of herself as Ann.

"You were abandoned by your mother?" Kevin still held her hands, as if to give her strength, and his kindness brought tears to her eyes again.

She nodded. "They said I was only a few hours old. The nuns named me Ann after St. Ann—that's the name of the church I was found in. My mother was never identified. My father . . . who knows?"

"Were you adopted?"

"I was almost adopted twice, actually. The couple who had me first ended up divorcing before the adoption was finalized, so I was returned to Catholic services. The second time, my almost-mother died and my almost-father couldn't cope, so back I went again. I grew up in foster homes. When I was eighteen, I was out of the system and on my own. I got a job, I lived with some other girls like me who had no one to help them out. . . . Long story short, I went through junior college in California while I was working as a file clerk for the police department in Silver Hill. I worked my way up in the department, then I asked to go to the police academy. I applied, and I qualified." She raised her head, gave Kevin's hands a final squeeze, then let go and crossed her arms over her chest. She looked at every face, met every eye. "Regardless of what you might think of me now, I was a damned good cop. That's one thing you have to understand about me. *I was a damned good cop.*"

"But why lie about your name? I don't understand." Susanna shook her head from side to side.

"Five years ago, I was working undercover in narcotics. I arrested a young woman for sale and distribution and brought her in. She was young—I think she was only seventeen at the time. She wasn't using, but she was selling, and I was afraid it was only a matter of time before she started sampling the goods. I tried to mentor her, I guess is the best word. Got her one of the better public defenders, tried to get her to find a different line of work. If other things in her life had been different, I think she might have moved on. But her boyfriend was a man named Anthony Navarro, who now controls a huge piece of the drug trade between Mexico and the southern United States." Her mouth was getting dry and she licked her lips.

Trula got up and went to the small refrigerator in the conference room and returned to the table with several bottles of water. She placed one in front of Emme and the others in the middle of the table for whoever might want them.

"Thank you." Emme twisted the cap off and took a long drink.

"Go on with your story," Trula told her when she finished.

"Tameka found out she was pregnant just about the same time that Navarro got tired of her. He set her up to be arrested with a large quantity of cocaine in her possession, which guaranteed her a prison sentence."

"What do you mean, he set her up?" Kevin frowned. "How could he do that unless he had—"

"A friend in the police department?" Emme nodded. "We could never figure out who it was, but there had to have been someone. Supposedly it was an anonymous tip, but it was too specific, the wheres and the whens and the whats. Anyway, Tameka goes to prison, and before you know it, she's ready to have her baby." Emme sighed deeply. "You have to understand, she was a really decent kid who got in over her head, and had no one to help her out. Her own mother was a junkie, she had no idea who her father was—she had no one in this world except her unborn child, and she was determined to do what was best for that baby."

"Chloe." Trula whispered.

Emme nodded. "Tameka asked me—begged me—to take her child and adopt it. She said she knew she wasn't going to get out of that prison alive, that she wanted her baby raised by someone who would give it a good life. She picked me."

Tears rolled down her face and she had to stop for a moment.

"So I agreed to take the baby after it was born. We had a lawyer and someone from children's services there to make it all legal. When Chloe was three days old, I brought her home. A few weeks later, Tameka was dead. They never did find out who actually killed her, but we all know that somehow Navarro had gotten to her."

She took another sip of water. "Fast-forward four years. Anthony Navarro has a bad case of measles and finds out he's sterile, and he's pissed. He's older now, and he's been thinking about passing on his name, his empire, and now he's bummed out about not having any offspring. And then one day he remembers Tameka and the baby she had in prison. He spread a lot of money around to find out what happened to this child. He found the social worker who handled the case, he has the records copied for him, and someone in public service gets a nice fat envelope for coming up with the goods."

"How did you find this out?" Susanna asked.

"I arrested a hooker one morning who offered to trade me a hot-off-the-streets news flash for letting her walk. The news was that Anthony Navarro was offering twenty-five thousand dollars to whoever brought him his daughter." She turned to Robert. "I was home that afternoon and thinking, what would I do if someone came for my daughter? I was waiting to go pick her up at preschool and was watching your press conference. I went online and filled out the application. I heard car doors slam outside and when I looked out, there were two men staring at my house. I was pretty damned sure it wasn't a coincidence. So I grabbed what I could and went out the back door. I went to my friend, Steffie's, and stayed there for a few days while I got everything in order."

"Would your friend Steffie happen to be Chief of Police Stephanie Jenkins?" Mallory asked.

Emme nodded.

"Please, please, don't do anything that would harm her. She agreed to go along with this for Chloe's sake. Over the past few years, we've both had to clean up some of the messes Navarro's men have left behind and we were terrified that he would find Chloe." She turned to look Mallory in the eyes. "I know that you're not going to keep me on and I accept that. I understand why you don't want me here. I'm all right with it. I deserve whatever happens from here on in. But Steffie will lose her job, and she'll never be able to work in law enforcement again, and that's all she's ever known. Please don't ruin her life because of me. She was only trying to save my daughter."

Her voice broke and she covered her face with her hands.

"It seems to me that that's all you were trying to do, too." Trula rubbed her back gently.

"I don't understand why you didn't call the FBI." Mallory sounded skeptical.

"The FBI has been trying to get their hands on Navarro for years, Mal." Emme turned to her wearily. "I could not count on them finding him before he found Chloe."

Robert cleared his throat and said, "I think we need some time to talk this over."

"I understand." Emme stood. "I just want you to know that I am sorry that I lied to you, that I disappointed you. But I'd do it again if I had to. There's no question in my mind that Anthony Navarro could have tracked me down if I used my real name. He isn't used to not getting what he wants. Right now, he wants Chloe."

"You're exhausted." Trula rose also. "You're going

to get a few hours of sleep. There's a spare room right next to mine."

"Trula, I couldn't sleep right now, not after all this," Emme protested.

"Nonsense. Just a few hours of rest, then we'll see." Trula took her by the arm and led her to the door, and then out into the hallway. Before she closed the door behind them, Emme heard her tell the others, "I'm coming back, and I'm going to have my say."

It was ten minutes before Trula returned, but she had plenty on her mind when she got there.

"I'm going to throw in my two cents," she told them as she sat back in the seat she'd earlier vacated.

"Please," Robert told her. "The floor is yours."

"I just want to say that if you fire that girl, I'm going to be one unhappy old woman."

"Trula, we have every right to fire her. She falsified her credentials, she got her friend to lie for her and help her pull off this fraud—the chief of police who should know better, for God's sake!" Mallory said, pointing out the obvious. "We have good reasons to fire her."

"And you have good reasons not to," Trula countered. "She was trying to save her child."

"You're just blind to what she did because of the way you feel about Chloe," Mallory replied.

"You're damned right I am. I think what Emme— or Ann or whatever name she wants to be called by— what she did was very brave. Gutsy. She pulled up stakes and drove across the country to find a place where she could safely raise her little girl. She gave up everything to do that—her home, her job . . . She had no way of knowing if you'd hire her, Mallory. And maybe I should remind you why you did."

"She submitted a résumé that belonged to someone else."

"She had an excellent reference from her former chief."

"Who was her best friend!" Mallory reminded Trula.

"But wasn't everything she told you about this woman true?"

"That's not the issue."

"Then what is, Mal? You needed a great investigator and you got one," Kevin said. "She solved this case in a matter of weeks and made us all look good."

"She's a fraud, Kevin. She should have told us the truth; we'd have kept her secret."

"And how should she have known that? Reading between the lines, who has she been able to trust in her life? Tossed away like trash after she was born, bounced around from foster family to foster family, then bounced out onto the street when she turned eighteen to make her way alone from there?" Trula felt her blood pressure take off but she couldn't help herself. "Does anyone here know what it's really like to have no one in their life they can depend on?"

The room fell silent, and Trula let them sit for a few minutes before turning to Mallory. "I know you had some rough times growing up, but you always knew you had a place to come back to at the end of the day—no one was going to toss you out. This woman didn't even have that small bit of comfort. The one thing she does have is her daughter, and she fought for her the only way she knew how. Just for the record, I'd have done the same thing, and I defy anyone at this table to tell me otherwise."

"Trula—" Robert said, but she cut him off before he could say what was on his mind.

"Robert, in all the years we've known each other, I've never interfered in your business or in your personal life, but I'm asking you now to think really hard before you let her go."

"Whether or not you've never interfered is open for debate," he replied, "but we'll let that go for now. But just so you know, I'm leaning toward keeping her on."

"Robert, if anyone finds out that she falsified her records, that we hired her even though we knew she was a fraud, we could lose our license and our reputation would most certainly be damaged," Mallory told him.

"Let's think this through. First, how would anyone find out?" he asked.

Mal rolled her eyes. "Robert, that is the most naïve thing I've ever heard you say. All it takes is for someone to recognize her, and it could happen. Or someone who knew the real Emme Caldwell—"

"Whoa. There are lots of people who have the same name, right?" he said. "And who in California, besides her former police chief, even knows that she's here at the foundation? No one."

"There is one person who knows," Mallory told them. "I called the chief earlier in the week, but she was out. I left a message with the desk sergeant that I needed to speak with her about Emme Caldwell. He said he and Emme—I'm sure now he meant the real Emme—had been partners early on. If he was wondering why someone from the Mercy Street Foundation was asking about a dead cop . . ."

"It probably went right over his head," Robert tried to assure her.

"I don't know that I'd want to bet on that," Mallory replied. "Her name is right there on the website."

Robert excused himself for a moment. "I will be right back. I want you to hold that thought."

He was back in a minute, his laptop under his arm. He placed it on the table in front of him and opened it to their website. He typed for a moment or two, then smiled broadly.

"There. All fixed." He turned the laptop around for them to see.

"What's all fixed?" Mallory frowned and craned her neck to look at the screen.

"Here. As far as the rest of the world is concerned, Emme Caldwell is now Elle Caldwell," he told them.

"You're serious. You think that's all it's going to take if someone comes looking for her?" Mallory was starting to get angry.

"No, but who's going to be coming after her?" Trula asked quietly. "It isn't going to be someone who's checking on her credentials as a former California police officer. The only reason anyone will be coming after her is to get to Chloe."

Her words hung over the room like a low-lying cloud.

"How would we even know if someone was out there?" Susanna wondered aloud. "I mean, if someone came to Conroy looking for her, how would we know?"

"There might be a way," Kevin told them. "Let me work on that."

"So have we decided to give Emme—er, Elle—a pass?" Susanna asked. "Shall we put it to a vote?"

"I say yes," Trula spoke up immediately.

"I never go against Trula," Kevin said.

"Me, either." Robert nodded.

"All right. But if there are repercussions from this . . ." Mallory looked directly at Robert.

"There won't be. But if there are, we'll find a way to handle them. Suse? What do you think?"

"Emme didn't set out to deceive us because she was trying to get a job she wasn't qualified for," Susanna said, "or to defraud us in any way. She is what she said she was, right?"

"What, but not who," Mallory reminded her.

"Still, as Trula said, we have to consider the motive. She was trying to save her child from being kidnapped by a drug lord. Can anyone at this table say they think it would be good for Chloe to be raised by someone like that?"

Her eyes skipped from face to face.

"That's what I thought. So yes, of course, I vote to keep her on."

"If she stays, there may come a time when we will have to protect her," Mallory told them quietly.

"If and when that time comes," Robert told them, "that's exactly what we'll do."

TWENTY-NINE

"Hey, sleepyhead, wake up."

Emme opened her eyes to see Nick leaning over her. He pushed the hair back from her face and kissed her.

"Trula said I could come see if you were awake, but that I couldn't stay up here. I don't know what she thinks we'd be doing with Chloe running around." He kissed her again. "On the other hand . . ."

"Nick," she pushed against him and tried to sit up. "We need to talk."

"In a minute."

"Seriously. We have to talk. It's important."

"Okay." He eased back and turned on the lamp on the table next to the bed. "Is something wrong?"

She sat and pulled the pillow up behind her back, and then she began. She told him everything.

When she finished, she sat back against the pillow, her face wet with tears, and waited for him to react. When he didn't, she said, "Nick, do you understand what I'm saying? I've been lying to you since the day we met. Aren't you going to say something?"

"Do I call you Emme, or Ann?"

"Nick, please don't make light—"

"I'm not. Does any of this change who you are? Or what you are to me?" He shook his head. "Not a bit."

"I'm going to lose my job, Nick." She held his hands. "They're not going to let me stay after this."

"Are you sure about that?"

She nodded. "Mallory is loaded for bear, and I don't blame her. I made her look like a fool. She was the one who checked my references, she was the one who hired me."

"She'll get over it."

Emme looked at him as if he had two heads. "I don't think this is the sort of thing one gets over. This was their first case. I was their first hire. I've made her look incompetent to Robert and everyone else. She has every right to be pissed at me."

"She didn't seem that pissed when she was in the kitchen awhile ago. She was asking if you were still sleeping."

"Probably because she's waiting to fire me."

"I wasn't getting that vibe, Em." He played with her fingers. "If the worst does happen, you'll find another job."

"I'm going to have to think things through a little better. I can't keep uprooting Chloe. She deserves better than that."

"Look, don't make any rash decisions. If you need a place to stay, there's the farm. You're welcome to stay there for as long as you want. And hey, if worse comes to worst, I can always teach you how to replace chrome, or tune up an engine."

She tried to smile, but was having a hard time pulling it off.

"You have to stay around at least long enough to help me put together a memorial service for Belinda, but I'm hoping you'll stay longer than that."

Before she could reply, the door flew open and Chloe blew in.

"Oh, yay! You're awake. Trula said it's time for dinner and we're all going to eat together in the big dining room." She turned to Nick. "Robert's dining room has a fireplace. And a secret panel. Father Kevin showed me. Wanna see?"

"I do. I always wanted to see what was behind a secret panel." Nick squeezed Emme's hands and stood. "We'll wait for you downstairs, Em."

Emme nodded and watched Chloe drag Nick from the room. *The gods must be having a fine laugh at my expense,* she thought. *All my life, I've been searching for what I've found here. Friends, a sense of belonging—and Nick . . . well, he's the man I always hoped I'd find.* The thought of leaving was almost too painful to bear.

She exhaled and swung her legs over the side of the bed and slipped her feet into her sandals. She needed a few minutes to splash some water on her face and compose herself, and then it would be time to face the music.

She was unprepared for what waited for her downstairs.

Robert had opened several bottles of champagne, and when Emme came into the kitchen, he was proposing a toast to Belinda's memory.

"Ah, you're just in time," he told her. "We're remembering Belinda. Well, Nick is remembering her, and sharing some of her with the rest of us."

Trula handed her a flute.

"She was a pretty happy kid," Nick said. "It's good to think about that right now, to look back on the good times."

"That's important." Trula patted him on the arm. "You need to think about the good times. It doesn't make the loss less painful—only time can take away some of the sting—but the good memories will keep her alive for you."

"I'll drink to that." Kevin drained his glass. Robert offered a refill, but he declined. "I have a meeting in about an hour at the church," he said.

"Since when do you have meetings on Saturday nights?" Robert asked.

"Since something came up that I would like to discuss with a member of my parish." Kevin put his glass on the counter and turned to Trula. "What can I take in to the dining room for you?"

"Everything's already there. We just all need to—"

"Wait a minute," Emme said. "I feel like the nine-hundred-pound elephant in the room, and all you can think about is eating."

She looked from one face to the other.

"Do you really think I can sit down to dinner with you all, then turn in my cell phone and leave?"

"You're not leaving, Emme." Robert put his glass down. "We understand that you did what you did because you felt you had no choice." He glanced across the room at Chloe. "We all agreed that given those circumstances, each of us probably would have done the same thing."

Emme turned to Mallory. "Is that how you feel?"

With some apparent reluctance, Mallory nodded. "I don't like it, but Robert's right. I don't know that I wouldn't have done the same thing. And you are exactly what you said you were. A good investigator. I don't know that I've worked with better."

"I don't know what to say," Emme told them. "I was so sure that—"

"Not another word," Trula said. "Dinner's getting cold. If you want to discuss this any more, you're going to have to do it over pot roast."

"Trula has spoken." Robert grabbed a bottle of wine from the counter and began to usher everyone toward the door.

"I'm afraid I can't stick around for the celebratory dinner, Emme." Susanna swung her bag over her shoulder. "I'm afraid I have another commitment. But I'm delighted that you're on board with us. I think you're a real asset."

"Thank you, Suse," Emme said, and hugged her before she left.

"I'll see you all on Monday," Susanna called to the others before leaving by the back door.

"Where does she go when she takes off like that?" Emme heard Mallory whisper to Trula, who shook her head and whispered back, "Beats the devil out of me."

•

She'd already missed the entire day, but Susanna had planned ahead. When she wasn't waiting for Emme to return, she was in meetings talking about Emme or listening to someone else talk about Emme. She was relieved when the vote was taken and everyone—even Mallory—agreed that Emme deserved a place on the staff. The time between meetings was spent on her computer, studying topographic maps and eliminating roads she'd already traveled. There were some she'd driven early on that she thought perhaps she hadn't investigated far enough the first time. Before she crossed them off for good, she needed to be certain. One road in particular had stayed in her memory. It had wound around and around a mountain on a narrow path, but had been navigable. Something she'd noticed on one of the maps she'd downloaded, however, seemed to indicate hairpin turns, the two lanes very tight. She'd drive much of the night to get to her destination, but she didn't really mind. She knew that someday she would find the place where Beth Magellan's car had been hidden all these many months—if not this weekend, then possibly another.

Susanna had asked herself a hundred times how much longer she'd make these trips, how many more weekends she'd spend driving alone on side roads, peering down ravines and checking guard rails for scrapes of brown paint that would match the color of the Jeep that Beth had been driving that day. She hated to admit how obsessed she'd become, but that was the truth of it. There would be no peace for Robert until the Jeep was found, so finding the car was the key for both of them.

In some ways, the trips were a comfort to her. She was doing something for the man she loved, and with luck, someday he'd understand just how much of herself had gone into these journeys. She wasn't unaware of the risk involved, of course. She knew it was possible that she'd discover what had happened to his wife and he'd still see her as his best friend, nothing more. But she clung to the hope that once the truth was known, once he knew for certain that Beth had left this life, when he looked for love again, maybe someday he'd look to her.

Susanna was smart enough to know that the odds might not be in her favor, but they were the only odds she had. She would look until she found, and then the next act would begin. She didn't know how the play would end, but she would see it through.

THIRTY

Needle in a haystack time.

Susanna took the exit from the turnpike Beth Magellan was believed to have taken the morning she disappeared. There'd been an accident eastbound between two exits that had resulted in the first one being closed and all the traffic diverted. Beth may have been one of the first cars to encounter the detour after the road was blocked off, and may have been directed off the turnpike before all of the detour signs had been put in place. That would have left Beth to figure out on her own how to find her way back to the turnpike with some twenty miles between where she got off and where she should have gotten back on.

Over the past two years, Susanna had considered most of the possibilities and traveled most of the roads that would have been the most logical choices, as had the state police and the private investigators Robert had hired. But Susanna figured she had one advantage over all of them: She'd known Beth fairly well for several years, knew how the woman thought.

The scenario that played out in Suse's mind had Beth finding herself in a line of traffic that was not moving. She'd have been in a hurry to get home. Maybe Ian was fussing in the backseat, maybe she was frustrated at not having her phone with her. She was always talking to someone when she was driving. It was the one thing Robert consistently criticized her for.

What would Beth have done under these circumstances?

Might she have decided not to wait patiently for the police to direct the cars off the turnpike? To Suse's way of thinking, she'd have driven on the shoulder of the road and slipped off the turnpike exit as quickly as she could. With no signs to direct her, perhaps Beth might have done what Suse could see herself doing under the same circumstances: she'd have asked the person in the tollbooth. There was a good chance she'd have been directed to the main road, and hopefully that would take her around the mountain.

The main road off this stretch of highway was a two-lane affair that went through one small town after another, and at first glance might have appeared to be the most logical, took her down the mountain, not up. There were signs that pointed toward this town or that, one state or county road or another, but for a stranger, the signs meant nothing. The last time Susanna had followed this same road, she'd taken the route that led her down the mountain. Today, she'd go in the opposite direction, and see where that would lead.

It wasn't long before she noticed that the road narrowed around those hairpin turns, and that some of the guard rails at several of the turns bore numerous scrapes, battle scars from vehicles that may not have fared quite so well as she had so far. She had to slam on the brakes several times to take the turns on all four wheels, and on more than one occasion, opposing traffic had caused her to hug the right side of the road a lot closer than was comfortable. On an icy road, drivers could find themselves one misstep from disaster.

The sudden blast from the horn of the SUV behind her startled her and caused her to jump, and she swerved even closer to the guard rail. The driver of the SUV was right up to her rear fender and made no effort to back off. As she rounded the curve, her foot on the brake, she saw a driveway up ahead on the right, and she practically slid into it to get out of the SUV's way. The driver laid on the horn as he passed her, his middle finger in the air, and she watched him disappear down the next hill at a speed she couldn't even imagine on a road like this.

That's how it happens, she thought as she caught her breath. That's how cars get pushed off the road. If this had been winter, any accumulation of snow or ice on these roads would have been deadly.

And then she recalled that Beth and Ian had disappeared in the dead of winter.

She checked her rearview mirror for oncoming cars, then drove back onto the roadway. Several hundred yards ahead was a slight clearing. She pulled over and parked. She stuffed her bag under the front seat and locked the door after she got out. She walked back to the curve where the SUV had crowded her and studied the metal guard rail. It was dented and bore the scrapes of many a passing car. She stepped over it and walked downhill a short distance. The bottom of the ravine was littered with old tires and plastic trash bags holding God knew what. From somewhere below she could hear the sound of a stream, but there was little else to break the silence.

It would have been a place like this where Beth went off the road, she thought, only higher up the mountain, maybe. Someplace where a car could go over and be hidden from view by trees or thick undergrowth that even in February would prevent it from being seen from the road.

She walked back to her car, knowing she was right, in theory. All she had to do now was find the right road, on the right mountain.

Three hours later, she stood behind a guard rail that did its best to wrap around an exceptionally narrow turn. On the opposite side of the road, a huge piece of rock jutted out from the side of the mountain and hung partially over the left lane. A driver coming uphill in the right lane, unfamiliar with the configuration, might well overcompensate if a vehicle was coming too quickly from the left. Susanna found a safe place to park and again set out to explore, the fourth or fifth time she'd done so that day.

Since she had been following possible routes Beth might have taken, Susanna assumed that Beth would have approached this particular curve on the right side. She walked along the road and climbed over the barrier, noting that there was ample room at the end of the guard rail for a car to slip between it and a tree that had apparently not only stood witness to a number of accidents, but had itself been a victim on numerous occasions.

"Everything from a Mini Cooper to one of those big mean pickups must have bounced off you," she said, taking note that the gashes on the trunk were of varying heights.

She stepped around the tree and looked down. The hill dropped off sharply and the trees grew in dense clusters, their branches and leaves forming a green wall. Now, in the summer, the foliage could hide just about anything down there. In midwinter when the trees were bare, however, she was pretty certain any car that might have gone over on this side of the road would have been visible. She started back to her car, then on a hunch, walked across the road and stepped over the guard rail, which was much lower on this side of the road.

"Oh, come on, Beth," she said aloud. "You could help me out here."

She stood at the top of the incline and studied the topography. Beneath her feet was solid rock, and looking down the mountainside, there were mostly rocks below for maybe fifty yards. Beyond the rocks an overgrowth of shrubs disappeared over a ledge. Susanna crossed the road to the place where the curve began, and thought back to the impatient SUV that had come up behind her earlier and startled her with a loud blast of its horn. What if she'd been driving into a curve like this one, on so narrow a road, and had been surprised by such a blast. Would she have swerved to the right, or to the left? If to the right, she'd have bounced off that tree, wouldn't she? But if she'd swerved to the left . . .

If she'd swerved to the left, might she have gone into the curve in the opposing lane? And if she had, she'd have looked up to see that rocky overhang right there. If she'd tried to overcompensate, if she'd hit ice . . . what might have happened to the Jeep? Might it have scraped through between the rock and the railing?

She stepped over the rail and made her way down the rock as far as the ledge and looked over. She almost missed it, but the sunlight bleeding through the clouds caught on something down below and sent a beam back up through the trees.

It could be nothing, she told herself as she made her way around the rocks and down into the ravine, or it could be chrome, or a mirror. She made her way down as far as she could safely go, but it wasn't necessary for her to go any farther. Through the thick growth she could see the back quarter panel of a brown vehicle, and she knew.

Susanna's heart all but stopped in her chest. She was torn between going down there, to the Jeep, and running back up for her phone to call for help. She took two steps down and three steps back. For as many times as she'd made the trip in search of this place, now that she was here, she was barely able to think. Most likely Beth and Ian were in that car, and if they were, they were dead. Should she know this before she called for help?

She eased her way down to the Jeep. It had apparently come straight down the mountainside until it smashed nosefirst into a rock that had held it in place for more than two years on the far side of the ledge. Suse crept forward sadly, her heart in her mouth. Robert's family had been found, after all this time, and now she'd have to tell him. The thought made her sick.

Almost against her will, she peered inside. Stunned, she blinked, not certain that her eyes weren't playing tricks on her. She cleared dross off the window with the front of her T-shirt and looked again.

Beth Magellan's remains lay across the front seat at an angle to the steering wheel. Ian's car seat was, as always, directly behind his mother's, but incredibly, Robert's son was nowhere to be seen.

A white-faced Robert sat on the hood of the car parked at the side of the road, numb with disbelief. After he'd gotten Susanna's call and her words actually sank in, he'd hired a helicopter to bring him and Kevin as close as possible. Once they landed, Susanna picked them up and drove them to the mountain where the Jeep had been found. He'd had trouble putting words together in a sentence since they arrived.

"What kind of person would take a child from a wreck and leave its mother there to die?" he asked the trooper who met them at the accident scene.

"Sir, we don't know what happened here. We're trying to find out." The trooper, Captain K. Carlson, had tried to calm Robert. "If you'd just wait over here—"

"I want to see my wife," Robert had protested.

"Sir, your wife has been removed from the vehicle and is no longer on the scene." Carlson had blocked his way.

"Where is she? Where did you take her?"

"To the medical examiner's, sir. He'll need to determine the cause." It wasn't necessary for him to add, "of death." It was understood.

"What are you doing to find my son?" Robert demanded.

"We're almost finished processing the car, then we'll—"

"I don't give a damn about the fucking car," Robert shouted. "I want to know what you're going to do to find my son."

"Sir, someone removed your son from the car," Carlson replied calmly. "The only way we have to figure out who that was is by processing every bit of trace evidence from that vehicle. We need to develop the fingerprints we've lifted so we can run a search through every database we have access to. I promise you that we'll do this as quickly as possible, but right now you're going to have to let my people do their jobs."

"Robert," Kevin touched his arm. "Let them work. Go sit with Susanna for a while."

"Standing around . . . sitting around . . . while Ian is . . ." Robert waved an arm to take in the scope of the entire mountain. "I feel like I should be doing something."

"What you should be doing is thanking God that there is a damned good chance that your son is alive somewhere," Kevin told him calmly. "What you should be doing is thanking Susanna for doing what no one else has been able to do."

"Didn't I thank her?" Robert frowned. "I thought I said thank you."

"Not sufficiently, no."

Robert walked to the car where Susanna sat on the hood watching the buzz of activity.

"I owe you an apology," he said when he reached

the car. "Kevin has pointed out that I haven't thanked you enough."

She put a finger to his mouth and said, "You did thank me, and once was enough."

"But Kevin is right, Suse. I *can't* thank you enough." He sat next to her on the hood of her car. "I owe you an enormous debt. I still can't believe you spent every weekend searching for them."

"It wasn't quite *every* weekend." She smiled weakly. "But it was many."

He took her hands and held them between both of his. "You know, in my heart, I think I've known all along that Beth was no longer with us. I was surprised, but not *shocked* that she's been found. But Ian . . . I've never felt that Ian was gone. I kept telling myself it was just because I didn't want to believe that my son's life had been cut so short. But honestly, deep inside, I felt he was still here, in this world. Now I don't know what to think."

"Want to know what I think?"

"Of course."

"I think that someone stumbled across the car. Either they saw the accident, or heard it, or were walking through those woods and found it. They looked inside and saw that Beth was most likely already gone. The car was old, Rob. There were no airbags that could have cushioned that fall. I don't know if the medical examiner can determine how she died at this point, but I think she probably did not survive the crash." She watched the crime-scene techs load their black bags into the back of a car. "But Ian . . . you know, there was no blood on the car seat. No blood on the backseat."

His head snapped up to look at her.

"I opened the door when I first found the car. I probably should not have done that. Now my fingerprints are on the door handle and the car seat. And yes, I did tell Captain Carlson, and he did take my prints for comparison, so I didn't really compromise things too much. I hope. And I hadn't meant to open the door. But when I looked through the window and I didn't see Ian in the car seat, I thought how strange that was. Trula and I bought that car seat, remember? We went online and found the one that had the highest safety rating, the one that was supposed to be able to survive a nuclear blast."

When he raised an eyebrow, she added, "Okay, that was an exaggeration. But the point is, it's supposed to be the best on the market. So why didn't the straps hold him in the seat? That's what I was thinking when I opened the door. But then he wasn't there at all. His diaper bag was gone. Beth's sister said she strapped Ian in herself, and that she put the diaper bag on the floor behind Beth's seat."

She paused. "There's only one logical conclusion, Rob. Someone took him, and he was alive."

He stared at her for a long minute. "Because a dead child won't need a diaper change."

She moved closer and put her arms around him. "So the next order of business is to find him."

"Someone's had my boy all this time," he said, his voice choked with emotion. "At least one person has known all this time where he was, and didn't tell. What kind of a person does that, Suse?"

"I don't know, Rob."

"All this time, he's been growing. Learned to walk,

probably. Learned to talk, too. Someone else got to be with him for all those important things."

She rocked him gently, side to side.

"He doesn't even know me," he said. "If we found him tomorrow, he wouldn't know me."

She stroked the back of his head, too choked up to speak.

"I want my son, Suse."

"We're going to find him, Robert."

They sat together quietly for a while, Susanna still holding him.

"You're the best friend I ever had, Suse," he told her, breaking the silence.

"I know, Robert," she whispered. "I know . . ."

EPILOGUE

Maria Clemente stood at the gate and waited for the children to come out of Our Lady of Angels for morning recess. She was glad Father Kevin had installed the new fence around the entire playground. The old one really hadn't been very secure. Anyone could get through at the far corner if they'd wanted to badly enough.

This new fence was just fine, with only one gate, facing the church office. Well, that was just fine, too. You never knew who might be about these days. When it came to the children, you could never be too careful. Besides, Maria liked to wave to Mary Corcoran, whose desk faced the playground, when she finished fixing the altar flowers. This morning she'd picked red dahlias the size of dinner plates, white gladiolas, and blue delphinium from her garden and arranged them in tall white vases in honor of the upcoming holiday. Father Kevin always got such a kick when she tied the altar flowers to some special day.

From the corner of her eye, she saw a woman approach, and she tilted her head to watch. Not that she was by nature a nosy person—God forbid—but she was very observant. Very little got past her, even now, when the arthritis made cutting the flowers so much harder than it used to be, and that cataract was starting to cloud the vision of her right eye.

The newcomer appeared to be in her late fifties, and wore a linen sundress, pretty leather sandals, and dark glasses. She carried a handbag that looked expensive, and when she came closer to the gate, Maria could see that the woman's nails—fingers and toes—were manicured and painted with a sunny coral color.

"Hello," Maria greeted her pleasantly, and the woman nodded as she reached to unlatch the gate.

"I'm sorry," Maria said, as she reached out and caught the woman's hand. "They don't permit anyone in the play yard during school hours. If you want to speak with someone, you have to go through the church office." Maria pointed to the window where Mary Corcoran sat.

The woman stared at Maria for a moment.

"I'm sorry," Maria repeated. "I just thought perhaps you were new here and didn't know."

When the woman spoke, it was with a deep accent. "I am new. I thank you. I didn't know."

"You are from Mexico, too, I see," Maria said, switching to Spanish. "Where are you from?"

The woman named a city over the Arizona border.

"I have not been there myself," Maria told her, "but I know people who have been. I heard it was nice."

"Nice enough," the woman agreed.

"Are you visiting here in Conroy?" Maria asked.

"Just for a while." The woman appeared to relax just a bit, and seemed more comfortable conversing in Spanish than in English.

"You have come to visit the school?" Maria asked, wondering if perhaps this was the one Father Kevin had spoken of. He hadn't said the threat would come as a woman, but still . . .

The woman nodded.

"It's a fine school. Mrs. McHugh is a fine teacher."

The door opened and children spilled out. The woman's eyes skimmed the twenty or so faces as if looking for someone. Her eyes lingered on Chloe Caldwell, narrowing as the child ran to the fence waving a piece of paper, and Maria knew for certain this was the danger he'd warned her about.

Maria's heart all but froze with fear. She could see Father Kevin near the church door but had no way of alerting him that the one he watched for was now here, and so close to the girl. Her fingers closed tightly on the rosary beads in her pocket.

Holy Mother, shield this child from the evil that threatens her. . . .

"*Mamacita!*" Chloe called out as she raced toward the fence. Maria held her breath. "I drew a picture for you."

"Chloe? Chloe?" the woman called to her, a broad smile on her face. She reached out to the girl.

If Chloe heard, she gave no sign. In her hand, she held a drawing.

"See, *mamacita*? It's the flag. We talked all about the flag today because Saturday is the flag's birthday. Mrs. McHugh read us the story about it and told us all about the lady who made it."

"Is your name Chloe?" the woman asked, and Maria's insides twisted.

"My name is Betsy." Chloe held up the picture and

pointed to where she'd signed her name, *Betsy Ross,* in red, white, and blue letters.

It was all Maria could do not to cry in gratitude. Her prayer had been heard.

"Are there more children inside? Some who have not come out for play?"

Chloe shook her head.

"Then perhaps there is another girl in this school with dark skin like yours?" the stranger asked. "This girl's name would be Chloe."

Chloe shook her head again.

"Betsy, that is the best flag I have ever seen," Maria said, to divert Chloe's attention away from the stranger.

"It's for you, *mamacita.*" Chloe handed the picture over the fence.

"Thank you. I will put it right on my refrigerator door the minute I get home. Betsy, it looks like Father Kevin is waving to you." Maria pointed at the priest who'd just come into the playground, a look of concern on his face. "Go see what he wants."

"Bye, *mamacita.*" Chloe ran off, then turned and waved to the woman who stood next to her friend. "Bye."

The woman continued to stare at Chloe. Finally, she said, "She is your granddaughter?"

"Yes. She is a lively one." It was all Maria could do not to raise her eyes toward the heavens to see if storm clouds were gathering, clouds that would bring lightning to strike her down dead for the lie she just told.

"You are certain of this?" Her eyes never left the child.

Maria injected as much indignation as she could into her reply. "Are you thinking perhaps I do not know my own flesh and blood? I carried this child home from the hospital in my own arms. How could I not be certain?"

"Of course, of course." The woman appeared flustered. "I apologize. It's just that, that little girl looks so much like my Elena did at that age. The resemblance is uncanny. My son . . . his daughter was taken from us when she was a baby." The woman shook her head. "I'm sorry. We were given bad information. He thought she might be . . . Well, when I saw her . . . and she looks so much like my daughter . . ."

"I've raised Betsy since she was born right here in Conroy." Maria could not stop yet another lie from rolling off her tongue. "You know how it is sometimes with your children. They don't always make the wisest decisions. My daughter was too young when she had this baby, and it fell to me to care for her. Not that I am complaining, of course. I love her dearly." That part was true. As for the rest, well, she would have to be first in line for confession before the next Mass. She patted the woman on the arm and added, "Perhaps someday you will find the child you are looking for. This child, however, she is ours."

The woman nodded, and turned to walk away. "May God be with you and your family."

"And with you and yours." Maria returned the blessing and watched the stranger walk past the church. When she reached the corner, Maria whispered, "Except for your murdering, drug dealing son."

*   *   *

The woman walked briskly around the block to the waiting car and got into the backseat. She waved a crisp "get moving" gesture at the driver and immediately opened her bag and took out her phone. She speed-dialed a number and sat back against the leather, which was icy cold thanks to the air conditioning that ran the entire time she was out of the car.

She did not bother with a greeting when the call was answered.

"You have idiots working for you," she snapped in Spanish.

"What are you—," her son began but she cut him off.

"Whoever told you this child is yours is a moron."

"You found her?"

"I found *a* child, not *your* child."

"I had it checked out. The daughter of this Emme Caldwell is—"

"I'm telling you this is a different child. I met this child's grandmother, Anthony. I spoke with the child herself. I asked her. Her name is not Chloe."

"Maybe she was lying."

"Her name was written on her school paper. I saw it. Anthony, it isn't her."

"Perhaps you were looking at the wrong child," he persisted.

"I was looking in the wrong *place*," she snapped at him again. "This is not the one you're looking for."

"My people—"

"Are fools. I'm coming home, Anthony, and I'm not happy about having spent the last twenty-four hours in this nowhere town on this wild bird chase."

"Wild goose."

"What?"

"The English expression is 'wild goose chase.'"

"Whatever. The bottom line is, someone gave you bad information. I hope you did not pay the reward money to this man."

"Fool me once," he muttered under his breath.

"What did you say?"

"I said, I'm sorry for having wasted your time, *mi madre*. It won't happen again. As for the informant, you can rest assured he will get exactly what's coming to him. . . ."

Read on for an excerpt from

ACTS OF MERCY

by Mariah Stewart
Published by Ballantine Books

Her high heels clicking across the hardwood floors, Mallory Russo walked through the quiet foyer of the handsome Tudor mansion that served as home to business mogul Robert Magellan as well as her place of business. Uncharacteristically silent, the house seemed to reflect the sad spirits of all who'd come under its roof today. Earlier that morning, Mallory and her co-workers had gathered here before filing into the limousines that took them to Our Lady of Angels Church a few miles away in Conroy, Pennsylvania, where Father Kevin Burch, Robert's cousin, conducted the memorial service for Robert's wife, Beth.

Mallory removed the wide-brimmed black hat she'd bought for the occasion and walked the length of the hall to the wing of the house where her office and several others were located. She snapped on the overhead fan as she entered the room and went straight to her desk. She tossed the hat on a nearby chair and tried to remember if she'd ever owned such a thing. Under the desk, her feet kicked off the heels she seldom wore and her cramped toes wiggled in the hopes of bringing back the circulation.

She wasn't sure when the others would be back but she hoped to get some work in between now and the time those who'd been invited back for a luncheon began to arrive. No one had seemed in much of a hurry to leave the cemetery after the service and gathered around chatting, but she'd been ready to leave even before the priest had begun to speak. There was something about holding a funeral for a woman who'd been dead but not buried for well over two years that had unsettled Mallory. So when Charlie Wanamaker, her fiancé and a member of the local police force, had whispered in her ear that he'd be taking off, she asked him to drop her off on his way to the police station.

As a former detective herself, one would expect that Mallory was beyond the point where death had the power to spook her, but there was something about this death that rattled her right to her soul. Beth Magellan and her infant son had been missing for more than two years, but the Jeep they'd been in had only recently been found in a deep ravine in the mountains of western Pennsylvania. Beth's remains still were strapped into the driver's seat when the Jeep was discovered, but there'd been no trace of the baby other than his car seat. That someone had come upon a dead or dying woman and had walked away without calling for help was beyond Mallory's comprehension, but the knowledge that this same person had most likely been the one who'd walked away with the woman's child was haunting her. Had Beth been alive, even conscious, when Ian had been taken? Had her last breath been spent calling for her son? Had she been aware that she was dying? The horror of it sent a chill up Mallory's spine. Robert was a good man, and she'd grown very fond of him. He didn't deserve to suffer like this. She suspected that the only thing that kept him going now was the knowledge that Ian most likely was still alive. Somewhere.

It was this last part that was torturing everyone: where was *somewhere*?

Robert Magellan had founded—and funded—the Mercy Street Foundation to provide private investigative services to those whose loved ones had gone missing and for whom the investigating law enforcement agency had made little or no progress. Robert knew the pain of not knowing what had happened to the two people he loved above all others—his wife and his son—but circumstances had blessed him with the means to hire professionals to search for them. That they had failed hadn't diminished the fact that he could afford to take those steps.

Not that any of the PI's Robert hired had had any success, Mallory reminded herself. It had been a member of Robert's own staff who'd eventually found his missing family. But the point had been that he could well afford to hire an army of investigators. Most people were not that fortunate. The foundation was intended to do for them what they could not do for themselves: get the best investigators on the case.

While still in its infancy, the foundation had taken only two cases, but both of those had met with success. There'd been an overwhelming response to their solicitation of applicants for their services as well as their call for experienced law enforcement personnel to add to their staff. Mallory was charged with the task of sorting through all the applications and pulling out those cases that might best benefit from their services. She was also responsible for reviewing the hundreds and hundreds of résumés to find those individuals she thought might be best suited to the foundation's needs.

On her desk, she had both their next case and, she hoped, their next hire.

The letter from Lynn Walker had captured her imagination even before she'd read through the copies of the news articles that had accompanied it. Lynn's husband had been murdered under very odd circumstances, and the cop in Mallory couldn't help but be enticed by the challenge. Even now, she couldn't stop herself from reading through the file again: the body of Ross Walker, a construction supervisor, had been found behind the soup kitchen where he and Lynn volunteered one night every week. The body had been stabbed repeatedly, the face unrecognizable, left posed against the dumpster, seated, with a very large hamburger from a fast-food restaurant stuffed in his mouth.

The police investigation had been at a stand-still almost since the very beginning. Whoever had murdered Ross Walker had been careful to leave no trace of himself, and interviews with the folks who'd been in and out of the kitchen had proved fruitless. No one had seen or heard anything.

Yet someone had gone to a lot of trouble to kill Ross Walker and leave his body in plain sight. The man's widow had submitted it to the foundation for consideration. After more than a year, she wanted to start to move on, wanted her children to be able to begin to move on with their lives. But not knowing who had killed her husband and why was keeping them all stuck in that moment when the doorbell rang and her seven-year-old son had opened it to find two police officers standing on their front porch.

Yes, this case would do nicely. Mallory hoped the others on the selection committee would agree.

Mallory turned her attention to the second folder on her desk and opened it. Over the past several weeks, she'd reviewed hundreds of résumés from law enforcement officers from every agency and just about every state. She'd been separating them into piles of *interview* and *toss*. At the top of the interview pile sat the résumé of Samuel J. DelVecchio, who in past lives had been a Marine, a lawyer, and most recently, an FBI profiler.

It was this last incarnation that most interested Mallory.

For one thing, a former FBI agent would have a lot of contacts within the Bureau, contacts that could prove invaluable, not only for this case, but for future cases as well. For another, he'd worked just about every kind of case imaginable, and would bring a wealth of experience to the foundation. Kidnappings, sex crimes, white slavery, serial killers—it seems Samuel DelVecchio had seen them all.

Mallory went back to Ross Walker's folder, and pulled out the newspaper article that contained part of an interview that the local chief of police had given three months after the murder. That the body had been carefully posed suggested that the killer was sending a message, the chief was quoted as saying, but what that message was and who was supposed to receive it, well, no one had figured that out. Mallory figured an FBI profiler might be able to do just that.

Yes, Samuel DelVecchio looked like he just might be the right guy.

Sam DelVecchio stopped at the gate that blocked entry onto the grounds owned by Robert Magellan and waited for the guard to wave him through. The gate swung aside and Sam drove his old SUV along the drive that wound past an island of newly planted trees. When Magellan's Tudor mansion came into view, Sam hit the brake. Although he'd seen pictures of the house on TV and in a magazine spread, he hadn't been prepared for how impressive it was.

"Nice," he said aloud. "Very, very nice."

He parked on one side of the drive, as he'd been instructed, and got out of the car, pausing to put on his dark suit jacket and straighten his tie. It had been a long time since he'd been on a job interview, and he wanted to make a good impression. He walked to the door and rang the bell. Almost as an afterthought, he removed his dark glasses and tucked them into his jacket pocket as the wide front door opened.

A woman of indeterminable age stood at the threshold.

"Samuel DelVecchio?" she asked.

"Yes."

"Come on in. You're early. But promptness is a virtue not everyone appreciates. Can I take your jacket for you? Must be warm out there." The woman barely seemed to take a breath before adding, "Late summer around here can be really toasty. Not to mention humid. You want to go right on up those stairs, second door to the left. Conference room. Mallory should be in there. If she isn't, give a shout and I'll find her for you."

She held out a hand for his jacket, and for a moment, he was tempted to hand it over. But he was meeting with one of the nation's most successful businessmen, and he wasn't sure the casual look was the way to go.

"I'm fine," he told the woman—the housekeeper, he assumed.

"Suit yourself." She smiled and waved and set off toward the back of the house, and Sam headed up the steps as he'd been directed.

At the second door on the left, he knocked lightly. When there was no answer, he pushed it aside slightly and took a step inside. A woman stood looking out the back window.

"Excuse me," Sam said, and she turned around as if startled.

"I'm sorry," he told her. "I'm Sam DelVecchio. I was told to come up here and . . ."

The woman laughed and waved away his apology.

"I'm the one who should apologize. I was daydreaming. Sorry. Please, have a seat." She walked toward him, her hand out in greeting. "I'm Mallory Russo. We spoke on the phone."

He shook her hand, then sat in the chair she'd pointed to.

"I have your résumé here . . ." She sorted through a pile of papers in a fat folder at the head of the table. "Just give me a second . . . here we are."

Mallory sat, her eyes scanning the résumé he'd sent in six weeks earlier.

"So." She turned to him. "May I ask why you left the FBI after fourteen years?"

He'd expected the question, but hadn't expected it to open the conversation. "Well, truthfully, I just had enough."

Might as well just toss it out there.

Mallory raised an eyebrow.

"If you've read my résumé, you know I've worked as a profiler for the past several years," he explained in answer to her unspoken question.

"That was what made your resume stand out from the others. We thought that someone with profiling experience would be an asset to the foundation." She paused, then asked, "You do understand what the Mercy Street Foundation was established to do, don't you?"

"It's my understanding that your purpose is to help find people who have gone missing. Cases that law enforcement has given up on, for the most part. People who have been lost, and never found."

Mallory nodded. "That's basically correct. Some of those people will be found alive—our first case involved two missing teenagers who we did in fact find and return to their families. Our last case did not result in a happy ending. We did find the young woman we were looking for, but unfortunately, we were too late by months to save her. The bottom line is that we're searching for answers. What happened to this person? Dead or alive, what caused them to go missing? If we know from the outset the person was a victim of a violent crime, our job is to find out who did it and why, if law enforcement agencies haven't been able to do so."

"I think your website describes your work as private investigation with a twist," he said.

"The twist being that if we decide to take on a case, it's because there's something about it that appeals to us, and therefore, our services are free." She sat back in her chair, her arms crossed against her chest. "Do you see where a profiler's skills might come in handy to an organization like ours?"

"Well, yes, but . . ."

"Did you think the cases we take on would be easier than the cases you worked for the Bureau?"

"I thought they were mostly missing person cases."

"You mean, someone is missing, here, track them down?"

He nodded. "Pretty much, yes."

"And that appealed to you?"

"To some extent." Sam shifted uneasily in his seat.

She closed the folder. "Mr. DelVecchio, I think you'd be better off working for another private investigative firm, if that's what you're looking for."

"Miss Russo, can we start this interview again? I've obviously gotten off on the wrong foot."